MY HA`
MIDNIGHT

By

Isobelle Cate

18 July 2015

Dear Caroline,

All the best!

Love,

Isobelle Cate

Isobelle Cate

Amaryllis Hart has lived a hard life. Falsely accused of theft, she decides to live the life thrown at her until one encounter throws her into a world she does not believe exists and into the arms of the immortal who steals her heart.

Colin Butler, Dux of the Leeds Cynn Cruors and his second, Craig Shaw, return to Leeds abruptly after a secret Colin has been keeping for centuries, returns. In their attempts to keep it under wraps, another situation blows up in their faces, bringing Colin face to face with his past and his future—a violet eyed beauty who heals his soul.

As luck would have it, Colin's secret is unearthed. To top it all, Dac Valerian and Herod D'Argyl are in Leeds and the Ancients' enforcer arrives to pass judgement on the Dux of the Leeds Cynn Cruors.

Colin has to make the hardest decision of his life. Either he walks away from the past that will forever haunt him or make up for a past he had no control of and lose the woman he loves.

This is a work of fiction. Names, characters, places and incidents are either the product of the author's imagination or used fictitiously, and any resemblance to actual persons, living or dead, business establishments, events or locales is entirely coincidental.

My Haven, My Midnight
All rights reserved.
Copyright 2015 © Isobelle Cate

Published by Beau Coup Publishing
http://beaucoupllcpublishing.com

Cover by JRA Stevens
For Beau Coup Publishing

ALL RIGHTS RESERVED. This book contains material protected under International and Federal Copyright Laws and Treaties. Any unauthorized reprint or use of this material is prohibited. No part of this book may be reproduced or transmitted in any form or by any means, electronic or mechanical, including photocopying, recording, or by any information storage and retrieval system without express written permission from the author / publisher.

Acknowledgements

To everyone in Beau Coup, you have been such a great blessing and moving force in my writing career, Jennifer Stevens, Orry Benavides, Emily A. Lawrence, Debbie Workman, Emily Kirkpatrick, Shirley Bastian, Elaine Robinson, the beta readers and proof readers who work behind the scenes, thank you.

Special thanks go to Emily A. Lawrence, Jennifer Stevens, and Dianne Dixon. Not only have you helped me make Colin's and Amaryllis' story come to fruition, but you've also enriched my life with your laughter, wisdom, and everything else in between. Thank you so much.

Jim Foy. Thank you very for helping me thresh out valuable information of Scottish history. It is always such a pleasure to talk to you.

Cinzia Marchetti, *grazie per l'aiuto*.

To the Cate's Renegades Street Team. You keep me going all the time. We shall go from strength to strength. Thank you for your support.

To my family. Thank you for the pizza, the coffee, the wine, your advice, laughter, patience, and insight even at 5 am. I love you both.

To all the authors I have had the good fortune to know in this incredible journey, thank you for allowing me to read and learn from you. To my readers, new readers, bloggers and to those who have been with me from the very start. My characters and I are truly humbled and honoured that you have allowed us to be a part of your lives.

I'm having such a fantastic adventure. Thank you.

Isobelle Cate

Chapter One

Loch Naver, Lairg, Scotland, 1747

Duncan Butler whistled while he walked along the Strathnaver, his grin widening the nearer he got to Altnaharra. Home. After visiting The Hamilton in Hamel Dun Uamh, he could not wait to see his family. Several swathes of crags complimented the thick green grass of the hilly plains surrounding the loch. Duncan breathed deeply, enjoying the sweet smell of the grass, the misty scent of the loch, the wind that whipped tendrils of his golden hair from the queue that tied his unruly mane at the base of his neck, and flapped the Butler tartan open. The Scottish sky had been kind, blanketing the heavens with clouds, allowing Duncan to enjoy a late afternoon walk without too much discomfort. Prickly, yes. The sensation akin to being too close to the hearth when he wanted to taste the food his beloved Euna cooked. He chuckled at the memory of having his hand rapped so many times with the ladle before he hoisted his mate over his shoulder to take her into their room.

The boiling stew forgotten.

They were relatively fortunate considering what the humans were going through. The *Crann Tara* or Highland Clearances that swept through the area displacing so many families was believed to be the punishment for those who had any Jacobite sympathies, those who sided with the Bonnie Prince. Duncan and the rest of the Cynn Cruors knew that it was not that simple. The clearances sporadically happened long before Culloden to break the clans, but blood loyalty ran deep.

Eventually it became associated more with English atrocities after the uprisings. The Cynn Cruors could not interfere, though they made it a point to aid those who suffered the confiscation of their lands by the English and the lairds who sided with them. So many times, the Cynn Cruors became involved in nighttime skirmishes against the Scatha Cruors who insisted on interfering, pretending to be English soldiers terrorizing hapless families who had no choice but pack their meagre belongings and leave the lands they tilled for generations behind. Duncan was only too glad that his family had more than enough food to share with those who came to their doorstep, grateful that the Cynn Cruors' resources were more than enough to spread around. So many of the families who travelled their way begged him to allow them to stay, willing to help till his land in exchange for his protection. In the end, he agreed.

Duncan Butler had become an accidental laird.

A scream rent the air.

Duncan froze for a split second before he whizzed up the hill away from the loch. He growled and felt his eyes turn into the red orange colour of bloodlust. Just by the footpath was a bedraggled family, the women screaming while the man was being beaten and kicked by several red coated English soldiers. But the stench that reached him told him otherwise.

Scatha Cruor.

Duncan spat on the ground with disdain, unsheathing his basket hilted broadsword from his side. The men, nay, vermin spawned by Dac Valerian never turned down an opportunity to take advantage of the hardships the *Crann Tara* foisted on the highlands.

"Och, Euna. Loving you will have to wait," Duncan muttered in annoyance before his mouth slowly turned up to a grin imagining how hot and ready he and his mate would both be once he got home. His smile softened as he remembered his sons. Soon Colin would join him to fight the Scatha. In a few more years, so would Mackenzie. When they came back from the missions assigned to them, it would be more feathers to the Butlers' cap. Duncan had already spent part of his immortal life teaching his sons what it meant to be a Cynn Cruor. He had the rest of his long existence to continue doing so.

The Cynn Cruor battle cry rent the air, immobilizing the Scatha and the family they were abusing. Duncan Butler sped down the knoll, swinging his broadsword in an opening salvo.

* * *

Mackenzie chortled when Colin's heel caught on a small rock behind him.

"Mack! Cease, for Ancients' sake!" Colin growled. He raised his sword just as Craig brought his broadsword down.

Clang!

"Aye, Mackenzie." Craig's voice whooshed out of him when Colin planted his foot square on his chest and kicked, causing to fall as well. "If no', Colin will lose his heid and he'll land on his arse again."

Mackenzie kept laughing so hard that he fell, rolling on the grass. All around them the people who found refuge in their small land in Altnaharra shook their heads in amusement before they continued to till the land and tidy their front yards. If they suspected something they kept it to themselves, only too happy to have a safe haven away from the hardships that followed the *Crann Tara*. It was difficult for grown Cynn Cruor warriors to spar during the day, but Colin insisted that he and Craig tried it out while the clouds were heavy with promised rain and covered most of the sunlight. Colin felt as though he was perpetually close to the brazier that warmed the humans surrounding them in the dead of winter, and he knew Craig felt it too. He did not mind the heat. They had both been human too when they were Mack's age.

Besides, they needed to keep appearances now that people were living with them.

Suddenly, he heard his mother scream and all laughter stopped. Colin and Craig rushed towards the hut, uncaring of the gasps that followed them as they ran like the wind. Mackenzie ran as fast as he could on his still human legs.

Colin and Craig reached the hut, and stopped in sinking horror.

"Mam!" Colin rushed to his mother, who fell as soon as she reached the last step outside their home. Tears ran down her cheeks that were slowly aging.

"Colin...*Faigh for air Da*," she said softly. "He's nearby...the loch. Go to the loch. I can feel him there." Anguish shadowed her face for a moment before she tried to smile. "Go. There isna much time."

"Mam!" Mackenzie cried before he too froze in shock. "Colin! What's happening? Mam...what's happening to Mam?"

Colin's mind raced, his breathing being squeezed out of his lungs. Ancients, he had to think!

"Butler!"

"Colin!"

Craig and Mackenzie's voices galvanized him. "Mack, *gabh cùram ri Mam*. Stay with Mam. Craig and I will look for Da."

"But—"

"Do as you're told!"

Mackenzie's eyes widened as though he had been slapped.

"Mack, Mam needs us both," Colin said in a gentler tone as he placed his hands on his younger brother's shoulders while Craig held Euna Butler. Though his heart was breaking he needed to be strong for them both. Emotion had no place in their world at the moment. "She's weakening. We have to hurry."

"I'm scared." Tears suddenly welled in Mackenzie's eyes.

"So am I," Colin said, his voice firm. "But we are Cynn Cruors. We cannae show fear."

Mackenzie blinked several times before he squared his shoulders and stood straighter. "Aye, we cannae." He swallowed and took a deep breath before allowing his mother to lean on him. "Come on, Mam. Let's get ye inside and I'll take care of ye."

"Aye, you will, Mackenzie." Their mother's voice was now a whisper.

Colin did not wait for Mackenzie and his mother to enter the house. He and Craig became two blurs charging to the loch but the exertion coupled with the sun's rays peeking through the clouds eventually slowed them down. They were breathing hard by the time they reached the top of the knoll. When Colin saw what was at the base of the knoll he roared in torment before running and falling down the slope, uncaring that he skinned his knees on the sharp crags, his vision blurred by the red wetness streaming down his face.

Because the only things left on the ground were his father's broadsword, his bloodied clothes and the Butler tartan.

Colin knelt brokenly by his father's remains, his hands clawing the ground in anguish and rage. He felt his eyes change, the heat of anger turning from dark green to red orange. He whipped his head around, his sense of smell stronger in his transformation. The Scatha were gone, only telltale traces of their stench lingered in the air. Then he noticed a movement. He was so wrapped up in his loss he had not realized there were people who witnessed his change. Humans. It did not matter. The vampire blood that ran through his Cynn Cruor veins would allow him to erase their memory of Duncan Butler's death.

Something that would stay forever with his son.

He looked down at what remained of his father's ashes. As he gathered them into a pile, his hands shaking, he tried to imagine the warmth of the body that embraced him, now reduced to dust. He gathered them into his father's bloodied shirt before wrapping it in the tartan. Colin stilled his heart, forcing himself to breathe slowly, to keep his heartbreak at bay so that his eyes returned to the green that they once were. He and Craig were about to finish gathering Duncan Butler's remains when they noticed the family approaching them with trepidation. Colin and Craig both stood up. The women clutched at each other, fear blatant in their eyes, but the man whose jaw had a telltale trickle of blood and was starting to bloom black and blue stood straight. Colin had to admire him for holding his ground even though his body was shaking and terror emitted from him in spades.

"Ye ur his son." The man's scraggly hair whipped against his face.

"Aye," Colin answered. "I hae ta go."

"He saved us." The man's tone had more conviction now. "He came at those who were hurting us like a man possessed. His eyes had fire in them like the devil and the men he fought." He shuddered. "When they turned on him….*samhanachs*! But he fought them and told us to run. He killed them all. He was walking towards us when another one flew in the air."

The women embraced the man as though gathering whatever strength he had left.

"Your Da, he dinnae hae ta time to turn." The man continued. "The *samhanach* killed him. Took his head." He stared into space and started to wail. "Took his heid...he dinnae hae time..."

"Go to your Mam, Colin," Craig spoke. "I will take care of them and follow."

Colin did not need to know what awaited him inside the hut. As soon as he arrived, the humans were around their house's entrance. He was just glad that they had not entered, respecting his family's need for privacy.

The peat fire burned low inside the abode. Colin entered the room his parents shared, carrying his father's sword, clothes, and remains. He knew that when a Cynn Cruor mate died, the one left behind would die soon after.

As soon as Euna saw him, tears started trickling down the side of her face, a face that was youthful that morning and had aged that night. Lines and furrows of a life lived long curved along her cheeks and the side of her eyes. Her body that had borne Colin and Mackenzie was gradually changing. Her skin was drying up, shrivelling. Her healthy flesh slowly disappearing and soon only skin and bone would remain. Beside her, Mackenzie kept at wiping her brow with the cloth he kept dipping in the bowl with water. His soft childlike face became harsh when the firelight struck it. He turned around to look at Colin, his eyes puffed and red from crying, his shoulders slumped in helplessness.

"Colin," his mother rasped. "My Duncan?"

"Here." He knelt on the floor and took his father's shirt with his remains from the tartan.

Euna's bony hand started to reach out, but Colin moved to give the shirt with her husband's remains to her. She clutched the shirt and sighed as she rested the shirt on her chest.

"I can feel him." For a while, her face glowed with happiness before she winced. She faced her eldest son. "Ye are the heid of the family now, Colin." Euna's voice was fading, coming out like a gentle wind. "There is much I hae to tell ye both about being a Cynn Cruor. While your Da and I go to the pantheon, you will join the rest of the brethren." Her eyes, sunken in their sockets, slowly darted from one son to the other. "Go to The Hamilton. He will keep ye both safe."

Colin knew The Hamilton and Hamel Dun Uiamh. It was the place he and Craig trained and had only recently left three moons past so that they could return to their families. He remained silent while Mackenzie bravely wiped the tears streaming down his face.

"Promise me, Colin."

"I promise."

Chapter Two

Leeds, United Kingdom, Present Day

The black Mercedes SUV eased into the Leeds Faesten's basement parking. Colin and Craig alighted from the vehicle before taking their gear out of the luggage compartment.

"*Grazie*, Paolo." Colin extended his arm in the Cynn Cruor handshake. "For taking care of things while we were away. I hope Liam and Cormac made you comfortable."

"Ahh, Butler, the pleasure was all mine." Paolo Aldebrandi Marchetti grasped his arm before turning to Craig to do the same. His dark hair was clean cut and complimented his northern Italian features or a chiselled face with dark eyes fringed with thick lashes. "*Si*, I was well taken care of."

"Are you sure you won't stay any longer?" Craig's mouth quirked.

"I'm afraid I have to leave. My little sister is getting married and she wants me there. Otherwise she will throw a tantrum, and when she does…" Paolo rolled his dark eyes, leaving his statement hanging, his hands raised gesticulating both defeat and a request for understanding.

The men laughed.

"Besides," Paolo continued. "My father wants to make sure that security is tight. Ever since Valerian resurfaced everyone has been very careful. Many of the Italian Faestens have been meeting to make sure that everyone looks out for each other."

Colin's brow arched. "Why, have you been having

problems?"

"Nothing we Italian Cynn Cruors can't handle." Paolo drawled much to Colin and Craig's amusement. Paolo became serious. "No one has seen Valerian and our intel has picked up a lot of Scatha activity jockeying for the top dog position."

Colin nodded. He did not like the sound of what Paolo had just said, but he had other things to worry about. One thing at a time.

Like that's going to happen.

"Is it true that the Ancients have found silver that will stop us from being killed?" Paolo glanced at them alternately.

Colin and Craig looked at each other.

"Not so sure about that," Craig replied, pursing his lips. "We left right after the battle for the Specus Argentum."

Colin shrugged as he scratched the thick stubble on his jaw. "The Ancients and Manchester are still in the Honduras and I still have had no communication with them so you're more informed than we are. Besides, the important thing is that Dac is dead."

Paolo's lips thinned. He shook his head. "I wouldn't be too sure. You know Valerian has done this several times. It's like the boy crying wolf."

Colin grunted in agreement. "And speaking of wolves, the Cynn Cruors have a new enemy. Werewolves."

"*Fanculo!*" Paolo swore, raking his hand through his hair. "I'd love to chat, as you Brits always say, but I have to get back to my own Faesten. We need a plan of action if the *lupi mannari* are now part of the picture. But the Deoré, she is one, isn't she?"

"Yes, but long story, little time." Colin nodded curtly. "I agree that we need to plan. Cynn Cruor intel is likely to spread through all the Faestens of what went down in La Nahuaterique. We'll all get the entire briefing soon. And Marchetti?"

"*Si?*" Paolo was midway into getting in the Merc.

"You're right. We can't be too sure about Dac being dead. I wasn't thinking straight."

"With the Scatha on one side and the werewolves on the other?" Paolo arched a thick brow. "Even with De Alvaro and the Trujillo Faesten, you probably had a lot on your plate. You're forgiven. Besides, you must be tired."

Craig snorted. "Tired? No, we'll only get tired and bored when there are no more Scatha left to decapitate. We'd be twiddling our thumbs like humans."

Paolo shook his head in wry amusement. "Yes, we will. I better go. Thanks again."

Colin and Craig watched the SUV make its way out of the basement parking. A Cynn mortal would be waiting at the airport to drive the vehicle back to the Faesten's garage where Colin kept a fleet of cars for visiting Cynn Cruors and mortals.

Colin breathed in the Leeds air and closed his eyes. His nose twitched. Rain. The much appreciated visit from the skies was well on its way to the north. Good. That way the immortals could risk moving out and about during the day. It was when the sun baked the earth and steam rose from the grass hovering over the ground that their blood could not take.

He turned when the lift opened behind them and two more of his men came out. Liam Stewart was a huge muscular Cynn Cruor warrior with nearly silver white eyes and a gentle disposition, unless he was in the battlefield. His weapons of choice were the flanged mace and battle axe. He was also Leeds' sniper as he had been born with sharp eyes that could see as far as three miles without a scope. Cormac Tavish was not as huge but had a honed body enough to become a human torpedo. His weapon of choice was his own body, which he hurtled against a Scatha before decapitating them with two misericordes, long narrow knives specially made and infused with silver. Cormac was very versatile in the use of weapons and if he had a choice it was the anelace or the poniard, a short sword used in close fighting. He was also the Faesten's explosives expert.

"Everything all right?" Colin asked after Cynn Cruor handshakes were exchanged.

"Relatively smooth sailing, Dux," Liam replied, his silver eyes twinkling. "Gave a few Scatha Cruors one way tickets to hell. Other than that, everything is peachy."

"Trumping a Scatha's arse is always peachy for you," Cormac deadpanned before his mouth widened in a genuine smile. "Good to have you back, Dux. How was La Na-whatever-the-tick? The Ancients?"

"The Ancients are good," Colin answered. His mouth quivered at Liam and Cormac's sighs of relief, his eyes crinkling in amusement. "La Na-whatever-the-tick?"

"Couldn't pronounce it." Cormac raised his hands, his tone defensive. "There are too many letters. Bet you couldn't pronounce it the first time you heard it."

Craig's shoulders shook when Colin grunted.

"Good mission?" Liam asked, hands on his hips.

"More than good," Colin said. "We've secured the Specus Argentum and the Trujillo Faesten's immortals were all over it when we left. That's all I know at the moment until we get further intel from Trujillo or Manchester. We came home as soon as we could without arousing suspicion."

An uneasy silence descended.

"Colin, about killing Scatha Cruors—"

"It's what we do, Liam." Colin assured him, understanding his fellow Cynn Cruor's uneasiness. "I wouldn't have it any other way."

Liam scratched his head in a rueful gesture. "I just didn't want you to think I was willing to kill all of them."

"Thank you." Colin clamped Liam's shoulder and looked at the rest of his men. "Let's meet up in the control room in half an hour."

"The feed's all set up," Cormac stated as all of them walked to the lifts. Cormac and Liam took one lift that would bring them to the command centre a floor below the underground parking, while Colin and Craig took the other lift to the main part of the Faesten. As the lift opened to the third floor of the Georgian inspired building, they veered towards their respective quarters, passing through corridors softly lit by sconce lights protruding from the walls. Colin passed the tapestry of how the Cynn Cruors came to be and his mouth tightened. He did not have to be reminded of the Damocles' sword hanging over his head.

Reaching his door, he turned the knob, entering his bedroom. His all-terrain boots thudded against the hard wood floor while he walked. He dropped his gear by the foot of the king size bed. When he turned, his gaze caught the Butler tartan hanging over the mantle. The blues, reds, and yellows had faded with time. Once the right technology had been available, Colin made sure that the tartan was preserved and encased in non-glare glass, sealed against the ravages of time. It was once used to cover a highlander when he slept under the Scottish sky while away in battle.

It was also the only lasting memory of Duncan Butler, Colin's father, and the only thing left when he disintegrated in death.

After unhooking his Beretta APX from his hip, taking out the cartridge and leaving them side by side on the bedside table, he walked to the windows overlooking the huge lawn, his feet braced apart. He flexed his shoulders, his neck ligaments popping in relaxation.

It was getting harder and harder living a double life. Well, not exactly a double life as opposed to keeping a secret that could jeopardize not only his position as a Dux, but the lives of his men for they knew the burden he carried. He had not expected Marchetti of the Tuscan Faesten to call when he did to say that he was visiting the UK. Neither he nor the Manchester Cynn Cruors expected that Zac McBain would have called to tell them that Dac Valerian had shot the Ancient Eald. He could not turn Paolo away because it would raise questions. Cynn Cruors never turned away fellow Cynn Cruors, mortal or immortal alike. So Colin had asked Liam and Cormac to keep Paolo occupied with observing how the Faesten's clubs and restaurants were run. Coincidence or not, after the Silver Cave battle, Colin had received a phone call from Liam that made him return to the UK. He had made his excuses saying that the Leeds Faesten had received reports of children being abducted to be groomed for prostitution and as the Leeds Dux, he needed to nip the operation in the bud. It had not been far from the truth. Colin just did not include the most important intel he received.

Mackenzie.

Colin's eyes narrowed while he surveyed the city lights, his bedroom having the unimpeded view of the city centre. The mansion was situated in a hilly area that sloped and at night the town was laid at the Faesten's feet like a tray of glittering jewels in black and green velvet. A thick layer of trees and a twenty foot wall surrounded the property. Cameras were attached to several trees to crisscross over the property area. Motion detectors were hidden close to the ground so that no square foot of ground escaped discovery. He liked the area his Faesten was in. Unlike the Manchester Faesten which was right dead smack in the centre of town, the Cynn Cruors' Leeds headquarters was tucked at the end of the road in Cannondale, an affluent neighbourhood a stone's throw away from the city. That is if the Cynn Cruors drove like the wind, which they were wont to do. It was close enough for Colin's guests to find when he had rave parties, but far enough from the neighbours that the police did not need to be alerted. Colin's mouth lifted in a humourless smile. Neither did he want the neighbours to hear the orgasms he could wring out from the women he brought to his bed. They would only be too envious of what they could not have.

He pivoted on his heel and strode to the bathroom, removing his black shirt as he did so and throwing it on the bed. The lights automatically switched on as he entered and went straight for the shower. He turned on the tap, letting the hot steam cloud the bathroom while he removed the rest of his clothes. Entering the large stall, he let the liquid needles pummel his tired body, weariness of battle and of travel flowing down the drain. If only it could ease his mind.

Maybe you should relinquish your leadership of the Leeds Faesten.

The taunt stopped him cold even as his hands methodically soaped his body away of grime. Colin was not prepared to deny that thought had crossed his mind after losing Mackenzie, but it would cause many things to unravel. He was in too deep, his men with him.

He could not let that happen.

He heard a knock on the door just as soon as he

stepped out of the shower. Wrapping a towel around his hips, he sauntered across, unmindful of the water tracking across the wooden floor.

"Ready?" Craig straightened in front of the door. He, too, had showered, minuscule droplets of water in his dark hair glinting under the corridor's light. He had shaved the growth of stubble from his beard, putting his angular jaw in sharp relief.

"Give me a sec." Colin left the door ajar to get dressed.

Craig sighed ruefully as he watched the Leeds Dux get dressed in less than three blinks of the human eye. Colin preferred to use his Cynn Cruor ability of speed to dress.

"What?" Colin scowled when he returned to the door.

Craig shrugged. "You're agitated."

Colin snorted. "You think?" He expelled a breath. "Let's go."

Cormac and Liam were talking into their headsets when Colin and Craig entered the command centre. Previously a wine cellar, the Cynn Cruors had converted it into an intel hub to monitor the Scatha Cruors' activities in the area. For a long time, no Scatha abductions had been recorded and it had been easy for the Leeds warriors to join missions all over the globe, leaving the Faesten in the capable hands of the Cynn mortals. However, when Eirene Spence, mate of the Manchester Faesten's sniper and second-in-command, Finn Qualtrough, discovered Dac Valerian's whereabouts, the Cynn Cruors returned to becoming battle ready. Colin was given the opportunity to engage Dac and the Scatha when the Leeds Cynn Cruors joined the Manchester contingent in the Isle of Man. He shot Dac in the head as soon as the Scatha leader attempted to kill Roarke Hamilton, the Manchester Dux. But it was not enough to kill Dac, who escaped. Graeme Temple had taken the silver bullet for Roarke, and Colin had offered to take the injured Cynn Cruor and Zac McBain, Manchester's resident medic, out of the isle. Graeme would have died had it not been for the Ancients arriving to help Zac heal Graeme.

"What do we have?" Colin stopped his musings, comfortably slipping into his role as Dux.

Liam swiped his finger on his computer pad and flicked the image towards the wider screen above the bank of monitors.

"This."

The interior of *Le Club Cinq Mille*, one of Colin's clubs and the most sought after night spot for those who were seen and who wanted to be seen, filled the screen. The club was named as such because the minimum amount anyone should spend was five thousand pounds. The amount was taken from its patrons before they entered the premises and anything they imbibed or ate was taken from the deposit. The club's music thudded and blared so loud that the warriors in the nerve centre could have been physically inside. Blue laser beams crisscrossed the dance floor. Nubile women gyrated above the four bars located at the corners of the club's ground floor. There were fire exits beside each bar counter and behind the DJ's stage as well as on the second floor, which housed the private rooms. Two huge stairwells led to the second floor that had private rooms for parties. Fire exits were also found on the second floor that led to the balcony. A stairwell led to an alley on the ground and to the street. All of the booths facing the dance floor were filled. Men and women were dressed to impress or be prepared to undress by the end of the evening. The women had enough makeup on to cover what they decided to leave bare.

Liam manipulated the small lever in front of him and zeroed in on a booth close to the stage.

"Scatha," Craig growled, his eyes slowly changing colour.

"Easy, mate." Cormac glanced at his brethren.

"I know they're being watched, but I hate the sight of them," Craig grumbled, his hands on his hips.

Liam nodded in agreement, his mouth in a straight line.

"Why focus on them?" Colin asked. "Scatha often come to our clubs not knowing they are surrounded by Cynn mortals."

"Because they have been coming regularly with him," Liam replied.

Colin narrowed his gaze on the person hidden in the shadows. Without being in the club, his eyes could only adjust to what the camera picked up.

"Facial recognition," he ordered. Liam planted a square over the shadowy figure then launched the programme that computed and matched the common characteristics against the Cynn Cruors database. The points made a grid all over the unknown visage before it stopped. The grids and shadows disappeared.

Colin inhaled sharply. "Mack."

Craig blew out a long breath as he moved closer to Colin. "How many times has he been in the club?"

"This is the second time," Cormac answered. "The Scathas have been in several times. It seems they have a lot of money to burn. We can't take them down without alerting the humans."

"They've been on a kidnapping spree?"

"They've tried several times," Liam replied, rolling his chair across the length of the desk to reach for his coffee mug. "The Cynn mortals have been deftly foiling their plans." He chuckled. "Cynn mortals have balls, I tell you. One time I saw a Scatha growl at them and once the Cynn women reached them they twisted their nuts."

"Ouch." Craig grimaced and Colin's lips lifted in a ghost of a smile, diffusing some of the report's brevity.

"The Scatha howled but the DJ pumped up the volume in the club. Everyone thought the howl was a signal to howl back and they did."

The Cynn Cruors snickered.

"Sorry, Dux." Liam cleared his throat.

"Bloody quit treating me like I was some fragile nutcase," Colin ground out.

"You're not fragile," Cormac quipped. "A nutcase, maybe, but definitely not fragile."

"I should be," Colin muttered.

"But you're not, Butler. Cut it out and do what you do best" Craig said. "Lead us."

Colin's chest tightened at the loyalty his men showed. They could have turned him in at any given time. They did not. They could have told the Council of Ieldran that Mackenzie was alive and absolve him of his burden and they did not do that either. It was his burden to bear, his decision to make and until then they stood beside him.

Colin nodded his thanks. "Let's kick some Scatha butt and find out what my brother is up to."

Chapter Three

Max Greene surveyed the dance floor. Women gyrated against each other, throwing their heads back as peals of laughter left their slender throats. Some had red ruby lips, others just had lip gloss and very smoky fuck-me eyes. Max's gaze travelled the length of their bodies encased in tight-fitting clothes that left little to the imagination, and his mouth lifted at seeing their feet encased in five inch platform heels that looked too heavy to carry while walking.

So ripe for the Scatha Cruors' picking. They would be thoroughly fucked, screaming as they came before they were dumped at the warehouse to be sold to a growing world market.

He looked at his companions, chortling at how the women gravitated to them. Max looked away, making a sound at the back of his throat. He could not hack their smell, well, part of the time. Their stench reminded him of rotting food and the muck filled streets of Edinburgh centuries ago when people shouted "Garde loo!" before dumping the rich man's bowel contents out the window. Sanitation and hygiene had come a long way since then, though it seemed not for his fellow Scathas. Surreptitiously, he smelled his armpits. Bloody hell, he was pathetic. He inhaled sharply and his senses went on overdrive.

Cynn Cruors.

Something inside Max battled for dominance. He growled, his heart starting to beat rapidly. He braced himself for the change, the pain that enlarged the beating muscle inside his chest and made evil flow through his veins like raw silk. Smooth and abrasive at the same time. A pain he had learned to welcome and even enjoy. But when the Cynn Cruor part reminded him of what it had been like before his forced transformation, the same pain he relished became torture. He had to bite down hard on his lip until he drew blood to stop himself from yelling. He felt that duality now and hated every bloody minute of it.

He scanned his surroundings, glad for the shadows that kept him hidden because his eyes were changing. Not that the Cruors, whether Cynn or Scatha would notice him. The Scatha were clueless that they had entered a Cynn Cruor dominated club, but the Cynn Cruors knew. Max scented Cynn mortals everywhere. It was something he could not understand. Why could his brethren not scent the Cynn mortals until it was too late, but he could? It might have something to do with his transformation, something he would rather forget or he would foam in the mouth. He was something of a hybrid in an already hybrid race that had vampire, werewolf, and human DNA. The Cynn Cruors wanted to hunt him down, the Scatha did not trust him. His eye colour made him different. It was not quite the Scatha's neon green eyes yet, but he was getting there.

He knew all along that they had entered a Cynn Cruors' club.

After all, it was Colin's club.

Max's mouth lifted in a sardonic smile. He had never told anyone who his brother was and even changed the way he spelled his name, a symbolic gesture of breaking away from all he loved for he did not belong to them anymore. Yet, he still had enough sense of loyalty to his mother and especially his father, who was murdered by the very being he had become. And his brother? Fury raced like wildfire in his veins. Max swallowed hard. This was not the place to let loose.

Innocent people could get killed.

What the fuck?

He hated his bloody scruples, an already bloated moral leech that continued gorging on whatever conscience he had left.

Badon Exton, the Scatha who sat beside him, moved. Max knocked back the Camus Cuvee cognac, poured himself another from the bottle on the table and waited for the Scatha leader's orders. Badon checked his phone, the instrument panel lighting his face.

"It's time." Badon's eyes glowed green. "We're meeting them at the back."

Max downed the cognac as he stood with Badon and two other Scatha Cruors. The faces of the two Scathas soured at the interruption of watching the striptease happening on the dance floor.

"Lighten up," Badon chortled. "Once we truss up the pussy we're getting you can come back and sink into all the pussies you want."

The two guffawed, their eyes lighting up as they followed Badon with Max taking the rear.

A van with two other Scatha warriors was waiting in the narrow alley. The vehicle was a tight fit with the community bins, taking a lot of space on the opposite wall from the club's building. Max snorted, trying to quietly cough the stench that seemed to cling to the back of his nose and throat. He forced his gag reflex down at the smell of the alley by the side of the club. A slight breeze made its way from the skies as though sensing his disgust, temporarily removing the offending stench. He sucked in a breath immediately. No way was he going to let go of that reprieve. Ahh, the promise of rain. He would keep the air and the promise it held inside his lungs for as long as possible. Immortals like him could do so. After all, he had the vampire's attributes in his

DNA.

His sharp vision and hearing sensed rodents scuffling and shuffling in the dark corners of the side street. They were not that different from who they were.

Scum.

He heard several motorcycles rumble along the street before its lights lit the dim alley. Three Kawasaki bikes blocked the alley entrance. Groups of men and women laughing amid their chatter walked along the main street, oblivious to what was going down in the alley. Neither did they look into the alley. Max knew the human psyche. Humans opted not to get involved, didn't want to be caught in the middle of something that might just mean trouble, or worse, death for them.

Max watched the group with wariness, his hackles rising. He exhaled in reluctance, letting go of the precious clean air inside his lungs and sniffed. Leather, sweat, traces of evil. Nothing different. Then he stiffened.

A hint of honeysuckle. A scent that brought back memories of happier days in Altnaharra. His father used to go to the Hebrides, bringing home posies of the flowers to give to Max's mother. Flowers that united them in eternal love. Max scowled. Those were memories of a boy long gone.

Long dead.

Max's hands changed, his ligaments stretching. The group that arrived was definitely human and evil. He should relax because he was in the company he kept. He could not understand why he did not like the vibe he got from them. He shot a glance at Badon and the rest of his brethren. At ease. He mulled over his unusual reaction when someone alighted from the bike which belonged to, he surmised, the leader. Someone petite was with him. Max's breath seized.

the money."

"What?" She huffed in disbelief. "Why? What did I do to you? You told me you'd keep me safe!"

Jack sighed. "I have my reasons."

"Bull fucking shit!" Ice trickled down her spine at the maniacal chuckle coming from one of the men facing them.

"She's got a mouth, hasn't she?"

Jack's lips quirked. "Badon here is looking for an exotic beauty."

"I'm no bloody exotic beauty," Amaryllis snapped. Her skin crawled at Badon's leer. What the hell was happening? Why was Jack doing this? She had never given him any reason to throw her out. She was his most trusted lieutenant, for God's sake, kicking ass for him when his men acted like pussies. They had become close after she escaped her uncle. Jack had taken care of her, had told his men that anyone so much as flicked her ass would be sleeping six feet under. They had had no strings attached mind-blowing sex on occasion, but both knew it was a tension reliever.

Now this.

"I am not a whore!"

"Such beautiful eyes," Badon murmured almost to himself. "They flash violet fire when you're angry."

"If looks could kill, you'd already be flayed alive." Her baleful glare landed on him.

Badon cackled. "I'm going to enjoy taming you."

"You won't get far. You'll be dead before you even lay a hand on me."

The slap made Amaryllis cry out, her head whipping back at the force, her vision exploding in brightness. She tasted blood and sucked her injured lip. She glared at Jack. His face was hard, the planes becoming harsher in the dim lights.

"I had no choice," he said softly, looking at her. "It's done."

Amaryllis glared at him then at Badon. She sure as hell was not going down without a fight. "Fuck you."

She gasped at Badon's eyes before her glance darted at his hand, ready to strike again. But the pain did not come. A shadow wedged itself between her and her assailant. She felt a prick of pain on her neck.

"Sleep."

* * *

Max felt his brethren's lust to take her. His hands balled into fists at the sight of Badon backhanding the violet beauty. While he could not help admire the spitfire, he also could not understand why it bothered him that she was being treated that way. It had never bothered him when other women were taken by his brethren. A low growl came from his throat as Badon prepared to slap her again. With Cruor speed, Max shoved Badon away and pinched the violet beauty's neck. The terror he saw in her eyes hit him like a sucker punch.

"Sleep," he ordered softly.

Just as she blacked out, Badon pushed Max against the wall. His hand clawed and dug deep into Max's shoulder. Max gritted his teeth as sharp claws hit muscle and sinew and groaned at the perverse pleasure he got from the pain.

"What the fuck!" Badon's eyes glittered, his jowls starting to transform.

"Change your appearance, Badon, or we lose the best source of flesh this side of Leeds."

"You think I fucking care?" Badon's voice became reed thin as his teeth lengthened and sharpened. His claw hit Max's collarbone. He jerked his arms by his sides, but he could feel his hands changing. He let Badon relish his moment of torture even though he wanted to break away.

Max growled. A second was all he needed. He impaled his claws into Badon's side and slid it upwards. Badon's roar stunned the humans, who watched in stupefied terror as the rest of the Scatha mutated.

"I care." Max pulled Badon's body closer with his claw before he whispered into his ear, "I don't like giving up my lifestyle."

Badon grunted then bellowed when Max slashed higher. Blood spurted from the lengthening wounds. He pushed Badon away, snarling as Badon's claws dislodged from his shoulder. Max twisted and swung his arm, taking Badon's head from his shoulders. The body disintegrated even before the head hit the ground. Max turned to the other Scatha, their eyes lighting up. He knew that without Badon to lead them, it was open season for anyone who wanted to be Scatha lieutenant, the person who headed the Lair. He saw Jack Crawley and his men getting on their bikes and flooring it, leaving his violet beauty in a heap on the ground.

Filthy cowards.

They were one less thing to worry about, for now.

The first Scatha lunged at him while the second catapulted himself from the wall to land behind Max.

He chuckled. "Boys, boys. I don't care to be a Cruor sandwich, but if you insist…"

The narrow alley was perfect. Max spun around with his arms outstretched, his claws slicing across the Scathas' abdomens, their yowls sounding like sirens against the backdrop of thudding club music. The moment they doubled over, Max hit them with an upper cut and swiped off their heads, turning them to ash as well. Straightening, he looked around. If it were not for the dank smell and the grimy building walls, he might have thought himself walking along a black sand beach. He looked at the unconscious woman. Some of the ashes blanketed her clothes, her face.

So not cool. She shouldn't be covered in filth. That's way beneath her.

Max exhaled slowly, his anger abating. The green tinge of his eyesight bled out replaced by the colours around him. His head jerked slightly when his jaw and teeth returned to their normal, more human form. He flexed his digits and his wrist to ease the stiffness after his claws changed back to hands. The club's sound that seemed to hover above him earlier while he fought, fell on him like the last curtain call, before guilt caused by his actions and wistfulness for the days he used to be a Cynn Cruor pressed from all sides. Gritting his teeth as though it would build a wall against any scruples he had left, he bent down and lifted violet beauty to lay her gently inside the van. He brushed away some of the ash from her face but it only served to dirty her further. Swearing, he gave up, securing the door. He got into the driver's seat and started the engine. He backed out of the alley, crunching over the remains of the Scatha, finding immense satisfaction at the sound of the ground mixing with immortal dust. He shifted from reverse to first gear then he eased into the street. Slowly, gently, not wanting to wake Violet Beauty, he headed north, away from the Scatha's pit. Max would deal with the questions later.

There was something he had to do first.

Chapter Four

Colin and the Leeds Cynn Cruors were an impressive sight crossing Merrion Place in a row. Men envied them, women lusted after them, both groaning when the bouncer let them into *Le Club Cinq Mille*. Once they were inside, they were bombarded with thudding music, the cacophony of voices, and Cynn Cruor mortals and warriors who greeted them with handshakes and back thumps, especially Colin and Craig who they knew had just arrived from the Honduras. Their laughter covered what everyone was aware of.

The Scatha Cruors in their midst.

The Cynn Cruors could not stop the growls coming from their throats. The Scatha froze when they saw him, their eyes glowing a neon green. They knew who Colin was. Colin looked up at the second floor. Even the private rooms had several Scathas partying. His eyes saw through the tinted glass, all oblivious to what was happening on the ground while humans got them off, or the Scathas got off them. He turned his gaze back to the ground floor where Seth Holms, the club manager and Cynn mortal, wove through the crowd to greet him. She was also in charge of all the Cynn mortals in Leeds.

"Dux," she shouted above the din of club music. She grinned. "Good to have you back."

"Annaseth." Colin smiled back, calling her by her full name and guffawed at her scowl. "Glad to be back. How's everything? Scatha Cruors in the crowd, I see. Have they been coming more frequently?"

"Since you lifted the ban No. Same ol', same ol'. Sometimes it's the only way to immediately catch them in the act and kill them before they kill us," she said with insouciance. Colin shook his head, his mouth thinning with displeasure, but he understood. He did not like the idea that Scatha Cruors entered the bars and restaurants controlled by the Cynn Cruors. Did not like how their hands were tied by human laws. Refusing them entry would lead to a lot of questions and protests about discrimination and they did not want that. Humans did not need to know of the war that brewed in their midst.

He raked his appreciative gaze down Seth's lithe body with curves in the right places. Her ombre coloured hair gleamed in the club light the same way her lightly kohl rimmed chocolate brown eyes twinkled. She did not have large breasts or a pronounced ass, but she had killer legs that no amount of money would be enough to insure it.

She was perfection in her simplicity.

Seth's dark eyes assessed Colin, the sweep of her lashes lowering to his shoes all the way to his face. A perfectly trimmed brow arched and a line ploughed her forehead. She cocked her hip and tapped one red lacquered finger over her Cupid's bow shaped mouth. Colin braced his legs apart, amusement twitching his mouth.

"Had I known that going into battle in some foreign country would get you to notice me instead of me doing my damnest to flirt with you, I would have done that a long time ago," he said over the din.

Seth raised her other brow and snorted. "In your dreams, Dux. California beach boy lookalikes aren't my type."

"Then what is your type?" Cormac's eyes glittered. He moved closer to join the conversation.

Seth rolled her eyes. "Definitely not you."

Cormac and Liam chortled. Craig kept silent, his

eyes narrowing at her. Seth turned her attention to Colin, her face serious.

She leaned up and placed her mouth against his ear. "There's something you need to see."

Colin nodded, indicating for her to lead the way. He had a pretty good idea of what Seth was going to show him. Mackenzie. But Colin wanted to find out why, after all this time, he decided to show up. Unless Mack did not realize that the Cynn Cruors' technology was advanced enough to lift an image out of the dark. No, that was impossible. Mack had been a Cynn Cruor before. If there was still any remnant of that left inside him, he would have the intelligence to realise that.

The group meandered through the sea of humanity until they reached the back of the DJ's stage. Slipping through the thick fireproof curtains, Seth placed her hand against the sensor pad on the wall. A door opened and they were immediately greeted by the low hum of Cynn mortals talking into headphones, leaving the thudding club music behind. Greetings rose from many of those inside the Club's security room, turning away from their respective screens to acknowledge the Cynn Cruors' presence before turning their backs to return to their work. *Le Club Cinq Mille* was the hub of Colin's club and restaurant operations. Each of the establishments he owned had security cameras directly connected to Le Club's communications link and the Faesten's command centre. The Cynn Cruors had their own telecommunications line that ran parallel to that of the humans and Colin made sure that all of his businesses were linked together. The Cynn Cruor network had so many encryptions that would make any self-respecting hacker become vertigo-prone for many years to come.

Except for Eirene Spence, Finn Qualtrough's mate.

Colin waited until three feeds came up on the bigger screen. One was of the dance floor and booths, the other was of the stairwell and corridor leading to the washrooms, and the third was the alleyway.

"Scatha's behaving?" he asked, his leather jacket creaking as his arms crossed over his chest.

"Nothing we can't handle," Seth replied.

Craig cocked a brow at her. She darted a glance at him. He kept silent.

"This happened a little while ago." Seth began before asking the Cynn mortal to bring up the alleyway feed. They watched as the Scatha Cruors exited the door to the alleyway to join two more of their brethren who were leaning against a black van. Colin's hands clenched at seeing Mackenzie among those who exited the club. His jaw was so tight that he thought it would break. A little later, he saw three motorbikes enter the alleyway, blocking the only egress.

And was stunned at the sight of the woman with a slash of iridescent violet in her hair. His gut curled in vexation because he wanted to see more of how she looked. Deep attraction started to map a beeline to his groin. He watched her body language, her agitation making her shake her arms at her sides like a prized fighter about to enter the ring. Then she froze before two of her companions grabbed her arms. A low growl came unbidden from his throat at the sight and he just wanted to smash his fist at the Scatha who backhanded her.

"Bloody hell," Cormac swore, his gaze widening.

"You should have interfered," Craig said with suppressed anger. He pointed an accusing finger at the screen. "I don't give a fuck if we start a war. They're in our territory and anyone in our jurisdiction is kept safe."

"Watch," Seth snapped, her brown eyes darkening to mirror her annoyance. "We would have, believe me, but a Scatha decided to do it for us."

With speed that any Cynn Cruor could follow, Colin watched in stunned amazement. Mackenzie had intervened. He pressed the woman's neck to make her unconscious. What ensued after caused the security centre to cease talking. They watched in stupefaction as Mackenzie singlehandedly turned his companions to ash before he picked up the woman and lay her gently in the van before he drove away.

"Where do you think he's going?" Cormac muttered. "Think he'll stake his position as head?"

"As the Scatha leader?" Colin looked at both Cormac and Liam. "What happened to Thorne?"

"Killed by Badon, who's just been killed by Ma— other Scatha," Liam replied smoothly, covering his near faux pas.

"Mother Scatha?" Seth snickered.

Liam gave her a dark look before speaking. Seth mouthed a "sorry," chastised. "Right after you and Craig left for the Honduras, there was a changing of the lieutenants. You know how quick their turnover in leadership is especially since Dac Valerian vanished."

"Valerian was a show in La Nahuaterique," Craig quipped. "He's very much alive. The Ancient Eald broke his neck and seems to have drowned."

Seth visibly bristled but shrugged. "Same M.O. different place. Until it's official, I'll think that he's still alive."

"You two do your table tennis some other time," Colin retorted. "We need to know where that Scatha took the woman. She'll get lost once she's exchanged. Seth, do you know if there have been other possible abductions in the other clubs? Restos?"

Seth looked around, checking on the reports coming in from the other establishments. "Nada. Just this one."

She nodded at the screen showing the empty alleyway. "He might have taken her to their stronghold south from here. With Badon gone, the Scatha might just proclaim his authority over the lot of them."

Craig swore softly and rubbed his face before he looked away.

"Got a problem with that Shaw?" Seth's eyes spat fire. "It was a statement of fact."

Before Craig could riposte, Cormac spoke, "Children...children. Cease thy quarrel."

"Shut up, Tavish," Craig growled before Cormac snickered.

"Look, I don't know what's going on and I don't bloody care," Seth's said with barely suppressed anger. She looked at Colin. "You want me to back off, tell me. But don't treat me like some dumb bitch."

"Farthest thing from my mind, Holms," Colin retorted, irate. "Stand down." He turned to Craig. "That goes for you too."

The tension caused by the heated discussion dissipated. The pressure of locating the woman increased.

"Have mortals case the stronghold," Colin ordered Seth.

"They've moved again," Liam said, his silver eyes narrowing. "We still haven't found out where they've set their new lair."

"Bloody hell." Colin's face became thunderous. "No matter. Check the old lair. "Don't get too close until we get there."

Seth gave him a curt nod, not bothering to look at the rest of the warriors. She snapped at several mortals, giving them their orders.

"She sure is pissed," Cormac commented.

Craig grunted.

Colin's phone buzzed and he checked it. "Manchester has just taxied," he said. "They're going to debrief us as soon as we get back to the Faesten."

"Good," Craig exhaled. "If Dac survived, we'll need to rethink how to protect Leeds."

The rest nodded. Then Colin's phone rang.

Liam snorted. "Guess they couldn't wait."

Colin shook his head. "It's not them. It's a private number." He brought the phone to his ear. "Butler."

"Hello, brother."

* * *

Luke watched the plane slowly ease into the hangar, the engine's whining sound bouncing off the walls. He arrived earlier with the Mercedes Springer van to pick up the Manchester Cynn Cruors. Jay Nevins, a Cynn mortal who worked with the Greater Manchester Police, volunteered to stay in the Faesten while Luke and the Cynn Cruor women went to Deanna's private hangar in the airport.

Luke leaned on the side of the vehicle with a wry grin on his face as he watched the three women waiting for their men to disembark. Deanna Logan, Roarke Hamilton's mate, was the most unflappable of the three women but right now, she was shifting her weight from one leg to the other, eager to see him. Eirene Spence was the excitable one. A foot shorter than her mate, Finn Qualtrough, Roarke's second in command and the Faesten's sniper, she was the Faesten's hacker, though she scowled at the phrase. Her incessant attention to detail had led Dac Valerian, the head of the Scatha Cruor, back into the open. Dressed in her usual black skinny jeans, tight shirt under a leather jacket, and ballet flats, her body thrummed with anticipation. The sound of the plane finally stopping and the whining of the engines brought collective sighs from the women. Luke turned to the last woman of the triumvirate. Kate Corrigan, Graeme Temple's mate. Though Luke could sense her joy of finally seeing Graeme home, she had a certain sadness tingeing her form and it made her shoulders slump a little. A very minuscule change in her body language, but he noticed it. Kate was still mourning the loss of her best friend, Thomas Mitchell. A friend who gave up his life to save their other friends, Anthea and Florence, by being the evil the Cynn Cruors were up against, a Scatha Cruor. The worst part of Tommy's death was not that he died a Scatha.

It was because he died by Kate's hand.

The plane door's air locks sighed as it opened, disgorging its passengers one by one. Eirene broke into a sprint and launched herself at Finn as soon as he stepped down the last step. Finn laughed and he had to let go of his gear, catching Eirene in his arms before giving her a ravishing kiss. Eirene looked as though she was literally melting in Finn's embrace. Deanna, on the other hand, kept her cool. Her deep red jersey dress and red bottomed high heels caused Roarke's eyes to flare with gold flecks. He crushed her in his arms when he reached her, his massive form enveloping her, his hand on the back of her head keeping her steady for his kiss. Kate walked slowly towards Graeme. Luke saw the love and tenderness in Graeme's eyes as the Cynn Cruor and his woman met halfway. Graeme held Kate as though he would never let go, their kisses interspersed with soft sighs and whispered endearments.

Three different men and women, three ways of expressing love.

Luke wondered when he would get a shot at what they had. The face of the woman he had only caught a glimpse of when they fought Elliot Hammond and his

Scatha Cruors, drifted across his mind.

Adara Kerslake. The only woman who kept his interest even after she was long gone from his sight. Hell, he was attracted to so many women but after a few hours between the sheets they faded from his memory. Ironic that he also did not know who he was, had no memory of where he came from or how he became a Cynn Cruor. Only Adara's face remained.

"Griffiths," Roarke broke through his thoughts. Luke grinned and took the Manchester Dux's arm in the Cynn handshake. He was still a bit uneasy about doing so because he did not belong to any Faesten. However, while they had a common enemy and while the Cynn Cruors had generously opened their archives and shared their resources with him to find out his past, it would have to do.

"Dux."

Roarke's eyes widened in pleasure. "Does that mean you've decided to belong to Manchester and not Leeds?"

Luke laughed. "For now, until I sort things out."

Roarke sighed. "One can hope. I gather Jay's holding the fort?"

"He is." Luke nodded. "Though I'm sure he can't wait to get back to Florence."

Roarke's eyes lit with amusement. "I'm not surprised. Cynn Cruor mortal or immortal, we love our women like no one else can. You'll understand it one day."

Luke's mouth turned up in an unconscious smile before turning to Finn and Graeme. He smiled in amusement to see Eirene still hugging Finn like a koala and the warrior did not mind. Finn had one arm around Eirene's waist while his other arm held his gear over his shoulder. Graeme and Kate were more sedate, their heads close to each other. Graeme was listening to what Kate was saying, but straightened when he reached Luke.

"Thanks for keeping an eye on our women," Graeme said.

"No problem," Luke said. "They've been worried about you three, but they just keep working on the charity and foundation."

"Where's Colin and Craig?" Deanna asked, her hand on Roarke's chest as she looked up at him.

A look passed between the three warriors.

"I saw that." Eirene's forehead crinkled. She slid down from Finn, her hands on her waist. "Where's Zac?" Eirene asked, looking around at the three men. When they did not answer, her face was pained before she looked at her mate. "Finn?"

"Zac's fine." Finn rubbed Eirene's shoulders, a hint of a smile on his mouth. "We'll talk about it when we brief Colin. He needs to hear this too."

"Is there something you need to tell us?" Deanna mirrored Eirene's worry.

"Not yet," Roarke replied. "Not until we know what's going on."

"Sounds ominous." Kate worried her lip. "Are they back on UK soil?"

Graeme nodded. "De Alvaro got them on a plane back here earlier."

"I've texted Colin to tell him we're debriefing them," Roarke said, looking at his watch. "It's just twenty-two hundred. He'll let us know when we can have the conference call. We need to let them know that Valerian is alive."

Deanna gasped, her face slowly turning ashen. Apprehension leapt out of her in buckets. "No..."

"He won't find you, my lady." Roarke let his gear

fall to the floor before cupping Deanna's face in his hands. "He will die first before he even lays his eyes on you."

"I'll carry your things, Hamilton, and we can continue the conversation back at the Faesten." Luke suggested, bending down to get Roarke's gear.

"Thank you." Roarke spared him a grateful smile.

Luke understood Deanna's anxiety. He had seen first-hand how conflicted she was when she returned to Roarke, having been Dac's prisoner and mistress. The Ancients had hired him to spy on Deanna to make sure that she was not working for Dac Valerian. He did not like the idea but the proposition was something he could not resist. Spy on Deanna Logan in exchange for accessing the Cynn Cruors archives to find out where he came from. Some good that did since he was nowhere near to finding out who he was.

The ride to the Faesten was relatively quiet. Luke gave the immortals their much needed time with their mates. Their whispered promises of what they were planning on doing once they reached their quarters made him envious.

"Guys, mind changing to your telepathic links? You know, the one you only share with your women?" Luke joked. "Have pity on your unmated chauffeur."

The warriors snickered and the women giggled.

"You'll have your chance soon enough," Eirene remarked.

Luke snorted. "Hardly likely."

"Listen to Eirene, Luke," Graeme added, his voice, wry. "She has this uncanny ability to give you a vaguely specific idea of what will happen."

"Vaguely specific, huh?" Luke glanced at his rear-view mirror when there was laughter behind him until he too chuckled before they finally fell silent. He exhaled.

There was no better time as that moment to appreciate the dictum that silence was golden.

Until auburn tresses and dark brown eyes floated to the centre of his mind.

Bloody hell, could his mind not give him a break?

As soon as they arrived at the Faesten, everyone alighted and entered the lift, except Luke.

"Coming, Griffiths?" Graeme asked, holding the lift's button.

"I'll meet you upstairs," he called back, partially swivelling to acknowledge the Cynn Cruor. He made his way towards the parking lot's entrance. "I'm going to take a walk."

"Be back in two." Roarke instructed.

"Will do." Luke didn't bother to face them but raised his hand in a wave before walking into the night.

Chapter Five

"Where are you?" Colin moved away from the group even as he opened his telepathic link with his men. He left the security room and made a beeline for the alleyway.

Keep Seth and the rest occupied.

"Wouldn't you like to know."

"Mackenzie—"

There was an angry growl. "I'm not Mackenzie. I haven't been for a very long time."

"Then why call me brother?" Colin knew he was goading Mackenzie. He could not help it. The need to know if his brother was still inside that Scatha shell was overpowering. He was desperate. He wanted his brother back. He wanted his fellow Cynn Cruor returned. Mack had always been a bit short tempered, ever since their parents died. Colin pushed the fire door and walked into the alley.

"Fuck you!"

Colin's hand rested on his hip and he looked up at the sky framed by the buildings' rooftops. Yup, his brother was still there. A humourless smile crossed Colin's mouth. "That's quite a unique name you've given me." When he heard a moan in the background, Colin lowered his head, his eyes narrowing at the brick wall in front of him. "Where are you Mackenzie?"

"I'm not—"

"No matter what you think or do or say, you're still *bràthair* to me."

A painful moan.

"What the bloody hell did you do now?" Colin asked, his voice furious. He paced the alley.

"Always my fault, isn't it?" Mackenzie accused. "I didn't want to be a Scatha. You made it happen but it will always be my fault. Why can't you get it through that thick skull of yours that you're to blame?"

Colin's chest tightened with the guilt that never left him since Mackenzie's transformation. Now was not the time or place to dwell on it. "Where is she? I swear to God if you hurt her—"

"I'm the worse Scatha there is. I've got a fucking bloody conscience! I hate it!" His brother snapped before muttering, "I don't know why the fuck I'm doing this."

Colin kept quiet, his empty hand curling. "Where are you?" He repeated. "Let her go. Leave her in a place where we can pick her up. I won't chase after you tonight."

"No. I can't do that."

"Why the hell not?" Colin blazed, pacing the narrow alley. He bluffed. "We know where the Scatha lair is."

"I'm sure you do, but I'm not there."

"We're just running in circles, Mackenzie."

"I'm here. At the Faesten."

"What?" Colin stopped dead. "Why?"

"Because I don't want the Scathas to know about her." He sighed, resigned. "She needs the Cynn Cruors' protection."

* * *

By the time Luke returned they were all in the Faesten's library and nerve centre. Finn and Eirene, Roarke and Deanna sat in opposing couches while Kate was on Graeme's lap on one of the wingback chairs closer to the unlit fireplace. The lingering smell of bacon wafted out of the open windows and Luke watched

Eirene, who popped the last bacon rasher into her mouth, with amusement. It was a cool spring night and nearly the entire city was asleep save for those clubbing. The smell of rain wafted through the windows. Soon Manchester would bask in wetness.

"Jay," Luke greeted the Cynn mortal who stood in front of the unlit hearth. "I thought you'd be long gone."

Jay lifted his hand in a wave. Anyone who saw him would think he ate people for breakfast, with his imposing broad shouldered physique and shaved head. He had gained a lot in bulk and muscle since the Elliot Hammond debacle. While he was no nonsense, the Cynn Cruors knew that he was as kind as a lamb especially when it came to women and his girlfriend, Florence, one of Kate's best friends. His skin was the colour of smooth molasses and he had a round but chiselled face. It was his kind hazel eyes that Florence had fallen in love with and his adherence to his duty as a Cynn mortal. He was a man the Manchester Faesten respected and trusted, their inside intel in the police force.

"Florence knows I'll be a bit late. She doesn't want me to disturb her reading another historical thriller slash romance novel. Like the danger of being a Cynn mortal's girlfriend wasn't enough." Jay's brow creased and he shook his head ruefully.

Graeme chuckled. "Just imagine what historical romances we could ply her with."

"Really?" Kate arched a brow enquiringly.

"That was before I met you, Corrigan," Graeme said softly, caressing the back of Kate's head. "If you existed then, I'd only have one historical romance to tell." He brought Kate's lips down to his, sealing his vow.

"Found what you were looking for?" Roarke enquired, his gaze assessing.

Luke shook his head. He had walked all over town,

from King Street, to Deansgate hoping to get a glimpse of the woman who now filled his every waking moment. If Adara Kerslake was a Cynn Cruor, then she would be more comfortable walking around at night when the sun set and the Kinaré did not make her blood boil from the inside out. She would be trawling the streets and bars looking for possible Scatha Cruor abductions and preventing them from happening. No such luck. He did get a good lay by the side of one of the office buildings, erasing the woman's memory of the tryst ever happening. He still felt unsatisfied. All he kept seeing was Adara's face. It was as though someone had branded her face inside his mind with an iron.

The phone beeped by the bank of computers.

"That must be Colin." Eirene moved away from Finn's side. She stood and brushed her hands against her jeans as she walked towards the controls. Soon Colin's face showed on the large LCD screen. "You're online, Colin."

Colin's face came into focus. "Eirene! Ladies," he drawled, his smile widening to show perfect white teeth. "Jay! How's it going, mate?"

"Doing brill, now that I have Florence with me." Jay grinned.

"Luke! Have you decided which Faesten you'd like to be a part of?"

Luke chuckled. "Not yet."

"Roarke," Colin said, turning his attention to the Manchester Dux. "Sorry for leaving you in a lurch, mate."

"It couldn't be helped, Butler, so don't sweat it," Roarke replied. "You did, however, miss one bloody battle."

"Damn!" Colin sighed. "That good?"

"Bloody good," Finn answered. "More werewolves

in the beach battle that would put Normandy to shame with the immediate surrender of the weres to the Deoré."

"No shit!"

"Yes shit." Finn's mouth quirked before he became sober. Even Jay whistled, shaking his head in wonder.

"Where's Zac?" Colin asked.

"He had to stay for a while longer," Roarke answered quietly. "He was nearly killed by Kamaria, the Deoré's aunt."

"Oh God, no," Eirene, Deanna, and Kate cried almost simultaneously. Jay straightened from his post by the fireplace, his face a picture of shock. Colin's face crumpled.

"He's better now." Roarke assured everyone. "If it weren't for Faith, he would be dead by now."

"Faith?" Jay asked.

"His mate," Finn said.

Jay rubbed his hand over his shaved head and shook his head. "Man, we seem to be finding our mates in skirmishes or battles lately. I'm just glad Faith was there. How did they meet? Does she know about us?"

"She does now," Finn replied. "She went to La Nahuaterique on a medical mission and was kidnapped. While Zac was healing after the battle, she told us more of how she came to be there. She said she sensed Zac when he and the Ancients tracked Dac Valerian and the Deoré's aunt. They killed her kidnappers, but she was able to escape of all places to the Specus Argentum. She's also like us."

"Another Cynn Cruor female?" Luke asked, taken aback.

"No," Roarke answered. "She's a firebinder."

"Say that again?" Jay's forehead ploughed. "A firebinder?"

"She has fire in her blood and uses it to heal. She

can also kill."

"How?" Eirene's eyes were wide as saucers. "Knives? Daggers? Stilettos?"

"That's your speciality, babe." Finn chuckled. Eirene scowled with impatience at him but blew him a kiss before turning back to Roarke.

"Faith has to be close to the ground so that when her blood siphons out the illness, it will flow to the earth and not stay inside her. If she's not close to the ground, not only will the disease return to the person she's healing, her fireblood will flood the person as well."

Eirene and the rest of the women, Luke, and Jay stared at Roarke, stupefied.

"Oh God." Eirene's breath came out in a rush. "I think I need a drink." She stood up and walked to the mini bar that had recently been built inside the nerve centre.

Finn's eyebrows rose in enquiry. "You sure about that?"

"Oh yes," she puffed. "Now more than ever."

"I'll have one as well." Deanna stood, surprising Roarke. "Surely with the Kinaré in us, it'll sharpen our minds just like yours and at the moment we need all our heads put together."

"Count me in." Kate got up from a bemused Graeme's lap.

While everyone was having a light-hearted moment, Luke watched Colin. The Cynn Cruor warrior joined in the laughter but his smile did not reach his eyes. It was as though he could not wait for the debriefing to begin.

Or to end.

There was something definitely wrong, and Luke did not take his gut instincts lightly. Being a spy had honed that trait, and with his ability to shift between parallel planes, he was formidable. No one knew that he was in their midst until it was too late. Watching Colin, he wondered whether he would need to use his abilities again the same way he did when he spied on Deanna. If it came to that, he hoped to God that it was not something that would test his loyalties. He was already beginning to feel a sense of brotherhood with the Cynn Cruors even if he had not committed himself to either Leeds or Manchester. They were a band of brothers that had each other's backs, something he never had as a field agent.

Something he wished for now.

"How have you ladies been?" Colin asked when the women returned by their warriors' sides.

"Better now that our men are back." Deanna smiled.

"Dux, can we take a rain check on that debriefing? We're still in the middle of trying to get the children back to safety," Colin said with a rueful grin.

Roarke took his arm away from Deanna's shoulders and leaned forward, resting on his elbows on his knees. "Need any help?"

"No, we're fine, thanks." Colin was looking down at something which the feed could not show before they heard the shuffling of papers. "Sorry, mate, I'm just preoccupied."

"Understood, Dux." Roarke nodded. "Let's debrief tomorrow."

Colin looked up and smiled, his relief evident. "Thanks, Dux. Sorry, I gotta run." He severed the link.

"That's not the Colin I know," Finn murmured.

"Why do you say that?" Kate cocked her head to one side after taking a sip from her scotch. "God, this burns." She pursed her lips, whistling inwardly. Graeme's mouth twitched in amused adoration.

"Colin has never, not once in his life, missed a chance of keeping abreast with what is happening in

Cynn Cruor Faestens all over the globe," Graeme replied.

"He seemed evasive," Luke commented.

"You noticed that too." Roarke's face was pensive.

Luke nodded and leaned against the mantle. "Did anything happen in La Nahuaterique that was out of the ordinary?"

"I was thinking the same thing." Jay agreed. "Something could have triggered this change."

"Werewolves were unusual," Finn said as he stood to walk towards the mini bar. "We have never battled werewolves before, but I don't see how that could have affected Colin."

"Colin has always been a joker," Graeme said. "He's the only warrior I know who laughs, literally laughs in the face of danger. Like he has a death wish. Good thing Craig has been his shadow to sometimes rein him in. Those two are like real blood brothers."

"Colin had a brother, Mackenzie, but he was killed by the Scatha," Roarke added.

"Oh, Colin," Deanna said sadly. "Could the Honduran mission have triggered a memory? Maybe something that reminded him of how his brother died."

Roarke's forehead puckered. "It could have. Information on Mackenzie's death was sketchy and I didn't want to pry. But I don't think what happened in Honduras is to blame for his change in attitude. He was already different en route to La Nahuaterique, quiet and sombre. Not his usual self."

"Craig was almost the same," Graeme said. "Still their attention was on the mission. They took out a lot of the Scathas and werewolves and for that I'm grateful because we were nearly overwhelmed. They just kept pouring in. Had it not also been for De Alvaro and the Honduran Cynn Cruors, shite! I don't even want to think that far." Graeme's eyes closed. "Whatever is happening in Leeds hasn't derailed them at all."

"But there's still something there." Luke concluded.

Roarke nodded. "Whatever it is, we can't interfere unless he asks us to. We have to respect that. After all, he is the Leeds Dux."

* * *

Colin could not get back to the Faesten quick enough. Instead, he ordered his men to take the Merc and he would use his speed borne from the Kinaré to get home. Craig soon caught up with him. They both looked at each other. Words were not needed where Mackenzie was concerned. They flew by humans who thought that the sudden gust of wind was a freak mini tornado at night. They stopped as soon as they reached the Faesten's grounds, their breathing relaxed for immortals running faster than the speed of sound. There was still the tree lined driveway to trek through before they reached the Faesten's huge doors.

"Go to the command centre," Colin ordered. "Watch me from there."

Craig nodded, although he showed his worry. "You okay?"

"When was I never?" Colin cracked a smile.

"How about now?"

"I'm fine, Craig." Colin jutted his chin towards the basement parking. "Now get your arse down there."

Colin and Craig whizzed forward, before Craig broke away to enter the underground parking entrance by the side of the house. Colin approached the entrance warily. The van he saw in the CCTV feed was parked properly by the door. He let himself into the Faesten, his gaze sharply assessing. Nothing appeared amiss. His feet moved stealthily across the wood polished foyer. He made his way through the hallway that ran beside the grand staircase. He peered into the huge dining room, the library, the unused and musty ballroom. Nothing. The doors to the game room were also undisturbed.

He felt for his dagger tucked snugly at the small of his back. All Leeds Cynn Cruor immortals had it. The urge to take it out was strong because of the faint Scatha stench, but this was Mackenzie, his younger brother. He would not. He could not. There was still hope for his brother despite what he saw happening around him. He tried to erase the thought of what happened to Kate Corrigan's best friend, Tommy, when he was transformed when he helped bring down Elliot Hammond a few months back. It had taken almost all of his willpower not to show how affected he had been, and when the Cynn Cruors honoured Tommy with a burial, he imagined Mackenzie in the same boat. At that moment, he had been united with Kate in grief more than any of the warriors present. Question was, would they also bury him with honours befitting a Cynn Cruor even if he was transformed to a Scatha? Tommy was forced to become one as well. The only difference between Kate's friend and his brother was that the Cynn Cruors immediately knew of Tommy's transformation. He kept Mackenzie's transformation a secret from the Cynn Cruors. And now he felt the noose tightening. Despite everything, he was going to make bloody sure he found a way to get Mackenzie back. The hell was he going to give up.

Even if he had to die trying.

"Mackenzie," he called, crossing the foyer.

There was no answer.

Colin inhaled and nearly choked against the sourness that threatened to rise up his nose. The smell was manageable, not as strong as the Scatha Cruors he encountered in the battle for the Specus Argentum. He followed the scent, the werewolf part of the Kinaré stalking its nemesis. He climbed the grand staircase that curved to the second floor and treaded stealthily along the corridor. He opened his telepathic line. Craig was close enough for him to communicate with.

Can you see him?

Negative. No sign. Craig telepathed back. *Not even in the dungeons.*

I'll check the bedrooms. He might be in his former quarters.

Be careful, Colin.

Colin scowled. *He's my brother, Craig.*

He's also a Scatha Cruor.

Don't remind me.

Colin heard Craig sigh. *Liam and Cormac have arrived.*

Tell them to keep their distance. This is my problem.

Craig snorted. *You do know that if Mack kills you, it's our duty to hunt him down.*

Colin came to an abrupt stop. *That's not going to happen. I'm not going to let it get to that point.*

Make sure it doesn't.

Colin thought that sometimes Craig would have made a much better Dux than he could ever be.

Chapter Six

Amaryllis moaned. She moved her head from side to side and winced when the right side of her forehead touched the pillow.

Pillow?

Her senses started to come into focus. The dank smell of garbage had disappeared and so did the last vestiges of feeling the hard cobblestones underneath her when she fell unconscious. It was replaced by the downy softness of the pillow under her head and the clean but musty smell—her eyelids fluttered open—of a room.

Amaryllis' gaze took in her surroundings, blinking so that she could put everything back into focus. She lay on what could only be described as a museum piece, something out of the opulent set of the Three Musketeers. A bed with a vaulted canopy with dark brocade and tasselled edges hovering over a mattress that was too firm as though it had not been slept on. Her hands felt the rich satin coverlet before drifting to the pillow case. Cotton. Contrasting textures. One rich, the other ordinary. She expected the pillowcase to be silk. Not that she had ever lain in similar plush surroundings. She knew the disparity because it was what spelled the difference between food and hunger, between what she stole and what she left behind, between a slap and being left in peace for just a few hours.

Amaryllis eased up on her elbows. There was a reading lamp, now lit, tucked in the corner of the room, close to a bookshelf built into the wall. Beside it, nearly facing the huge windows, was an upholstered wingback chair. She swivelled her head slowly, unsure if the movement was going to make the world spin. As it was, the bruise on her forehead was throbbing and felt as though some dumb bird made a nest and left an egg.

A love seat stood in front of the bed facing an unlit fireplace. There was another door off the room where she could see a marble sink and the plexiglass partition of what looked like a huge shower. A huge wardrobe and chest of drawers completed the ensemble of bedroom furniture. She slowly swung to a sitting position on the side of the bed. A vase with fresh lavender sat on the bedside table, its faint scent tickling her nose. With the mustiness around her, the flowers looked out of place. Amaryllis' head jerked to the right when she heard the bedroom door open. The light from the corridor bled into the room and silhouetted the figure that strode in.

"Don't come any closer," Amaryllis croaked.

The stranger gave a throaty laugh. "You're in my bedroom, well, former bedroom, so I can do whatever I want."

For one moment, confusion blanketed her mind. "Who are you? Why did you take me here? Put one finger on me and you won't need the surgeon's scalpel to change into a girl." Amaryllis' heart thumped so hard in her chest that it clogged her throat.

"Ouch," he said with mock pain, cupping his groin. He chuckled. "The name's Max Greene. You're very feisty, Miss Hart—"

"You know my name?" Amaryllis tracked his movements with wary eyes.

"But then again, your wanting to turn me into a girl is nothing." Max continued as though she did not speak, walking into the room until the lamplight showed his features. "You see, I thrive on pain. Pain makes me...breathe."

Amaryllis gasped. His sandy brown hair was

brushed back to show a widow's peak while he kept it short at the sides. He was handsome in a dark way, his chiselled cheekbones and angular jaw complimenting a cruel mouth, yet there was an air of vulnerability around him despite his leer. Dark brows slashed over eyes that were glowing green.

"Oh my God, you're one of them!" A flash of memory. "You were the last person I saw before I passed out!"

"I saved you."

"From what? From them when you're the same thing?" Adrenaline was pushing Amaryllis, her voice becoming shriller.

"If I didn't knock you out you would have been hit one more time and fucked by all of us at the back of the van," Max retorted, his tone turning her blood to ice. "Had I known you wouldn't mind getting gang banged, I wouldn't have bothered."

"Fuck you." She seethed.

"Gladly." His eyes glowed further. "When? Now's a good time as any."

"I'll kill you first before you do." She shot back. "Besides, you stink."

Amaryllis' squeal stuttered and her eyes bulged when, in less than a blink of an eye, Max was suddenly in front of her with his hand around her throat. She gasped when she felt something sharp slowly slice into her neck.

Oh dear God. I'm going to die.

"Aside from pain, I thrive on fear, and yours," he moved closer, his tongue swiping her cheek all the way to her earlobe. He grinned when she shuddered, "is an elixir I'd like to taste. I can see your terror in those irises, my violet beauty." Max pressed his body closer, hip to hip, chest to breasts. He laughed softly when she whimpered. "I'm going to enjoy fu— enjoy...enjoy...fuck!" He suddenly moved away.

Amaryllis stumbled forward but caught herself, her hand going to her throat. She winced when her fingers touched the gash on her neck. She looked at her hand. Blood. She could feel it slowly making its way to the hollow by her collarbone. She watched Max with fear and wariness. She could not believe her eyes when he was just in front of her one second and by the edge of the room the next. Unless he knew how to do those martial arts things that allowed them to fly.

"I'm sorry."

She stared at him blankly.

"Did you hear me?"

She tried to swallow, but her throat was so dry she coughed.

"I'm sorry."

"Excuse me?" Amaryllis stared at him. She was not sure she heard him right.

"I hurt you."

Her jaw slackened. *Bloody hell, is that remorse in his voice?*

"Didn't you say you liked pain?" she blurted. Okay, so her brain to mouth filter was not working.

"Shut the fuck up!"

That's it!

"Seriously, arsehole, you're giving me whiplash, not to say you've also given me a bloody hickey. Literally!" She was not scared shitless anymore. She was downright pissed. "Now show me how to get the out of here and I won't tell anyone you abducted me."

Max barked out a laugh. "And where will you go, bitch? Back to Crawley who easily gave you up? He's been our source of pussy to sell in the black market for years! He'll only find another buyer and you won't be lucky the next time around. By the time men are done with you, the miner forty-niner won't need explosives to enter the cave that used to be your hole." He laughed when Amaryllis flinched at his sordid joke. "Believe me, you're safer here."

Reminding her of Jack's betrayal and what he had intended for her made Amaryllis bleed inside. She felt the sharp bite of tears at the back of her eyes. Where would she indeed go? Go back to where she grew up? No, she would move to another place where no one knew her. Heck, she would make her way to the Shetlands if that was what it took to escape this growing nightmare. She had a little saved. She could go back to Crawley's hideout and sneak inside the secret passage she knew of, grab her things and then leave. So many questions plagued her mind about Jack and she would wait. After what he did to her? There was no more honour among thieves. She would spill everything she knew about Jack's operations. She had to find a way to get out. She could not stay.

"Since I don't know where 'here' is, you won't have to worry. Just let me go."

Max raked his hand through his hair, closing his eyes briefly, conflicted. "I can't," he exhaled the words as though they were being dragged from his mouth. "The Scatha can't know you're alive."

"What's the Scatha?" She blinked in bafflement.

"My brethren." He darted a glance at her. "You were going to be placed in the open block for men and women to bid on you."

"You're joking."

He looked at her, the smile tugging at his lips making him look sinister. "Do you think I am? I'm not."

Amaryllis' gut clenched. She shook her head, shock making her stare unseeingly.

Dear God, please make me wake up from this nightmare. Wake me up!

"I assure you it isn't a nightmare."

Amaryllis stared agape. Shock immobilized her. Bloody hell, who were these people? Correction. Who were these freaking beings? The hell she was staying a minute longer. She saw Max's eyes turn to slits, the sides of his mouth lifting to what could only be described as a diabolical smile. She closed her eyes and concentrated on imagining a blanket over and around her thoughts. As soon as she opened her eyes she vaulted and slid over the bed and got to the door before she screamed. Max's hands clamped over her upper arms. She struggled, her heart racing in fear. With one swift move, she kicked Max on the shin.

"Bloody fuck!" he snarled. "You can't go! You're safer here!"

"He's right. If you want to live, you'll have to stay."

Amaryllis' stumbled backward when Max roared as he let her go. Blood drained from her face as she watched him transform into something straight out of a horror movie. His face became more cruel, if that could still happen, and his mouth. Oh God! His mouth started filling up with sharp teeth, reminding her of vampires and werewolves. And his fingers…they elongated and curved into…claws! Was that how he sliced through her skin? Amaryllis felt like a deer caught in the headlights of an oncoming lorry. She could not move. It was an effort to even swivel her head to look at the man who spoke.

A man who looked like Max.

Max's voice sounded like wheezing. "It's repugnant to see you again, Colin."

Colin treaded slowly into the room. "It's good to see you again, *bràthair*."

* * *

Colin kept his distance from Max. Still, elation filled him at finally seeing his brother after such a long time. Then, pain pushed the happiness away. It hurt him to see his younger brother transform to the very thing he vowed to kill. He looked at the woman, his mouth tightening at the sliver of blood trickling down the side of her neck. Her eyes bulged in horror, her terror palpable as she watched Max morphing. It was so thick that Colin could cut through it. Her heartbeat was elevated and soon she might just pass out without someone pinching her nerve. When he spoke, her eyes darted to his face and he was floored. Her almost feline eyes were the colour of deep amethysts that seemed to burn a hole through the darkness of his existence to flood it with bright light. Her cheeks were flushed, accentuating her oval face. His groin tightened at the sight of her perfect mouth in the shape of Cupid's bow, parted, soft, and moist. She was more beautiful than Colin had ever imagined. Her black hair slightly tousled from sleep had that streak of purple he saw on the CCTV. It was parted to the side to flow down her shoulders in soft natural waves. He had to stifle a groan at seeing her hourglass body encased in leather. What treasures lay beneath that layer of clothing? Colin wanted to find out.

"Brother?"

Colin's musings were cut short by the lilt of her voice. Somewhere between a woman and a child. The strong urge to protect her hit him in the gut, blindsiding him. Damn, she was sexy even when she spoke.

"Aye, Mackenzie is my brother," he said quietly.

"I am not your fucking brother, Cynn Cruor! My name is Max Greene. Mackenzie Butler is dead."

Colin's jaw tightened so much he thought it would break. Had Mackenzie really forsaken their heritage? Their name? It was enough that he ached and suffered Mack's jibes. He did not know what he would do if his parents were still alive to see Max now and hear the vitriol that spewed from his mouth.

"You called me and came to the Faesten," Colin said, instead refusing to rise to the bait. "The Faesten has sensors to know whether a Scatha has broken through or not. You're here and it didn't. You are as much as a Cynn Cruor as I am, Mack."

Max screeched and Colin saw Amaryllis cover her ears as she winced. "Never."

"We can discuss our bloodline later." Colin changed the subject again. "Now that she's here, you have my word. No harm will come to her."

Max straightened from his crouching position, dark neon green eyes burning into Colin's soul, a reminder of a mistake he had had no control of. Colin watched the woman's eyes widen so much at Max's metamorphosis as his teeth receded and his claws became fingers once again. By the time he was through, Max was breathing hard. Colin saw Craig, Liam, and Cormac enter the corridor, but he gave an imperceptible shake of his head. They slowed down. He did not know whether the Scatha could tap into their telepathic link and at the moment he did not care. He did not want to spook Max. Colin just had this need to see Max after he escaped from them almost two hundred years before. He also needed to keep Max safe from the Cynn Cruors until he could find a way to remove the Scathas' hold on him.

"I can only imagine how painful that must have been," Colin murmured, watching and cringing when Max gave him such a look of hatred that could make even strong men wither.

"I thrive on pain, Butler." Max watched him with wariness before a smile pulled one corner of his mouth. "You should try it sometime."

"No thanks, I hardly go to the dentist or the salon," he said. "I'll pass."

"Dickhead."

Colin's brow arched. "And you are?"

Max growled, his eyes changing again, his head jerking when he saw the rest of the Cynn Cruor moving.

"Macken—Max." Colin sighed. "You're here inside the Faesten, outnumbered four to one. Do you really want to fight? In front of her?" He nudged his chin at the dumbfounded beauty.

Max looked at the violet eyed beauty before turning his attention back to Colin. His mouth widened to a shit-eating grin. "Let's do that...*bràthair*. To the victor, the spoils. No, let me amend that. The ashes."

"I won't kill you, Mack." Colin reverted to the name he called his brother since they were children. "Neither will I raise a hand or sword at you unless I have to impress into that bloody skull of yours that you're one of us. I swore that I would find a way to bring you back."

"I don't want to go back," Max bellowed in a shrill voice that made Colin wince and the woman grimace. "The Scatha are now my brothers, Butler. Get your head around that fucking fact!"

"No! You are not one of them!"

"You are now my enemy," Max continued as though Colin had not spoken. "So you better watch your head because I intend to take it!"

"Mackenzie! Don't do—" The rest of Colin's sentence gushed out of him the moment Max barrelled into him. Colin registered a scream like it came from a tunnel before he and Mack toppled to the floor. He roared as white hot pain seared him when Max swiped his claws against his mid-section before diagonally slashing across his chest with inhuman speed. The agony and the Scatha's stench that covered Max made it difficult for Colin to control the bloodlust in his veins. He could feel his eyes change. Did not know how long he could parry Mackenzie's blows without hurting him. Blood fell in rivulets from every wound Mackenzie inflicted on him. His arms bled. His leather jacket was torn to shreds. He raised his arms to protect his head and neck from Max's blows. But when Max buried his claws into his stomach, Colin bellowed. The bloodlust was now in full force, unable to do anything about it until it was satisfied. The gloves were off.

Mackenzie was going to die.

Chapter Seven

What did I get myself into?

Amaryllis' mind swirled at the scene transpiring in front of her. She screamed in reflex when the fight between brothers started. Brothers? She heard Max mention his brother's name. Colin? But Colin had called him Mackenzie. How could they be so different from each other? Were they separated at birth? She could not move, riveted at the scene unfolding. Then Max's brother howled and the vice that seemed to grip her in place shattered.

"Stop it!" she screamed. The growls and roars of torment drowned her plea. She shrieked again when Max catapulted over his brother, crashing heavily against the lamp and the bookshelf, splintering the wood, books sliding open on the floor. There was another roar, this time from Max. Amaryllis saw the flash of metal before a dagger met Max's gut.

"Oh God, please stop fighting!"

They did not stop, did not heed her. Their growls and snarls bounced around the room. Amaryllis whipped her head towards the door when three men with evil looking swords casually walked into the room. One of the men flicked a switch by the door and the room flooded with light, which did not even stop the fight. They stood a few feet apart from each other, watching the brawl with cautious eyes. Amaryllis threw all caution to the wind, rushing to the three men.

"Stop them," she cried. They ignored her. She grabbed the jacket of the man with silver eyes, who looked down at her like she was a pesky fly. "Why are you not doing anything?"

"Let them finish," one of the men with dark hair replied, his voice hard.

"One of them is going to die!"

He looked at her, his mouth curling. "None of them will die."

"But can't you at least stop it?" She was getting desperate. Blood flowed freely from both men.

"How do you propose we do that?" His brow arched and raised his sword. "Slice through them?"

Blood, a mixture of red and green spilled from the two men, splashing against the walls and floors. It splattered on the Persian rug on the floor and flicked against the walls and the now upended wingback chair. Amaryllis gave a short scream when the standing lamp toppled over, crashing on the floor.

Oh my God...dark green blood? Are these people aliens?

Amaryllis snapped, fear turning to anger. "God, I can't believe I'm surrounded by arseholes," she muttered underneath her breath. The man who refused to help gave her an amused glare while the mouths of the other with him lifted in lopsided grins. Amaryllis looked around, stepping back when the brothers fought near her. In a burst of inspiration, she vaulted on to the bed. She took out the flowers from the vase, inching her way to the brothers before she threw the water on the two men.

"What the fuck?" Max roared.

"You didn't want to stop!" Amaryllis shot back. "You were going at each other like dogs. Now calm the fuck down!"

Max glared at her. His horrific appearance should have scared her, but Amaryllis was past beyond caring. She had never fainted in her life and she would not be surprised if she was about to. Right in front of her, the wounds inflicted by Max on Colin gradually healed, his tattered shirt and leather jacket the only evidence of their violent fight. Max's face also morphed, his teeth returning to their normal size, claws changing back to long tapered fingers. His wounds also closed, the skin stitching together like tendrils of fibreglass before they melded together, leaving new pinkish hued skin. He was devilishly handsome again.

Lord, please let this just be a nightmare. I'd do anything to not wake up in this hellhole.

"What the hell...are...you people?" The adrenaline rush was waning and the words came out choppy, like she had been crying so hard she could not stop the hiccups clogging her throat. Panic threatened to drown her this time. Gritting her teeth, she pushed it back down. She knew of people who had their teeth sharpened and wore red contacts to look like vampires, but she had never come across anyone who could make those same teeth recede or the eyes return to normal. What would she know about the latest inventions in cosmetic surgery? She was not interested in the latest procedures to make a person uber-perfect. She was more concerned with putting food in her stomach and a roof over her head.

She watched the two men glower at each other before Colin took a deep breath and exhaled loudly. He raked one had through his hair and wiped the greenish tinged blood from his dagger.

"Are you sick? That's green blood. You might have developed an infection." Okaaay...her brain to mouth filter was so not working again.

Max glared at her, pinning her in place. Colin and the rest of the men visibly stiffened. Amaryllis saw Max shudder, his hands balling into fists. There it was again, the vulnerability she saw before he took on a cruel persona. Jekyl and Hyde in the flesh.

"Stay away from him," Colin ordered her.

She approached him slowly, still holding the vase, drawn to the helplessness that seemed to cloak him. Max's eyes narrowed and watched her every move. A deep sound rumbled from his chest. She hesitated before she continued. The one thing Amaryllis trusted above anything else was her gut instinct. Without it, she would not have gotten out of the many scrapes she found herself in. Her gut was telling her now that Max was not dangerous despite his ability to become Mister Ugly Face.

She continued to approach Max. "He isn't going to hurt me," she said softly. "He saved me. Didn't you, Max?" Why she was talking to him as though he was a child, she had no bloody idea. All she knew was that it was the right thing to do.

Max straightened and stood taller. The change he went through was subtler, the cruelty dissipating. He was someone with looks that girls would fall over for, preen, and try to catch his attention but that was not what Amaryllis felt. She felt sympathy, empathy.

"I know what you're going through," she said.

Max's brows rose. He looked at Colin and the men by the door. "Really? Have you been killed only to resurrect as someone else?" His voice was soft and dangerous. "I don't think so, violet beauty, because you would not smell as fuckable as you do now."

Amaryllis dropped the vase that thumped on the carpeted floor instead of breaking into pieces. Her hands were on her hips and a scowl on her face.

"Seriously? Wash your mouth with bloody soap and water," she snapped. Her ire was further fuelled by Max's slack jaw. "And close your mouth. It's not polite."

The silence was deafening. Amaryllis swore she could hear all their heartbeats. She turned to Colin and the other men. They appeared to find difficulty hiding their amusement, their mouths twitching. She turned to Colin. Holy shit, the way his half lidded eyes looked at her made her want to melt to a puddle in front of him. He was hot. His beach boy looks were out of place in this windswept Georgian mansion. His short cropped blond hair looked like it had been bleached with gold. His green eyes were inscrutable, yet Amaryllis could feel the heat in them. Her body warmed before it became a slow burn starting from the pit of her belly close to her pubis that steadily spread out and up to her breasts. She swallowed. If only he would...

He cleared his throat. Her eyes widened when his eyes glowed with gold. She blinked. The gold was gone. Had she just imagined it? A thought occurred. Damn, could he read minds too? Holy shit! She flushed, so sure that she looked like a tomato. Then he frowned as though he was...conflicted. She wanted to smooth the furrow between his eyes by kissing it. She felt the blood rushing to her cheeks and averted her gaze when Colin cocked a brow and a minuscule smile formed on his mouth, which she nearly did not notice because of the sexy stubble that shadowed his jaw. He crossed his arms over his broad chest, his biceps bulging against his tattered clothes, leaving her without a doubt of his strength, his masculinity.

His virility.

Amaryllis had to concentrate. There was too much testosterone in the room, not that the other men were bleeding that hormone in buckets. All the testosterone she could handle came from Colin. She had to leave the place.

"You really can't leave," Colin spoke with regret.

thigh before settling on her hip. His other hand moved further upwards and Amaryllis' stomach tensed at the fire from his palm, her skin coming alive at his touch until his hand slowly made its way to cup her breast. She moaned and closed her eyes as his thumb rubbed her painfully hard nipple through her thin T-shirt, making it ache for his mouth. She hovered just an inch above his erection, her thighs straining, her body aching for the contact.

"Ride me," he rasped. "Hard."

Amaryllis did not need further prodding. Her sex was slick and wet inside her jeans and when she grazed her core against Colin's arousal, he hissed. She closed her eyes, air leaving her in a moan. Her clit felt engorged against his hardness, and the more she rubbed, the more the ache grew.

"I…need," she breathed.

In an instant, Colin unzipped her jeans and his hand dipped inside her panties.

"Oh God," she whimpered when Colin's finger found the centre of her arousal, swirling it lazily. She kept dry humping him, his length heating her opening. Then his finger slid inside her. She gazed down at him and saw that his eyes had more gold than green. Her breathing became erratic, soft sounds coming out of her as he finger-fucked her.

"Yes." She closed her eyes when Colin placed two fingers inside her.

"You're wet. I like that. I like wet pussy," he murmured. "Makes me want to taste you and fuck you with my tongue."

She moaned. His dirty words made her feel wanton. She lifted her hips and opened his fly. Dear Lord, he was not wearing anything! He bucked his hips and Amaryllis closed her hand around his thick hot shaft, the skin like velvet, the rod like steel. It was Colin's turn to groan, his eyelids closing over his unusual eyes. Amaryllis firmly moved her hand up and down his erection before circling her palm over the head slick with pre-cum.

"Ancients!" Colin pressed himself against her hand. "Yes, Violet, give me that hand job."

Amaryllis complied eagerly. The harder Colin finger-fucked her, the firmer her grip became, jerking him while her other hand went down to cup his balls. She fell beside him on the floor, each one heavily petting the other. Amaryllis licked her lips when she looked down at his cock's glistening head.

"Sweet Jesus!" Colin growled.

Amaryllis' eyes snapped back to his. Their gazes locked, refusing to let go while their hands pleasured each other. Colin kept his fingers inside her while his thumb teased her clit, then he moved his fingers in a come-hither action.

"Oh…" Amaryllis could feel her orgasm building, intense pleasure coiling tightly inside her pelvic area, the sensation rising towards her belly and her centre, her sex clenching against his digits. Colin moved faster inside her and she could feel the heat starting to burn her, delicious tremors making her clench her thighs. Her hips undulated against his hand while her hands kept up the pace on his granite hard shaft.

"That's it," Colin growled. "I'm going to fuck you soon enough. I will have my cock inside your pussy and I will ride you hard. Oh yeah, jerk me, baby. I love your hand on my cock. Make me come."

They matched each stroke, every touch, every hard caress taking them higher.

"Yes!" Amaryllis felt her orgasm overpower her, catching her unawares at the last minute, her vagina clamping against Colin's fingers. Two more strokes and she heard Colin growl, the warmth of his seed spurting and flowing against her hand. She continued her strokes until he became semi-flaccid. Her eyes, half lidded flared with lust when Colin placed his fingers inside his mouth.

"You taste good." His tongue swiped between his fingers and Amaryllis felt an answering twitch on her clit. With mischief in her eyes, she slid her fingers along Colin's cock, wet from his spurts. She watched his eyes flare gold again, tracking her fingers before they disappeared into her mouth. Amaryllis moaned in appreciation, the salty tang of his essence bursting on her tongue.

"So do you," she said against her digits, sucking them as they went in and out of her mouth.

Colin chuckled, his eyes turning back to green. "You still can't leave."

Amaryllis felt as though she had been slapped. She shoved off him. "Damn you."

Colin stood up and fixed himself. His smile did not reach his eyes. "I already am."

He pivoted to the door. "Stay here," he ordered again. "If you attempt to escape, I'll put you on my knee and spank that sweet ass until it becomes pussy red."

"Ugh!" Amaryllis gasped, anger making her blood boil. In a fit, she looked around and saw a glass vase by the side of the bed. She sprinted for it and hurled it like a cricket ball at Colin's back before it shattered on the floor. She gasped, fear suddenly spiking her heart rate.

Oh shit.

Heart in her throat, Amaryllis stared wide eyed at him when he turned around. Instead of ranting, Colin laughed softly before closing the door.

Chapter Eight

Ancients! Amaryllis was the hottest woman he had the pleasure of fingering for a long time. Colin's cock stiffened just at the thought of Amaryllis' hand on it. His brother's push to get away had landed him where he wanted to be. If Mack was not his enemy he would have thanked him. He would cuff him around the neck and pull him into an embrace like he used to do when they were young. His mouth lifted unconsciously. Mack hated being hugged, said that it was only for girls. Then he would run away, taking the crags so swiftly, Colin always had to pull him short using their telepathic link.

Easy, Mackenzie, humans are watching, Colin would message.

Then Mack would stand still by the side of the hill and climb to the top at a more sedate pace.

Seducing Amaryllis Hart was not in the initials cards he had in his hand. Keeping Mackenzie in the Faesten was. But when he lost his balance and felt her soft body against his, the Kinaré roared and demanded that he taste and take her, to appease the lust that ran wild inside him. God knew he needed the strength that sex gave him, gave all the Cynn Cruors. He did not get a chance to sleep during the flight back to the UK, worried about what he would find. Then he was hit with a double whammy. Mackenzie.

And Amaryllis Hart.

He never intended to read her mind, never intended to know who she was or where she came from. Even when he saw her on the camera's feed and he felt the stirrings of desire traipsing through his blood down his spine and snugly thicken his cock, he had no intention of knowing her other than making sure that she was free of the Scatha Cruors. Hearing her scream and seeing her in the flesh in Mackenzie's old room and all his vows disappeared. Talk about lip service. He watched her stamp down her fear. She was definitely afraid, terror oozing from her pores when she saw Mack transform.

Bloody hell, Mack. You just fucking gave us away.

Despite Mack's physical transformation, she held her ground, challenged his brother and treating him like a child. Amaryllis Hart was either really brave or she was extremely stupid to take on the Scatha, and Colin could not stop the grudging admiration he felt. Hysterical women were a dime a dozen in the streets, screeching like banshees as though men found breaking their eardrums endearing. Amaryllis was of a different mould, a woman who refused to run away in the face of one of the most grotesque transformation any human was likely to witness. Colin also felt protective of her, not the kind of protectiveness he felt for the women he bedded, making sure that they were safe after their tryst. With Amaryllis, it was more. He wanted to protect her and possess her. The way that a man possessed, protected, and placed a woman on a pedestal. To kiss the very ground she walked on. So when Mack said that she was good enough to…

Colin halted mid-stride. Early on he had been willing to bring Mack back to the Cynn Cruors fold. Towards the end, he was ready to send Mack to the beyond. Bloody hell, his mind was about to explode, as though his head was a tennis ball being whacked back and forth at Wimbledon.

He entered the command centre, the glass doors opening with a swoosh. He shucked his shredded jacket from his shoulders, slightly wincing at the pull of new skin over his wounds, which felt no different to a sunburn he occasionally had when he stayed too long under direct sunlight. "Talk to me."

He stood before the huge LED screen on the wall, legs braced apart, arms crossed over his chest. A muscle in his jaw ticked at the annoying sensation of tightness all over his body.

"Mack left the van behind." Liam noted, enlarging the camera's feed showing the Faesten's entrance. He walked to Colin, a syringe in his hand. "Here, you need it." Colin looked down and took the adriserum, nodding his thanks before he plunged the needle in the crook of his arm.

"He'll be starting a bloody war," Cormac muttered, his eyes slowly turning into the colour of bloodlust.

"We're already at war." Liam huffed.

"I meant on our doorstep," Cormac retorted.

Colin's mouth tightened, proof of the truth he refused to accept right in front of him. He remained silent. What could he say? Cormac was right. If the Scatha saw the van used to abduct the woman within the Leeds Faesten, they could easily put two and two together. That is if their small minds could see the ramifications of Mackenzie's actions. They would not understand how one of their own kind had willingly sought the Cynn Cruors' protection for a potential victim. Protection and justice had never been part of the Scatha Cruors' vocabulary.

"Why was he here, Colin?" Cormac's thunderous frown could not hide the puzzlement reflected in his eyes, the bloodlust almost gone.

"Amaryllis. He wanted the Cynn Cruors' protection for her."

"What?" Cormac and Liam's jaws slackened.

"It's why he called," Colin said, his face grim. "I could hardly believe it myself. After all this time..." If

Mackenzie had still raked up enough scruples, that meant all was not lost in bringing him back to the Cynn Cruors' fold. A renewed spark of hope lit up inside Colin's heart. He also could not help but think that for Mackenzie to live as long as he did in the Scatha's' midst, no one probably knew his connection to the Leeds Faesten. For that he was grateful and for that, Colin believed there was still hope for Mack.

"Well, that's a first." Cormac drew out a long breath before raking his tapered fingers through his hair and scratch the back of his head.

"A first for everything, bro'," Liam said. "First time Mack returned after Crimea."

Colin sucked in his breath. The helplessness he felt more than two hundred years ago still tightened his chest at the memory of when Mackenzie turned.

"Sorry, Dux."

"Treat me one more time like a pussy and I swear I'll punch you all," he growled.

Liam flushed. "Aye, so—Dux."

Colin exhaled and shook his head. He clamped his hand on his friend's shoulder as remorse replaced his anger. "I know you mean well, Liam. It's I who should apologise."

Liam's mouth turned upward slightly. "I cannot even begin to comprehend how you've done it. What it feels like to live with the guilt. But you have my word and it's as strong as the day I pledged my fealty to you eons ago. I will follow you."

"As will I," Cormac added, nodding before inclining his head at Liam. "You know, what he said."

He did not deserve Liam and Cormac's loyalty. Hell, he did not deserve their fealty. Craig, whom he had known for the longest time could have left right after the Mackenzie incident, but he stayed. All of them, vicariously carrying the same burden through him and trying to make sense of the conundrum his brother started. By abiding by him, they had sealed their fates as well.

"I lost him."

They all turned to see Craig walk through the automatic doors, agitated. The only sign of exertion was his wind ruffled hair. The vampire part of the Kinaré fuelled their speed effortlessly.

"How far did you get before you lost his scent?" Cormac asked.

"As far as Call Lane before he merged with the bar crowd."

Colin rubbed his forehead with his fingers. He could feel the onset of a headache coming. Shit. Cynn Cruors never had headaches. They were immune to any human affliction, no matter how small. "Liam—"

"Last known Scatha lair was just outside Bradford. They've moved again and so far we haven't found a track. They keep moving before we can even put a fix on them. You know that."

"God dammit!" The Scatha Cruors were getting savvy.

The phone on the console beeped.

"Annaseth."

"Dux, Scatha's are crawling all over town both in Cynn Cruor owned and human pubs." A frisson of anxiety laced Seth's tone. "It's like they're rejoicing and they don't care."

"Suit up," Colin ordered his men before speaking to Seth. "We'll be there in ten."

"We'll keep them occupied," Seth said before ending the call.

Craig by then had whizzed to the far right wall, pressing a code into the wall console. Soon the wall separated, opening into a recessed chamber filled with weapons. M249 Squad Automatic Weapons were locked in place beside smaller hand guns like Desert Eagles, Glocks, and SIG Sauers. PK2000 hand guns were placed side by side with CZs and Beretta APXs. To the side of the assault weapons were various swords from the Turkish kilijs and scimitars, to broadswords, wakizashis, and katanas. There were misericordes, dirks, anelaces and even the medieval double balled mace. Craig, Liam, and Cormac started packing weapons. Two guns strapped to their thighs, smaller swords on their backs and several rounds of ammunition in their pockets. Cormac took two parrying daggers and inserted them in the scabbard attached to the belt at the small of his back. He then took two misericordes and attached them to his waist.

"What about Amaryllis?" Craig kept fitting weapons on his body.

"I'll deal with her." Colin secured a longer dagger on the small of his back. He walked to the door. "Meet you in the foyer."

He breezed up to Mack's room, both dreading and anticipating this confrontation with his violet spitfire.

Amaryllis isn't yours. She belongs to Mackenzie.

"Mackenzie never said anything," he muttered, making his way to the room.

He should have felt remorse at their heavy petting, but it just felt so right. Colin hardly placed any importance in destiny but at that very moment, it appeared that his true north pointed to the woman with the unusual violet streak in her hair and amethyst coloured eyes. And even if Amaryllis was not his destiny, he still could not allow her to leave until the danger had passed. Not that it would be easy to hide a violet eyed beauty within the confines of the British

Isles. If push came to shove, he would ask one of the Faestens to take her in. Something that left a bitter taste in his mouth. The door swung open just as he arrived and Amaryllis' soft body collided with his.

"What the—"

"Bloody hell," Amaryllis yelped, surprise and guilt mirrored in her thickly lashed eyes.

"Where are you off to?" He cocked his brow at her, appreciating the deep flush that crept up her neck to land squarely on her cheeks.

"The bathroom."

Colin did not stop the frown that ploughed his forehead. "There's a bathroom off the bedroom."

"I'm not staying here." Amaryllis pushed against him, all pretence washing away from her face. "Step...out...of my way! God it's like pushing a bloody wall!"

Amaryllis' warm hands on his chest were going to be the death of him. Her touch flooded Colin's body with such strong urge to rut that all he wanted to do was to carry her over his shoulder, throw her back on the bed and fuck her so hard until she screamed her voice box raw. He watched her with half lidded eyes, taking pleasure in the dusky rosiness of her mouth, the concentration that marred her features while she continued to push against him. He did not have to read her mind to know that despite her vehemence she was as affected as he was. He heard the rapid beating of her heart like a hummingbird's wings that deepened the flush on her cheeks. He knew she remembered their short, hot intimate moment. He ground his teeth. For once, his zipper was a welcome wall that stopped his cock from tenting.

But fuck, it hurt.

Not as much as it hurt not being buried inside

Amaryllis' warm pussy.

"I told you, you can't leave." It was an effort to pull away from her. "The Scatha are about to overrun the city. If they see you, they will take you and you'll wish they killed you instead."

"I don't care about some bloody gang war you have going on here. Hey! You're hurting me," she cried out when Colin gripped her upper arm.

"Did you see the way my brother changed?" Colin's tone was dangerously soft, his face so close to hers, he could see the pale dusting of freckles on the sides of her nose, could smell the trace of honeysuckle on her skin and his mouth watered. "Does that look like someone from a bloody gang to you?"

"No, he looked more like some fucked up radiation experiment," she snapped, not backing down, her ire deepening the violet hue of her eyes. "Or he decided to celebrate Halloween at springtime."

Colin shook her, annoyance splashing against the lust wreaking havoc inside his jeans. "This is not a game! Those were real teeth that can tear you into shreds and those claws can slash you open. Jack the Ripper's exploits would look like child's play. Or maybe I should go for something modern. How about the Yorkshire Ripper?"

Amaryllis swallowed, her eyes widening.

"Yeah, got your attention now, did I?" Colin saw Amaryllis attempt to stem the fear that leaked into her eyes, earning his grudging admiration. This was a woman who did not scare easily. He wanted to stay longer to see what other retort came out from her sassy mouth. The thought of her mouth on him, taking him and pleasuring him beamed out of nowhere. He wanted to explore her body, map out her curves with his hands and mouth, taste a bit of her blood to see if she was a potential Cynn Cruor mate. His carnal thoughts would have to wait because right now he was losing precious time just thinking about the woman in front of him, writhing in ecstasy under him.

"Amaryllis, look at me." He spoke so softly that he thought she did not hear him. She stared back. Waiting. Anticipating. He deepened his voice, entering into a mesmerizing mode. "You are not to leave this house until I come back for you."

He watched while her mind protested against his command.

"No…"

"Yes, Amaryllis. This is your haven. This place will keep you protected. There are men outside this place who want to harm you. Stay. I command you to stay."

Her lips parted, a soft sigh leaving her before her eyes fluttered close.

"Do you understand?" Colin eased his grip on her arm, sliding his hand down to her wrist. Amaryllis shivered.

"Yes."

Colin's jaw tightened, wishing that her breathy voice was agreeing to something else.

"What do I want you to do?" He was powerless to stop his other hand from cupping her face and brushed his thumb across her lower lip, delighting in the softness of her mouth.

"You want me to stay…"

"Good," Colin breathed then bent his head, giving in to the need to kiss her. His lips softly brushed her mouth, just a brush before Amaryllis nearly crumpled to the floor.

With a disappointed sigh, Colin took her in his arms and carried her to the bed. He stared down at her bathed in the room's gentle light, appreciating every curve and every rise and fall of her chest, letting him know that she was sleeping deeply. Colin bent down and removed her jacket. It would make her more comfortable without having the leather tighten around her. He sucked in his breath as his fingers touched her satiny skin. Hardening his resolve, he finally straightened and laid the jacket on the bed before he strode back to the bedroom door and switched the lights off, allowing the light of the nearly full moon to bask her in its caress. A beautiful form amid the pale bedspread.

"Much better." His mouth quirked to one side before he closed the door.

Chapter Nine

Max got out of the stolen car and headed inside the Scathas' lair. He stepped on rubble and blocks that broke away from the edifice, going deeper into the heart of the condemned building. The colder it became the better he should have felt. Max growled. He hated this feeling as though his soul was hovering over him, torn between two bodies. Undecided. His steps faltered. Squaring his shoulders, he inhaled sharply, trying to centre himself. He cleared his mind, imagining a broom in his hands, sweeping his Cynn Cruor memories and replacing them with the diabolical deeds of the Scatha. Abduction, auction, rape, termination. Max balked at a memory, the one time he forced a woman. When he had just been newly transformed. The act had given him a permanent bitter taste in his mouth, vowing never to do it again. But on the night of the full moon, when the urge to rut was so strong, he could feel himself sink further into a darkness he was afraid he would never come out alive from. Negotiations and auctions, those were more up his alley and the never ending promise to eradicate the Cynn Cruors. Max inhaled deeply again. This meditation to ground oneself mumbo jumbo bullshit actually worked.

This was building number how-the-hell-would-he-know? Sometimes he thought the Scatha Cruors were nomads. No permanent addresses because of the bloody fucking Cynn Cruors being able to get a fix on where they were in only a few months. The longest they had stayed in any one area was six months tops before the Cynn Cruors found their lair again.

Max went down the flight of stairs that led to the

bowels of the building. Dark and dank, no human would be caught there in the dead of night. Entering here was akin to being caught in a spider's web. Intruders were caught to be turned or sold and if they refused, they would never see the sun again peeking through the vacant holes that passed for windows. Max saw the door to the lair straight ahead. He was not afraid that Badon was dead. Kill or be killed was their circle of life. He was more worried about whether he could lead them. A Scatha with a guilty conscience? That was unheard of. And if he got killed? Max snorted. Death might just be a better option to end the beat of his blackened heart.

Max entered the lair to the blaring sound of La Traviata, the soprano's voice nearly breaking his eardrums. Scatha Cruors lazed around in couches. The wails and plaintive cries of women about to be shipped out of the British Isles could be heard in another part of the building together with the moans of teenage boys and girls destined for the same plight. Scatha Cruors often 'dipped' into the merchandise unless there was a 'Do not Touch' order imposed. It was why he brought Amaryllis to the Faesten. With her unusual beauty, the 'Do Not Touch' command would never be enforced. His brethren would fight to the death to have her. Max was not stupid enough to believe he could take out all of them.

His brethren watched him warily, taking in his dishevelled appearance.

"Where's Badon and the rest?" Lee Harris, a Scatha stood from his stool by the bar. He was one of those whom Max spoke to on a regular basis. If there was any notion of honour among thieves, Lee was the only one on Max's list.

"All dead," Max replied. "The Cynn Cruors jumped us."

"Fuck!"

"Tell me about it."

Lee assessed Max. He pulled at his red hair. "And the girl?"

"Taken by them as well."

"How the fuck did that happen?"

"Exchange went bad." Max shrugged, walking towards the bar to pour himself a cognac. "It's not like it never happens."

Lee swore again. "Fuck the Cynn Cruors to kingdom come!" He looked at Max. "Why aren't you pissed?"

Max's brows rose enquiringly. "Should I be? Scathas die all the time. That's our way of life. Besides, there's a lot of flesh to be had out there. Young or old they're willing to get fucked or be fucked. No big deal. We'll get another batch together."

"That's not what I mean, Greene," Lee hissed. "I don't care if it happened any other time. Not tonight."

"What's so special about tonight?" Max took a swig from his tumbler, appreciating the burn of the amber fluid down his throat. His hair ruffled softly when Lee whizzed to stand in front of him.

"Because Dac Valerian is here, asshole, and he's in the office looking at the books!"

Max felt the blood drain from his face. Apprehension settled squarely in his gut. He had never met the Scatha Cruor leader before or after his transformation. As a Cynn Cruor, Valerian posed a threat to their kind and to mankind, the nemesis of the Ancients after he nearly killed the Ancient Eald. As a Scatha Cruor, Valerian was a man to be feared and pleased no matter what. He only heard of Dac's exploits and his proclivity for staging his death only to resurrect unannounced to slay the Scatha who dared to take his place. Max heard of Dac's penchant for indiscriminately killing his own men for no reason other than for his pleasure or because a Scatha dared question him.

Max went through all the possible reasons he could give to explain what happened during the exchange and at that very moment he was glad that he followed his instincts to keep Amaryllis Hart away and to keep her alive. His need to protect her puzzled him, the distaste to take her and slake his lust even more so. But one thing he was sure of was that in order to keep Amaryllis safe meant that he had to keep his thoughts of his connection to the Leeds Cynn Cruors hidden from Dac Valerian. Otherwise, there would be hell to pay.

"That's a first," Max remarked, swirling his drink. "Of all the lairs why pick this one?"

"Fuck if I know," Lee ground out.

"You keep at that and your fear will be thick enough to make a terror jacket." Max's glance swept the pit over the rim of his glass. He swallowed. "Keep your cool, Harris, if you value your life."

Lee nodded, exhaling. "Now that Badon is dead, it's going to be a free for all. I would have fought anyone for the post—"

"Including me?" Max's lips twitched in amusement.

"Especially you." Lee snorted.

Max's shoulders shook.

"But with Valerian here…" Lee left the statement hanging.

"You're such a bloody coward."

Lee flushed. "I won't be answerable to Dac while he's here," he retorted. "Cowards get to live another day."

Max caught a movement from the corner of his eye and froze.

Dac Valerian and the only Scatha he trusted with

his life, Herod D'Argyl, appeared outside the office door. Dac swept his gaze over the Scathas in the room, his eyes taking in everything, his mouth curled in a perpetual smirk. Max had always thought that Dac had a full head of hair, but the man he saw had a shaved head that shone under the room's lights. Dark brows slanted over eyes that were fathomless black. He had an aquiline nose slightly huge for his face and thin lips that at the moment clamped on a Cuban cigar. His broad muscled body was packed into a pair of low cut jeans and muscle shirt that clung to his chest and biceps.

He was not the image Max imagined him to be. Max expected him to look like a Roman general in twenty-first century clothes, not some bad ass dude who could be at ease behind the controls of a motorbike.

Herod was no different, save for the hair on his head that brushed the base of his thick, corded neck and framed his harsh and war ravaged face. His body belonged to a warrior that saw many battles and lived to tell the tale. Naturally arched brows came down on dark brown eyes and his mouth was straightened to a line. His eyes did not miss anything either.

"Ahh, Greene," Dac spoke still with the cigar between his white teeth, the smoke curling upwards and slightly blurring his features from view. "What have you brought back?"

Max knelt in front of Dac. The urge to praise and laud the killer facing him was so strong even when part of him recoiled.

"Sire." Max kept his head bowed. "You do us the honour of being in our midst." His pulse raced and his heart struck his ribcage like the sonorous Big Ben. Goosebumps prickled all over his skin when Dac cackled.

"Stand up. I want to look at you."

Max stood but kept his head bowed.

"No need to pull the bashful act, Scatha Cruor." The room tittered. "Let me see your eyes."

Max's mouth twitched and he had to force it into a thin line. Dac's tone reminded him so much of human actors portraying vampires. Coaxing. Getting the prey to trust him. Speaking to him like a little child before the kill. Then again, did they not all have vampire blood in them? Humans had no idea what vampires really were.

Centuries of perfecting the ability to close his thoughts against any invasion kicked in. Max raised his head and looked directly at Dac's fathomless depths. He waited dispassionately. Dac's eyes narrowed. Max felt it, the insidious entering of his mind, like a stiletto thin line of black smoke that dispersed and covered every cell in his brain. Prodding. Seeking. Coaxing. Trying to unearth whatever secrets he had. Dac would fail. He would not find the memories that would expose his links to the Cynn Cruors. Max had immediately kept under layers upon layers of Scatha reminiscences.

For Mam and Da. Always for ye both.

Dac grunted. "Your mind is too clean."

"I don't really think, Sire," Max said, head bowed. "I just follow."

Dac closed in on Max's personal space. The stench that marked a Scatha was not apparent in the leader. The sensation of being enclosed inside the smoke that tightened around them both to the point of suffocation did, and the examination of his mind continued. Max tamped his panic down lest he give himself away.

"You were supposed to be with Badon," Dac began. "Where is he?"

"Dead, Sire. Killed by the Cynn Cruors."

Max flew across the room. He grunted and growled when his back and his head hit the stone wall. Bits and pieces of the concrete wall fell around him before they reached the floor. He looked up. The wall looked like an upright pillow indented by his head when it hit. He wanted to whip and lunge at his attacker so badly but that was out of the question. At least he was out of the black void's grip. He was not sure how long he could still take the continued exploration and he was starting to believe he had become Dac's science experiment. He swiped the blood from his split lip with his thumb, feeling the wound close even before he wiped his hand on his jeans.

"You allowed them that honour." Dac seethed. He pulled Max up by the collar of his shirt and slammed him against the wall once more. Max winced at the claws that evenly sliced through his skin. "You're such an incompetent fuck!" The claws were closing in on his vein.

Do it. End my life.

"Dac, we might have use of him. He can show us where the Cynn Cruors killed the rest of the Scatha then we can retaliate."

Herod's reasoning got through Dac, like water quenching the dry silence of anticipation and trepidation that befell the lair. It was a spectacle the Scatha Cruors enjoyed when they saw someone dying. It was a treat if the death was meted out by the Scatha Cruors' leader.

Max was thrown a second time against that opposite wall and could just imagine how an abused doll felt. His brain matter seemed to shake inside his skull at the impact and his skeleton seemed to rattle against his muscles. He grunted with the searing pain his body was subjected to, welcoming the discomfort and dislodging the Cynn Cruor part of his psyche that wanted to tear Dac Valerian from limb to limb.

"I have you in my sights, Greene." Dac brushed his

hands together as though removing dirt. "There's something about you that doesn't ring true."

"I'm at your disposal, Sire," Max replied, not a hair's breath after Dac spoke. "You have seen my mind, explored it to no end. I cannot keep anything from you."

"Yes, yes..." Dac murmured, his expression derisive. "That's what worries me." He strode to the bar, the Scatha parting like water sliced away by a cigarette boat. He took one of the bottles of cognac and turned to the direction of the office. "You are going to tell me what went down tonight and if I catch even a whiff of disloyalty, your ashes will be at my feet."

Max straightened from his crawled position on the floor and eyed his brethren, who looked at him with malice and curiosity, uncertainty and amusement.

"Yo, Greene. If you can come out alive, you can fuck me."

Hoots and catcalls flew across the room.

Max smirked. "When I come out alive, I'll kill you before your next breath. How's that?"

The Scathas guffawed, including the one who threw down the gauntlet.

"A thousand quid says you won't get out," the Scatha said, his shoulders shaking with arrogant mirth.

"Why do you insist on digging your grave and loading it with shit piled higher and deeper?" Max furrowed his forehead in bemusement. "Put some distance between the turd and your sorry face because no one will know the difference."

"Enough!" Herod snapped. "Now get your sorry arses out of here and find more humans to sell."

The Scatha scurried to do his bidding, almost tripping over themselves in their haste to get to the door.

Max angled his head towards Herod, who was loping to his side.

"Dac's right. You're off." Herod looked at Max evenly, sweeping his gaze from Max's shoes to the top of his head.

"I probably stink. I haven't changed or showered since the Cynn Cruors' attacked." Max raised his arms and smelled his armpits, snorting. "Yeah, it's my stench."

Herod stared at him. Max stared back. Finally Herod nodded. "You better get in there. You wouldn't want to die before your time."

"Time is immaterial as long as the job is done." Max brushed off unseen lint from his jacket.

"Hmmm." Herod surveyed him critically. "Watch your back, Greene. You don't know how the cards fall with Valerian."

"Is that a friendly warning?"

Herod did not reply. He was already making his way to the office.

Dac was behind the desk when Max arrived. He riffled through several documents sprawled on the table, pausing to read the contents of one before moving on to the next. Herod was on the couch that faced the desk, his pose relaxed with one arm resting over the back.

"It says here that Badon was picking up a woman given to him by a Jack Crawley." Dac pierced Max with a glare.

"We did. The drop off point was the side street by *Le Club Cinq Mille*. That's where we went."

"So what went wrong?"

"Like I said, Sire. The Cynn Cruors." Max stood with his feet braced apart, his hands clasped low in front of his groin. "We were not expecting them and I don't know how they got wind of the exchange." He paused. "We know which areas are Cynn Cruors strongholds and which are places we can hunt. That area was Cynn Cruor territory."

"Whose fault was that?"

"No one knew the meeting place until the last minute, Sire." Max raised his hands helplessly, his voice insistent. "Only Badon knew. He never said anything before last night. All I know is that he got a call and then we went to meet with Crawley."

"Bloody imbecile." Dac dry rubbed his face. "I'm so sick and tired of being surrounded by incompetents!" He drew out a long breath. "And this Crawley, where is he?"

"He hightailed out of the alley when fighting broke out." Max shifted his weight from one leg to the other. "He's human, Sire. It will be easy to track him down. He's one of our sources for our…auctioned items."

"Find him. I want to speak to him to get to the bottom of this."

"As you wish, Sire." Max lowered his head and pivoted to leave the room.

"One minute," Herod spoke, pivoting from the couch. "How did you escape while the rest were killed?"

Max bristled, really bristled. "Are you implying that I had anything to do with Badon's and the rest of the Scatha Cruors' deaths?" He felt Dac's eyes regard the scene unfolding as Herod stood and turned around to face him.

"I wasn't implying anything, Greene." Herod's left brow lifted a fraction. "It was a simple question that needed a simple answer. Being defensive means you're not telling us something we should know."

"I'm nothing but true to form, D'Argyl." Max's response came out in a low growl. "We are a defensive and suspicious lot, are we not?"

Max's response seemed to appease Herod because he turned back to face Dac as though nothing happened.

"Then how did you escape?" Dac took up the interrogation.

"At the risk of courting your ire, Sire, humans call it luck. I call it self-preservation." Max continued quickly. "When I realized that I was already outnumbered, I scaled the building wall and threw off my scent. I stayed out of sight, knowing that they would keep track of me up to a certain point. What happened in that alley would have flagged up in their systems since it was within the Cynn Cruors territory.

"How would you know that?" Herod shot over his shoulder.

"When Badon took us to *Le Club Cinq Mille*, I already knew we were in Cynn Cruor territory." Max fidgeted. "I told Badon several times to change the venue, to tell Crawley to meet up somewhere else, but he refused. Who was I to question him? He was your Lieutenant here in Leeds. Like I said, I only follow orders."

Herod stood to lope slowly to Dac's side.

"If I had the authority to change things early in the game, I would have and the woman Crawley brought would be here ready for procession instead of being snatched by the Cynn Cruors."

Something passed Herod's eyes. Max only caught a glimpse of it before it disappeared, but he could swear that it was a tinge of sadness.

Why the hell would Herod be sad? Was it possible that he was another one with a conscience among the Scatha Cruors? A possibility. Max shook his head dispelling the notion.

"You want more authority to make decisions for your lair, Greene?" Dac challenged. "That's tantamount to saying you want the position as the head of the Scatha Cruors."

"If I can get the job done, so be it." Max stood straighter. "However, I am not presumptuous to proclaim myself the de facto lieutenant of this Scatha branch just because Badon is dead, although even I have every right to do so. I was Badon's second in command and under our rules, I become the interim lieutenant until it is confirmed by the Scatha High Council. Namely you, Sire, and Lord D'Argyl."

Dac barked with laughter. "That's the first refreshing thing I've heard for the longest time." He looked at Herod. The sides of his eyes crinkled. "Lord D'Argyl? I haven't heard you called by your title for centuries."

"Only because you refused to allow those around you to call me so."

The light in Dac's eyes dimmed and his smile dipped. Max eyed a bored Herod. Man, this Scatha could really say anything and Dac would not even lift a finger to throw him out. Lord Herod D'Argyl had balls of titanium.

"Compared to you, I am a young Scatha Cruor. But as soon as I was able to get back on my feet, I read as much as I could about our kind."

"How did you become one?"

"The Crimean War," Max replied. "I was attached to the 93rd Sutherland Regiment. I didn't care about the war, only the adventure and the spoils that came with it." Max swallowed to keep the bile threatening to discharge from his throat down. The lies he was saying were tightening around his neck like a hangman's noose.

I hate having a bloody conscience!

"I killed a man when he found out I had slept with his wife. His friends came after me and I was lynched to an inch of my human life. A man I met during the war nursed me to health and turned me. I didn't know he was a Scatha Cruor. But he was also killed. By the Cynn Cruors."

At least that part was the truth. The rest, an embellished story. The more Max thought about the death of his maker the more his anger grew inside him.

He continued, "I will not rest until I kill the Cynn Cruor who killed the one who changed me."

"Who is this Cynn Cruor? Do you have a name?"

Max almost spat his name. "The Dux of the Leeds Cynn Cruors. Colin Butler."

Chapter Ten

Roarke entered the kitchen to the sweet scent of freshly baked cookies. Deanna, Eirene, and Kate were licking the batter off the baking spoons, giggling as they did. Deanna turned, her eyes lighting up.

"My Lord! I didn't expect your sparring session to end so soon. We were just preparing something for a repast before supper or a midnight snack if you prefer."

Roarke chuckled. "Not that it matters that it's one in the morning now but aye. I came up to take a shower only to see you three here." He pointed at her. "You've got batter by the edge of your mouth." He rushed to her side and licked the batter from her skin before slanting his head to take her mouth in a toe curling kiss. Moments later, he raised his head, amused at Deanna's dreamy visage. "Much better."

Eirene snorted while Kate laughed softly. They heard a buzz coming from the nerve centre before the light just above the kitchen door lit up.

"Incoming." Eirene jumped off the stool and went to the sink to wash her spoon.

"Leave that." Kate gathered the rest of the used baking utensils and bowls. "I'll wash them. Go. It might be important."

"Cheers!"

Roarke kept his arms around Deanna's waist, cinching her to his side. His hand travelled down her pert derriere and he felt the stirrings of lust in the centre of his groin. He growled softly when Deanna turned and rubbed her pelvis against his hip.

"You need a shower, my Lord." Her mouth lifted in a seductive smile.

My Haven, My Midnight

Roarke bowed his head to whisper in her ear. He grinned at the shudder that went through his mate when he sucked on her earlobe. "Aye, I'd like that," he whispered before he telepathed. *Why don't we make it a bath? It's nearly the full moon, my lady, and I need your tender loving care. I will enjoy you lovingly surrounding my cock with your tight pussy.*

Oh, Roarke. Deanna turned her head towards his ear. *You do like me getting wet.*

"Seriously? Go to your room." Kate rolled her eyes, smiling while she filled the dishwasher.

"Which is exactly what we're going to do." Roarke continued to look down at Deanna's eyes where gold flecks were starting to surface, showing her need to mate. His heart was close to bursting. It happened every time Deanna was near.

"Damn, it smells good in here." Graeme took a deep breath when he entered the kitchen then saw Kate. His grin turned wicked. "Now I know why. I can never resist your scent, Kate Corrigan." He swept her into his arms and gave her a resounding kiss. When he released her he brushed his knuckles against her jaw. "I'm glad you're smiling."

"How can I not when you're by my side? You're my strength, Graeme Temple." Kate lovingly cupped his cheek.

"As you are mine," he replied softly.

"Wow, it doesn't smell like bacon in here." Finn chuckled. He went to one of the cupboards and took out a glass before putting it under the fridge's cold water dispenser.

Graeme snorted, keeping Kate by his side. "Be glad Eirene isn't here."

Finn downed the entire contents of his glass. "Where's my minx?"

"I was in the library." Eirene had an irritated frown when she entered the kitchen. "And thanks to the Cynn Cruor blood inside me, I heard that."

"Babe—" Finn immediately placed the glass on the kitchen counter and sped to his mate amid the chuckles of his brethren.

"Later." Eirene gave him a sweet but annoyed look before she faced Roarke. "It's Luke. He found something."

"What did you ask Luke to find?" Finn looked at Roarke while his arm was around Eirene's waist, refusing to let her go even when she squirmed and tried pushing away.

A crease appeared on Roarke's forehead. "I didn't."

Finn allowed Eirene to leave his grasp. Eirene preceded them to the library. Finn sighed and followed, shaking his head when Graeme gave him a friendly and sympathetic smack on his shoulder. Once they were all in the library, Eirene returned the phone on the receiver and keying in a command, brought the feed up on the LED screen.

"Luke, what's up? Where are you?"

"In Leeds."

Finn's brows arced, his eyes widening. "Leeds? You're a long way from home, my friend."

"But you were just here a while ago." Graeme scratched his head. "We were just sparring..." He smacked his palm on his head. "I shouldn't have asked."

"Get used to it, Temple." Luke chuckled, making his voice louder against the falling rain.

"So what are you doing there?" Roarke's gaze flickered to the windows. Rain had started to fall, the water clinking and dribbling against the glass. "There's lots of entertainment here." Roarke tutted. "For shame, Luke."

Luke laughed. "I decided to check out Leeds and find out what was happening. It's raining here like anything, so I'm good."

"Happening to what?"

"Not to what Roarke. To who."

Roarke's smile slowly melted away as a slight frown furrowed his brow.

"Hear me out, Hamilton," Luke said quickly. He took a deep breath, expelling it as he talked. "I did some digging only because I felt that this is my way of showing my appreciation for what the Cynn Cruors have done for me. It doesn't look that way but that's the truth."

"Go on." Roarke removed his arm around Deanna's waist and folded both arms over his chest.

"You said something was bothering Colin and I wanted to see if maybe I could help."

"I didn't order you to spy on Butler, Luke." Roarke's voice became cold.

"No, you didn't," Luke agreed, but his countenance brooked no argument. "But I've not pledged allegiance to Manchester either. At the moment, I'm a free agent."

"Ouch," Graeme said softly.

"Hey." Eirene had her hands on her hips. "What gives? Why'd you do that?"

Luke heaved a sigh. "I didn't do this out of spite. Sorry, Hamilton, but it had to be said. I appreciate your hospitality, but I've not agreed which Faesten I want to belong to. My loyalty is to the Cynn Cruors."

"It's okay, Eirene. Luke is right." Roarke acknowledged in a grim voice. "He isn't under my command. Every Cynn Cruor is welcome in any Faesten, including ours. I don't like what you're doing, Luke. I don't like spying on other Cynn Cruors."

"Dux, I'm not spying. I just want to find out how I

can help."

"And you think spying is going to do that?" Eirene asked, displeased.

"Eirene, let's listen." Kate touched her friend gently on the arm. "I did the same thing to get to the bottom of Elliot Hammond's operations. It isn't something I was proud of even when it served a purpose."

Eirene's mouth thinned, but she nodded, backing down.

Roarke nudged his head at the screen. "Go ahead. What did you find?"

"Colin's in trouble."

The Cynn Cruors and their mates looked at each other.

Roarke's mouth lifted to one side. "He always gets into trouble, mate. But he's the Leeds Dux. I can't interfere unless he asks me to. He can take care of himself and his men."

"This is different." The rains slowed, the sound relegated to gentle pelting on the roof of where Luke had sought shelter. He moved away, the visual on his phone erratic as he walked, avoiding some of the people who strode past him. "Roarke, you said Colin had a brother?"

"He died during the Crimean War." Roarke nodded.

"And his body, obviously, couldn't be found," Luke added.

"Because we disintegrate," Graeme spoke. Kate laced her had with his. They looked at each other briefly before turning back to the screen.

"Only if we are beheaded."

"What are you getting at, Luke?" Finn asked softly, his voice jagged as shard glass. "Tread carefully."

"Before you all start giving me crap, hear me out first," Luke ground out. "I want to help."

"Some help you're showing," Finn snapped, his countenance bristling with anger. Eirene held on to him and he visibly relaxed, though not enough to continue throwing dagger looks at the screen.

"Well, he wasn't going to come right out with it, was he?" Luke was the epitome of calm. "He was hiding something, from all of us and y'all just didn't want to rock the boat."

"Your time in America is showing, Luke," Deanna said softly.

Luke puffed out a breath in frustration. "Something which I still need to decipher, but we're not talking about me."

"Fine," Roarke said. "Though I can't understand what Mackenzie Butler's death has anything to do with this."

"Because Mackenzie Butler is alive, Roarke." Luke rubbed his forehead.

Gasps of disbelief reverberated around the room.

"That's impossible." Roarke scoffed. "Colin was devastated when Mack died. He refused to talk about his brother. He felt it was his fault that his brother was killed. We all mourned him."

Luke's face disappeared. A little while later, a portrait of Colin and Mackenzie Butler flashed on the screen.

"Is this him?" Luke's voice came through.

"Where the fuck did you get that?" Finn was livid.

"When I was researching my roots."

"And you happen to carry a picture of Colin and Mackenzie on your person?" Finn's voice dripped with sarcasm.

"No, I took a detour to the archives before returning here," Luke said.

Finn was about to say something before the

enormity of Luke's gift made him shake his head. He raked his fingers through his spiky hair instead.

"Why the hell would you look into Colin's background?" Finn shot back.

"It's not like I did it deliberately," Luke retorted. "I had to go through so many tomes to find out who I really am and Butler's was just one of the families I looked at."

"No shit, Sherlock." Finn thundered. "I'd beat you to a pulp if you were here."

"Babe," Eirene said softly, trying to placate him, her face troubled.

Luke disappeared from the screen, the place where he stood, empty. "Go ahead."

Everybody whirled around to see Luke brace himself just by the library's glass doors. Finn took one step forward, his huge fists trembling at his side.

"Finn!" Eirene went in front of him, pushing against his huge chest.

"Enough!" Roarke bellowed. His eyes were stormy. Deanna held him, her face dismayed.

"Stand down, Finn," he ordered. He turned to Luke. "At this very moment, Griffiths, I don't particularly like you."

"Why can't you let sleeping dogs lie?" Graeme asked, disappointment marring his voice.

Luke's mouth pulled to a sad smile. "Because it affects all of us. Not just Colin."

"What do you mean, Luke?" Eirene spoke, upset and bewildered. "I don't like to see you warriors fighting."

"I really wish it doesn't come to that." Luke's shoulders slumped and he looked away.

"Tell us, Luke." Kate straightened beside Graeme. "Why does it affect all of us?"

Luke pinned them with his gaze.

"Because not only is Mackenzie Butler alive, he is now a Scatha Cruor."

* * *

Amaryllis' eyes moved underneath her lids before she blinked to wake up. The dawn's watery sunlight filtered softly into the dim room, the dust motes haphazardly floating around like the tiniest of pixies in its rays before alighting gently on the wooden floor. In the distance she heard the faint sound of rolling thunder. She could not remember if it had rained the night before. Amaryllis sighed and shivered. There were telltale rain trails down the window and soon the deluge would come back. She rolled on to her back, stretched, and sighed. She stared at the ceiling. She was still in the same predicament as she had been in the night before. Inside a strange house, with strange men.

And one man who gave her the best orgasm with his fingers. Just the thought made her belly flutter and her nether lips throb.

Standing up, Amaryllis walked to the bathroom to relieve herself and wash her face. She saw a bottle of mouthwash and took a swig from the bottle cap then rinsing it. She surveyed her reflection while she let the mouthwash do its job. Spitting, she straightened once again and wrinkled her nose in disgust at the smears under her eyes. Taking a towel from the rack, she dampened it and gently cleaned the offending eyeliner to make her look less of a panda.

"Right," she muttered. She returned to the room and grabbed her jacket from the end of the bed.

Then stopped.

She had no recollection of taking her jacket off. She frowned but then became more concerned with worrying if the door was locked. She sighed in relief when it opened.

The hallway was eerily quiet and cool. Behind her, daylight filtered through the stained glass window with a design of two oak leaves criss-crossing each other. It threw a carpet of browns, blues, and greens on the floor. She continued walking and stopped at the door to Max's room. The door remained ajar and Amaryllis peered inside. She gasped. The room had been cleaned and devoid of any blood splatter. The bookshelf was fixed with the tomes neatly returned. The walls were pristine. The standing lamp that had fallen the night before was in its right place, a thin sentinel against a dark corner, and the wingback chair was by the side of the window, waiting for someone to sit. The only sign that something had happened inside was that the Persian rug on the floor had vanished, exposing the original wooden floors of the room that had been polished to a sheen. Amaryllis continued down the hallway, reminding her of a posh hotel corridor. Even the plush carpet underneath her feet made her want to remove her boots as though it was a sacrilege to even step on it. The dark wood panelled walls were bare save for a long and narrow embroidered tapestry encased in non-glare glass stretching all the way to the stair's landing and continuing again on the opposite wing of the house. She regarded the tapestry in rapt fascination.

"Bloody hell..." she breathed, her eyes widening at the figure of a woman changing into a wolf mid-air. The wolf landed on a man and nearly cut him in half. Thereafter, scenes of battles dominated the rest of the cloth.

Between men and creatures that were half-man, half-beast.

"Oh shit," Amaryllis repeated under her breath.

"Wonder how much this would fetch in the market."

She continued to make her way slowly towards the landing. Several portraits on the opposite wall caught her eye. She moved closer and gasped. There were five portraits of men who had the uncanny resemblance to the men she met the night before, their poses strong, confident, with more than a hint of arrogance. The paintings appeared to have been done a long time ago. Parts of the oil had the tinniest fissures brought about by time and its exposure to the elements. Amaryllis scrutinised the two portraits in the middle. They were the doppelgangers of Max and Colin. The one who saved her. The other who touched her. They were as different as night and day. Max had sandy brown hair while Colin had sun bleached blond hair. Where Max had amber coloured eyes, Colin's were dark green.

"Good morning."

Amaryllis gave a small squeal and whirled around at the female voice. A woman with long flowing dark ombre hair and lithe body encased in tight jeans and a figure hugging shirt stood behind her with two steaming mugs.

She swallowed. "You always creep behind people like that?"

The woman arched a perfectly trimmed brow in mock amusement, her mouth quirking to one side. "That was a friendly good morning."

"Wonder what your greeting would sound like if you were in a downright foul mood," Amaryllis quipped.

The woman laughed, assessing her. "Try not to get on that side." She extended a deep red manicured hand with a mug. "Tea? It'll make you feel more human. For the moment."

Amaryllis looked at the brew with suspicion.

"Oh, bloody hell, there's nothing in it." There was laughter in her shrewd eyes.

"Bloody hell, indeed." Amaryllis expelled a breath. "If I faint, you're going to have to drag me back to the room."

"Or I might just leave you here on the landing."

Amaryllis gawked at her and the woman burst out laughing. "Get used to it." She chuckled. "You might hear a lot of that kind of ribbing around here. I'm Seth Holms."

"Amaryllis Hart. Unusual name."

"It's Annaseth actually, but people who call me by my full name normally die."

"Okaay." Amaryllis' forehead furrowed slightly as she gave Seth a weird look. "I'll keep that in mind." She turned back to the portraits. "Waterloo?"

"No. Crimea."

"Oh shit, I don't know my history." Amaryllis reddened with embarrassment. "I would have wanted to learn more, but…"

Seth shrugged. "It's not like history is going anywhere. It'll come."

They scrutinised the portraits that hung on the wall.

"It's amazing how the portraits look like the men I met last night." Amaryllis observed. "I've never seen ancestors look so much alike."

Seth's mouth pulled to a grin. "Who said those are their ancestors?" she murmured before taking a sip from her mug.

Amaryllis looked at her and scoffed. "They can't be the same. The pigment in those paintings have been cracked by time." She took a sip from her mug and closed her eyes. "Bloody hell, this is good!"

"Thanks," Seth remarked wryly. "Right, before I tell you a story about Mary Morry—"

"Who's Mary Morry?"

"Never mind," Seth said on a breath. "Let's go to the kitchen where we can talk comfortably instead of standing here like misplaced statues. I'm baking and I don't want the bread to burn too. I need to de-stress after all of the action last night."

"What happened last night?" Amaryllis asked curiously. Damn, talk about being dead to the world.

"Same ol' ass kicking in and around the clubs and restos in town." Seth stopped and grinned ruefully. "Forget I said that. Don't want Dux to cream me."

"Dux?"

"Colin," Seth replied.

What the hell was a Dux?

They went down the long flight of stairs to a simple but elegantly appointed vestibule. Two Queen Anne period chaise lounges flanked the walls with identical mirrors above them. Their heels clicked loudly against the wooden floor as they turned into the ground floor corridor leading to the huge wood panelled and steel kitchen. They were welcomed by the aroma of baking bread that had Amaryllis' stomach growling and blanketing her with comfort. She had been too dead tired last night to even think of food. Suddenly, she felt bereft, causing her eyes to smart with unshed tears. When was the last time she entered a place that reminded her of the comforts of home? She could not remember.

Amaryllis stood by the kitchen counter as she watched Seth take out the bread from the oven.

With her bare hands.

"Holy shit!"

"What?" Seth turned to face Amaryllis.

"Are you crazy?"

"I've been called that on occasion." Seth watched

her with amusement. "That's the second time your mouth has been moving without any sound coming out. You sure you're not related to the fish?"

"That's not what I meant." Amaryllis shook her head with impatience and pointed at the pan. "That! You're holding the pan with your bare hand!"

"So?" In a split second realization cleared Seth's face. "Oh. Sorry, I forgot."

"Forgot what?" Amaryllis asked, disconcerted. She set her mug down, frantically looked around and grabbed the nearest tea towel she saw. She rushed to Seth and got the hot pan from her hand. Even with the tea towel, Amaryllis felt the growing heat about to singe her fingers. The pan made a thudding clanging sound as it hit the counter.

"You need to put your hand under running water—"

"Yo! Hey, Amaryllis!" Seth grabbed her shoulders. "Stop! Look. See, nothing has happened. I didn't burn myself and it isn't going to blister."

Amaryllis stared blankly at Seth's hand before she stepped back. Alarm sounded like the clanging of bells again inside her head. "What are you people?"

"I just have thick skin."

"Don't patronise me, Seth." Anger quickly flared inside her. "Even thick skinned people would have reddened hands."

"I'm not patronising you."

"No shit."

"Amaryllis, sit down and have something to eat," Seth said firmly even as she continued to slice the bread, the heat curling upwards and adding to the air's aroma. She walked to the fridge. "Butter?"

Seth's sangfroid only added to Amaryllis anger. "No."

"Please," Seth said gently. "I know all this is

difficult to take in. Just because I can hold a pan straight out of the oven doesn't make me a figure from Hell. Believe me, I'm not here to hurt you. Colin asked me to stay and protect you."

"Where is he?"

"Indisposed at the moment, but you'll see him later. I can't let you go. Colin's orders."

"I don't give a fuck what Colin ordered you to do." Amaryllis seethed. "You're keeping me here against my will."

"It's for your protection."

"No, Seth. It isn't for me. You have some gang war going on here and I refuse to be in the middle of it." She walked away from the kitchen and from the mouth-watering bread. "This is not my fight."

"Amaryllis, please."

She whirled around, her body vibrating with so much rage her hand trembled when she raised it. "Don't."

"Where are you going?"

"I'm leaving."

"Oh, bloody hell." Seth swore, a scowl forming on her forehead. "You're making me miss a good slice of fresh bread."

"I'm not stopping you from eating." Amaryllis shot over her shoulder. "I'm stopping you from making me stay."

"Well, I can't let you go without me." Seth followed her out of the kitchen with a disgruntled sigh. "I don't want to lose my head."

Amaryllis turned around, eyeing Seth sceptically. "So apart from thick skins, cosmetically implanted Halloween masks, and people with long lives, you also have decapitations."

Seth turned her face away, frustrated. "It's not as

cut and dried as that."

Amaryllis resumed walking, flicking her hand up to say she had enough. "You want to come with me? Fine. I just want out of here."

"How are you going to get where you want to go?" Seth stopped and cocked her hip. "It's a long way to town."

"I'll walk."

"Who's walking?" Three young men came through the entrance door.

"No one's walking," Seth replied, scowling. "I'm taking Amaryllis to where she wants to go."

"Hey," a man with wavy black hair and twinkling dark grey eyes said. "You new?"

"No, she isn't. She's under the Dux's protection," Seth said. "Amaryllis, meet Gareth."

"Wow, the Dux's protection," Gareth whistled. "You must be someone very important."

Amaryllis could not help the frisson of pleasure that filled her. Colin's protection? Yeah right. He only did that because his brother asked him to. Talk about a damper.

"Meet Donovan and Etienne. Guys, this is Amaryllis Hart."

"Hello, Amaryllis." Donovan extended his hand, smiling. "Nice hair. For real?"

His warm hand enveloped hers, his blue green eyes assessing her with interest. Amaryllis shook his hand, instantly liking him. "The streak of violet? Yeah, for real. Don't ask me how."

"*Mademoiselle. Enchanté.*"

Amaryllis laughed softly when Etienne took her hand and kissed it. Thick lashed dark eyes roamed her face and body with more interest than was proper. "Uhm...hi." She pulled her hand away.

"Where are you guys going?" Gareth asked.

Seth looked at Amaryllis, who rolled her eyes. "Since you're not keeping me out of your sight I have to go to Crawley's place."

"Who's Crawley?" Seth asked.

"Long story," Amaryllis replied. "But he's partly the reason why I'm here."

"He was there during the Scatha Cruors exchange," Seth stated.

"You know?" Amaryllis looked at her in surprise.

"Not only do I know, I saw what went down. CCTV footage of the alley. So why the hell are you returning there?" Seth frowned. "He was the man who gave you to the Scatha Cruors."

"The Scatha?"

"Oh shit!"

"*Merde!*"

The three men's faces contorted with ire. "Why the hell would you want to do that?" Donovan scowled at Amaryllis.

"My things are there. I need them because I don't have anything here," Amaryllis retorted.

"I'll buy what you need."

Chapter Eleven

Everyone whirled at the voice.

"Dux," Donovan greeted, glancing at the window before flicking back to the man who had just entered the kitchen. "Awake already?"

Colin's mouth twisted to a wry smile. "I was on my way back to the basement when I heard voices. He turned his attention to Amaryllis. "Going somewhere?"

What's in the basement? Coffins?

Amaryllis clamped her lips together to stop the smile threatening her mouth at the sudden thought. Her heart plummeted before it rose, thudding in the presence of the only man who could play her body, eliciting the most erotic sensations she had ever experienced. She shivered at his deep voice, a caress whispering over her skin. She watched him saunter towards them, every step making her heart beat louder in her ears. She balled her hands into fists when his dark gaze that held so much secret promise made her body thrum with need and her sex pulse with longing.

Colin stopped in front of her, their bodies so close that Amaryllis could feel his heat against her front. "I can't let you leave because I can't let you die."

"You keep saying that. I can take care of myself," she complained, crossing her arms over her chest as she stepped back.

Was that momentary hurt passing through Colin's eyes? Before she could decipher what it really was, it disappeared and a smile lit his face that sent her pulse racing again.

"Until we know what we're up against, you need to stay here," he murmured.

"That is all well and good but there are things that I need to get from Crawley's place," Amaryllis said while trying to calm her racing heart at Colin's nearness. "Please."

"Wait until later. I will take you myself." Colin obdurately turned on his heel, making his way to the shadows. Amaryllis' eyes widened a fraction at the sight of Colin rubbing his forearm as though he was easing some discomfort before turning his face away from the weak daylight that flooded part of the hallway. Amaryllis wanted to pull at her hair in frustration. "I can't wait until this evening. There will be more people there and it will be difficult to get my things out. Jack sleeps until midday. All of them do."

"Dux, she's right," Seth spoke, planting her hands on her hips. "With everything that's happening, going in tonight might not be a good idea. We'll be with her." She nudged her chin at Gareth, Donovan, and Etienne. They all nodded and ran where Colin had come from. "You have my word. She'll be safe."

Colin glared at Seth then looked at Amaryllis. "Fine," he gritted. "Be back in an hour."

Amaryllis gasped. "But it'll take half an hour to get there!"

"One hour." Colin scowled before he stormed off.

"Really now?" Amaryllis huffed, looking at Seth.

"He'll be less grouchy later." The three men returned. Donovan handed her a *sgian dubh*.

"What's this for?" She looked at the blade. "I've got a stiletto."

The three men grinned at each other. Seth looked at her pointedly. "Just take it. It might just come in handy."

"Fine." Amaryllis blew out a breath. No harm in packing another weapon.

"Let's go." Gareth nodded. "We'll follow on bikes.

* * *

Colin could not shake the sense of foreboding he felt about Amaryllis leaving the walls of the Faesten even if Seth and the mortals were with her as back-up. His thoughts continued to whir and lag. With the weak sunlight creeping like a living carpet along the hallway and despite the specially made glass that should have stopped the orb's heat from touching him, it still did. He was weakening and he knew it. Normally, the poor light would not have affected him. He could have stayed longer in the kitchen, could have been on the ground floor without having to hide in the shadows. But without sex's healing attributes, he was no different from a human not having eaten or drunk the whole day. The headache he never thought he would be subjected to intensified. In a few nights it would be the full moon and he had still not found a willing partner to strengthen the Kinaré. Having Amaryllis even for that brief moment in time had tipped his lust over. Tasting her on his fingers was like ambrosia found in a desert oasis, but it was not enough. It teased his senses, his body hungering for more. The Kinaré seemed to have a mind of its own and refused to have anyone other than Amaryllis. Bloody fuck. Colin was having a difficult time stopping himself from completely taking Amaryllis so that he could feed his craving. His first objective was to keep her safe as Mack asked him. Some bodyguard he was, cracking that unspoken wall of not touching her, but what happened was not his fault. Amaryllis had instigated it the moment she lifted her legs.

Admit it, Butler, you wanted her for your own. You're in deep shit.

This would not do. Tonight, Colin had to find a woman willing to join him for a few hours of pleasurable sex. That should keep his lust for Amaryllis at bay.

He was still rubbing off the soreness from his arm when he entered the nerve centre.

"You allowed Amaryllis out?" Craig intercepted him with two mugs of coffee. He handed Colin one. "There's food at the bar."

Colin nodded his thanks and sipped while he went to the bar and pinched a piece of breakfast steak from the platter. The flavour of the meat with spices flooded his mouth. "You know that Seth is one of the best female Cynn mortal warriors we have. Amaryllis will be safe."

Craig grunted and sipped from his own mug.

"What's it you object to with Annaseth?" Cormac asked from his seat, glancing at Craig, baffled. "You seem to keep being on her case."

"I have no objection at all." Craig shrugged. "Like Dux said, she's one of the best."

"Gareth, Donovan, and Etienne are with them, so they'll be fine," Cormac added as though assuring them. "Those three are excellent marksmen." His fingers flew over the keyboard as he resumed checking the Faesten's perimeter and looking at the different feeds of the Faesten's clubs and restaurants. Rain began pelting the streets with fat drops from the heavens. Now that it was day, not much was happening. Cynn mortals as well as human workers were cleaning up after another night of bodies crowding each other on the dance floor. Over at the restaurants, vans made deliveries, bringing in ingredients for the breakfast and lunch crowds. The exchange of crates to hands rushed so that the produce did not get wet, let alone the people involved in the exchange. People under umbrellas quickly entered coffee shops. Some shook their wet brollies out of respect for the floors while others breezed through, uncaring whether the water trickling from their umbrellas became immediate future health hazards. They fell in line, ordering their preferred cups of poison before another day of drudgery at the office. Some of the men raked their fingers through their damp hair. Women glided their fingers against their lower lids, making sure their mascara didn't run. Others who had too much the night before staggered into breakfast bars to get some food in their gullets to counteract the effects of too much alcohol.

And probably increase their depleted energy after a night of unbridled sex.

Liam was doing the same thing, inspecting a different quadrant of the city where the Cynn Cruors owned establishments. With the advancements in technology and with their own fibre optic cables snaking through the entire city, they were able to monitor Scatha Cruor activity in the safe and welcoming confines of the nerve centre.

"Dux, what do we do about Mackenzie? Roarke?" Craig asked the question no one wanted to pose to Colin. "He'll be calling to brief us and I'm sure he's starting to wonder what's happening here."

Colin shrugged and swallowed before he spoke. "He'll take our word for it. Valerian's appearance after a long hiatus has put all of the Faestens on amber alert at the very least. He won't suspect anything. For now."

Cormac swivelled his seat around to face them. "If Dac is alive, the Faestens will start webbing together again."

"They already have," Liam said. "Marchetti's arrival here can hardly be termed a coincidence. Now that they know and with the Cynn Cruors' communications spanning the globe, we already have interlocked."

"We'll call Roarke," Colin instructed. He took a swig of his piping hot brew, the caffeine easing his headache somewhat before swiping more of the food. "We won't be able to do anything at the moment without any cloud cover. The Scatha are likely to do the same thing as will Mack."

Colin became lost in thought while Liam contacted Manchester, sipping his coffee at a more sedate pace. Things seemed to be crowding him from all sides as though he was fighting a losing war in several fronts. A battle against his growing desire for Amaryllis. A war with Mackenzie. A possible war that could destroy his position with the Cynn Cruors. He wondered if the decision to keep Mack's identity a secret was the right thing to do back then. In an instant he knew it was, hands down. At that time, even innocents who became Scatha Cruors were killed, executed by the Cynn Cruors without compunction. The premise the Cynn Cruors adhered to was once a Scatha Cruor, always a Scatha Cruor. All scruples, all thoughts of good deeds disappeared and those converted were merely Dac Valerian's pawns in a war he was treating like a game. That was what Colin believed, what he and Mackenzie believed. They hacked their way through many Scathas, their anger about their father's and eventually their mother's death unabated for almost four hundred years.

Then things changed.

"Liam."

The sound ricocheted through the Leeds command centre. On an ordinary day, the greeting would not have mattered, just another call to debrief other Faestens about Scatha activities in the area. With Mackenzie's reappearance and Colin still undecided whether to tell Roarke that his brother was alive, it was ominous. The

Leeds warriors became careful underneath their relaxed exterior.

"Graeme," Colin greeted the Manchester warrior jovially. Liam transferred the call onto the screen. Colin chuckled at Graeme's bleary eyed appearance. "Tough night? We Cynn Cruors don't need much sleep. What gives?"

"I'd say the same to you." The sides of Graeme's mouth pulled at the corners. They could hear the rains in Manchester. "You look worse for wear. Still haven't kicked the jet lag?"

"Getting there." Colin raised his mug, the strong aroma giving him liquid courage. Who would have thought? He sipped before speaking. "How's Manchester?"

"As can be expected. Raining but quiet on Deansgate and other places so far. The mortals haven't reported any possible abductions. Jay Nevins is monitoring the police channel. Still nothing. Your end?"

"A bit serious, mate," Colin admitted. "Annaseth has just told us that the Scatha Cruors seem to be celebrating. We caught a few in the clubs."

Graeme whistled. "Looks like your work's cut out for you, my friend."

"Indeed. Look, Temple, can we get the briefing over? With Scathas going all apeshit, I don't know when I can call back."

"Already done. Telepathed Roarke and the rest as we were talking niceties."

As if on cue, Roarke, Finn, and Luke came to the library.

"Roarke, Finn, Luke," Colin greeted them. "Good to see you. Dux, you wanted to brief us. What happened when we left? We were torn between staying to see the Deoré through and my responsibility as Leeds Dux."

"Believe me, the Ancients understood." Roarke leaned back on one of the couch's armrests with a coffee mug in his hand.

"How is she?"

"The Deoré made a full recovery with Faith's help."

Craig's face broke into a smile. "Well done, McBain."

"Where is he?" Cormac's gaze swept at them, bantering. "Quiet McBain finally took the arrow." He chortled. "Congratulations are definitely in order."

"He's still in Trujillo," Finn answered, taking a seat on the couch, the leather creaking under his weight. His arms rested on his thighs, his hands holding his mug. "They should be back in a few days. Zac had to stay to heal."

Colin was grim. "Yes, you mentioned that the first time I called."

Roarke rubbed his forehead, his face suddenly weary. "We almost lost Zac, Butler, just like we nearly lost Graeme. What I didn't tell you was that his head was nearly severed by Kamaria."

"Shite!"

Colin was aghast. The silence that followed in both Faestens could have rivalled that of a tomb.

"Sorry, Hamilton," Colin said softly. He could empathize with Roarke. One of his men had already been lost to him and he wanted him back. Mackenzie. If any of his other men had been in the same situation, it would have compounded the burden he was already carrying. That was the yoke of a Dux. Full responsibility of the Faesten and the men that belonged to it was a must. "How is he?"

"Recovering nicely, thank the Ancients." Roarke's mouth pulled to one side.

"You said Faith was a firebinder." Craig spoke.

"And Zac was nearly beheaded," Liam piped in.

Roarke nodded. "The fire in her blood can heat up beyond boiling. Anything she touches combusts, but she was able to focus the fire to cauterize Zac's wounds and set them back, reattaching what had been severed."

"Zac's lucky," Craig agreed. "And Faith is a welcome addition to the ranks of Cynn Cruor women we will protect."

"Thank you." Roarke smiled.

"I take it that the Specus Argentum will be our main source of bullets and weapons now." Colin opined before he sipped his coffee. He grimaced that it was lukewarm and set it on the table beside him.

"Not exactly." Finn shook his head. He chuckled in disbelief.

"Once the Ancients have had more time to heal, all Dux and seconds will head to Anglesey to discuss the silver further," Roarke said. "The special silver will be a weapon but it won't be used for bullets."

"Securing the cave against Dac claiming it was one of the best campaigns, I have to say," Liam said. "Unexpected though it was."

"Among other things. Zac will be heading a team to develop something from the silver when he returns."

"To look at how to combat its effects if we get hit." Cormac concluded.

"No," Finn said. "To find a safe way to inject us with it."

"What?" The Leeds Cynn Cruors exclaimed, dumbfounded.

"That's bloody going to kill us!" Cormac was incredulous. "Are you out of your freaking minds?"

"Tavish!" Colin snapped.

"Beg your pardon, Dux." Cormac darted a glance at Colin. "But seriously?"

"Hamilton, the silver." Colin's eyes narrowed. "What gives?"

"That silver was used in the bullet that nearly killed me," Graeme said.

"We know that," Craig said, eyes narrowing with impatience.

"You can see it didn't."

"Because of the Ancients' magick and Zac's healing you," Colin affirmed.

Graeme shook his head. "It took me a long time to get back on my feet even after when I would have already been back to form in forty-eight. That was only part of my healing. The silver in La Nahuaterique was altering my system so that my body could accept it. It has made me stronger than I have ever felt in my entire existence. It has also made me immune to lesser forms of silver."

"Holy shit." Cormac ran both his hands through his hair. Liam slouched deeper into his chair, his mood bemused and disbelieving. "That's going to make us invincible! Well, barring we lose our heads."

Finn nodded. "Trujillo has secured it. De Alvaro and Hector have been beefing up security."

"Does Dac know about this?" Colin asked.

"We can only speculate," Roarke admitted, sighing. "The Ancient Eald didn't kill him. He was able to escape."

"Ahh fuck!" Cormac swore.

"Here we go again," Liam murmured, his mouth pulling to a sour grin. "The next time Dac dies, he better stay dead."

"The silver serum—"

"Silver...serum?" Colin arched a brow, clearly amused. "We better not be called silver surfers."

"That's flat, Butler." Roarke's mouth quirked.

"Let's call it that for the moment. The possibility of extracting a safe dosage that won't kill any of us is big. Zac will begin as soon as he and Faith return to Manchester."

"Butler, mind if I come over for a visit?" Luke piped in.

Colin slapped his thigh. "You are more than welcome to stay with us, Luke. You've finally decided on the Leeds Faesten? Told you we're better than Manchester." He winked.

The Leeds warriors guffawed when the Manchester immortals snorted and shook their heads. Craig did not smile. His mouth thinned as he looked at his watch.

"Still can't forget how you were able to wheedle your way into the team." Admiration filled Liam's eyes. "Nicely done. You should teach us how you do that."

"I don't know if I can, but we can try." Luke's smile widened. His gaze went to Craig. "You sure it's okay with everyone? Craig doesn't seem too happy about it."

"No, no, it's not that." Craig assured them. He looked at Colin, worry flickering in his gaze. "It's been over an hour."

"What was supposed to happen in an hour?" Luke asked, curious.

Just then the other phone line beeped. Liam pushed the button.

"Seth, you're on speaker phone."

"Stewart, the gates! Get ready to close the gates!"

Amaryllis.

The Cynn Cruors stood, even those watching from Manchester.

"Where are you?" Colin's voice was hard, his heart sprinting.

"E.T.A. two minutes from the Faesten." The sound

of the car speeding and tires screeching was in the background. Screams and expletives from pedestrians diving for cover and the blare of furious vehicle horns added to the melee. They also heard tires going through water. "Gareth, Donovan, and Etienne are behind me. They're taking fire."

Metal hit metal. Gunshots.

"Amaryllis!"

"She's fine, Dux," Seth spoke, her voice tight. The tires screeched, the car engine almost drowning the sound. "Amaryllis, brace!"

Cormac's face slowly contorted to a cringe, anticipating a crash. Liam froze in his seat. Everyone waited with bated breath. Then they heard the car accelerate once again.

"Fucking moron," Seth shouted. "Bloody watch where you're going!"

A car horn furiously blared in response.

Cormac sighed, chuckling. "That's our Annaseth."

"Tavish, you're dead." Seth gritted. "And who else is snickering there?"

"Manchester is online, Seth." Liam had a wide smile on his face. "They heard you too."

Liam's fingers flew over the keyboard, bringing the camera feed by the gates on screen and the road outside leading to the Faesten. The rains had begun in earnest, rivulets of water running down or splattering the CCTV lenses. Liam typed in another code.

"Manchester, here's your ringside view of what's happening," he drawled.

Roarke, Finn, Graeme, and Luke stood side by side, watching the action unfolding before them.

"Oh shit," Seth said. "No time for chit apologies chat. Gareth, Donovan, Etienne are inside the gates." Three black Ducati Panigale bikes screamed through the

Faesten's barriers. About five yards away, the Cynn mortals skidded to a halt, threw themselves off their bikes and sprinted to the gates, their weapons primed.

"What the bloody hell are you still doing outside?" Colin and Craig bellowed at the same time.

Liam and Cormac looked at each other before they stared at their Dux and his second in command.

Seth was not listening to either of them. The Porsche came squealing through the gates, speeding up the tree lined driveway to the Faesten's entrance. Gareth, Donovan, and Etienne started shooting at three cars and five Kawasaki bikes that were hot on the Porsche's tail.

The sound of metal pinging against metal and tires screeching to a halt filled the command centre.

"Get your arses back here!" Colin bellowed.

"What do you bloody think I'm doing, Dux? Stewart, the gates! Now!"

Liam pressed several buttons on the console by the keyboard and the Faesten's gates began to close.

"I'm going out there," Colin shouted, already whizzing out of the centre.

"Dux! Damn it!" Craig followed in pursuit.

Liam's mouth quivered at the various faces of admiration and enjoyment filled his brethren's faces. He raised his mug at them.

"And that, Manchester, is how we do things in Leeds."

Chapter Twelve

Colin and Craig sucked in harsh breaths once they left the confines of the dark corridor behind them and out of the lift. The rain beat down on the Faesten's roof, but they could still feel the sun's lingering heat. Oppressive and cloying, they seemed to have entered a greenhouse without any respite from the oxygen emitted by tropical plants. A blanket of uncomfortable warmth seemed to stay low, refusing to rise to the ceiling. They stood for moments to acclimatise to the change they felt keenly against their skin and in their blood. The thin muslin covering the windows was a poor excuse of protection for any immortal walking around the house during the day. It had been placed there for aesthetic reasons so no one knew they were in the midst of a race that had vampire, werewolf, and human genomes. Colin felt his skin prickle with the heat. He and Craig sped through the cooler but not much better confines of the hallway. He gritted his teeth. He was getting weak faster than he normally would, the Kinaré's strength close to empty. They heard more shots fired and a bellow of pain. They were about to sprint but abruptly halted before they crossed the foyer. Rain showered the dome above. Then suddenly the rains stopped and the sun broke through the clouds. Colin and Craig inched their way towards the entrance door, hugging the wall as much as they could. Both Cynn Cruor warriors' breathing rasped.

"Bloody hell, this is the one time I hate being an immortal," Craig growled. He looked out one of the glass walls by the entrance door, pacing in the narrow space he was in. They were both taking a risk of getting close to the rays of the sun that struggled against the clouds until it broke out in triumph. Colin looked at Craig.

"We've been through worse, Butler." Craig sucked in his breath.

Nodding, Colin opened the front door. Although the porch was covered, the ultraviolet rays felt like they faced the harsh orb in the desert. Pain burned its light into Colin's eyeballs and he had to squint where a human would have basked in its soft rays. Not even the slight breeze brought by the rain's respite was enough to ease his discomfort.

Fuck! Etienne was down and men were scaling the Faesten's walls. He turned away, closing his eyes to let moisture seep through his drying irises. Colin swallowed before looking back at them.

"Seth, on the wall!" He heard Amaryllis scream. But Seth, Gareth, and Donovan were too intent on treating Etienne.

No! Colin's heart stopped. The man who had jumped ran towards the group in the driveway.

Towards Amaryllis.

Protect her. Mine.

What he saw next rooted him to the spot.

* * *

As soon as the Porsche Boxster GTS zoomed up the driveway, Seth screeched to a stop, locking the wheels and kicked a lot of gravel. Splatters of mud and stone surrounded them, rapping sharply against the door and hitting the windows where spider cracks formed. The car halted right by the Faesten's door.

Amaryllis got out of the car just in time to see Jack aim through the closing gates and fire.

"Etienne!" Seth screamed, bolting out of the car,

running headlong to where the Cynn mortal fell.

Amaryllis watched wide eyed as she saw grappling hooks then Jack's men starting to climb the twenty foot walls. Gareth and Donovan ran towards the gate as soon as Seth knelt beside Etienne. They started shooting back, felling those who successfully entered the compound, who became heaps on the ground. They pivoted and sprinted to Etienne's side, helping Seth stem the blood flow. Suddenly, Amaryllis noticed a movement and her heart lodged in her throat.

"Seth, on the wall!" Jack was able to enter, squeezing between the gates before it closed, letting his men take the fall before he came blazing in. He ran forward and saw Amaryllis. Slowly, his mouth lifted to a maniacal I-am-going-to-get-you-this-time grin. Seth did not appear to have heard her, too engrossed in caring for her fallen comrade. Panic gripped Amaryllis. Jack had the gun pointed ready to take a closer shot.

"Oh, fuck it!" Amaryllis bolted to a run. If Jack wanted a fight, well bloody hell, she was ready for a freaking fight. She may not be good in the martial arts, but she was going to hit Jack where it hurt the most for giving her to creeps that had faces that would make Freddie Kruger run with his tail between his legs. Dimly Amaryllis remembered Seth telling her that they did not kill humans, only rendered them unconscious. Amaryllis just hoped that Etienne's gun only had tranquilizers. If not, she hoped Jack lived. It did not matter if he was a dickhead. No way was she going to be convicted of murder. Theft, been there, done that. Not murder. She refused to go to jail for that.

Seth and the rest did not notice her until she was nearly on top of them. With a distance of four metres between herself and the group, Amaryllis vaulted herself towards them, grabbing a gun by Etienne's side before rolling upright.

"What the fuck?" Gareth bellowed, scowling in anger.

There was no time to retort as Amaryllis planted herself in front of the group on the ground and pulled the trigger. Jack gave a guttural growl and an almost feminine squeal. Shock registered on his face before it went slack and he crumpled to the wet ground.

"How is he?" Amaryllis turned to them, bending down on her knees, looking at Etienne's ashen face. The adrenalin spike caused her heart to race and sweat to coat her in a thin sheen. The wind whistling through the trees that lined the driveway brought droplets of water over them, seeping into their clothes and marking them like polka dots. She noticed Gareth gawking at her. A drop felt on her crown and made its way down her forehead. She flicked it away. "What?"

"Seriously? You had to tranquilize his balls?" Gareth shook his head, a slight grimace contorting his face. "Bloody hell, woman, I wouldn't want to catch you on a bad day."

She snorted. "Yeah, make sure you don't."

Seth gave her an assessing look, a new found respect in her eyes. "Thank you. You've bought us time."

"Annaseth," Craig yelled.

"Dux, Craig, get the fuck back in the shadows!" Seth's head snapped up at the two immortals trying to make their way out of the portico.

Amaryllis twisted around and gasped.

"You come back in here," Craig roared at her then hissed, stepping back. "Ancients, dammit! This fucking hurts!"

"Etienne's down," Seth cried. "He's my responsibility." She looked up and noticed the sun sending stronger rays down to the earth. Then in a gentler tone, "I'll be fine, Craig. You won't be. Please go back inside." Then she was all business like, tearing the hem of her shirt to make a tourniquet.

"No!"

Everyone whipped their attention towards the portico.

"Dux! God dammit, Butler, don't go out!"

But Colin seemed far gone.

Sarcastically chiding Seth earlier about Halloween masks and vampiric teeth did not prepare Amaryllis for the way Colin started to burn under the sun. She refused to believe what the woman said. When Colin was about to step out of the door with Craig shouting for him to get back, and when she heard the sizzling sound and smelled the acrid odour of burning flesh, Amaryllis could no longer deny the truth. She sped back towards the house, slid over the Porsche's hood, vaulted over the short flight of stairs and encircled her arms around Colin's waist and back. Air whooshed out of her when his body slammed against hers, her heart squeezing at his grunt of pain.

"I've got you," Amaryllis whispered.

Colin looked at her with pain in his eyes mixed with gratefulness. He tried to smile but grimaced instead.

"What the hell were you thinking?" Amaryllis moved to allow Colin to sling his arm around her shoulders.

"Must...protect...you," he gritted. "Can't...let you...die."

"Here you go again with the death shit. You're in more dire straits than I am and closer to death than I'll be. I can worship the sun. You can't." She nearly heaved at the smell of singing skin, trying as much as possible not to touch the raw patches to prevent herself from adding to Colin's suffering. She needed to move away. The sun was warm with the breeze cool on her skin. It was turning to be a beautiful day for her, a nightmare for the man she held close. Amaryllis had the sudden urge to make sure he was all right. Worry gnawed at her and the strange surge of wanting to protect him frightened her. It did not matter at the moment that he could be a pain. She wanted to stay by his side.

Her brow creased in confusion at that fleeting thought.

They entered the cooler confines of the vestibule but the danger was not over. Two of the men she saw the night before were across from them, their hands balled into fists, trying as much as possible not to expose themselves to the sunlight streaming from the domed skylight above the foyer. There was another man with them, someone she did not recognize.

"Amaryllis," the man who scoffed at her the night before spoke, his voice gentle. "You have to bring Colin over to Luke and Cormac without having to go across the foyer. You can't cross because the sun will burn him. Can you do that?"

She nodded in mute assent. There was only enough space for them to move by the walls. Colin's harsh breathing fanned her cheek and her temple while he tried to keep his head up. She looked up at his half lidded eyes, raw with pain. His jaw was tight with the effort of not making a sound even as his mouth tried to pull into a grin. And even in the midst of his discomfort, he could still make her heart jackhammer for a different reason. He was getting heavier by the minute and she had to support their weight so that they did not fall. Her heart pounded and made a vein pulse in her temple. Her legs strained with effort. With razor like mindedness, she pulled more strength from the reservoir inside her, the same way she concentrated on a difficult parkour move so that she did not falter.

"Ready?" Her soft voice floated between them.

Before Colin could nod, Amaryllis hauled him by the wall and quickly scooted them towards the stairwell. He grunted and she winced at the sound and unpleasant smell of more burning flesh when she almost tripped and Colin's hand flailed towards the weak sunlight. Soon they were at the stairwell. The two men grabbed Colin from her and dashed into the shadowed corridor. Amaryllis bent from the waist, taking huge gulps of air, feeling the strain in her muscles, the ache in centre of her back, her heart running a thousand miles a second. If she was not a traceuse that trained almost every day to strengthen her muscles and increase her stamina, she doubted if she could have carried Colin as she had done.

"Bloody hell, Dux, haven't seen you this fried since Iran in '41." One of the men winced. He looked at Amaryllis. "We haven't been introduced. Cormac Tavish at your service. This mean monster holding up Dux is Luke Griffiths. Just arrived from Manchester via a parallel portal. That grouchy man in the shadows is Craig Shaw. Don't mind his face. He always scowls." As though on cue, Craig did just that.

"Hi." Amaryllis blew several gasps, raising her arm in a half-hearted wave.

Luke stared at her. A threatening growl rose up Colin's throat, surprising Amaryllis. She watched all three men in perplexity when their mouths twitched. Even Craig's frown lightened.

She turned to Craig, her voice laced with anxiety. "Where are you taking him?"

"His room," Craig said, a muscled ticking on his jaw after having a better inspection of Colin's arms and face.

137

Just then, Seth burst into the foyer, followed by Etienne being dragged between Gareth and Donovan. Etienne's left leg was matted in blood that soaked his jeans and trailed the floor. His head was angled towards Gareth, his face ashen.

"Cormac, get the adriserum and bring it upstairs then see to Etienne," Craig ordered. "Seth—"

"We're okay, Shaw." Seth stopped in front of him, encompassing all of them in her gaze. She looked the longest at Craig. "Talk later." She gave him a short smile and followed the mortals to the end of the hallway that led to the Faesten's hospital wing.

Colin's quarters were located in the opposite wing from where Amaryllis stayed. Craig flung the door open, allowing Luke to precede him to put Colin on the bed. Amaryllis hung back by the door. Her hair blew against her face when Cormac sped by before leaving the room again. Craig plunged the syringe in the centre of Colin's chest and her gut clenched at the hiss of pain coming from his lips.

"No finesse at all, Craig." Colin sighed.

Craig grunted. He looked at where Amaryllis stood. "He's going to be okay."

"Back to the control room for us, Shaw. I'll inform Manchester what's happened and that Butler's okay," Luke said, nodding.

Craig's mouth pulled up in a rueful grin. "Do that. I'll stay—"

"No," Amaryllis blurted, embarrassment burning her cheeks. "You both go ahead. I'll stay." She paused. "It's the least I can do."

Craig and Luke looked at each other before walking to the door.

"Thank you," Craig said then pointed to the phone by Colin's bed. "That connects to the command centre.

Call if you need us."

"I will."

Amaryllis closed the door behind the two men then made her way to Colin's side. His eyes were closed. She never realised that his lashes were thick. His forehead still creased with discomfort. Parts of his jaw, the skin on his cheekbones as well as beneath his stubble and the exposed skin on his arms looked like they were scrubbed raw, the skin as though having been eaten away by bacteria. She flinched and sucked in her breath when she felt the pain Colin was feeling. She could feel the soreness of each part of Colin's body on her own as though they were psychically connected.

"It's not as bad as it looks."

Amaryllis' gaze flew to Colin's. He watched her, quiet, waiting. His chest rising and falling rhythmically. Amaryllis' senses went into overdrive, a flush rising to her cheeks at Colin's scrutiny. The tip of her tongue moistened her lower lip and she was sure she heard him growl softly.

She swallowed, her mouth suddenly dry. "How long before your wounds heal?"

Colin continued looking at her. "In about a minute."

"A minute?" Her eyes widened. She looked at his wounds. "You were roasting! How can...that...be...?" In the dim coolness of the room, she watched in fascination when the open wounds started to close, healthy skin creeping over the burned areas.

"This is so freaking me out," she whispered, turning away to stand, but Colin's hand closing over her wrist stopped her. A delicious shudder pierced her at his touch.

"Stay." His deep voice was like hot, dark chocolate.

Amaryllis' lips parted, incapable of stopping her sharp inhale when Colin circled his thumb sensuously

139

over the erratic pulse on her wrist.

"Like it?"

Damn, why does his voice have to be so sexy? The initial excitement Colin elicited slowly settled in her belly and caused a deep throb between her thighs.

"Yes." She sighed. Her gaze locked with his, drowning in those dark green depths. She had to get away, her gut telling her she was in danger of wanting to continue where they left off. "You need to heal, need to rest."

"I am resting and healing, Amaryllis. Touching you helps me heal."

"I'm sorry?" Her forehead furrowed in confusion.

Colin sat up, still holding her wrist. "Look at me, my skin. The serum Craig injected me with helped, but I need something more."

"I can call Craig to get you what you need."

Colin chuckled. "I doubt if Craig could give me what I need."

"Then what do you need?"

"You."

"Me?" She gasped. "I don't understand. What can I give you so to help you heal?"

"Your pussy."

Amaryllis drew in a shocked breath. The dull throb between her thighs that occurred every time Colin was near intensified and she felt her heat seeping and moistening her nether lips. Bloody hell, he was crude. And hot. Blood rolled like thunder in her ears and she felt the wetness slowly soak her knickers. "What...why?"

"Sex helps me heal. Finger-fucking you earlier was not enough. I need to taste you." He inhaled sharply. "I can smell your sweetness, Violet." His gaze stoked the growing fire inside her. "Let me eat you, I need your cream. I need to play with you and make you come. Will you let me? Let me taste how delicious you are?"

Damn, that soaked her knickers all the more.

"This is madness," she breathed, hating the way her body was begging Colin's touch after he reminded her of their heavy petting.

Colin's closed his eyes and lay back with a sigh, letting go of her hand. "Yes it is," he admitted. "I've told you what I need, but I can't force you. I'm sorry if I scared you with my crassness."

Whoa. Talk about a sudden turn around.

"Don't be. I mean…it's okay. I mean…bloody hell." She felt as though she was adrift at the loss of Colin's touch. Just the thought of Colin's mouth on her was starting to drive her insane.

"Do you want me to touch you?"

"You were touching me a while ago," she said softly.

"I held your wrist, Amaryllis." There was smile in Colin's voice. "I didn't touch you." He sobered. "I have no right to ask this of you. You belong to my brother."

She slanted him a glance. "I don't belong to anyone, your brother least of all. Your brother rescued me. That's all there is to it."

Why did the sexual banter suddenly dwindle to seriousness? God knew how much she wanted Colin to touch her but what did he expect her to do? Take off her clothes and lie down so that he could eat her until she screamed?

"Yes, if you'll agree to it. I'll make you cum so hard with my tongue that when you're with someone else, you'll only think of me."

"What the—" Amaryllis moved away, her eyes wide with amazement. "Right, you read my mind. I forgot." She said on a breath.

"Couldn't help it."

Amaryllis sank down by the foot of the bed.

"I won't stop you if you want to leave the room," Colin said quietly.

"I didn't think of that."

"I don't need to read what was on your mind when you're about to vault."

"I can't leave you."

"Why not?" He looked at her.

"Because I said I would watch over you."

Colin sighed, looking up at the ceiling. "It's okay, Amaryllis. I'll be fine. I don't need a nursemaid."

Okay, that stings. Humiliation slowly heated her cheeks. "Fine, suit yourself." She stood and walked to the door. She had to leave before Colin noticed the telltale mistiness in her eyes. She left, not bothering to give Colin a second glance.

* * *

I'm such a bloody asshat.

Colin covered his eyes with his arm, grimacing at the pull of new skin over the places that had been exposed to the sun. He was going to make it a point to have the bloody dome fitted with the special glass. He had never given it much thought before but back then, there was no Amaryllis to speak of. Most of the time, only the Cynn mortals occupied the ground floor and any immortal worth their salt normally avoided the foyer on sunny days, preferring to walk through the dim hallways to get to where they wanted to go. It was the one thing Colin and, he was sure, the rest of the warriors missed after their eleventh birthday. The moment they started training and lost their mortality was the moment they lost their invulnerability to the sun. If they had to go out during the day, they would have to stay in the shade or side streets, like shifty individuals hiding from the law.

He relived the moment he thought he would see the violet beauty get maimed inside the Faesten's walls. In the centuries that the Cynn Cruors had lived in the place, no human had ever died within the confines of the bailiwick. Colin had seen Amaryllis take on the man hell bent on killing his people despite her misgivings and scepticism about who they were. Grudging respect was like a bubble expanding inside his chest, wanting to explode. He had a sudden need to take Amaryllis in his arms and punish her for risking her life by kissing her thoroughly until she was breathless with need for him as he was for her. But the only thing he could do was to grasp the doorknob until he felt warmth starting to heat up and burn his palm. He had hissed, his eyes rolling in his head. He could not breathe and when he did it felt like fire entering his lungs instead of air. He had the ability to stop breathing for long periods of time if his strength was optimum, but with the sun approaching its zenith and in his weakened state, it had been torture. Colin's knees had buckled, unable to stop from falling. That's when he felt himself buffered by softness so sweet and a voice so gentle and soothing.

"I've got you." Amaryllis' voice floated inside his mind.

He did not expect himself to be attracted to Amaryllis as much as he was. He swore underneath his breath as his thoughts constantly returned to the violet eyed beauty underneath his roof. The only reason why Amaryllis was with them was because Mackenzie asked for his help. Some help he was giving, his desire to possess the violet beauty his brother had brought to him for safekeeping was consuming him by the minute. He was a slave to her siren call.

His skin stretched taut over his arm. Colin could feel the same thing happening on his face. He blew out a breath, tiredness seeping into his bones. He just had to grin and bear it until he could find a willing female to assuage his hunger tonight. But first, he needed to allow his body to heal.

Chapter Thirteen

Amaryllis made her way downstairs to the kitchen. The farther she was from Colin's room the more she wanted to leave.

The more she wanted to stay.

"You're such a bloody idiot, throwing yourself like a slut." She was furious at herself, the memory flushing her cheeks and causing her body to tighten with shame.

She paused just by the door when she saw Seth taking out a mug from the cupboard and an herbal teabag from one of the canisters on the counter before filling the mug with hot water.

"How's Etienne?" Amaryllis went to the cupboard to get a mug as well before pouring hot water over the herbal profusion teabag she took out from the canister. Making tea would be good. It would take her mind away from the warrior upstairs.

Seth smiled. "He'll live." She took a sip from her mug, sighing in appreciation. "He just won't be able to enjoy whatever delights there might be tonight. He should be okay in a day or two."

"But he was shot." Amaryllis was aghast. "Surely you wouldn't allow him to get back on his feet after having a bullet go through his leg."

Indulgent understanding filled Seth's eyes. "We didn't really get to talk about who we are this morning. You've been thrown into the deep end without a rope to haul you back."

"So throw me a rope. Not sure if you'll get to haul me back. I'm still finding it hard to believe all that I see even if I know it's the truth."

"As Cynn mortals, we heal quickly. With the

amount of adriserum injected into him, Etienne's wound is closing up, any torn ligaments stitching themselves, any damaged muscle mending as we speak. It was a clean wound and didn't hit any bone. He should be fine." Seth walked to the breakfast table. The bread she had baked that morning had been placed in a bread basket and covered with a cloth to keep it moist. "Besides, he's going to chew my ass off if I don't allow him to train. Last night we ploughed the clubs for Scatha Cruors. Colin and Craig weren't in good form, but we were able to temper the Scathas' celebrations."

Envy uncoiled inside Amaryllis. "So you guys went out while I was asleep," she said flatly.

Seth shrugged. "Part of the job and we do it all the time. It's not like there was anything special save for the Scatha screaming their jowls out." She looked at Amaryllis curiously. "Would you have wanted to go? Join us?"

"No, no," Amaryllis said with a quick shake of her head, her brow slightly meeting in the middle. She gave a short smile. "Just curious." How could she tell Seth that she wished she could have seen Colin in action? Suddenly, she clamped down on her thoughts. If Seth was a Cynn mortal, she might read minds too. But Seth seemed unconcerned. There was no knowing look or snicker forthcoming.

"Is something going on tonight?" Amaryllis asked, blowing the tendrils of heat away from her cup before taking a tentative sip of her tea.

"The clubs are open." Seth shifted her weight, leaning her hip against the counter. "There's normally a lot of action happening at night, though I don't think it will be as hectic as last night. We kinda put a damper on the Scathas." She cocked her head to one side. "How's Colin?"

My Haven, My Midnight

Amaryllis felt her cheeks warm. "He's resting. I couldn't do anything more, so I decided to leave. "

Seth nodded. "We still haven't tried the bread I baked. I can toast some if you like."

"Thanks." Amaryllis nodded. "That'd be nice."

Seth placed her mug down to slice a few pieces of the bread. "The butter is in the fridge. Could you get it?"

Amaryllis got the butter and opened a few more cupboards to get plates and took some butter knives from the one of the drawers. She watched Seth and sighed.

"You know you don't have to flaunt the fact that you have thick skin," she said.

"What?" Seth looked at her vacantly before realizing that she was fixing the bread inside the toaster while the coils were red. "Oh. Sorry."

"This is crazy." Amaryllis blew out a breath and swung her head to look out the nook's window.

"After what we did this morning, you still distrust us." Seth's lips lifted in a sad smile.

"I don't distrust you, Seth." Amaryllis gathered her hair behind one ear. "I just can't believe you guys exist. You're like close encounters of the fourth kind."

Seth giggled. "Believe me, no one here is going to hurt you. And like I said, I'm no figure from Hell." She sat down on one of the chairs, setting the toast in the centre of the breakfast table.

"I didn't say you were."

Seth snorted. "Can we just have something to eat in peace? I love baking and not being able to eat what I've baked pisses me off." She lathered butter on one thick slice of bread before biting into it, closing her eyes, moaning in appreciation. "You're missing a lot, you know."

Amaryllis relented when her mouth watered as the

faint smell of toasted bread tickled her nose. She had been around danger all her life, so what difference did it make for her to be around people whose skin did not burn with electrical appliances but sizzled under sunlight? Or whose eyes glowed, changed colour, and who had claws for hands? Everything reminded her of a body snatchers movie. And the Cynn Cruors? Who were they? The only way to find out was to break the deadlock with buttered bread and herbal tea.

"Is there jam anywhere?" she asked.

"Also in the fridge." Seth nudged over her shoulder while she continued to munch on her bread.

Jam in hand, Amaryllis placed the bottle on the table, removed her jacket and draped it on the back of the seat before sinking down. She prepared her own piece of bread and bit down. A burst of flavours, sweet, slightly salty, and all-around goodness coated her mouth. She could not stop her own sigh of satisfaction. She had never tasted anything so good. She felt Seth watching her with amused indulgence while she ate five slices before she leaned back on her chair, replete.

"Told you it was good," Seth stated wryly before getting up. "Care for another cup of tea?"

"Thanks." Amaryllis nodded.

While Seth boiled water in the kettle, Amaryllis looked at the expanse of the garden unencumbered by a wall for what looked like miles. The rains had made the entire place a verdant green. Fresh, lush, and beautiful, the colours more vibrant. Flowers and trees were allowed to grow in something like shabby chic fashion, converting the garden into a riotous canvas of colours. A soft smile played on her lips. She could run and parkour all day. She could twirl around in place until she fell on the ground dizzy and allow the sun and wind sluice her face instead of having to hide in cramped quarters that felt more like a prison than a room at home. Good thing she was small enough to fit into the secret passage she found beside her room, which led immediately outside Jack's hideout. Amaryllis often made her way through the narrow passage and out into the moonlit night when her bedroom became too claustrophobic. She would climb to the building's top and watch the stars at night, often dreaming of a better place where she could walk at her pleasure, where no one told her what to do, when to leave, or when to hide.

Maybe someday she would find her own haven where no one would find her. Where she could live in peace.

"So," Seth began. "What's your story?"

"Don't have any." Amaryllis continued to look out, hitching her shoulders while she took a tentative sip. "What's yours? What's theirs? And don't tell me your real name is the Halloween gang." Her heart started to race at the memory of Max's transformation.

Seth gave a laugh that sounded between a snort and a puff. "Wish it were that simple."

"Tell me. I can be a good listener as long as you don't tell me any bullshit."

Seth leaned back, looking at her thoughtfully. "After what you did in the driveway, you don't deserve any bullshit from me or anyone else here." She pursed her lips. "What did you think of the tapestry along the upper hallway?"

"It was fantastical to say the least. Like in the realm of fantasy or sci-fi." A crease rested on her forehead. "But I don't see what the tapestry has anything to do with you or them."

"It will because it has everything to do with us. It's our history."

"No shit."

"Yes shit."

Amaryllis huffed. "So you're telling me you belong to a group that has monsters that do your bidding if someone as much as gives you the finger."

"Finger flicking is nothing. We are a race of both mortals and immortals. And no, we don't have monsters." Seth paused, taking another sip from her mug.

Amaryllis' stomach churned. Could there even be people like this? Correction. Creatures? Otherworldly beings? Despite what her mind refused to accept, everything that made them real was all around her, especially Colin's skin burning as though he had been near an inferno. What she had witnessed in the alleyway, in the bedroom, and in the foyer was too much of a reality check for her to dismiss it as a costume party for weirdos.

Amaryllis stood shaking her head, unable to refute what her eyes saw.

"I saw what happened in the alley, how the Scatha killed all his companions to take you away." Curiosity tinged Seth's voice. "And yet you are here."

"The monsters."

Seth nodded. "They were once like us, the Cynn Cruors. Mortals and immortals. Colin and the rest who live here are immortals. The first eleven years of their lives are lived as mortals. After that they become immortal."

"How?" Curiosity was getting the better of Amaryllis.

"The Kinaré gene. It mutates, making the vampire and werewolf parts of the DNA more dominant." Seth smiled kindly at Amaryllis' amazed visage. "It is a lot to take in but it's true. I've lived it my entire life and this is the only way I know how to explain who we are to you."

Colin's name being mentioned further stoked the flutter of excitement in her belly and heated her cheeks.

"Ahh." Seth's eyes twinkled. "I gather you noticed that Dux can charm the knickers off even the coldest of women."

"Dux? I noticed you call Colin that earlier."

"It's his title as head of the Cynn Cruors here in Leeds."

Amaryllis hummed then worried her lower lip.

"No."

"Sorry?"

"No, I'm not sexually attracted to Colin."

Amaryllis looked sheepish. "You read minds too." It was more of a statement.

Seth shook her head. "Your pinched expression says that you're jealous."

Amaryllis gawked at her before she covered her heated face with her hands.

"Sweetie, Butler is sexy as hell with a body to die for, but he's just my Dux. My leader. I will follow him wherever he goes. It's our oath." She shrugged. "He's just been to the Honduras on a mission and now this. He hasn't really rested at all. And with the night of the full moon nearly upon us, he'll need to renew his strength."

"Full moon." Amaryllis could not stop her sceptical look.

"There are so many things that I have to tell you which can't be told in one sitting. What I can tell you is that a few days before, during, and after the night of the full moon, an immortal needs to regain his strength to be in fighting form."

"How does he do that?"

"Sex." Seth said it so matter-of-factly that Amaryllis laughed in disbelief. The memory of her conversation with Colin made her heart skip. It was one thing to hear it from a guy, like it was some outrageous pick-up line. Hearing it from a woman was a different matter all together.

"Sex. Seriously?"

Seth shrugged. "It's who we are. We are a very sexual race, but we will only have sex with those who are willing. We don't force ourselves upon others."

"And if Colin doesn't have…you know?"

Seth's mouth pulled to one side, then she sobered. "The adriserum will do in a pinch. But knowing Dux? He'll be prowling the clubs tonight to get a partner or partners for that matter."

"Well, I guess that solves it then," Amaryllis said.

Jealousy sucker punched Amaryllis' gut. No freaking way was she going to allow the green-eyed fiend distort reality. There was nothing going on between Colin and herself. Sure he had pleasured her but that was brought by the moment. Nothing more. Besides, she was such a plain Jane she doubted if men who really mattered, those who treated their women right would give her a second look. Most of her adult life, Amaryllis had to fend off those who just wanted to get inside her knickers and boast that they banged a violet eyed bitch with a streak of violet hair.

But you want it to be something more.

Amaryllis felt inadequate beside Seth's beauty. Her face was heart shaped with a widow's peak that made her tresses fall softly down the sides of her face and down to her shoulders. She had alabaster skin and a naturally musk rose flush on her cheekbones. Amaryllis was not one to swing towards the same sex, but she recognized beauty when she saw it.

Wow, talk about big time insecurity. She was like a woman putting two and two together to make a thousand about a man with just one encounter! She was such an overthinking pathetic so and so.

Seth stood up and placed the dirty dishes and mugs inside the dishwasher. "I have to go and check on Etienne then brief Gareth and Donovan. Are you sure you'll be okay here?"

Amaryllis gave her a short smile. "I'll be fine. I'll just go around the gardens."

Seth looked at her warily.

"Oh, for God's sake." Amaryllis huffed in irritation. "Now that I know Jack is after me, I'm not that dumb to even venture out the gates. I just need a little exercise to release some tension. Besides, I take it that there are a lot of cameras all over the place so you'll know whether I've left the place or not. Then you can hunt me down."

Seth exhaled a laugh. "Well, it's not going to be me. If my hunch is correct, the only Cynn Cruor who'll hunt you and make you his is going to be Colin Butler. The way he looks at you and that soft growl whenever another man looks at you? That's staking possession the Cynn Cruor way."

"You." Amaryllis pointed an accusing finger at her. "Need to have your eyes checked. I was dumped here to be protected, remember? Mr. Butler hardly welcomed my presence."

"Right." Seth rolled her eyes as she washed her hands in the sink. Turning to the woman still by the breakfast table, she chewed her lower lip.

"What?" Amaryllis asked.

"Something doesn't make sense."

"Yes," Amaryllis agreed. "All of you don't make sense. All this doesn't make sense. I need to have my head checked."

"No, not that." Seth stared at a point behind Amaryllis. Doubt flickered in her eyes, then as though she finally resolved a conundrum, her eyes cleared. "I gotta go. Please don't give us any more trouble. I need to re-energize too, you know."

"By having sex in the morning?" Amaryllis grinned, liking the banter developing.

Seth gave a dismissive wave. "That's for tonight. I'm hitting the gym at the back of the house. I mean it, girl. No more trouble."

Amaryllis gave her a mock salute. "I'll try."

Chapter Fourteen

The sunlight sent its gentle warmth down as Amaryllis exited the entrance door. She stopped on the first step and raised her arm. The light breeze skittered over her skin, causing goose bumps while she focused on the orb's heat, glad for the respite from the rain. There were still clouds that threatened to unload their contents but for the moment the pale blues of the sky and the muslin thin white clouds dominated the heavens, a far cry from the dark greys moments before. Amaryllis loved the sun. She was not too keen on the rain but it was a given living in the North. What she could do without was deep, dank darkness that seemed to siphon her very soul. Ironically, it was one of the tools of her trade, the cover giving her protection from those after her after a successful heist or those who wanted to pounce on her after seeing her eyes. She was close to telling Seth who she was and what she did but telling was akin to giving up a part of herself, a truth that could be used against her, to be distorted, chewed, mangled and spat out. Then she would have to hide again in the very darkness she abhorred.

Never again.

Going down the steps lightly, she raised her arms to stretch before twisting and flexing her body in preparation for what she was about to do. She felt her heartbeat start to increase, excitement in her veins, determination in her stance. She took out an elastic band she always had inside her jacket pocket and gathered her hair into a ponytail.

Hanging her jacket on a protruding tree branch low enough for her to reach, she stretched one more time and started to run. A smile broke on her face before she reached her first obstacle. A low lying branch that looked as though it had been hit by lightning and remained attached to the tree trunk. Sobering, Amaryllis blocked her surroundings and zeroed in on her target. There was a nearby tree beside and she veered toward it, flowing like the wind that rushed against her face. Taking the trunk, she planted one foot then another before catapulting herself over the trunk as though she was about to dive into a pool. She hurdled the obstacle, tucking her entire body as compact as possible before executing a flawless barrel roll.

"Not too challenging," Amaryllis muttered when she straightened. Irritation creased her forehead. Her eyes narrowed, scanning the expanse of the garden, the driveway, and the sculptures dotting the landscape. "Let's make this more interesting."

* * *

Colin woke up with a start, his body clock telling him that dusk had passed. He bolted up from the bed and grimaced, looking at the offending spots on his body.

"Fuck." He swore softly, looking at his skin. The healing seemed to have stopped. He did not need the light to see that the patches on his arms made them look like limbs of a short giraffe. It didn't matter. He'd use a long sleeved shirt even if the weather was warm. The vampire's attributes in his blood would keep him comfortable in his own skin. Besides, when did the weather stop Cynn Cruors from a good fuck?

He was about to make his way to the bathroom and prepare for the evening when he heard laughter outside his window. Curious, he looked down. His eyes widened in surprise and disbelief. The Faesten's grounds had been transformed into an obstacle course. Lights beamed down on the garden like a huge football pitch at night while at the edge of the horizon, the night was slowly pushing the day to bed. Craig, Liam, Cormac, and Luke watched from the sidelines while Seth and the other mortals fixed the challenges. Stone seats that had dotted the opposite side of the garden were now stacked up on top of each other in walls of different heights. Amaryllis was running headlong towards the stacked seats. Colin's heart lodged in his throat, his hand planted against the window ledge, fingers digging until he heard the crunch of wood underneath.

Amaryllis.

Just like what he saw happen in the driveway, Amaryllis launched herself at the obstacle and vaulted cleanly over the seats, going back to them from a different angle. Colin's gut clenched when she sprinted at full speed, slipping through the narrow gaps between the stacked seats cleanly, tumbling and curving herself into a tight ball before gracefully kneeling on one knee then standing. The crowd around her erupted in applause and whistles. Colin's heart seized at the sight of Amaryllis laughing, her whole countenance happy. Not once did the seats fall on her. Colin relaxed his stance and placed his hands on his hips. Amaryllis was a traceuse. No wonder she was so sexy.

Craig.

Craig straightened from his relaxed pose and looked at Colin's bedroom window. Colin saw his brother in arms smirk.

Remarkable, isn't she?

Colin grunted. *We need to talk.*

Yes, we do. Annaseth is starting to ask questions. Craig sobered.

Colin nodded. He knew that even from afar his second in command would see it.

The men that were shot...

Their memories have been wiped out, Dux. Even before they regained consciousness, we started working on them.

Good. Thanks, mate. Not much of a leader, am I?

I won't dignify that with an answer, Butler. Colin saw the annoyance in Craig's face. *Anyone of us suffering from ultraviolet burns wouldn't have the strength to even move. You've never shown any sign of weakness such as self-pity.*

"Humans crack, Shaw. Cynn Cruors do as well," Colin snapped before raking his hand through his hair.

"Yes, they do and we're part human. But we've been through so many situations that would have made me give up and you didn't."

Colin looked over his shoulder at Craig, who ambled into his room. He gave a mirthless laugh. "I have no fucking idea why this situation is any different."

Craig kept silent, eyeing and waiting for Colin's instructions.

"There must have been people from outside who saw the car chase."

Craig chuckled. "Leave it to the mortals to think of something. Told those busy bodies that there was some filming going on. One woman asked Donovan why they were not informed. Donovan just cracked his smile and she was all gooey before she left."

Colin gave a lopsided grin then sobered. "Craig, if anything happens." He hesitated then expelled a breath. "You'd make a great Dux."

"Oh, don't go through that shit all over again, mate." Craig's lips thinned, his hands rubbing down his face. "You look like shit and you're feeling like shit because you haven't had a good fuck."

"I feel like a whole pile was dumped on me," Colin

replied over his shoulder. "I just need to get Manchester off my tail and fix this thing with Mack." He removed his clothes, leaving them in a heap on the floor. He flexed his shoulders, feeling stiffness settling in. He turned on the shower tap and waited for the cubicle to steam.

"We'll keep an eye on Luke," Craig said. "You sure you want to go out?" He sauntered nearer to the bed and leaned on the post.

"I need to go out, mate." Colin stepped into the steaming water. This was the only heat Cynn Cruors could tolerate and which they welcomed. "Full moon and all." His voice echoed from the enclosed stall.

I'll wait in the library. Craig's telepath held a dry tone. *We're not in the loch bathing in the buff anymore.*

Colin chortled. *Fair enough.*

By the time Colin trotted down the grand staircase, night was on its way to lording it over the skies. He buttoned the cuffs of his dark button down shirt, leaving it untucked over his slacks. He felt more at ease in his skin after his shower. The patches of new skin had disappeared. "Luke," Colin greeted him, entering the library. His smile widened with pleasure when Luke took his arm in the Cynn Cruor greeting. "I'm sorry for the shitty reception earlier, mate. I was being barbecued."

Luke's eyes held a wealth of understanding. "I know how that feels. You okay?"

"Better but will be more so after hitting the clubs." Colin moved towards the mini bar. "Scotch?"

"Please." Luke nodded his thanks after getting his glass and waited for Colin to give Craig his glass. "*Slàinte!*"

Colin and Craig gave pleased grins. Colin raised his glass. "*Slàinte mhor a h-uile là a chi 's nach fhaic!*"

Luke arched his brow in question.

"Great health to you every day that I see you and every day that I don't." Craig supplied.

"I'll drink to that," Luke said wryly. The three men laughed and drank before there was a commotion outside, the steps of the mortals clicking on the tiled floor of the foyer before they thudded against the hallway's wooden floor.

Desire shot through Colin the moment he heard Amaryllis' voice and laughter. Ancients! The sounds coming from her throat coated his body like a lover, ensnaring him in her thrall. His cock noticed and Colin had to grit his teeth to beg his member to be obedient particularly since he was commando. He moved to the window and looked out. A muscle in his jaw tightened when he felt his cock stubbornly rise in greeting. He looked down. Yeah, his hard on might just as well sing "Scotland the Brave" at ten in the evening.

"Damn, girl, you need to teach us all of your moves." Donovan's awed voice reached Colin's ears. He did not like it one bit.

Amaryllis laughed. Colin closed his eyes and stifled his groan, imagining that same laughter surrounding him if they were in bed after bringing her over the throes of ecstasy.

"Keep tumbling about, Donovan, and you'll get the hang of it," Amaryllis replied in amusement.

"Donovan can't dance to save his life." Seth's voice filtered through. "Your expectations of him perfecting his tumbling moves are short of a miracle."

"Hey, no fair," Cormac said in mock affront. "I can't dance either, but I vaulted through pretty well."

"So did I," Liam piped in, his silver eyes crinkling at the corners.

Amaryllis snorted. "For a big guy you had the grace

of a ballet dancer."

Riotous laughter followed.

"Seriously, I mean, c'mon." Amaryllis reasoned. "You're more than human. Donovan, I dare you."

Gareth guffawed. "This I gotta see."

"You're on," Donovan spat. "Put your hand on mine to close the deal."

"Ugh! Shake your own hand," Amaryllis said in disgust.

"Hey, Dux, feeling better?" Seth asked in greeting.

Colin did not speak. He kept his back to them. His heart raced. He shut down his telepathic communication, not wanting the warriors to know what he was thinking. He could feel Amaryllis' stare on his back, a delicious heat wave spreading across his shoulders and down to his already engorged shaft. All he wanted to do was to order all of them out, except for Amaryllis so that he could taste her, pleasure her, take her near the precipice over and over again. He wanted to be inside her, surrounded by her slick, sweet heat, his orgasm building with her every moan, sigh, whimper until she screamed his name that would take him with her to the place where only the two of them existed.

"Much better, ta," he finally said. He closed his eyes. Silence still permeated through the room, the camaraderie a few minutes ago deflating.

"Seth, can you tell me where I can put my things? I'm tracking mud inside already as it is and need to take the sweat and grime off." Amaryllis' voice was so soft, meant for Seth's ears only, but Colin's sharp hearing heard her bewilderment.

And hurt.

"You can still use the room you had earlier. I'll join you to make sure you have everything you need," Seth replied, puzzlement in her voice. "Guys, we need to gear up soon after. Meet you in the foyer."

The footsteps receded, the loud thuds of shoes diminishing the farther they were from the library. Donovan continued to ply Amaryllis with questions, which she answered, though her initial enthusiasm was gone, replaced by polite and friendly reservation. Colin heard the swish of the lift open in the hallway before it closed with a soft sigh.

"You okay, mate?" Craig clamped his shoulder, disconcerting Colin for a moment.

"Yeah." He downed his scotch and swung his gaze. "Why wouldn't I be? Just too much on my mind."

"That girl." Luke stared at the door. "She's a Cynn mortal?"

"No." Colin pivoted, facing the warriors. "She's under my protection."

"Whoa, Butler." Startled, Luke raised his hands. "Just asking."

Colin pinched his nose with this thumb and forefinger, a very human headache knocking the back of his skull. "Sorry, Griffiths. I'm just about depleted." The memory of fingering Amaryllis to orgasm made his mouth salivate. He moved to the bar to get another shot of scotch to keep his mind sharp.

"What are you protecting her from?" Luke asked, his face curious.

"She was almost sold to the Scatha Cruors by the men who attacked the Faesten earlier." Liam volunteered.

"Bloody hell." Luke swore, a gathering storm on his face. "Those bastards have to be stopped."

"And they will," Liam agreed.

"Let's get ready, mate," Cormac suggested cheerfully. "I'll also show you your room if you're staying. Unless you plan to parallel back to Manchester, dress up there then come back here. That is so cool."

"It gets tiring, too, you know." Luke snickered as he spoke. "Show me my room, I'll get my stuff from Manchester and meet you in the city. Where will you all be?"

"*Cinq Mille*," Cormac said. "I'm taking one of the Ducatis. See you there." He sped out of the library, deciding to take the stairs to his rooms, five at a time.

"Looks like our young Turk forgot to show you your quarters." Liam pushed away from the wall, sighing. "Come, my friend. Allow me do the honour." They walked out of the room.

Craig walked over to the door then turned to Colin. "Coming?"

"Go ahead. I'll follow."

Craig gave him a long look. He nodded curtly before speaking. "She isn't Mack's, you know."

"She's still under my roof. I won't use her because I need to get my strength back."

Craig hummed in acquiescence. "What if she comes to you? Will you turn her away?"

With that parting shot, Craig left Colin in the library.

* * *

The latest house music blared from several speakers all over the cramped place. Lee Harris made his way through the crowded low ceilinged underground club, grinning from ear to ear when his fingers swiftly fingered the women between their thighs while they danced whether they wanted it or not. Before the female could react, he was gone, moving on to the next unsuspecting cunt. He chortled as his sharp hearing heard sharp slaps against cheeks catching the men off guard and stunned why they were being womanhandled. Hey, the way Lee saw it, he was doing them a favour. Either they started fighting or they went to the side of the building getting off each other.

He licked his finger, tasting the women's various essences before fixing his tie. His eyes narrowed before they alighted on the person he wanted to see.

"Crawley," he shouted.

His Cruor eyesight watched as Jack Crawley paled when their eyes met, the strobe lights occasionally passing him. His eyes turned to slits. He wanted to go into full Scatha mode and rip through as much of the humans as he could. Unfortunately, today was not the day. Today, he'd find out what Jack had to say.

Jack stood, jerking his head in a nod. He wiped his nose on his sleeve as though he had a constant cold. He inclined his head towards the toilets and did not wait for Lee to follow. Lee grinned. He swung both ways. No reason not to mix a little pleasure with business.

Stopping just inside the doors leading to the lavatories, Jack waited. His hands were in his pockets and he fidgeted. Lee gave two women who had just come out from the ladies' washroom a cursory glance.

"What was it you wanted to tell me?" He continued watching their pert bottoms, giving him an enticing view of their swells. And humans wondered why their women got raped. He snorted, turning his attention to the man in front of him.

"How's my sister?" Jack's eyes were partially glazed from the coke he had imbibed. "Is she okay?"

"She's fine." Lee assured him, switching to mind control. His voice soothing. "As long as you deliver, she will be treated well."

"You said that over a year ago," Jack snapped before remorse took over. "Sorry...sorry....don't hurt her, okay? She's the only family I've got. I've not seen her for such a long time."

"As long as you supply us with meat, we're good." Lee shrugged. "Here." He fished out his phone and opened a video. "There she is with the rest of the women on a holiday in the Canarias. Look, she's having a good time."

Jack grabbed the phone like a man starved of water. He swiped his nose once more before his eyes glimmered.

Lee watched Jack's face.

"I don't see her."

"Yes, you do." Lee's mind connected with Jack's coke drugged one. "You see her with the rest of the women. They're laughing and having a really fab time."

Jack squinted and blinked several times. "I don't…" Nothing came out of his mouth. Confusion cleared and his gaze lit up. "There she is." He looked up at Lee, laughing and happy. "God, my sister's still pretty."

"Yes, she was…is." Lee corrected, but Jack was too engrossed in the video. Around them, clubbers went in and out of the washrooms unmindful. Lips retouched with gloss, hands adjusting junk, shrill laughter meant to draw attention to those who sorely lacked it. Discordant sounds masked their presence along the hallway.

"When is she coming back?" Jack swallowed. His grip on the mobile phone seemed cemented, not wanting to let go of the only connection he had with his own blood.

"Tell me what you know and I'll send word to her you want her back. Although." Lee shook his head. "I can't see why you want her to leave the good life she has."

"You kidnapped her from me!" Jack slammed Lee against the wall. Passersby screeched and bellowed but no one wanted to get involved.

165

Not their fight.

"You didn't have to do that to guarantee my bloody good behaviour." Jack was nose to nose with Lee. "I want her back!"

"Okay! Okay!" Lee feigned fear. "But you have to give me something to work with. I can't go to my boss and ask that he allows Corinne back without anything in return."

"I have kidnapped a lot of men, women, and children for you." Jack grabbed Lee by the collar. "I have grappled with my conscience doing so because of my sister. Give her back or I go to the police."

Lee cackled immediately. "You'll turn yourself in?"

"Yes." Jack's eyes were wild. "Because you've been dangling my sister like a carrot in front of me, promising me that she'd be back."

Lee's eyes turned to slits. Involving the police would get the Cynn mortals on their tail and as it was, their numbers were dwindling. And when the Cynn mortals got involved, the Cynn Cruors wouldn't be far behind. Dac Valerian wouldn't be pleased. That's what scared him shitless. It didn't matter if Lee wasn't the head of the Scatha Cruors in Leeds. They would all be dead if it suited the Scatha Cruor leader. "Tell me."

"What?"

"Tell me what I want to know. What have you got to lose?" Lee kept his cool.

"Do you know your breath stinks?" Jack pushed away, nearly heaving.

"You won't get your sister back, mate." Lee moved to go.

"No! Wait!" Jack pulled at his hair and scrunched his eyes shut. "Amaryllis is still alive."

"Who?"

"Amaryllis Hart. I gave her to Badon in exchange

for my sister."

"Badon is dead," Lee said pointblank, walking away.

"No, you don't understand." Jack grabbed his jacket. Lee wrested his arm away, his brows meeting in the middle. "Badon was killed by someone with him."

Lee froze. "How do you know this?"

"I was there when Badon's companion killed him. Badon…he…changed." Jack stepped back in disbelief. "He looked like he was going trick or treating." He scoffed. "You may be a bastard, Harris, but you're not monsters. Are you?"

"No, mate." Lee laughed. "You've been so high on coke, you're just hallucinating." He slung his arm over Jack's shoulder. "Buy you a drink. Tell me more and we can arrange for Corinne to come home, say in a week?"

An hour later, Lee lit a joint and inhaled deeply. The info Crawley gave him was a gold mine and Lee was only too glad to ply him with coke and promises of seeing his sister. Jack gave Lee the edge he needed to get into the good graces of Dac Valerian and take the place of Max Greene.

Lee looked at Jack slumped against the side walls of one of the Victorian buildings that housed expensive independent boutiques. He looked so wasted, his eyes glassy, his system filled to the brim with snow but anyone would think that he passed out after a pint too many. Someone only had to peer at his face and see that his eyes were so much like his sister's on the night she took her own life, refusing to be used and allow the Scatha to sink between her thighs.

Like Corinne, Jack was dead. OD'd on crack.

Lee took another drag and soon disappeared with the club crowd. Time to put his plan in motion.

Chapter Fifteen

Amaryllis' things were already in the room when she and Seth entered. She was dead tired. Still being able to free run her tension away was worth it.

"I requested Gareth to bring your things up," Seth answered her unspoken question before smiling. "He was all too willing." Seth observed the chamber they were in. "Nice. Colin placed you in the Duchess room."

"The what?" Amaryllis looked at her blankly as she threw her jacket on the bed. Her face cleared. "Oh right. They did have a penchant for giving names to the rooms back then, I think. Sorry, my boots are tracking dirt. I'll wipe the floor down later."

"Goodness, don't bother! And for naming the rooms? Hmmm…not unless there was some significance," Seth replied, surveying the soft pink and pale green silk bedspread on the four poster bed, the white dresser and wardrobe made of Scottish oak and birch and the thin pale pink curtains that billowed softly against the open windows. "This was a special room in this mansion's history. The original owner of this house was so in love with his wife, he called her his very own duchess." Seth's eyes became dreamy. "She didn't want for anything. Her husband literally placed the world at her feet. Do you know that they died almost a week after each other? The wife fell ill from the ague and passed away. The husband, unable to bear the loss of living without the woman he loved drank himself into a stupor. A servant found him sprawled in the library already dead. Unfortunately, they didn't have any children to carry the name and their fortunes were inherited by a relative who was a wastrel. That's how the Cynn Cruors came to buy this property. It was in a very sorry state, except for this room."

"That's a sad story," Amaryllis murmured.

Seth agreed. "Yes, it is."

"How do you know all this?"

"I read it in a journal somewhere. The builders found it in a secret compartment on the wall they had to demolish. It was inside a steel case, the key still inserted in it. They handed it over to the Cynn Cruors. But what I'm trying to say is that it's not a coincidence Colin would have made you use this room." A knowing look crossed her face. "Uh huh."

"Oh, please." Amaryllis rolled her eyes even though pleasure suffused her. "I was only placed in this room because..." Something told her to shut up.

"Because what?"

"I guess it was the only room he could shove me into." Amaryllis reached for her things. *Well, that wasn't a lie.* "I mean, look at him. I bet you if he turned around from that window he seemed to want to cling on to, he would've snapped my head off. Probably saw me wreck his garden to make obstacles for free running."

"Yeah right, like you didn't see his boner."

"Oh, bloody hell, Seth." Despite herself, Amaryllis blushed and laughed uneasily. She pointed at the other woman. "You need to wash your mouth—"

"Sure I will. With a bottle of Jack when I hit the club."

Amaryllis shook her head, her smile widening with mirth.

"You have to forgive the immortals," Seth said. "They hardly have any female guests."

"I'm not picky." Amaryllis stopped in the middle of the room. "A roof over my head is better than staying in the streets."

Seth cocked her head to one side. "Is that how you became involved with those men who came after us?"

"In a way," Amaryllis said after a slight hesitation. She stopped from taking out some of her things from her bag. "I'm a thief, Seth. Well, a cat burglar."

"How did you become one?" Seth sat down on the bed, one leg under her while the other dangled on the side of the bed, her heart shaped face filled with curiosity and interest.

"By accident." Amaryllis deadpanned, rifling through her bag.

Seth looked at her blankly.

Amaryllis sighed. "I was walking around trying to find a job. Anything to tide me over after leaving college."

"What did you finish?"

"Business Administration."

Seth blinked in surprise. "You could have found a job right away."

"That's what I thought." Amaryllis walked into the bathroom with some of her toiletries. "Until I was accused of theft." She re-entered the bedroom. "Someone bumped into me and left what he stole inside my bag." Her voice was bitter. "I was the one hauled off to jail. Ironic, isn't it?"

"Didn't the police do anything?" Seth queried in dismay.

Amaryllis snickered and did not say anything.

"Damn, I'm sorry."

Amaryllis shrugged. "Long time ago. You try to be as honest as you can, not hurting anyone as you go through life then you're thrown a curve ball not of your own making and bam! Your reputation is in tatters when you've not even started building it. Cruel world out there."

"Parents?"

"Too boozed and drugged out to care. The only thing they were good for was to make sure I went to school. That way they'd have the house all to themselves to shoot crack up their veins. Social Services belatedly got wind of my situation because someone ratted my parents to them. So my uncle took me in until he wanted to be inside me."

"Oh, Amaryllis." Seth reached out, squeezing Amaryllis' hand. Amaryllis smiled and squeezed back.

"So I left. I did odd jobs and made sure I got my degree then I was falsely accused. I didn't realize I could be good at it, so I didn't stop there. If I was going to be a thief, I needed to learn to determine the value of what I was stealing." She pointed to the door. "That tapestry outside? That can go for millions and it still won't be an accurate estimation of its value."

Seth's mouth twitched. She stood, giving Amaryllis a long hard look before sashaying to the door. "When this is all over, let's talk. I might have something for you that will stop you from dipping into your trade."

Amaryllis smiled. "Jack told me the same thing. No offence, Seth, but I think I'll pass."

Seth pirouetted to face her. "Ahh, but there's a difference."

"What's that?"

"I'm not Crawley," Seth said with a gentle smile. "I'll leave you to freshen up. I'm afraid you can't come with us."

"I wouldn't want to come with you either." Amaryllis gave a small laugh while she took more things from her rucksack.

"Gareth and Donovan will be here to keep you company. The rest of your clothes will probably be here tomorrow."

"But I didn't bring anything more other than these." Amaryllis looked down at her bag.

"You didn't," Seth agreed. "Dux bought you new clothes."

Amaryllis was stunned. "Colin? Why would he do that?"

Seth grinned. "Because he protects what is his. And he did say he was going to buy you what you need. The Cynn Cruors always keep their word. So you see, Miss Hart. Even if you deny it or even if Dux denies it, you are his duchess." With a wink, she opened the door and left.

Amaryllis plopped down on the bed.

Holy shit.

Colin Butler was an enigma.

It was so clear from his body language that he did not want her in the Faesten, that she was an imposition. He did not even turn around to talk to them when they came from outside after a fun afternoon of teaching the Cynn Cruors and Cynn mortals the fundamentals of free running. Damn the way his clothes fit him, his dress shirt stretched over his broad shoulders and narrow hips. And his ass. Oh my, those slacks fitted him perfectly down to the leather shoes he wore. Amaryllis wanted to go to him and put her arms around his waist and lean her check against his back, to feel his butt against her hips, to feel them tense against her touch. But Colin had been aloof and it brought a pall over the fun she had. Seth had commented that Colin was looking at them while they were on the Faesten's grounds. It made Amaryllis' heart race, a thrill running through her at the thought of Colin watching them. Good thing that their session was about to end because she was getting more and more conscious of Colin's presence by the bedroom window. Yup, she had sensed him watching. Even from afar, she could feel his gaze burning into her, possessing her, and she had relished the thought. It was as though Colin was right there, his gaze running down her body, admiring the roulades or rolls, the *passe muraille* or wall run, and other movements she did with the obstacles that had been built for her exercise. Maybe Colin did not like the stone seats being stacked on top of each other. She had protested when Gareth and Donovan started taking the seats from all over the place, but Seth said it was okay. When the sun dipped, Cormac, Luke, and Craig came out with the silver eyed muscled man, who introduced himself as Liam. With Colin's men watching her teach Donovan and Gareth parkour, Amaryllis got the impression that things were okay.

Until she saw him in the library. His sexy broad shoulders and back that stiffened the moment they arrived. All of that wrapped into one unapproachable individual.

And now he was buying her clothes?

She walked into the bathroom, flicking her hand in the air. She was going to have a word with him. She was not his. She did not belong to anyone other than herself. Amaryllis wrinkled her nose. Immortals, if they were to be believed, were complicated and a bunch of annoying alphas. She wanted nothing to do with them.

Problem was her mind kept on going back to wishing Colin gave her a second glance.

Amaryllis removed her clothes, putting her stiletto by the sink and the forgotten dagger Gareth had given her before she entered the shower stall. Unlike the bedroom that harkened from a bygone era, the bathroom had twenty-first century fixtures and fittings. The shower stall was deep, almost recessed into the wall, looking more like a sauna room. Amber tiles walled the shower, separated by the same colour tile divider that reached her waist. She turned the tap and water showered her from the showerhead above as well as from holes on both sides of the wall. She closed her eyes, sighing at the warm water surrounded down her body, beating the tiredness out of her. She intended to make the most of all her showers while she was under the Cynn Cruors' care. Who knew when she would have a shower all to herself again. Taking her shampoo and body wash, she lathered herself clean of almost twenty-four hours' worth of grime and sweat. She got out of the shower and wrapped the thick towel around her. She wiped the mist from the mirror, surveying her appearance. Deep violet eyes stared back at her. The violet streak in her hair looked almost black against the rest of her hair, rivulets of water dripping from the tendrils to be soaked by the towel covering her. Her nose was slightly upturned at the end while high cheekbones accentuated her oval face. At the moment her dusky rose lips were parted, her breath fogging the mirror again. Amaryllis loved her eyes because she loved the colour violet but sometimes she wished that she had brown, or blue, or green, or hazel eyes just like the rest of humanity so she did not have to be the target of creeps who wanted to get inside her knickers and be an object of conquest.

Moments later, she was dressed in one of the two T-shirts she brought with her and jeans. Her hair fell down the middle of her back in soft waves after she blow dried it, using the dryer she had brought with her. She went down the stairs intent on looking for Gareth or Donovan. Thinking that they might be with Etienne in the hospital wing, Amaryllis explored the house on her own before checking on Etienne as well. She made her way to the kitchen but stopped when she passed the door leading to the library, her feet faltering just at the threshold. Her gaze automatically centred on the window where she last saw Colin. Embarrassment heated her face and knotted in her gut at the memory of how cold he had looked, how aloof he had become. Maybe he was one of those men who played with women, teasing them before throwing them off like yesterday's newspaper or worse, today's fish and chips wrapper. Man, she really had such lousy luck with men. At least he was not around to demean her some more. Amaryllis was sure he was with the rest of the Cynn Cruors getting their kicks in the clubs. Seth had said so earlier about the Cynn Cruors' need for sex on the nights leading to the full moon and the times after. Thinking of Colin with another woman made her heart constrict with the green eyed monster. Huffing, Amaryllis forced the thought away. No point in wishing for someone she could not have. And why the hell should she be jealous? It was not like she and Colin were exclusive or an item just because he had shoved his expert fingers inside her wet and waiting quim. No point in believing she had the right. It was just one finger fuck session, for God's sake!

Resolutely, she squared her shoulders. She snorted. Like that was going to help her forget what happened. She shook her head, walking into the library and noting the rich red and cobalt blue hues of the huge Persian rugs on the floor and the authentic Queen Anne furniture suite made of chintz. The chandelier light above her glittered against the crystals that adorned it. There was a mirror above the fireplace that multiplied the light in the room. Amaryllis could easily imagine the lords with their powdered wigs and ladies with their hooped skirts playing whist or listening to the katzenklavier. A baby grand, it would have probably been placed by the window, its tinkling melody resonating even outside of the room to draw more people in. She perused the books that lined the shelves, the phantom sound of the ghostly piano playing Bach in her mind. Her eyes widened and she gasped with delight at the rare collection of literature. There were first editions of *Dante's Inferno*, the *Book of Urizen* by William Blake...

"Holy shit..." Right in front of her was one of the seven original manuscripts of J.K. Rowling's *Tales of Beedle the Bard*.

"Oh my God..." Amaryllis could not stop herself. She knew a copy had been auctioned for millions. But that was not what made her heart thud with awe and excitement. She was not wearing her thief cap at the moment. She was wearing her cap of wonder, the thrill of being in the presence of a masterpiece that brought tears to her eyes. She raised her hand to take the book out, but stopped mid-way. She wanted to touch it, her fingers and her palm burning with need, her pulse racing at the thought of...

"Like what you see?"

Amaryllis whirled with a scream, heart in her throat, her hand on her chest. "Why the hell do you have to scare me like that?"

"What did I do?" He raised a brow while he leaned against the door jamb. "I only asked if you liked what you saw. I didn't bellow."

"I have no doubt you can do that." She sniffed, eyeing his delectable enough to eat body from head to foot. Damn, he smelled good. "I thought you'd gone with the others."

"I thought about it." He nodded, moving into the room. "I decided to stay. The men need their R and R. Etienne is still in the hospital, though. I told him not to go to the clubs tonight."

"But Seth said—" Amaryllis felt heat rise up her cheeks.

"Seth said what?" He cocked his head, his gaze boring into hers and suddenly Amaryllis felt a different kind of heat suffusing her.

"Nothing." Her throat became so dry that she coughed when she swallowed. *Keep your thoughts to yourself...keep your thoughts to yourself...*

"You okay?" He ambled towards her. Confident. Sleek.

Dangerous.

"Yes." Why did her voice have to squeak? She pointed at her neck. "Dry throat."

"Drink?" He kept walking.

"No, thank you." She stepped back, her heart racing, the strong attraction she felt in his presence weaved languidly through her system. *Damn him for doing this to me.*

Colin's deep jade eyes studied her, raking her body with that gaze that made her pliant as a violin would be in the hands of a virtuoso. Yup, the sounds of the piano had disappeared and in their place was an image of Colin strumming her clit and making her gasp and moan.

They were now less than a foot apart.

"I don't bite, Violet." He spoke so softly that Amaryllis nearly did not hear it, but the thrum of his voice rippled through her, sending waves of desire lapping at her skin, teasing her to test the waters she knew could drown her. And damn if she cared. Her body arched out of its own volition, her breasts swelled and strained against her cotton bra, her nipples beading as though he was already touching her and she had this ache for his hands to cup them. Tease them. Taste them.

"My name isn't Violet." Why did her voice have to sound seductive? Her breath hitched in her throat when Colin moved in and bent his head, his breath fanning her hair at her temple.

"You are to me." His voice was getting deeper, drowning her in a whirlpool of longing. Deep and sensual. His voice mesmerised her. "That violet streak that coils through your hair flows through my hands like the finest silk." His hand moved to her scalp while his fingers snaked through her hair. Amaryllis' mouth parted, a soft groan escaping. He leaned back, his gaze boring into her as though claiming her very soul. "Your eyes are the colours of the deepest amethysts I've ever seen. Yes, Amaryllis, your name is Violet."

Amaryllis' belly tightened, the stoked coals inside her becoming incendiary. She wanted to close her eyes, but Colin's gaze now veined with gold flecks locked with hers, keeping her anchored, not allowing her to pull away. She felt her pussy weep, soaking her knickers. His eyes had that predatory glint that branded her everywhere. Her five foot five frame was ensnared between the bookshelf and Colin's over six feet mass of hard muscle that epitomized SIN.

Oh Lord, I want to suck him. Her mouth watered at the thought of tasting him deep inside her mouth. To feel his hard shaft on her tongue. To lick the soft skin that covered it. He smelled heavenly, his aftershave mixed with his unique scent made her want to jump his bones. Her hands gripped the lower shelf behind her. She needed the leverage, otherwise she would just melt in a puddle at his feet. The heat of Colin's body surrounded her in a cocoon of lust, tightening around her, keeping her bound.

And there was no place she would rather be.

Her breathing ratcheted up when he bent his head, his breath hot against her neck, feeling him inhale a slightly cooler air and exhale a much warmer one that had her breathing in shallow gasps. His arms bracketed her against his body. There was no doubt of his hard cock prodding her stomach was a sign of his own aroused state and the thought brought a flood of cream from her pussy. Colin inhaled sharply.

"Fuck, you smell good."

Oh yes, I want you to fuck me. Hard.

"I heard that, baby," his voice rasped against her ear, sending ripples of desire down her spine and flooding her veins. Amaryllis bit her lower lip to prevent the moan from rising from her throat. His breath skittered against her jaw, the side of her neck, her ear. When Colin sucked her neck by the back of her earlobe, Amaryllis gave up stopping the moan. She was soaking wet, her hips following Colin's every move. She held on to his narrow waist, his muscles hard and unyielding. His chest brushed against her breasts, the whisper of touch enough to ignite her body once more, her nipples puckering into tight buds, desperately seeking his mouth. Her breasts craved for his hands to cup them. She was about to combust and Colin was just seducing her with his breathing.

"Amaryllis..."

She was now under his spell. She was a willing victim, impatient for the fuck fest to begin. The back of her head tingled where his fingers brushed. She heard more than felt a sliding noise.

"Yes." Her voice was husky and expectant.

Colin stepped back, the rare copy of *Beedle the Bard* in his hand. He had a mischievous smirk on his face.

"I believe you wanted to look at this manuscript."

Chapter Sixteen

You're such a bloody fuck, Butler.

Colin groaned inwardly. He watched the emotions that flickered like a silent movie across her face with half lidded eyes. From passionate, to disoriented. Flustered to embarrassment to annoyance. And every feeling wormed its way inside his heart. He did not know if he wanted to tease her more or kiss her senseless.

Ancients, she was beautiful!

"Seriously? You seduced me just to get to a bloody book?"

Colin pressed his lips together to stop the grin from coming out. "I have that effect on you?" Damn, she was hot even when she was angry and he felt his cock agree.

"Don't flatter yourself," Amaryllis retorted, moving away from him towards the table with a reading lamp. She switched on the light and carefully placed the book on the table top. "If that's all you've got for foreplay, I'm not buying."

Foreplay, huh?

"I agree," he drawled. "Fingering you until you came in my hand isn't foreplay either. That was just antipasti."

She looked at him. "Antipasti?"

"An appetizer," he clarified. Damn! He loved the way she blushed, her eyes glazing with need. Colin did not care anymore if his slacks could not hold his raging hard on bulging against the zipper. "If I placed my tongue inside and sucked on your clit and finger-fucked you at the same time, that's not foreplay. When I play your body like a harp, eliciting the sounds of pleasure from you while my mouth and tongue alternately suck on your tits before I nibble my way back down to your beautiful pussy, holding your ass in my hands and devouring you like a man starved, my tongue flicking inside you, going in and out of you, and gently biting your nub until you scream and come in my mouth."

Amaryllis' chest rose, her breath suspended.

"That's foreplay."

Amaryllis visibly swallowed before turning her head away. "Okay." She exhaled. "Let me look at this book now."

Colin made his way to the bar while Amaryllis prepared to open the collectible. His cock continued to strain against his slacks and he could feel some of his pre-cum being absorbed by it. The remnants of his words still showed on her face, still affected her body, but he admired her at seeing the huge effort she was putting on moving away from his verbal seduction. When she edged away from him, he suddenly felt adrift. As though a part of him had flown away like an errant balloon. He watched Amaryllis reverently feel the folio's intricate cover, tracing the edge like a lover tracing the contours of her man's body. He watched her carefully open the book, her fingers lightly touching the pages, and watched her face. His heart smiled at the joy and wonder in her visage, her chest rising and falling with every breath she took, her sighs of pleasure swirling in the library's air as her body vibrated with excitement.

If only she looked at him that way.

He took out the rare single malt from its wooden case, taking out the black ceramic decanter of the rare fifty-year-old Dalmore scotch. This moment deserved a rare drink. The honey coloured liquid complimented with cinnamon and spices reminded him of the woman perusing the book across the room. Sweet and spicy, hot and exquisite. He could feast on her for days on end and not want to come up for air.

Because she was the only air he would breathe. The only air that would keep him alive.

Holy fuck. Colin's gaze narrowed, his eyes staring in confused realization at the floor. No fucking way! But his whole being, his mind, his body, his heart told him one thing.

Amaryllis was his.

No, it was not possible. This was just the Kinaré going haywire. Colin hated himself for giving in to wanting and touching her when he was meant to protect her. Damn, the woman was making his thinking process convoluted! He poured himself a hefty amount of scotch and swallowed it in one go. Fire raged through him, the alcohol sharpening his senses even more.

Why do you want to stay away when she really belongs to you?

Colin shook his head imperceptibly.

Like that stopped you.

"Shut up."

"Excuse me?" Amaryllis swung her head at him. Hurt flickered in her eyes. She closed the book slowly. "Sorry, I didn't know you didn't want me to talk while I enjoyed the book." She gave him a fleeting smile that did not dispel her wounded look. She gave the book one last caress then she left.

"Amaryllis—" What the hell was that all about? Shit, was she talking and he was so caught up with what he was thinking that he did not hear her? He placed his glass on the bar and followed her out of the library. "Wait."

"No, I will not wait!" She hurled at him, pushing him away and causing him to stumble backwards.

Damn, she was strong. She was talking again. Colin listened.

"I understand you don't want me here." Her voice trembled but her eyes sparked violet fire. "Fine! I never wanted to be here but what did you do? You posted bodyguards to watch me while you and your men slept. Vampire and werewolf blood. Ha! You could all belong to a cult for all I care." She poked at his hard chest. Colin's eyes twinkled when she winced and held her finger.

Her eyes snapped. "Arrgh!" She stormed away before returning and slapping him.

Colin roared, the shock and shooting pain almost making him immobile. He cupped himself. "You slapped my dick!"

"Because you bloody think with it," she screamed, her chest heaving. "That should teach you a lesson to stop leading women on." She ran away from him.

"Where the hell are you going?" he thundered. He took one step, wincing at the pain weaving its way up his belly. Shit, if Craig and the rest found out that a slip of a girl had taken a swipe at their leader's cock. He closed his eyes in consternation. He would never hear the end of it.

"None of your goddamn business!" She took the stairs three at a time.

With whatever strength he had left, Colin gritted his teeth and chased after Amaryllis. Just as she reached the top of the stairs, Colin grabbed her arm.

"What the hell?" She wrenched away from his grasp. "Not only are you a dickhead you've got caveman written all over your face!"

"Before you start foaming in the mouth," Colin snapped. "Hear me out."

Amaryllis sucked in her breath as her eyes widened,

stunned. "God, I can't wait to get out of here."

Colin held both her shoulders, forcing her to stop her furious fidgeting. "If you want to go, then go, but not until I know you're safe."

She wriggled.

"Amaryllis, please. Stop."

She did not listen.

"Or I can use mind control on you." The harsh tone of his voice stopped her. "Your choice."

"Spit."

Colin sighed. "You've got some mouth."

Amaryllis snorted. "You haven't heard what I think about you."

"Heaven forbid."

She scowled. "Unless you really have to say something or show me how to balance on the top step of the stairs before you come flying to my rescue, I suggest you start talking."

"I'm sorry."

She blinked. "Say again?"

Colin relaxed his grip from her shoulders and brought his hands down. "I'm sorry," he repeated quietly. "My saying 'shut up' in the library wasn't addressed to you."

Amaryllis lifted her chin. "You can say whatever you want. It doesn't matter to me."

"Doesn't it?"

She turned away. Colin inclined his head, bending a little to get her to look at him, but she refused. He gently took her chin and swivelled her to face him. "I saw the hurt in your eyes, Violet. Hurt before it disappeared and you left in a huff."

Amaryllis looked down.

"Do you know you're still beautiful when you have your eyes lowered?" Colin looked down at her mouth, tracing her bottom lip with his thumb. "When the dusky pink colour of your lips entices me to taste them?" Damn, his heart was running a million miles a minute. And his cock. It did not matter that it had been physically chastised. His cock wanted inside her. Hard.

"Colin—" She looked at him entreating, her creamy skin flushed. "It doesn't matter."

"It does." His jaw hardened. "I wasn't telling you to shut up. I was saying 'shut up' at myself."

"Why?" She looked at him as though he had fallen off his rocker.

Colin clenched his jaw, blood roaring in his ears. "Because God help me I want you." He bent down to kiss her, but the Faesten's alarm went off. He growled, leaving Amaryllis at the top of the stairs and rushing to the door. When he opened it, the stench hit him and his anger spiralled.

Scatha!

"Get down here," he barked at her. "Don't bloody argue, woman, because the men who want you are back."

Amaryllis paled before resolve covered her. Nodding, she vaulted over the banister to land softly on the wooden floor of the hallway. She turned to him, with an arch of her brow. "You coming?"

He went to the lift, Amaryllis running close behind. "I need to put the shields up. Go to the hospital wing and check on Etienne. You know where it is?"

"I'll find my way," Amaryllis said quickly. "But there are other mortals patrolling the area."

"No, Violet," he said softly. Colin could feel his eyes change. "They went to the clubs as well. Etienne is alone. It's only you and me here against the evil that's about to knock on the Faesten's door."

* * *

It took sheer will to vault over the banister landing softly on the ground floor, but it deserted Amaryllis when Colin told her they were alone. Colin's mouth tilted to one side, amused. His eyes were in the middle of changing colour. "After giving me an earful and whacking me between the legs, you're running scared?"

Irritation flared in a scowl on Amaryllis' face. She flipped the bird at Colin as she walked out of the library.

"I don't even know why I bother," she muttered under her breath.

Like the upper corridor, the hallway was softly lit, with small tables strategically placed along its length. She passed the doorway to the kitchen, the huge formal dining room to her right and what looked like a ballroom to the left side of the hallway until she reached the end of the corridor. The path veered to the left where she was met with a set of glass doors. The faint scent of antiseptic tickled her nose even from the outside of the hospital wing. There was a console to the right with several buttons. She pushed against the glass door but it did not budge.

"Now what?" She exhaled.

There was a buzz before the glass doors clicked open.

"It's open, Amaryllis," Colin's disembodied voice came through hidden speakers. "No matter what happens, stay inside. Understood?"

She nodded.

"Good girl."

For some reason those two words made her feel giddy that she had pleased Colin.

Weird.

"What about you?" she blurted. "You're only one against God knows how many there are outside."

"I'll be fine." Colin's voice was gentle, soothing a little of the anxiety she felt. It was different from the arrogance she had sparred with a few moments ago.

"You can't take them all down," she protested, looking around for the speakers until she saw the camera.

"The Faesten's shield is up. The walls and the gates are electrified. The rest of the Cynn Cruors are returning soon."

She opened her mouth to speak.

"Amaryllis, please for once, stay put." Colin's sigh filtered through. "I can't defend the Faesten when I worry that you might escape again."

She grimaced. "I wasn't planning on escaping. I was thinking of helping." She relented. "Fine, I'll stay put. Please, be careful."

Colin did not reply anymore. Amaryllis pushed the door open, this part of the corridor a vast contrast to the plush corridor just outside of the glass barriers. This part of the wing had the stark yet pristine decor of a private clinic complete with a nurse's station that was empty. She moved along until she saw Etienne's room.

"*Allo?*"

She rushed to him. "Good heavens! Why are you already on your feet? You've got a hole in your leg."

His thickly lashed brown eyes crinkled in amusement. He raised his hospital gown, exposing his leg. "What hole?"

Except for the reddish round imprint on his skin, there was no gaping hole.

"Oh, shit…" Amaryllis wanted to crumple on the floor. "I get it, you guys are different. Seth told me. Geez."

Etienne's boyishly handsome face lit up. "*Je suis bien.*" Before giving a dramatic sigh. "But Colin did not want me to leave." He walked slowly, testing his leg. "Why are you here? Ahh, *mademoiselle*, you are very sweet to visit me." He continued in his heavily accented English.

"Not exactly."

He clutched his chest. "Argh…you wound me."

"Cut the drama." She could not stop the smile that tugged at her mouth before she sobered. "Colin told me to stay here because the Scatha are here."

Immediately, Etienne's playful mood disappeared.

"*Merde!*" Without preamble he started to dress, shucking in his still bloodied jeans as though he had never been injured. Amaryllis looked away when she caught a glimpse of Etienne's firm ass. He strode ahead of her as he pulled on his black shirt, covering his lean muscular frame.

Do all men go commando here?

The sound of an assault weapon's safety sliding back broke through Amaryllis' thoughts. Etienne placed his Glock on the station counter. He pushed several buttons on the console by the side of the desk. The desk top opened and a computer rose from its depths. His fingers flew over a few keys and Colin's face appeared on the monitor.

"Dux"

"Etienne," Colin greeted. "How are you feeling?"

"*Bien, merci.* Ready to bring down the Scatha." Etienne's face was grim. "How many?"

"About six." Colin's eyes darted from left to right, checking the camera feeds. "Etienne, you have to keep Amaryllis safe."

I'm not a bloody Dresden doll!

Amaryllis was about to pull her hair in frustration.

"Shit, they've breached the wall!"

Amaryllis gasped. Colin's eyes were now red

orange. Two Cynn Cruors. One immortal. One mortal. And one human the Scatha were after. Colin's face disappeared. In its place was the camera feed of the gates. Men, no, creatures were on top of the property wall. Their glowing green eyes looked like mutant fireflies darting around in the dark. She stifled a scream. She and Etienne jerked back when a face with glowing eyes and a maw filled with long, razor sharp teeth instantly dominated the feed. The head moved from side to side, making Amaryllis think of the possessed in the Exorcist. Moments later, the feed disappeared before the screen blacked out.

"Etienne, you know what to do." Colin's face came back online. "You don't need to look for the Scatha. They have already morphed."

"*Monsieur*, you hurt me," Etienne reproached. "You should not always believe what Seth and the rest say."

Colin laughed, moving away from the screen.

"I can't believe you two. How can you laugh at a time like this?" Amaryllis watched Etienne press another button on the desk.

Etienne walked to the back of the nurse's station. He leaned against the wall, giving Amaryllis a lopsided grin. "What do you want us to do? Cry? We are warriors, *mademoiselle*. This is the life we enjoy and we aspire for." The wall slid to show a hidden compartment. Fluorescent lights blinked open, showing a cache of weapons and daggers.

"You keep weapons in a hospital," Amaryllis stated flatly, her face belying her disbelief.

"The Cynn Cruors keep weapons everywhere. We never know when we will need them." Etienne pulled weapons out, checking their chambers before clipping them to his waist and inserting them into the holsters he tied around his thighs. He pulled a dagger from the row of knives and clipped at the small of his back. He stopped mid-way. "*Mademoiselle, qu'est-ce tu fais?*"

"What does it look like I'm doing?" She knew enough French to know what Etienne asked. She continued to finger the daggers before strapping two thigh holsters on her person and sheathing the daggers into them. "I'm helping."

"*Merde*, you cannot." He protested.

"Etienne, there are only two of you. The CCTV picked up six. God knows how many Scatha we've not seen in the feed." She took a Sig Sauer. "Got any bullets?"

"You know how to use a gun?" He gave her a disbelieving look.

She rolled her eyes. "Humour me."

Etienne shook his head before handing her a magazine.

"Silver, I presume."

"*Oui*," he said, still sceptical. His brow arched, watching her hands.

Amaryllis inserted the magazine until it was fully engaged. Next, she deftly pulled the slide back fully and released it before allowing it to fly forward. She cocked a brow.

"I'm impressed." A grin pulled the side of Etienne's mouth.

"Before I met you people I had a lot of opportunity to hold guns. Being around Jack Crawley and his men was enough reason to have a weapon."

Etienne gave a rueful shake of his head before they briskly walked towards the glass doors. "Butler will kill me."

"Not if he gets killed by the Scatha first. And if he even as much as threatens you, tell him I forced you at gunpoint."

Etienne's brows rose.

"Well, you didn't stop me from getting a gun now, did you? You gave me the bullets as well."

"Ahh, Amaryllis. I am so glad that you belong to Monsieur Butler."

"Why does everyone think I belong to him?"

Etienne snorted and started talking fast in French. Amaryllis could not follow what he was saying. Just as they reached the front of the hospital suite, they heard screams and gunshots.

"*Merde,* they've entered the house!"

Chapter Seventeen

Etienne punched the code in the console and the doors clicked open. He swung around to face her. His boyish face was gone, replaced with harsh and hard planes of a man going to war. He seemed to gain height and bulk. "*Bien*, you want to help, stay behind me. Only when I am overwhelmed will you come in. *Comprends?*"

Amaryllis bristled, a frown creasing her brow.

"*Comprends*, Amaryllis?"

What is it with this alpha male beating-my-chest antics?

"*Comprends.*" She nodded, swallowing against the apprehension lodged in her throat. Her body tensed. Her pulse raced. Her focus threatened to desert her when the noise closed in. She had to remind herself that this was just like preparing to escape after a heist or practicing free running. Easy peasy lemon squeezy. She flexed her neck from side to side and in a circular motion to allow her tension to bleed out. She loosened her limbs but not too much and held the gun firmly in her left hand.

Silver bullets. Monsters. One hot sexy man that takes my breath away. Wow...

She was ready.

But she was not ready to see Colin flying through the air and landing hard against the wall in front of them that she gave a startled scream. In a split second he was up in time to parry the claws of a Scatha that nearly slashed his face. Amaryllis winced at the frustrated scream coming out of the fiend. If it weren't for the glass doors that shielded them, she would have experienced the full blown attack of nails scratching on a chalkboard.

Colin was getting weaker and at that moment, something grew inside her. Anger at how Colin was being attacked. She needed to protect him. She needed to help the man she belonged to.

She rushed headlong and pushed the glass door open.

"*Mademoiselle, non!*"

"Amaryllis!" Colin looked at her, a flicker of fear and dread in his red orange eyes.

This time it was Amaryllis who was far too gone. Gun pointed at the Scatha who was momentarily stymied by Colin's roar and who twisted his head at her, Amaryllis took advantage of the lull and shot the Scatha broadside, the silver bullet passing through his rib, his skin sizzling at the impact while green blood spurted from the hole. It screamed as the bullet's force propelled it sideways. Colin was on the Scatha as it bounced away from the wall, slicing the head off its shoulders with his sword. Amaryllis raised her arm and turned away at the explosion of ash. She heard nails on a chalkboard screams again and saw three Scatha advancing at full speed but halted abruptly that they bumped each other in their haste. Amaryllis sprinted at them when they stalled, the Sig raised to shoot.

"Blood hell, Amaryllis! Don't!" Colin shouted.

At the last minute she planted her foot high against the wall and used her kinetic energy to propel her over the three Scathas, who gaped at her. She landed behind them and discharged her weapon in rapid succession. The Scatha screamed, writhing on the floor, their skin sizzling around the bullet wounds on their backs, ribbons of green bleeding on the floor.

"Why aren't they dying?" She stared at them.

"*La tête*, Amaryllis! Cut off the head!" Etienne

rushed to her and decapitated the Scatha closest to him. An ash cloud surrounded them. "Go for the head and they die."

The Scatha close to Amaryllis turned to face her. Just as she unsheathed the dagger from her thigh, he flipped himself to a stand and swiped at her arm. With a scream, she let go of the dagger and crumpled to her knees. Pain raged like a forest fire along her arm. Amaryllis gritted her teeth, holding her injured hand close to her chest. Etienne had frozen, but there was a movement beyond him. Colin's face was filled with rage and torment. He was too far to get to her on time, but he still ran to her. A sense of peace filled her as she looked into his eyes through the distance. Her heart swelled inside her chest at the unvarnished truth. She did belong to him. She could feel it in her bones, in her very sinews until the feeling suffused her. She looked up at the monster who was about to kill her, letting all of her fury burn in her eyes. No way in hell was she going to give the arsehole standing over her the pleasure of seeing her in agony. Knowing that she belonged to someone gave her strength to face her fate. Too bad she could not enjoy it more.

* * *

Luke's senses were tingling. Not even the thud of the speakers booming out the latest club musing or the mindless chatter of the clubbers could dispel the prickling sensation at the back of his neck. He had joined the rest of the Leeds Cynn Cruors to town, leaving Colin to man the Faesten. His mouth twitched. Knowing what he knew now of what a Cynn Cruor was, Colin would need sex soon. It was T-minus two days to the full moon and without the sexual gratification the Kinaré needed, any Cynn Cruor would weaken tremendously. Still, he understood Colin's decision to stay.

Amaryllis.

She was beautiful to say the least. Luke understood how she drew Colin to her purple flame. However, he still didn't know why a mortal was under a Cynn Cruor's protection when they both parried each other. Everyone could see the attraction was there and everyone gave Colin a wide berth. He was like a caged animal, a growl at the ready every time the warriors even as much as looked at Amaryllis longer than they should. But she could not hold a candle to Adara.

Luke closed his eyes. Adara Kerslake was driving him to distraction. Where was she? Why couldn't he find her? He remembered the sway of her hip and how her auburn tresses fell down the middle of her back, bouncing gently as she strode the length of King Street. That was the first time he saw her. The last time was a glimpse on the rooftop when they went to support Graeme kill Elliot Hammond. Adara had seen him, a flash of recognition in her eyes from across the space between them. Then she jumped off the rooftop and disappeared into the night.

The only female Cynn Cruor.

Until he found her again, he had to fight. The more he saw what the Scatha Cruor were doing, the more he wanted to stop them. He was still haunted by the faces of the children who were saved after he had come to Deanna's rescue in the Isle of Man. Haunted by the paranoia in the eyes of the women and children, Deanna and Eirene continued to rescue through their charities, Kids Come Home and the Haven Foundation. And it was not only females the Scatha abducted. Even young men became victims of human trafficking. Devon, Eirene's solicitor friend had started to draft the papers for another charity for abused men. He could only imagine what those who were abducted went through. Their lives would never be the same again.

Having been given a room in the Leeds Faesten, Luke had paralleled back to Manchester to gather a few things. Before he left, he spoke to Roarke, Finn, and Graeme. Telling them that there was no sign of Mackenzie.

"If you ask Butler about Mack or the Scatha, he will become suspicious," Graeme commented.

"No reason for them to be now." Luke grabbed some shirts from the nearby chest of drawers. "The Faesten was attacked today." He dumped his clothes into his duffel bag.

"Oh shit." Graeme exhaled. "In broad daylight? Scatha mortals, I presume."

"Can't say if the Scatha have mortals like the Cynn Cruors do," Luke said. "It was someone by the name of Jack Crawley. They were after a woman Colin had under his protection." His mouth tilted to a wry grin. "Quite the looker. Has deep violet eyes."

Graeme whistled and Finn chuckled from his position by the door. "Finally, Colin Butler has received an appointment from Cupid."

Roarke, who stood with his back to the window, allowed himself a small grin before sobering. "Do what you can to gather intel, Luke." He pinched his lower lip between his thumb and forefinger, his face thoughtful. "We can't help Butler if he refuses and I hope to God we're barking up the wrong tree. But if you're right about this, we need to prepare. If the Council gets wind of this, Colin might just be stripped of his leadership."

"That's the worst that can happen?" Finn's face was sad.

"That will be the least of his problems." Roarke

turned his back on them to face the window.

"What's the worst?" Luke asked quietly.

"Death," Roarke said over his shoulder before he bowed his head.

The silence in the room was deafening.

"So, Griffiths. Pray that what you unearth doesn't come to this."

Luke nodded, the weight of what he was beginning to discover was like an albatross on his shoulders. "I better get back." He zipped his bag shut and slung it over his shoulder. He bent, reaching for his sabre that lay on the bed. "Will keep you posted."

He shifted planes but not quick enough not to hear Finn say in awe, "Damn, that's incredible."

A hand clamped over his shoulder, invading his thoughts. The club's sounds rolled in like a gentle crest before it thundered around him.

"Those women have been eyeing you," Cormac shouted.

Luke followed Cormac's gaze. Two women in tight dresses short enough to catch a glimpse of the swell of their bums were dancing seductively a few feet from where Luke and Cormac were. They writhed and swayed against each other. Other men on the dance floor had also seen them and gravitated behind them, sliding their lean bodies against the women's backsides. Luke felt the stirrings of lust pool in his groin, imagining the two women going down on him. Suddenly, he thought of Adara. His need to satisfy the Kinaré was too much and Adara was gone, probably a figment of his imagination. It didn't matter. He would think of her when he was pleasured. He would wish for her when he gave pleasure. For now practicality dictated.

Luke's eyes lit up and he felt his eye colour change. He knew it would be burnished gold. His pupils warmed. His breathing accelerated, the Kinaré taking hold of him. With purposeful strides, he left Cormac's side and approached the women. He hooked them both by the waist and dragged them away from the dance floor much to the anger of the men dancing with them. Cormac rushed to the scene and spoke to the men. Instantly, the men moved away in a daze until other women started to gyrate against them. Luke whispered in the ears of both women, who giggled as they made their way to the second floor. He was ready for the lust fest to begin.

Several moments later, Luke left the private room. He twisted to look at the satiated women, their dresses bunched around their waists, the rest of their bodies exposed, their eyes glazed with the aftermaths of their orgasm. They would only recall how fantastic the sex was. They would not have any memory of Luke. He closed the door behind them. He frowned.

His Spidey senses were still tingling.

The Faesten!

Fuelled by his sexcapade, he fixed the coordinates of the Faesten in his mind and shimmered just in time to see the Scatha zipping over the gates. He shifted back to the Club and saw Liam's thunderous face as he spoke into his phone. Luke zoomed to him.

"The Faesten," Luke shouted over the din.

"On our way," Liam shouted before turning away towards the security room. "Meet you there!"

Luke made a detour to his room and got his sabre. Rushing back to the ground floor, he heard a scream before he saw Amaryllis fall.

* * *

"Beautiful toy." The Scatha's guttural voice only added to the grotesqueness of his smile. He swayed from side to side, his shirt mottled with his blood. "Mine to play with."

The last thing Amaryllis saw before she closed her eyes was the Scatha raising his arm and his claw rushing towards her. She waited for death to strike her, but the only thing she could feel was the pain in her arm before she snorted and coughed. She dared open one eye and saw herself covered in ash. Her executioner had disappeared. Suddenly, she was being hauled up on her feet and her mouth was covered in a kiss that was desperate as it was passionate.

Colin.

Her mouth opened to welcome him, her knees weakening at his onslaught. Colin was like a man starved and the blood sang in her veins, her heart thudding with desire. Only too happy to know that she was his oasis. But then she winced when her wounds nudged her back to reality. Colin suddenly let go of her mouth.

"Don't bloody do that to me again," he growled. The shade of his eyes were between the colour of bloodlust and dark green. But when the gold flecks became more prominent, it reminded her of the sunset. Amaryllis could only nod, still too caught up in Colin's fiery kiss. She saw the strain around Colin's mouth and knew that he was close to collapsing, but he held on like a true leader. Her heart swelled with pride. Colin looked beyond her and she turned. It was the other man Cormac introduced as Luke.

"I owe you Amaryllis' life," Colin said in gratitude. "Thank you."

Luke grinned, his sabre pointed down at the floor. "Story of my life. Rescuing damsels in distress."

"I wasn't…" Amaryllis winced and relented with a sigh. "Thank you."

"Come, *ma cherie*, we need to clean your wound." Etienne walked to them. He raised his hands as though in surrender when Colin gave him a baleful eye. "Dux, I know she belongs to you, but her blood is dripping on the floor and we don't know if the claws will infect her."

Colin's jaw tightened. He nodded. He looked at her, his gaze gentle. "Go with Etienne. I have to check the periphery."

"Liam and the rest are on their way." Luke provided before pivoting. "See to your woman first then back me up." He rushed to the entrance door. Amaryllis could see green lights flickering in the distance. Dread plummeted in her stomach.

"I'll be okay." She licked her dry lips, blushing when Colin tracked the movement with his eyes. "Go."

Colin cupped her head and gave her one more hard kiss then he was gone. The emptiness Amaryllis felt disoriented her like an elastic band snapping. It was like she had a sudden out of body experience and could not rightfully return to her physical self.

"*Cherie.*" Etienne touched her shoulder.

Her shirt was soaked with her blood as she tried to stem the flow. Suddenly, she stopped. Etienne looked at her quizzically.

She hesitated before she spoke. "You're not going to drink my blood, are you?"

Etienne chuckled. "I am as human as you. Even the warriors will not want to drink your blood. Blood exchange only happens when you mate."

"Oh."

"Truly, *cherie*, you don't need any makeup when you blush that beautifully. With your eyes' rare colour? You'd make even the haughtiest model jealous." They entered the hospital wing. Etienne led her to the treatment room, taking down antiseptic and bandages before putting them in a tray. He went back to where Amaryllis sat on the trolley waiting, her weapon beside her.

"Ever the Gallic and gallant French."

"I'm pleased you think so." Etienne's smile widened. He placed on a set of gloves and worked on her arm, a muscle in his jaw ticking when she winced, but he continued without let-up, efficiently cleaning the deep claw marks before bandaging them tightly. "All done."

"Thank you." She sighed, wrinkling her nose. "I'm a bloody mess."

"Take the lift by the end of the wing." Etienne gathered the bloodied pads and snapped his gloves off before sliding the tray's contents into the medical refuse. "It will take you up to the rooms."

Amaryllis jumped from the trolley and took her gun with her other hand and gave it to him. "Guess I won't be able to use this for the moment."

"Keep it," Etienne said, nudging his chin towards the weapon. "You never know when you'll need it again." He held his gun. "I better go."

She nodded and he left.

Amaryllis got out of the lift moments later and rushed to her room. She had one more clean shirt left and then she would need to find the laundry room. It was all well and good that Colin had decided not only to house her but to clothe her while she was here. While she appreciated the gesture, she was still not comfortable with it. Besides, the clothes had not arrived and with the ongoing skirmish, she doubted if the delivery service would even think of bringing the stuff to the Faesten. Who knew how the Faesten would look like after tonight?

She went to her bedroom window that overlooked

the other side of the garden with the maze. She gasped when she saw something fly from one tree to another. She was right. There were more than the six Colin had earlier noticed and they had broken through whatever shield the place had. She did not dare open the lights. No way was she going to make herself the prey. There was enough moonlight streaming through her window to know where she was. Leaving her weapon on the bed, she snatched the shirt from her rucksack and rushed to the bathroom. She hissed at the pain crawling in her arm as she removed her soiled T-shirt and dumped it on the counter by the sink. She fumbled for the towel on the rack behind her and opened the tap to soak it, still nursing her injured arm against her chest. She dabbed the wet cloth against her stomach and chest, stopping when she was satisfied that she did not feel sticky from her own blood. Throwing the towel away, she took her fresh T-shirt and gingerly inserted her injured arm into the sleeve. She grunted at the discomfort and gritted her teeth until she could put the T-shirt over her head. Sighing in relief, she returned to the bedroom, grabbed her gun and took one last look through the window. Headlights loomed from vehicles driving towards the Faesten at full speed before they screeched just outside the gates. Relief washed over Amaryllis when the gates opened and the familiar figures of the immortals and mortals sped through.

Leaving her room, Amaryllis ran swiftly along the corridor towards the stairs. Pressing herself against the wall with her injured arm close to her chest, she peered from the corner. The ground floor was ablaze with lights but was empty. She whipped her gun in front of her as she stepped down the stairs, her back to the wall. Her eyes darted from left to right, checking whether someone would be coming from the corridor just below the stairs or from the open doorway. The ornately carved door was hanging precariously by one hinge. Amaryllis could hear the fighting outside but not too near the house. She swivelled right to look at the corridor, weapon at the ready, but save for the upended tables, the scratches on the walls and the ash scattered on the floor, the place was empty. Stealthily, she made her way outside. She felt very exposed coming out from a glare of lights to the darkness. She just hoped that everyone was fighting the Scatha and that they were too busy to look at the house. She was about to sprint towards the direction of the fighting when a hand gripped her upper arm and whirled her around to face her attacker. But a claw clamped over her mouth before she could cry out.

Chapter Eighteen

Colin emerged from the haze of the Scatha's ash he had just killed, leaving the confines of the maze where the close infighting had occurred. He sucked in his breath, coughing when he inhaled some of the ash, causing him to bleed some more. He was not healing as fast as he should. The stolen kisses with Amaryllis were not enough. He needed more.

He looked down. His blood oozed from between his fingers clutching his side soaking part of his shirt before it dripped in spots on the ground. He looked at the moon tantalizing him through the break in the trees. All around him the Cynn Cruors were dispatching the Scatha Cruors that breached the Faesten's walls. Thank God, Craig, Liam, and Cormac had arrived with Seth and the rest just in time because Colin was not so sure whether he could hold on. He was glad for Luke's ability to parallel shift. They had fought back to back, taking down as many Scatha as they could before reinforcements arrived. Craig wanted him to rest. Colin refused and look what it got him.

"Colin, you need the adriserum now." Craig's forehead furrowed in annoyance.

"Like this ever stopped me." The pain was subsiding to a dull ache. He stepped forward and nearly stumbled. Craig's hand shot to stop him from stumbling, grunting with the effort. "You need the adriserum too. Have you fed?"

"I'm not injured," Craig said. "You've been hit by the Scatha twice. One was from Mack. That's not a laughing matter."

"I'll double dose later." Colin looked around. His

eyes narrowed. "Seth's coming this way." He felt Craig stiffen beside him and it suddenly dawned on him. Colin looked at his second in command in stunned amazement. "Bloody hell, Shaw. Why didn't I notice that?"

Craig grunted. "Shut up."

"How the hell did this happen?" Seth panted, running towards them, her blade soaked in ash and murky blood. "How did the Scatha know where the Faesten was?" Her gaze moved back and forth.

"There must be some intelligent Scatha now in Leeds," Colin quipped.

She accepted his response with a dark look and eyed his wound with concern. "You need to get that attended to." She turned to Craig. "You okay?"

Colin noticed Seth's voice softening.

"When wasn't I okay?" Craig raised a mock brow.

Seth's lips thinned. Colin saw the flicker of raw hurt in her eyes before she banked it. She turned away, flicking her hand in disgust. "I don't know why I even bother. Really!"

"All the Scatha are dead." Liam's huge muscular frame approached them, holding his broadsword resting on his shoulder. The red orange glare slowly morphed back to silvery white. "Let's get back to the house. Cormac can arrange for clean up by the mortals in the morn."

Their sharp hearing heard a stifled scream.

Luke shimmered by their group, his face, grim. "Colin, a Scatha has Amaryllis."

* * *

Amaryllis wanted to pull away from the Scatha but the claw over her mouth dug into her face and her arm hurt like a mother. Her stomach churned. She dry heaved. Oh my God, what did he dip his hands into?

Revulsion shuddered through her, nearly paralyzing her at the Scatha's odour. She had no choice but let the Scatha drag her along the tree-lined driveway. Her eyes darted to the maze, her fear jacking up the farther they were from the brightly lit mansion. She dragged her feet on the gravel strewn path but had second thoughts when her face stung at the claw digging into her skin. She had let go of her gun when she was captured and she did not dare take out her stiletto for there was no way she would be quick enough to maim the monster who held her. She winced against his claws the excruciating agony of her raw wounds making her want to crumple to the ground. The Scatha had thrown her dagger away but had not noticed the stiletto she kept hidden in her boot. They weaved like drunks moving deeper into the dark, the moon's brightness lighting their way.

"I'm taking you somewhere where I can fuck you." The Scatha's voice was reed thin. "Need to check the merchandise, you know." He laughed at his own sordid joke.

Amaryllis shuddered and harrumphed behind the claw, clasping the offending limb so that it did not dig deeper than it already was.

"Going somewhere?"

Amaryllis screamed behind the claw. Tears smarted her eyes at the sting of the Scatha's claw piercing her skin when he turned around, taking her with him. Relief flooded her at the sight of Colin and the rest of the Cynn Cruors, who began to surround them in a loose circle. Their swords glinted under the moonlight. Etienne, Gareth, and Donovan trained their weapons at the Scatha's head, the laser dancing red on its face. Her sonorous heart was heavy inside her ribcage. Were they pointing at her head too? Amaryllis hoped that if they were lousy shots, they would allow her to die quickly.

Death had never weighed constantly on her mind until now.

A sound which Amaryllis could only describe as a cross between a screech and a growl rose from the Scatha. She did not stop the heaving gag of her throat, unable to inhale the air without getting a whiff of sweat and urine coming that made up the Scatha's breath. She squirmed against him, but the Scatha clamped his other arm around her waist. She sobbed, angry tears beginning to take shape and threatening to spill from her eyes. Everyone watched them. She hated being the cynosure of attention.

Colin tutted. "What a coward. Using the female's body to shield yourself." His mouth tilted to a smile. "You know we can still take you down from behind. Or was that too difficult for your pea brain to comprehend?"

The Scatha hurled Amaryllis away in fury, launching himself at Colin.

Liam stopped her fall before Amaryllis kissed the ground.

"Thank you." Her breath caught in a squeak. Liam acknowledged her with a short smile, helping her to stand. Amaryllis watched as Colin battled it out with the monster who had held her. They both rolled to the ground with Colin gaining the upper hand, straddling him to bash his fist with his sword hilt against the Scatha's jaw. A few of the Scatha's jagged teeth flew, making it screech in fury. Colin winced at the noise and that was enough time for the Scatha to turn the tables. Colin bellowed when the Scatha's own claws sank deeply into his thigh. Hardening his jaw, he lifted his sword and sank it into the Scatha's thorax. The Scatha gurgled against the blood that spurted from his throat. Colin grunted when the claws shucked out of him but it did not detract him from raising his sword again, twisting the handle in his hands and slicing through. The Scatha immediately disintegrated to dust, causing Colin to land on his ass.

"Colin!" Amaryllis rushed to him, unmindful of the soreness in her arm. She knelt before him, her heart squeezing at the rivulets of blood soaking his trousers.

Colin looked at her. Even in the dark, Amaryllis could see his eyes return to their normal colour. His mouth lifted in a lopsided grin. "Hey." He huffed a laugh. "Some fight, eh. Damn, I'm tired." He cupped her face, brushing his thumb against the shallow cuts on her face. He frowned. "You're hurt...sorry I couldn't get to you in time." He tried to stand up.

"Don't move," Amaryllis said softly, the aftermath making her voice tremble, tears forming in her eyes at his sweetness. "You're bleeding a puddle."

"I don't feel anything." Colin shrugged and attempted to stand up.

"You've always been a stubborn mule, Butler." Craig bent down on his hunches, shaking his head. "Let's get you to the hospital."

Amaryllis felt a hand on her shoulder. She looked up and saw Seth. Mutely, she allowed the woman to raise her up. She watched Craig and Liam carry Colin between them. Abruptly, the adrenaline rush disappeared and she started shaking, hunching against a phantom coldness she felt. The tears fell down her cheeks as she tried to stifle the sobs wanting to explode from her. She was such a self-absorbed bitch. She was such a fool. It had to take a car chase and a home invasion for her to see that the Cynn Cruors were sincere in protecting her. It had to take both mortal and immortal to be hurt to make her realize they did not mean her any harm.

It had to take Colin Butler to spill his blood for her.

It was time to pull herself together and apologise. Time to move away from her need for self-preservation and allow someone to take care of her. Problem was, it was such an alien feeling of letting someone protect her. Partly allowing someone to take the cudgels for her was similar to wrenching a piece of herself away.

She would miss that Damocles' sword.

Seth placed an arm around her shoulders, a small smile on her mouth.

"I'm so sorry, Seth." Remorse covered Amaryllis in her shame. Her throat constricted when she spoke, halting the words. "If I didn't...return to...Jack's place—"

"We're not sure it was Jack who did this," Seth replied as they walked back to the mansion. Cormac carried Colin's sword, quietly talking to the mortals before they spread out across the grounds.

"That evil incarnate who took me...he looked the same as the one who took me here."

Seth stiffened beside her, removing her arm around Amaryllis. They stopped walking. "Took you here?"

Amaryllis nodded. "The one tonight wanted to take me for himself before I was going to be sold." She shuddered in revulsion. "The one the night before couldn't make up his mind whether he wanted me for himself or...if he wanted to protect me. I strongly felt that he brought me here to protect me from the very demons that they were. Mackenzie. Colin's brother."

Seth froze beside her. "That's impossible. Mack's been dead for centuries."

Amaryllis looked at Seth in alarm. "But...oh God." She was so damned confused. "Seth." She looked at her friend, worry worming its way into her already fragile state. "Did I say something wrong?"

Seth had a blank expression. Amaryllis was about to say her name again when she pulled back. Shock still marred her face. She jerked her head in the negative and did not speak.

"I don't want to cause any more trouble than I already have." Amaryllis thought back to Colin.

"No, you haven't." Seth assured her, her voice cold. "But the immortals might just have."

* * *

After more than a few injections of the adriserum, Colin limped towards the lift back to his floor. He refused any help. No one offered knowing that the adriserum would enter his system faster the more Colin used his injured limbs. The adriserum had broken through his fatigue, feeding and giving the Kinaré temporary relief. He just had enough energy to strip off his clothes, his face crunching as he made cautious movements to lie on the bed, sighing in relief as he lay flat on his back. He winced as new tissue was created, stitching old and new muscles together. Lines ploughed his forehead as he felt new skin cover his wounds. However, the pain was nothing to the abject sadness he felt the moment he saw the Scatha scale the Faesten's wall.

"Mack, what have you done?" Colin murmured.

Had he really lost Mackenzie for good? The whole time he had kept the faith that he would be able to save his younger brother from turning completely Scatha. This evening's attack threatened to cut through the very frayed rope of hope he had. Each decade since Mackenzie had turned unravelled more of the rope until only the thinnest of threads held Colin's belief together. He was close to giving up his promise to his mother before she died. Only the friendship and brotherhood of his men kept him from reneging. Colin suddenly felt as old has his real age. A nearly three hundred year old immortal inside a thirty-five-year-old body of muscle and hard planes, honed by war and the fickleness of time.

His thoughts went to his mated brethren, those who comprised Manchester aside from Luke and Blake Strachan who was still missing. Grudgingly, he admitted that he envied the peace and love Roarke, Finn, and Graeme had found in Deanna, Eirene, and Kate. He saw the same between Andres de Alvaro and Bianca in the Honduras. And now Zac had found his Faith, in more ways than one. All of the Cynn Cruors found strength in their mates. It was something he was starting to look for.

The moment he saw Amaryllis take on Mackenzie.

She was beginning to fill his every waking moment when he did not think of the Faesten, when he allowed his mind to rest worrying about Mackenzie. All he could think about were her curves, her soft skin. His fingertips tingled at the memory of touching her, curling automatically, when visions of her face suffused with desire, her body hovering over him while he finger-fucked her, filled his mind. The muscle between his legs twitched and his balls started to feel heavy with the concomitant discomfort of being unable to unload. His mouth watered remembering her taste. If only he could really lick her sweetness straight from the source. And the feel on her mouth when he could not stop himself from kissing her, only too relieved that she had not been killed by the Scatha. His tongue remembered her sweetness, how pliant her lips were, how welcoming her mouth was, how his cock twitched when her tongue played with his even only for that brief moment. Colin groaned. He had to stop thinking of Amaryllis. There was still so much that needed to be done. The Faesten needed him. The Leeds Cynn Cruors and mortals looked up to him for his leadership. Mackenzie needed him even if his brother refused to admit it.

But Colin Butler needed Amaryllis Hart. And despite his vow to stop thinking of her, she was the last thing he remembered before sleep claimed him.

When Colin woke several hours later, he ached everywhere. He likened the feeling to being thrown, chopped and pureed through the meat grinder. That was exactly how he felt every time he pushed himself harder than his men, when he knew that he had to let go because he was weakening. His stubbornness was forever Craig's bane even when they were training in The Hamilton's Faesten. He had not felt the pain during his fight with the Scatha, his adrenaline and bloodlust erasing the harsh torment associated with any wound inflicted during a battle. Now, the agony bloomed, his sorry carcass feeling like a rough terrain where mines detonated, scourging him. The last time he felt this way was when he and the rest of the Leeds Cynn Cruors were part of Operation Countenance, the British-Soviet invasion of Iran in 1941 to secure the oil field and supply lines for the Allies against the Axis powers. The adriserum they had was dwindling. Colin would not survive the heat but at the last minute, Cynn mortals had come to their rescue with the much needed adriserum and orders for them to return to England. They had all stayed in one of the hulls of the navy ships returning from the Persian Gulf. Good thing the Admiral was a Cynn Cruor mortal. No one except Cynn mortals entered the secret compartment of the ship to bring the Cynn Cruors food.

Speaking of food, he needed to eat. He needed sex. He needed a whole lot of things. He looked at the window and swore. Dawn was breaking. It did not matter. The special glass would protect him when he got food from the kitchen or anywhere he cared to go inside the mansion, as long as he did not attempt to commit suicide again by walking through the foyer. But just as he was about to sit up, the door to his room opened.

Chapter Nineteen

Amaryllis slowly entered Colin's bedroom. After what Colin went through and talking to Seth about why sex played a pivotal role in warriors' healing, she decided to bite the bullet. The fact that the Cynn Cruor warrior got pleasure and strength from the woman they took to the pinnacle or orgasmic delight caused need to pulse through her and down to the aching flesh between her thighs. Frustration smacked at the back of her head when she recalled the satisfying but short moment she and Colin had before all hell broke loose.

"But it's so soon," she murmured.

Since when did it stop you from your one night stands? What's the difference?

Yeah. What really was the difference? She became all shy and retiring. She scowled. No way was she a shrinking violet. Taking a deep breath, she looked down at what she wore. The clothes Colin had bought for her arrived earlier that day. Donovan had picked them up from the gate because the morning after the attack, the Faesten's grounds looked like a freak tornado decided to become an interior decorator and threw statues and bushes haphazardly against tree trunks in its interpretation of shabby chic. There were several Cynn mortals outside cleaning up, many who she did not know. The immortals were inside the house, safe from the sun.

Her T-shirt was soiled. She tried to brush away the dirt and the Scatha's stench but it was no use. She had washed her face, arms, and hands as much as she could and winced when the towel hit her sensitive arm and the forgotten welt she had on her throat when Mack closed his claw around her. Now she had more recent slashes on her cheek. She tied her hair in a pony tail that swished over her shoulder when she bent down, conscious of how she looked. If only Colin found pleasure with her, inside her.

Consuming her.

"You're thinking again." His deep muffled voice came from the bed.

She froze, not realizing he was awake. Oh shit. He was freaking naked. Heat and building excitement stained her cheeks. Immediate desire trickled down her spine and pooled in her mons. She licked her lower lip before she spoke, trying to get her emotions under control. How the hell could she win this round when the man she desired was on the bed, in the buff, a feast for her eyes?

"You read my mind again," she said, averting her gaze.

"No, I didn't." He said it so softly, she thought she misheard him. "Shouldn't have done it the first time."

She kept silent, indecision making her to stay by the door.

Colin lifted himself on his elbows and looked at her. There was an odd mingling of wariness and amusement in his eyes. "Excuse my impropriety. I didn't expect company or else I would have worn something, unless you don't mind seeing me in the buff."

"Arrogant much?"

When he laughed softly, her heart turned over. "You seem to like that particular part of the room." He paused, his voice curious but deep and it made Amaryllis want to melt where she stood. There was just something about his voice that did delicious things to her. She would not be surprised if Colin just used his voice to make love to her and she would combust. As it was, she was already wet and needy.

"How's your arm?"

She looked down. "I'll survive."

Colin grunted from the bed before he let out a long breath. "Why are you here, Amaryllis? Don't tell me we'll be going through the same ridiculous argument of having to keep you here."

"No." She sighed. "I'm not going anywhere. I came to heal you."

"You're offering me sex?" Surprise flickered in his voice. He lifted his head to look at her.

"As sordid as it sounds, yes, I am." She fidgeted under his cynosure. "Take it or leave it."

With a sigh, Colin lay back down. "Amaryllis, you're not a piece of meat I can eat and then throw away if I didn't like the presentation or taste. I don't treat women that way."

"But Seth said—"

Colin growled. Amaryllis sensed he was keeping his irritation in check. "I'm going to have a long talk with Annaseth…what did she say?"

"Sex healed the Cynn Cruor, strengthened the immortal."

"And you believe I'm immortal?"

"You should have died when that monster sank his claws into you, but no. You could walk with Liam and Craig's help even with blood soaking your trousers. With everything that's happened around me and as stupid as it may sound, I'll take what everyone says to be true."

"I can always get sex outside."

Amaryllis looked away. Strike two. Colin's rejection should have relieved her, but she was past caring. To her surprise, it stung. Colin was right. She was not meat.

"Fine." Her voice was cool. She could not stop herself. "I guess women who don't live up to your quality of meat had to have thick skin to be discarded that way."

She pivoted, her hand on the doorknob. She gave a short scream when a strong breeze brought tendrils of her hair to her face, and Colin pushed her none too gently against a wall. She cried out softly at the pain in her arm.

"You are not just any woman," he ground out. She gasped when he pushed his hips against hers, his arousal hard as marble, lust immediately flooding her. "Feel that? That's what happens to me when you're near. I want to fuck you so hard and make you scream until you become hoarse and make you scream again until you have no voice left." His green eyes darkened to almost black before gold flecks started to appear in them. "From the moment I touched you, I have wanted nothing else but have my mouth devouring your pussy and my cock to sink into you." He kept pressing himself against her. Colin cupped her face in both hands, his forehead resting on hers. "There," he breathed through his mouth. "I want the air you breathe as the only air I breathe. Your mouth the only one I kiss, your body the only one I worship. I don't think I can have any other woman now. You've ensnared me, Amaryllis Hart. Ensnared me and I come willingly even if I'm not supposed to do so." Colin brushed his lips against her jaw, his tongue leaving a wet trail, his teeth grazing the nerve endings on her face, her ear, her throat. With a groan, he captured her mouth.

Amaryllis opened against his mouth, giving him full access. Her pulse thundered as unadulterated desire filled her. She moaned against his lips, her tongue sparring with his. She held on to him, her fingernails raking his chest before her arms crawled around his neck, desperately bringing him closer. She whimpered as pain and pleasure filled her. In the end she could only encircle his neck with one arm. She slanted her head, giving him more access. She nibbled at his firm lips, smiling against them when he groaned. When he let go she protested. Colin chuckled, smiling against her skin, his hot breath trailing down her throat before he opened his mouth and licked at the fresh welt against her cheek, then her throat, growling when his tongue swiped it before he sucked the skin at the base of her neck. Amaryllis moaned, turning her head to give him more access. She gasped when he tore her T-shirt.

"Colin." She gasped, dazed with desire. "My arm."

"Oh shit, sorry." He rasped, huffing a chuckle. "I got carried away."

"But I want you to take me," she breathed. She watched the passion flare in his eyes, their breath suspended between them. "Please. Don't stop. Feed yourself with me. Build your strength from me. If only for this moment."

Colin looked down at her arm then took off the bandage. Amaryllis' heart thundered like a waterfall in her ears when Colin bent his head. There was a tingling in the pit of her stomach when Colin's tongue languidly swiped at her wounds. She gasped, desire coiling strongly where his tongue licked. She mewled, her breath coming short and fast. She held on to his head, glorying at the feel of his sun bleached hair against her fingers and her palms.

Then it was over.

Colin lifted his head and he seemed to be peering at her intently. Only then did Amaryllis notice that the wounds in her arm were slowly healing, the pain dissipating. Her body sorely needed his touch to ease the craving building inside her. To hell with the tightening skin in her arm and her cheek. She needed him, wanted him. She could not wait any longer. She took Collin's face in both her hands, willing for him to look into her eyes. Her heart pounded an erratic rhythm as his eyes seemed to burn into her very soul. His eyes were predominantly gold now and the sight raised her libido higher.

Something in Colin seemed to snap. In less time that it would have taken to undress, he removed Amaryllis' clothes. His golden eyes devoured her, raking his gaze up and down her body, his hands sending electricity over her exposed skin. When his eyes stopped at her nipples they pebbled even more under his gaze and her lips parted in a sigh. Her stomach concaved with excitement, her heart pounding so hard, she thought it would burst from her chest. She trailed her fingers up his chest until her right palm lay over his hammering heart. Anticipation made her tremble, the craving inside her was coming close to pain and she could not wait for pleasure to begin.

"Ancients, you're beautiful." He rasped. He took hold of her ponytail, pulling gently to expose her neck once more. Amaryllis felt the fast pulse beating against her skin and moaned when Colin's tongue licked at it. After having no compunction demanding what she wanted with her sexual partners in the past, she felt like it was the first time with Colin.

"I'm going to suck and lick every inch of you," he growled against her ear, nipping at her lobe. He burned a trail to her collar bone and down the swell of her breasts, putting open-mouthed kisses against her flesh. Colin's other arm went around her waist, bringing her closer and rubbing his hot, erect shaft against her.

That's it!

She could not wait another moment. She pushed Colin away much to his surprise before she knelt down. She heard his harsh intake of breath as she kept her gaze locked with his. He leaned against his arms on the wall, his stomach moving in and out with every sharp breath he took. She broke their eye contact and looked at him.

Damn he was big...deliciously big. His manhood stood proud and erect in front of her. A hot treat that made her salivate.

Amaryllis cupped his balls, gauging the weight while she encircled her fingers around his cock. It was hot, hard, needy for her mouth. She pressed her cheek against its length before letting it trail against her chin. Colin hissed when she licked from the middle of his sac all the way up to the tip of his cock before opening her mouth to graze her wet lips back down his length.

"Fuck," he groaned, throwing his head back when Amaryllis hummed against him, running her tongue and lips up and down, making him slick before taking his cock inside her mouth.

Amaryllis closed her eyes, savouring Colin's taste. The more she sucked him, the more her mouth watered. Heat started from her chest, suffusing her entire body with a hunger she could not put her finger on. All she wanted to do was to pleasure Colin, twisting and pumping her hand around his cock while simultaneously bobbing her head as she sucked. He growled when his cock reached the back of her throat, keeping him there for a while before she started sucking him again.

"Holy fuck!" he hissed.

She popped him out of her mouth, her hand sliding up and down his wet aroused member. She smiled seductively. "You taste good." She flicked her tongue against his tip before swirling and sucking more of the pre-cum that coated the tip. He continued to lavish her

My Haven, My Midnight

mouth on his head humming to send vibrations through his cock.

"Enough," Colin growled, hauling her up and plundering her mouth with his. Amaryllis moaned greedily, sucking his tongue, duelling with it, allowing him to venture into her mouth's secret places. His cock was hard, wet, and hot against her stomach and she was drenched and needy. One of her legs rose, trying to hook itself against his hip so that her desperate core could find some friction. Colin pulled her hair once more causing her to arch her back. She released a strangled cry when his mouth found her already hardened peak and sucked on it. Hard to the point of pain. His tongue laving and grazing against her nipple brought a bolt of electricity down to her pussy. Her clit throbbed with every spear of pleasure coursing through her from Colin's mouth on her nipple. One of her hands took hold of his shoulder while the other held his head to her breast. She gasped when his groan vibrated against her sensitive nub before he went for her other nipple.

God, she was so wet. Her nether lips were thick with desire, her channel aching.

"Colin," she moaned. "Please...I need..."

His mouth moved from her breast and his stubble grazed her chin. "Yes, Amaryllis, talk to me. What do you want?"

"I want you inside me." She could not help her whimpers. She did not care if she sounded like she was begging.

"My tongue...or my cock?"

Bloody hell, how can I think at a time like this?

"Both." She groaned when her clit rubbed against him, her heat sliding up and down, Colin's hard shaft. He chuckled and eased back. "You're such a bloody tease."

She yelped and opened her eyes when she felt herself being lifted and carried to the corner of the wall. Higher she went until Colin had her ass in his hands. Her thighs were over his shoulders and her bare pussy was directly in front of his mouth.

"Colin! You're still weak."

"You think?" He arched a sexy brow.

"Put me down."

"A tease, huh." Colin's wicked smile and his head between her legs made her inside quiver in anticipation.

Her breath hitched.

He stepped away a little to allow her to lean against the wall. He breathed then sighed. "God, you smell good and you are beautiful." He sighed, his breath blowing against her quim making it clench. She shuddered when he nipped at her inner thigh before easing the sting away.

"Colin, I think I'm going to fall," she whispered.

His golden gaze darkened, lust swirling in their depths, threatening to drown her.

"Yes, you will." His voice deepened. "Into my mouth."

The verbal foreplay was too much. The moment Colin tongued her pussy, she came. Hard. She had never been a screamer but Colin's touch made her let go and she cried out softly at first before she screamed. She whimpered when she felt herself flood, her juices coating his mouth. She slowly came from her high, but Colin was not finished.

"Damn, you taste so fucking good."

Amaryllis moaned when she felt his tongue swipe every sensitive inch of her sex, sucking gently on her labia before languidly swirling and strumming her clit with the tip of his tongue. Liquid heat flowed from her when she heard the sucking noises Colin made as he ate her, He flattened his tongue and licked her from her hole up to the pleasure point just above her opening. He did it over and over again before opening his mouth and letting his tongue enter her as far as it could. She writhed against his hold when she felt his tongue flick inside her several times before coming out to strum her clit again.

"Oh God, Colin…" Her hand raked through his hair and she opened her eyes to watch the erotic man below her. She became wetter at the sight of his mouth glistening with her cream. Then he moved his face away, showing his taut tongue before he moved back to insert it into her hole. Her orgasm started to build again, swirling in the pit of her belly, coiling and tightening.

Amaryllis threw her head back, giving in to the expertise of his mouth. He gripped her ass tightly as his mouth continued to fuck and kiss her.

Amaryllis' breath came out in pants, following the beat of Colin's tongue inside her.

He ravished and demanded.

She moaned and whimpered, raking her fingers against his sun bleached hair, sobbing towards fulfilment. Her orgasm tensed tightly inside her, the promise of sweet release increasing.

He flicked and sucked.

Amaryllis came. "Yes! Colin, yes!" She bucked against his mouth, her hands on his hair. She shuddered and sobbed, feeling her pussy weep when Colin hummed and took her clit between his lips.

"Your pussy is a delight to eat," Colin's voice rumbled against her, making her take short and quick breaths. He placed kisses against her thighs, chuckling as he felt her quiver. "Now for the second course."

Her eyes opened in a daze, her breath hitching. "Second course?"

* * *

The moment his tongue tasted the blood in her skin, desire streaked through him like a meteor. The taste of Amaryllis' blood was the sweetest thing that ever landed on his tongue. The more important thing he realized was that she was a Cynn Cruor mate.

And she was his.

Colin held on to her waist as he brought her down, her thighs sliding from his shoulders, down his arms to encircle his waist. He pinned her to the wall. She moaned when she felt her lips bump gently against his hot and silky erection. Just as she placed her hands on his shoulders, the tip of his cock teased her entrance before he slid into her, inch by thick inch, letting her get used to his girth and length. He watched her irises enlarge and growled softly when the tip of her tongue licked her lower lip. He swooped down to capture it while he continued to rock into her. And when he filled her to the root, they both sighed. Fuck, she was so tight. So good. Her core clenched hard around him, her walls squeezing his length, desperately wanting to keep him inside.

Colin's voice was deep against her throat. "Fucking you hard until your pussy becomes all mine is the second course."

She could not do anything but purr.

"Seeing that you like this wall so much, I'll fuck you here." Colin eased out then plunged back inside Amaryllis, his cock hardening even more within her warmth, savouring her pussy's grip. "Do you like me fucking you here, baby? Do you like my thick cock inside you?"

Colin grinned against her throat when Amaryllis could only whimper, her eyes limpid pools and glazed with her desire. He leaned up. His grin slowly disappeared as his hips thrust against her, his cock sliding in and out of her tight sweet heat. His own breathing became shallow. Fuck, he had never felt this good with anyone else. The way she gripped him...it was like a velvet caress, the sensitive nerves in his cock head gaining pleasure from thrusting into her. Eating Amaryllis the way he did was an experience Colin did not think existed. It was an epicurean delight. She tasted and smelled sweet. The moment her cream laced his tongue, he knew he would never get enough. Her flavour exploded through him like the most expensive ambrosia that could probably rival Olympus'. Her essence flooded his system like jet fuel, invigorating him in less time than the adriserum did. Tasting and having her against the wall raised above him was a sight to behold. The more he pleasured her, the more he felt her excitement thrum through her body, trembling against his hold. Her firm belly undulated beneath the swell of her breasts. And those delicious globes...Ancients! They were perfect for him, bobbing slightly above him with every move Amaryllis made, her nipples pointed peaks of desire. And then she came. Colin drank everything she gave, his mouth greedily sucking, demanding more. His throat contracted with every swallow, her essence gently sliding down into his system and lighting him up. Now as Amaryllis surrounded him, he wanted more of her to strengthen him.

"Harder," Amaryllis mewled. "Please."

Colin withdrew and slammed back inside her, eliciting a soft cry from her. She took him all the way to the root. She raised her head, her neck exposed. Colin sucked at the skin on her throat. "Oh God, yes!"

His teeth dug deeper, unable to stop the urge to taste her blood once more. She gasped when his mouth pulled against her neck, drawing a little blood that would mark her flesh and he closed his eyes. And emotion he could not put his finger on exploded inside him.

Knowing that Amaryllis was his mate nearly made him fall to his knees.

He carried her weight in his arms. Amaryllis held on to him while he spread her legs further apart. He growled at the sensation of sinking more deeply into her, his balls slapping against her with every buck of his hips. Her eyes were glazed over, violet pools he could easily drown in and never resurface. Her lips were parted and soft, her sweet breath caressing his face. The more he rode her, the more his lust was beginning to turn to something more primal. More meaningful.

Possession.

Mine.

His body flared in response to her sheath's velvet vice. His cock glided against her walls deliciously, squeezing him as he thrust into her over and over again.

Colin closed his eyes, unsure of how long he could last. "Damn, Amaryllis, I'm going to lose myself in you," he growled. "Your pussy feels so good around my cock."

"Yes! More," she breathed, holding him against her. Their bodies slicked with sweat from the heat they both made.

Colin gave what Amaryllis asked for. He looked down at where they connected, watching his cock wet with her juice going in and out of her, taking his pleasure and strength from her cries of ecstasy. He hissed, feeling his balls tighten. When Amaryllis' hand came down to play with herself, swirling her bundle of nerves while he thrust into her, he felt his orgasm ready to explode from him.

"Yeah, baby, that's it."

"Colin." Her eyes mirrored her wonder. "Oh shit…you're getting longer…and thicker?"

He grunted, feeling her pussy tighten around him.

"Oh yes." She arched her back, continuing to play with herself. "Hmmm…oh yes!"

Colin took one nipple and sucked hard, his control slipping. Amaryllis stopped playing, her hands gripping his shoulders, her body's tremors shuddering though Colin as well.

"Yes!" Her core squeezed him tight before her walls throbbed fast around him, her climax coaxing to join her. With a guttural groan, he followed her, his warmth bathing her in long spurts as his balls emptied his essence into her. His body pulsed with the healing that sex gave a Cynn Cruor warrior. He was coming alive. Colin's knees almost gave way at the intensity of their joining, his heart still racing. His cock flexed inside her and she moaned, gripping him in response. He reclaimed her lips, pliant and yielding, a willing slave to his tongue's masterful strokes. He felt Amaryllis give herself freely to the kisses he demanded from her. Raising his head, his mouth lifted in a lopsided grin at the way she looked. Her mouth swollen because she had been thoroughly kissed. Her pussy dripping and satisfied because she had been thoroughly fucked.

Still inside her, Colin walked to the bed. He sat on the edge before twisting to lie down gently on the dark blue silk sheets with Amaryllis on top of him. He closed his eyes at the pleasure that movement made, his cock still sensitive with their afterglow. He turned to his side, taking her with him so that he and Amaryllis lay facing each other. Her leg draped over his hip and thigh. Coming down from his high, he inhaled deeply then stopped mid-air. He blinked several times, making sure his eyes were not playing tricks on him. But it was there for him to see. For him to realise. For him to accept.

A thin opalescent film covered Amaryllis, connecting her to him.

As his mate.

He blew out his breath slowly. He stared without seeing, the ramifications of what was happening sinking into his gut. Now that they had both satiated their lust, dread and elation churned in an elixir. One he was afraid and desperate to drink at the same time. He caressed Amaryllis' arm then shoulder, looking in wonder at the prism of colours that seemed to float in a thin sea of white.

Bloody hell, I'm in so deep.

Colin looked up at the ceiling, the emotions crowding inside his chest making him want to squirm, but Amaryllis' body beside him trumped the misgivings that threatened to cover the joy that gave him peace. A peace so beautiful in its simplicity, it hurt.

What kind of life would he give Amaryllis knowing that Mackenzie was still a problem he had to deal with? Colin had no doubt that everything would soon go pear shaped and he would be in the middle of the storm. He was likely to lose Leeds and even his head for keeping Mackenzie's existence a secret, but he sure as hell was going to make sure his men were spared. This was his burden to bear. It was never his men's.

Amaryllis opened her eyes. The violet pools that were dark and deep with contentment now had traces of the gold flecks that further solidified her position as his mate. A tranquil wave whispered over crags of Colin's immortal soul. The muscle inside his chest increased in size at the emotion he felt. She was the most beautiful woman he had seen in his life. Slight disappointment flickered in their depths when he eased out of her. He reached for the duvet to cover them both. Amaryllis snuggled against his side and he chuckled at the small adorable noise she made when she draped her leg over him.

"Sleep, Amaryllis." He kissed her hair, caressing her shoulder and back. "Thank you."

But her deep breathing indicated to him that she had left him to enter sleep's realm. Colin wrapped his arms around her, holding her close, inhaling the scent of her hair, his breath stirring the violet streak at her crown. She squirmed and softly mewled in protest. Damn, he was holding her too tight. He eased his embrace and Amaryllis' lips parted softly, sighing. Even though Colin never felt the cold, the were blood tempering the coldness of the vampire's blood inside him, ice seemed to coat his spine in increments.

Would the Council of Ieldran even give him a chance to be with her? More importantly, would Amaryllis want to stay with him after he was condemned? Bloody hell, who was he kidding? Before he could even think that way, Amaryllis had to come to him willingly.

Which she has already done.

No. Colin shook his head imperceptibly. He had to hear it from her lips. He needed to hear it and when he did, he would keep those words in his heart to sustain him wherever and whatever judgment befell him.

Chapter Twenty

Colin came down the stairs and to hear Seth and Craig shouting. For once, he welcomed something that would take his mind off the inevitable feeling of losing his mate. He exhaled long and slow as he sauntered to the kitchen and stopped dead. He did not know whether he was going to laugh or snap at the Cynn mortal and immortal. Seth held an empty bag of flour. Craig looked like the ghost of Christmas present.

Colin swallowed his amusement and said in an ill disguised attempt at annoyance, "Care to tell me what's going on?"

Their gazes darted to him.

"One of us looks like a cat who got the cream." Craig went to the sink to brush off what he could of the flour in his hair.

Oh yes, I got the creamy pussy and lapped it all up. It took sheer strength of will not to return to his room and make love to Amaryllis again. To wake her with his hand between her legs, stoking the wetness back while he mouthed her nipples to hard peaks was a temptation he was ill equipped to refuse, giving it to the temptress in his bed, enjoying how she held on to him, her thighs encircling his waist as though never wanting to let him go. He breathed in her climax that fuelled his own. And as he filled her with his essence he watched the opalescent glow that joined a warrior and his mate become thicker. And stronger. They floated back down from the pinnacle enclosed in their afterglow's embrace.

His jaw clenched as he tried and nearly failed to get a grip on his lust, as his cock begged him to return. Her cries of release swirled inside his mind, reminding him of how she beautifully unravelled, clenching around his length as her orgasm rippled through her and into him. The strength that surged into him was different to holding a live wire. At that moment, Colin thought he would explode from the power Amaryllis gave him.

His jeans were definitely tight now.

"Who brought Amaryllis Hart here to the Faesten?" Seth faced Colin, her eyes reflecting her bewilderment and denial of a truth she wanted to hear.

The question was enough to switch the tap of Colin's lust off.

"Tell me, Dux. I have every right to know."

"Is that why you threw the bag of flour at Craig?" Colin gave Craig a long look. "I assure you, you've just wasted a good amount of flour."

The fight left Seth. "No. That was an accident."

"You're on the opposite sides of the island." Colin left it at that and walked to the fridge, taking out a cold can of beer and a plate of ham and cheese sandwiches covered in cling wrap. Tearing the film, he grabbed one and bit into it before snapping the ring and taking a swig. The saltiness of the food mixed with the slightly bitter taste of the beer burst inside his mouth. Having had so many missions in America, he developed a liking for cold beer.

"Dux."

"What?" He took another sandwich and continued eating, looking at his Cynn mortal second over the rim of the can.

"I'm not stupid."

Colin's brows rose, his ire slicing the surface. He continued chewing as he leaned against the counter. Craig continued to clean himself by the sink. Seth stood her ground.

"I have always been loyal to you. I didn't bat an

eyelash when you allowed Scatha Cruors into the club." Seth continued.

Colin's hand slightly hesitated before bringing the beer back to his mouth.

"I saw a Scatha take Amaryllis from the club. Everyone in the security room saw it, Colin. They have been asking questions."

Colin continued drinking from his can. He contemplated the departure of the dusky pinks and oranges of the day and the arrival of the dark blues and purples of the night. So much like the eyes of the woman lying in his bed. His mouth straightened. There was no getting around this one. If Mack had not shown himself this would not have happened.

Neither would you have known where he was.

"Meet me in the command centre." Colin threw the can in the bin and walked out of the kitchen, then he called over his shoulder, "You bloody well better clean up this mess before you do."

Liam and Cormac were in the centre, checking on the feeds coming from the clubs.

"Luke around?"

"Haven't seen him," Cormac replied, his eyes still trained on watching club activity.

Colin was dead sure that even if he told Seth about Mackenzie, Luke would get wind of it not because there was a snitch among the Cynn Cruors he led. It was because of Luke's ability to parallel shift. He perused the cameras, his gaze moving from the clubs to the security feeds of the Faesten's perimeter. Even if he opened his telepathic channel he still had no way of knowing if Luke was in the premises. Until a Cynn Cruor warrior pledged his fealty to a Faesten, telepathy would not work. Colin was also of two minds telling Luke. This was his problem, his fight, his burden which his men insisted they carry with them. He dry scrubbed his face, feeling the stubble on his jaw. Amaryllis had liked the way it abraded her skin, begging him to deepen his licks against her pussy.

Amaryllis. She was never far from his mind.

Colin's chest tightened. The strength he got from her was more than he could have had from ten vials of adriserum. Okay, that may have been an exaggeration and Zac might just whoop his arse, but Amaryllis' essence was nothing compared to what unmated Cynn Cruors took if they were wounded or if they expended more energy than was necessary. And he wanted to kiss her again. By the Ancients! His mouth tingled in memory, the need to feel those lips under his, strong. He wanted a repeat, and if possible, numerous repeats of savouring her own unique taste that fired his blood and quickened his pulse unlike any woman had done to him in his immortal life. He wanted to lick her tongue, play with it, tease it so that she moaned against his mouth. One of the most erotic sounds that came out from her.

Colin sucked in his breath. Never had he wanted a woman to be his for his entire immortal life than Amaryllis. Was it her violet eyes that drew him to her? Eyes that appeared to look into his very soul, seeing it with all of its scars, its ugliness brought on from killing Scatha Cruors who turned willingly, some whom Colin had known since childhood. Friends who had fallen for Valerian's lies. Or was it her sassy attitude of taking on monsters after her initial fear? Fear that she fought so hard to hide. Was it her vulnerability? Amaryllis would probably chew and spit him out if he called her vulnerable. Colin had only caught glimpses of her life and she definitely was no shrinking violet. She met her apprehension head on and stood shoulder to shoulder with people she gave her loyalty to only to be thrown into the streets.

No. Colin wanted her because she was his Cynn Cruor mate. The blood he had been able to extract from her skin and her sweat was proof enough. When she was about to climax, she gave out her blood's unique scent and the moment Colin inhaled her, his gums itched as his incisors descended. And he could not help himself. With a swipe of his tongue against the beating pulse at her throat, he sucked, drawing blood out of her skin.

And she came.

The doors to the nerve centre opened with a whoosh of air. Cormac chortled.

"Cake baking gone awry, I gather." Liam deadpanned but his eyes crinkled in amusement.

"Shut up," Craig growled, casting a sidelong glance at Seth, who refused to look at him. Seth went to the couch and sat with arms and legs crossed, her face petulant.

Cormac shook his head. "Why you guys can't just give in, I'll never know." He turned his back to them, still chuckling as he checked the camera feeds once more.

I'm telling Seth.

Liam and Cormac stiffened, both glancing at Colin with serious faces. Colin went to the mini bar and took out both the Dalmore scotch and a glass. He saw Craig approach and reached underneath the counter to get another glass.

Are you sure? Craig nodded his thanks at the proffered glass of scotch.

"I have no other alternative, Craig." Colin did not bother to telepath. "He attacked the Faesten. He may not have been here, but I'm sure as hell no one knows where we are except him."

"You do have an alternative."

"What? Not let the mortals know?"

"You've been doing that for a long time."

Colin's jaw hardened.

"That was uncalled for." Craig blew out, contrite.

"Yes, it was." Colin left Craig by the bar. "Are the mortals patrolling the perimeter?"

Seth nodded, immediately in leader mode even if her eyes held her wariness. "Even outside the walls."

"What about the clubs?"

"Gareth, Donovan, and Etienne are taking teams around the city centre. There are a lot of students and people about."

Cormac looked at his watch. "It isn't in full swing yet but it will soon be."

"Dux, how did the Scatha find us? No one knows this is the Faesten." Seth gave them all hard looks. "Who was the Scatha that took Amaryllis? How did Amaryllis get here? I know there is a connection, so please. Cut the bull fucking shit."

"You don't mince words, do you?"

"Shut up, Tavish," Seth hissed.

Liam smacked Cormac at the back of his head. "Ow! Shit, okay! Sorry, Seth."

She stood looking at Colin. "You want me to lead the mortals, you need to level with me. You don't then tell me and I'll hand over to the one you choose." Hurt glimmered in her eyes before it disappeared and her chin lifted.

The silence in the room was palpable, almost tomblike.

"You might want to sit down."

"I prefer to stand."

Colin nodded.

Curiosity and slight apprehension widened Seth's eyes.

Colin took a huge breath.

"About the Scatha Cruor you saw on the CCTV…"

* * *

Luke shifted to the Manchester Faesten's foyer, nearly bumping into Finn.

"Whoa! Hey, mate." Finn jumped back, surprised. He expelled a long breath. "Couldn't you have chosen a different spot to morph back?"

Luke smiled ruefully. "Sorry. I was in a rush…not concentrating too much."

"Let's just hope you don't leave your waist down in Leeds while you're waist up in Manchester. That might just freak us all."

"It doesn't work that way." Luke laughed before he mellowed. "Roarke in? I need to speak to all of you."

Finn's smile faltered. "He and Deanna went to Scotland. To talk to The Hamilton."

Luke's face was grim. "Because of what I said?"

Finn sighed, hands on his hips. "He's worried about Colin. All of us are. It's impossible that his men don't know."

"They do," Luke acknowledged. "They don't have to tell me anything for me to see it in their faces. Sense it in their movements. They're very protective of Butler. Especially Craig." They started walking to the library. "But I think they're starting to get overwhelmed."

"What do you mean?" Finn pushed the glass door, inclining his head for Luke to precede him.

Luke's gaze was steady. "Scatha Cruors have attacked the Faesten. Whether Colin needs our help or not, I think we should give it to him."

* * *

Seth ran as fast as she could. Tears streamed down

her face, the surface of her heart breaking, her mind in a turmoil. She just had to get away. What Colin told her, confessed…God dammit! It was just too close to home. The Cynn mortals patrolling the perimeter watched in shock to see her ruffled to the point of waterworks.

"Annaseth."

Without hesitation, she turned around, letting her fist fly. Her knuckles slammed against the hard jaw and she found satisfaction at hearing it crack. She toughened her face, refusing to wince. Shit, her hand was going to hurt like a mother.

"I told all of you nobody calls me by that name." She stormed away but a vice-like grip clamped on her arm. "Let me go, Craig!"

"No," he grounded out. "You are bloody going to listen to me." He dragged her towards the maze. Seth had to raise her other arm to protect her face from some of the protruding branches of the hedges that rustled as they turned corners. The night birds Seth had dimly heard when she bolted from the confines of the mansion were suddenly silent. Only the occasional breeze whispering through the trees lining the driveway could be heard from where they were.

Craig loosened his grip once they reached the centre of the maze. Seth wrenched her arm, striding away from him, putting the two marble benches in the middle of the clearing between them. She rubbed her arm, casting Craig a baleful glance. Craig held his ground, his legs a foot apart, his arms by his sides, but Seth was not deceived. She would no sooner be able to escape for Craig to flash in front of her in less than a second. That thought brought a tingle down her spine.

A delicious tingle down her spine.

Despite the wretched feeling that made her hug herself, awareness of Craig in the middle of the maze with her was making her heart do somersaults.

"Why are you crying?" Craig tilted his head to one side.

Seth furiously wiped at her face. "None of your damned business."

"Seth…"

"Why didn't Colin tell me?" she asked, unhappiness in her voice. Whether it was because of her past or because of what was happening in the present, she did not know where the anguish came from.

"Not telling you or the rest was to keep you safe from the Ancients' and the Council of Ieldran's anger. What do you think would happen to you if they found out you knew about Mackenzie and you didn't report it?"

"Why tell me now?" She scuffed her boot at the base of the marble seat. She swiped her hand against her nose.

Craig arched his brow. "You want me to answer that?"

Seth did not answer.

"You quickly placed two and two together," Craig said. "And because Mack came back. We didn't know where he was until a few nights ago. Colin has been looking for him all this time."

"If he didn't show up you wouldn't have told me," she stated.

"It wasn't my story to tell." Craig raked his hand through his hair. Seth stole a look from underneath her lashes. She blanketed her mind from the Cynn Cruor's mind intrusion, a talent she had honed to keep the immortals' inquisitive minds at bay from the secrets she kept. God, how she wished she could rake her fingers through Craig's tousled hair. "Like I said, the burden was ours alone."

"Why?" Her laugh cracked through the air. "Because we are just mortals?"

"No! You know we treat you as equals. Even thinking that way is stupid."

"So I'm stupid now."

"Annaseth, you're not bloody thinking straight!"

"You want me to make your jaw even and hit you on the other side?"

Craig roared. "Why the fuck do you twist my words? You know damn well that's not what I meant."

"Stay away, Shaw. Please." Her voice was breaking again. She disguised it with a laugh. It came out nearly hysterical. "You're right, I'm not thinking straight. I need to be alone. And if you think I will betray Colin, I'll say this now. Fuck you."

"I didn't say anything." Craig's face was thunderous. "I followed you because I wanted to see if you were okay. You're very strong, Seth. No one ever doubted your loyalty. Not then. Not now. That's why you were chosen to lead the mortals. Whatever chip you have on your bloody shoulder, you better get rid of it. It doesn't become you. Everyone needs to gear up because from the looks of it, we're about to go to war that will include the mortals."

"I get it. Suit up, right. No problem. I'll have the mortals ready. So quit the posturing. I don't need a lecture." She sniffed.

Craig was suddenly in front of her, the breeze bringing tresses of her hair to her face. "Yes. You don't need a lecture. You need this." He grabbed her by the waist and held her head in place before taking her mouth with his. Seth gasped against his mouth, stunned and Craig swept in, devouring her, his tongue twirling against hers. Excitement fired in her belly and pierced her core. She lit up, returning Craig's kiss hungrily, grabbing his shirt collar, twisting the cloth, her red nails digging into the fabric and ripping a part of it. Her toes curled at Craig's kiss. A low moan surfaced from her throat when his hands drifted down to squeeze her ass, pressing her closer to his hard and thick shaft. She sucked on his lower lip, moaning when Craig slanted his head to deepen the kiss. His muscular scent pervaded her senses, igniting her blood. He tasted of man and scotch and a tinge of flour. Seth would have giggled at the fleeting thought, but she was so wrapped up at the way Craig was making her a puddle at his feet.

Oh God, I can't give in. Not again.

She ended the kiss and opened her eyes. Craig held her for a moment longer, his forehead leaning against hers, their breaths mixing. Seth sucked in the air Craig gave, taking it into her system, hoping it would ease the ache knocking at her battered heart. How could she do this? What was happening to her?

How could Craig crack through her wall?

Craig let go of her slowly, stepping back. Seth looked at his eyes, her soul lightened by the tiny gold flecks in his warm brown eyes before they disappeared. Craig became unreadable again.

"I shouldn't have done that." His voice bore no emotion. "I'm sorry." Then he was gone.

Seth sank down on the marble bench and looked up at the sky.

"Why do things have to be so complicated?" she whispered before tears started rolling down her cheeks again, sobbing her anguish softly.

* * *

"Seth okay?" Colin's eyes narrowed at Craig when he returned.

Craig walked to the bar, not answering. He poured a

liberal amount of scotch in a glass, knocking it back in one huge swallow. The amber liquid fired the neurons in his brain, the heat spreading across his chest.

Damn, that feels good.

"What happened to your jaw?" Cormac arched a brow.

"Hit it somewhere," Craig said. "Seth will be okay. She just needs time to absorb everything you've told her."

Colin nodded. "Seth won't bolt."

"No, she won't," Craig agreed. "She needs to be brought in, in everything from now on." He clenched his jaw, slightly wincing. After Colin told her about Mackenzie, the last thing they all expected was to see her eyes tearing. Shock, anger, maybe even fury, but not the waterworks. He had followed her out, wanted to find out what the hell was wrong.

He got punched instead and damn, she did pack a wallop.

You called her by her full name.

There was something else. Craig's gut told him there was more to Seth's erratic behaviour. But at that moment she looked so vulnerable he just wanted to hold her. Problem was she always rubbed him the wrong way and it felt right.

"Do you know why she left?" Liam queried. "First time I saw Annaseth cry."

"No, I don't." It was a partial truth. Craig had no idea why Seth had cried when she left, but he knew why she cried after he left her.

Because he kissed her. His blood sang in his veins when she returned his kiss and then she ended it. She closed in on herself.

His chest ached, loneliness carving a gaping hole in it.

He vowed he would not make the same mistake again.

Chapter Twenty-One

Amaryllis woke with a start from the wafting chill against her back. Her body was deliciously and decadently sore. Her cheeks heated at the remembrance of the explosive sex she had with Colin. That Colin had left the bed was understandable. After all, she had offered to heal him. This was just sex.

It did not stop the hollowness that Colin's absence carved inside her, taking a piece of her with him.

She sighed, her body languidly gliding against the silken sheets. The last thing she remembered was Colin stoking the fire between her thighs and making love to her once more before he had enveloped her in his arms. Tightly. As though he never wanted to let go, still deep inside her, holding on to his shoulders like a lifeline, with her head resting on his muscled chest. She remembered the sudden loss of him easing out of her, the memory of the silken sheet over their satisfied bodies. The gentle kiss on her hair. She stretched her arms up and above her head then stopped. An opalescent sheen appeared to coat her skin, like she had placed one of those glittery lotions on herself. She switched on the bedside lamp to look more closely.

"What the...?" she murmured, frowning. She tried rubbing it. Her eyes widened in surprise when the sheen merely displaced around her fingers, returning to coat her when she removed her hand. Sighing, she plopped back down on the bed closing her eyes, a smile curving the corners of her mouth. Then her eyes snapped open in horror.

Holy shit, they did not use protection. Damn it! Seth was starting to become her go to friend. Amaryllis now had to find a way of delicately telling Seth that she had to leave the house to go to the chemist's. She knew that Seth was blasé about sex but still. To let Seth know that she and Colin had...

"Arrghh..." Embarrassment made her cringe. She lay on her back, her lips parting as her breath came out softly, a groan coming unbidden at the soreness between her thighs. She could not help the smile that teased her mouth. Damn, he was big and long, filling her up that she thought she would not be able to take all of him. And the way he tasted inside her mouth, oh man. If she had a chance to give Colin head again, she was going to make damn sure he came in her mouth.

She groaned at her aching muscles. Who would have thought there were still parts of her body that her parkour regimen had not reached?

Hello! That's free running. Not a sexcapade with an immortal.

True. A hot guy that burned in direct sunlight whose eyes turned nearly all gold when he fucked.

"What the fuck did I get myself into?" She was not really one for the "F" word. She was more of using 'shit' or 'bloody hell', but she was saying the effing word more times than several months staying with Jack did combined. Thinking of Jack Crawley was like having an outrageously sour pastille in her mouth that she pursed her lips at the thought. It was the one thing that dampened her bliss after Colin's lovemaking.

No. Strike that. This is pure unadulterated lust.

This was all that was. She gave him healing and he gave her wish, satisfying her need to continue where they left off.

She threw the silk sheet aside and sat up, swinging her legs to the floor. Her knees threatened to give way under her, her legs feeling like jelly. She finally made it to the bathroom. She turned the shower tap and entered the huge shower stall, sighing as the warm liquid kneaded her body. Then she gasped.

Except for the red welts that marked where the Scatha had slashed her, her wounds had disappeared.

Wow.

Done with her shower, she went back to the bedroom to use her T-shirt only to remember that Colin had torn it asunder. Even her bra had not been spared. Sighing as her body warmed at Colin's possession, she made a decision. Finally dressed, she made her way out of the bedroom barefooted to go to her room. Her gaze fell on the tapestry once more, focusing on a figure that looked like a magician and a she-wolf standing beside him atop a hill. They appeared to be lording it over the assembled. In the distance were those Amaryllis had seen the night the mansion was attacked.

Freddie Kruger's long lost relatives.

She went down the flight of stairs, the new ballet flats she got from her room tapping lightly on the wood. The front door had been replaced earlier that day and the ground floor hallway looked as though no skirmish had happened the night before. She went to the library, checked the formal dining room and ballroom. She turned around, puzzled. Where was everybody?

Like you're the only one who needs sleep.

But it was evening. Her mouth twitched, acceding that point to her conscience.

She made her way to the kitchen and switched on the coffee maker. Seth's bread was long gone. She smirked at the thin film of flour on the counter.

Seth must really be stressed. Not surprising after a visit from the monster squad.

Amaryllis foraged in the fridge, taking out some butter, eggs, cheese, and a can of mushrooms she noticed in the cupboard filled with dry goods. She found a clean glass bowl from the dishwasher and cracked the eggs over it, adding cheese gratings and the mushrooms. Soon the strong aroma filled the air and the soft sizzling of pan when she poured the omelette mixture. Her thoughts were half on what she was cooking and on what her next steps would be.

She transferred the omelette on to the plate, taking the utensils from the drawer before plunking down on one of the chairs by the window.

The grounds beyond the kitchen window looked serene, peaceful. She could just hear the last few chirps of woodland birds in the trees before dusk surrendered to the night. She looked up at the sky. The moon was getting fuller and close to it was a lone star. She closed her eyes and made a wish. The beginnings of a smile tugged at the side of her mouth. Her childhood was not that bad. She still believed in wishing on a star. If her wishes had come true, she was not aware of them. She was too hell bent on her survival after leaving her parents.

She placed a slice of the omelette into her mouth, chewing thoughtfully before taking a tentative sip from her coffee.

Seth had offered her a job. Maybe Seth could give her some references or point her in the right direction. Amaryllis was under no illusion that things between her and Colin would progress. They both needed each other at that particular time. To scratch an itch, to fuel a killing machine. Amaryllis refused to acknowledge the feeling of being discarded. She did not know how she would look at working in the Leeds area, seeing Colin hook up with other women for the night. No, it was better that she moved away and this became an anecdote in her scrapbook. That was, if she took up the hobby.

She finished eating and bussed the used plates, pan, and bowl to the dishwasher before switching it on. Taking her mug with her, she wandered through the house. It was eerily quiet. Was she the only one left? Had they all gone out? Apprehension shivered down her spine. No. Mortals would be guarding the mansion. The Cynn Cruors would not risk another attack.

The Georgian house was huge. While hedgerows lined the front of the house and ivy nearly covered the façade, the edifice had a long corridor beyond what anyone could initially see. Amaryllis already knew that the hospital was housed at the farthest end of the house. She noticed a set of double doors after the library. Fresh scratches on the intricately carved wood were the only evidence that the doors had not been spared. The wood was antique and Amaryllis knew that its value would sharply depreciate because of its battle scars. Now if those scratches had been made centuries ago…she chuckled. She was hardly an expert. A certificate of provenance and a history behind the scrapes might just save it. Any *chi chi* or *noveau riche* individual who wanted to look cultured would snap the doors in an instant. She turned the doorknob and switched on the lights. She gasped in pleasure.

A game room.

It retained the wood panelling prevalent in the rest of the house. An empty pool table dominated the room with two bright lamps overhead. The triangular rack and balls were neatly placed it their shelf beside the pool sticks rack. Beside the pool rack was a wet bar with shelves of various scotch and liquor and two taps facing the counter. A sofa and coffee table set in deep green was placed in the opposite side of the room. At the farther end was another sofa set with a huge movie entertainment suite.

Amaryllis knew how to play a little, but she was out of practice. She placed her mug down on the bar counter and proceeded to arrange the balls and she racked them on the table. She manoeuvred the rack into place and slowly lifted it. She went to the stand and selected a cue stick that felt comfortable in her hand. She chalked the tip and bent down to make the break. She pulled her shoulders back, relaxed and took aim. With a crack, the balls scattered all over the table with balls five and twelve neatly shooting down the pockets. Several minutes later, her brow furrowed, her teeth worrying her lower lip. She walked around the table, trying to find the right angle and darted her gaze between the cue ball and the one she wanted to put into the corner pocket. Damn, she would have to overextend herself over the table. Resigned, she tiptoed and bent down, wriggling her backside to get more leverage.

"I didn't know you played."

Startled, Amaryllis hit the cue ball out of position. She sucked in her breath. That tenor, oh God, it was making her body warm. She was very much aware of Colin's presence. His scent reached her from the door, starting to cloak her the closer he moved. Amaryllis inhaled deeply and closed her eyes. Lime and his cologne teasing her senses. Damn...

Amaryllis despised interruptions when she played. Then again, she did not like the cue balls angle. A smile pulled at the corners of her mouth.

"You made me hit a foul." She straightened from her bent position, sparing him a sideways look from beneath her lashes before placing the cue ball in a different angle.

Colin chuckled. "The way I see it, I did you a favour."

Amaryllis looked over her shoulder with a sly grin.

"Perhaps."

Excitement grew in increments at the thought of what she was about to do. Would Colin take the bait?

Heart thudding, core throbbing, body switching to seduction mode, she lowered her gaze, her lashes fanning her cheeks. She spread her legs a foot apart, rose on her feet then bent over.

Slowly.

She heard Colin's sharp inhale and the sound caused her heart to pound harder against her ribs, feeling it through her chest dipping against the table's velvet.

Her eyes were on the cue ball, her hands cradling the cue stick, pushing it in and out through her fingers.

Until the butt of the stick hit something hard and Colin's hot hands were on her hips.

He bent over to her ear, his breath making her shiver.

"You're wearing one of my shirts," he murmured.

Amaryllis gave a long sigh when the bulge in his pants brushed between her ass.

"Because you tore my T-shirt," she spoke, her voice husky.

"You look damn sexy in my shirt." He licked the shell of her ear. "I'm jealous of it for covering your skin and brushing against your tits." One of his hands trailed under the shirt. Amaryllis closed her eyes when Colin cupped one bare breast and rubbed her already hardened nipple. "Oh, baby, yeah."

Her sex flooded when Colin pinched her nipple, the sweet pain zinging down to flick on the switch of her lust in her clit.

The cue stick suddenly became too heavy for her to carry, the game too difficult for her to finish. Her mind zeroed in on what was happening down south, or rather what was happening in the region of her sex. She tried to keep her breath normal but how could she when Colin's hand was hot against her hips before squeezing her ass. She heard Colin inhale.

"Sweetness pervades the air between us, Amaryllis," he stated softly. His hands continued their seduction. "Mmmm…I bet your pussy's dripping wet."

The cue stick rattled, falling on the table, nudging the cue ball that rolled a few centimetres away.

The seductress was now the seduced.

Colin continued. "Legs spread apart, my cock against your ass. Your scent is very enticing. Tell me you're wet. Tell me it's all for me."

Amaryllis moaned and gasped. Her thong was soaked. She knew it without a doubt. Before she could reply, Colin spoke.

"Can't speak?" Colin tutted. His hands moved from her ass and breast, to her hips and around her waist to unbutton her jeans. "I'll just have to check if you're soaking wet."

"Oh…"

Colin's finger eased into her jeans. Amaryllis' breathing sped when he brushed against the drenched fabric of her thong. "You are wet and hot. Hhmm…your thong is wet. Let's see if your pussy's wet too."

"Colin, I am soaking," she breathed, her hips beginning to move, her sex seeking release, despairing with the need to be petted. She shuddered. "Oh…"

"Oh yes, baby," he said appreciatively. "You are wet. My fingers feel so good surrounded by your pussy's heat and nectar."

Amaryllis whimpered.

Colin hummed. "That's it. Feel how my finger is tapping and swirling against your clit?"

Amaryllis' eyes were closed. Her body arched following Colin's beat, electrified by his strumming.

Her thighs clenched to keep herself from falling in a heap on the floor.

"Amaryllis." Colin stopped. She groaned in frustration. "I asked you a question. Can you feel my finger…make that two fingers playing with your sweet clit?"

"Yes."

"Will your clit be my fingers' plaything?"

"Yes!"

"And if it isn't my fingers, will it belong to my tongue?"

She nodded, her fingers clawing against the table's velvet cover. "Yes…oh…yes."

"My mouth?"

She moaned. "Damn…"

He stopped.

"Colin!"

"Damn wasn't the answer I was looking for."

"Yes!"

"Good girl." His voice husky. "I want you so bad. Feel that…oh yeah…you're squeezing my finger. Let's make it two."

Amaryllis' breathing ratcheted, her sex dripping.

"Damn, you squeeze hard. I'm going to tongue fuck and eat you. Will you let me do that?"

Amaryllis was spiralling to meltdown. Colin continued playing with her, pleasuring her until her entire being felt centred in her sex. She was helpless to stave off her impending release.

"Don't come yet."

"What?" Her head jerked towards the sound of his voice, confused. She opened her eyes in bewilderment before closing them again at the sheer pleasure of Colin's fingers on her. "Oh dear God…" Colin took out his fingers and flicked her clit in rapid succession, before inserting them inside her again. "Yes!"

"My hot Violet." Colin increased the pace while his thumb continued to rub the pleasure just above her entrance. "You're dripping with cream. We don't want to go to waste, now. Do we?"

Colin did not wait for her to acquiesce. He peeled her jeans off, almost tearing them in his haste. Amaryllis looked over her shoulder. Colin had his fingers in his mouth. Damn. Seeing Colin lick her juices from his fingers was so erotic. His eyes had the gold flecks that bore into her. He held her hips with both hands before disappearing from her sight.

"Oh shit!" she breathed. Without preamble Colin entered her with his tongue from behind, flicking her inside before nibbling and eating her pussy. She keened softly, her eyes closed, her forehead on the table, her hands trying to find something to grip so she did not fall. She allowed Colin to roughly pull her hips and her pussy into his face. Her thighs dug into the table, but she did not care. Colin hummed against her clit and her knees almost buckled. His tongue swiped at her from her clit to her hole and back. He opened his mouth and sucked at her labia, swirling his mouth against all of her.

"Colin...please."

"Tell me what you want, Violet," he said against her pussy, every vibration shooting her up higher in ecstasy. "Need my cock inside you?"

"God yes! Fuck me hard," she keened softly.

She heard him open the zipper of his jeans, moaning in gratitude when she felt the tip of his shaft against her. With one thrust he buried himself deep inside her. His arousal hard and hot, sinking into her, and easing the edge of her need. They both groaned at the connection.

Colin withdrew and slammed back inside her, her hips hitting the edge of the table. He did it again, making Amaryllis gasp in pleasure.

And again.

And again.

The tempo increasing.

The heat rising.

No words were spoken.

Their moans the only communication as bodies and minds shifted and collided.

And became one.

Colin rapidly thrust into her soaking quim, gripping her hips hard. Amaryllis felt her release resurface but this time she knew it would be much bigger than the last. Her pussy felt full and pampered by Colin's delicious stabs, her euphoria growing every time Colin's hips bumped against her, his sac slapping against her until finally, she reached the end of the cliff and fell off the precipice. She screamed her release, her vagina clamping against Colin's marble hard cock, bringing him with her as he roared his orgasm. Amaryllis felt the ribbons of his essence spurt hotly inside her, bathing her with the intensity of their foreplay, culminating in their joining.

Suddenly, tears squeezed against her closed lids at the intensity of what she felt. Colin fell on her back, his breathing laboured, his heart running, beating furiously against her skin. Her own heart kept pace with his before starting to come down from its high.

Fuck, she was so screwed.

"Well, the fact that your manhood is hard against my stomach means it's working."

Colin barked with laughter.

Colin could not get enough. He would have wanted to stay longer. To take her to his room and sink into her warmth. To make her scream while she made him shout. To pleasure her until she begged him for rest. Colin watched emotions dance across her face. Seduction, anticipation, and another emotion he never saw in the eyes of the women he bedded, paraded like a silent movie in her gaze and he wanted it. Needed it. A different kind of warmth seeped into his skin, wrapping every sinew of his immortal body until he was covered with it. Terrifying and comforting him. Shaking him to the core to leave him weak yet so light, so freeing that he wanted to soar. To shout. To roar.

To be free.

In Amaryllis' eyes he saw his future, his strength, his life.

His death.

And he would not have it any other way.

Colin's gaze skimmed her face. From her forehead, her brows, her delicate nose, the sweep of her cheeks still blushed with fulfilment, down to her enticing rosy mouth. He cupped her neck. She tilted her head, a soft smile on her lips ready to accept him again, her eyes lighting up once more.

A sound only a Cynn Cruor could hear pierced the air just as Colin bent to grant Amaryllis her wish. He groaned as he rested his forehead on hers.

"Something wrong?" Amaryllis held on to his waist, leaning back to look at him.

"Duty calls," Colin said against her forehead.

She rubbed his chest with her palms. "Come back to me afterwards?"

He pulled back, looking at her throat down to his shirt that gave him a fetching peak of her cleavage, her delicious pert breasts puckering against his pale pink dress shirt.

"I will." His voice deepened as he whispered in her ear, enjoying the shudder that ran through her. "You better get dressed. Properly. Only I should see you fuck ready."

Her soft laughter went straight to his groin and he rubbed his straining dick against her. "Next time, maybe you should prepare."

He arched a brow. "For what?"

She tiptoed and sucked his ear, making him growl softly. "You've not come inside my mouth. Be suck ready." He inhaled sharply. With a light brush of her lips against his jaw, she slinked towards the door, her hips swaying, and out of the room.

Bloody hell, Amaryllis was going to be a handful.

* * *

Max could not understand why he was being given the run around. Suddenly, he did not have access to Dac Valerian. In a span of a few days, he had fallen from grace with the Scatha leader already? The hair on his nape rose and his spine tingled. There was something very wrong. The rest of his Scatha brethren watched him with suspicion, some with open hostility. It did not bother him. That was how the Scatha Cruors were, kill or be killed. What he could not understand was that whatever semblance of camaraderie they had, if it passed for camaraderie, had disappeared.

"Hey, Greene, found us any more flesh for the market in Grimsby?" one of the men slouching on one of the couches called to him.

"Yeah, fish flesh." Max smirked. "I was sent on a

bloody goose chase. No contact arrived. Where are the others?"

"Looking for cock and pussy. It's nearly full moon," the Scatha said, earning chortles from the rest.

Max pursed his lips. He went through one of the corridors leading to the sleeping quarters. With Badon gone, he had moved up. Not much of the kind of digs he wanted. Badon had been filthy. Used syringes and empty cognac bottles littered the floor. Mac had thrown them away together with Badon's flashy clothes that harked back to Saturday Night Fever. The elegance of the room shown through after Max made Badon's hovel to his pad. Amber and cream furniture and soft lights with a huge sleigh bed dominated the room. A dark rug partially covered the concrete floor. Off to the left was a small bathroom with a glass shower stall. Badon hardly bathed, giving the en suite an unused feel. After Badon died and Valerian promoted him, Max checked the entire room for weak points. There were none. The one thing he liked about the hovel was that Badon had installed a camera feed to spy on all the rooms of the pit, including his office. Max had never realized he had done so until he found the feed console by accident. Badon had hidden it in his closet behind his flashy clothes.

Max watched the feeds, absently putting his push dagger on the table by the bed, the only remnant of his Cynn Cruor life which he could not let go of. A low growl came out softly from his throat. He enlarged the feed showing Badon's office. Dac Valerian, Herod D'Argyl, and Lee Harris were talking. Lee's clothes were torn in several places.

"...the Cynn Cruors killed a lot of the men," Lee said. "I barely got out with my life."

"You shouldn't have given it up," Dac snapped.

"Then there wouldn't be anyone to report to you,

sire."

"He's right," Herod spoke, then to Lee. "How did you find the Cynn Cruors?"

"I got it out from Jack Crawley. He was asking about his sister and wouldn't give me intel until I assured him that she'd be back with him soon."

"And how are you going to arrange that, hmmm?" Dac invaded Lee's personal space. "They've been sold. We can't demand them back."

Lee straightened to his full height. "I know that, sire. Corrine Crawley ended her life the night she was abducted coming home from school. I used mind control to project a perception in Crawley's mind. I gave him my phone saying I had a video of his sister and that she was happy. In truth, he was looking at a blank screen. He was flying so high on crack it was easy to fiddle with his brain."

"I'm impressed."

"Thank you, sire." Lee bowed, his face beaming with pleasure.

"So did he tell you?" Dac queried. "We have several of the best tech savvy minds only too willing to sell their souls to us and we still can't find them. I don't think we're getting our money's worth. And now a human who's fried his brain is able to tell us. "

"We've been too busy avoiding them," Herod commented softly. "Maybe we should go on the offensive?"

"Calling the shots now, are we, D'Argyl?"

"No, Dac," Herod said. "A suggestion you may wish to take or leave."

"There's more," Lee said.

Both men looked at him.

"Badon was not killed by the Cynn Cruors. He was killed by a Scatha Cruor."

"Who?" Dac's eyes narrowed.

"Max Greene." Lee grinned.

"Bring him to me." Dac's eyes blazed with fury.

By the time the Scatha barged into Max's room, he was already gone.

* * *

The condemned building looked very much at home in the run down area south of Leeds. Some of its glassless windows were boarded up. Others looked like empty eye sockets, the lights coming from the distance eerily illuminating the space. The building's walls or whatever was left of them had so much graffiti that would make Banksy cringe.

Leaning against one of the exposed pillars, he watched the comings and goings of the men from afar. Even from his vantage point, he could smell the ammonia from the urine that had dried against the wall and other things that dried up in the daylight. He snorted, his throat constricting. All things considered, he preferred the ammonia than the stench coming from the men because no matter what they did, evil clung to their skin, coating it like sunscreen. Earlier, he watched the Scatha load up a van filled with young men and women who all looked like they were drugged as they obediently entered the recesses of the vehicle. He curled his hands into fists, helpless and unable to do anything, knowing that if he confronted them without backup, he would meet his end. He could not allow that.

Not when he needed to know the truth of what happened almost three hundred years ago.

He scratched the itch that flared from his beard. His hair curled around his head, unruly. It was not necessary to keep his dark locks tamed in a clean cut. Better that he was not recognized by the Cynn Cruors.

Rebelling after so long? He hitched his shoulder. *Maybe.*

He flexed his neck muscles before pushing away from the concrete twisting his upper torso to ease his fatigue. How long had he been waiting? He could not tell anymore. He had watched, waited, and wondered. He had lost his quarry for several weeks, could not understand where Herod D'Argyl had gone. He had deliberately searched for Scatha Cruors throwing off his scent so as not to alert them that a Cynn Cruor was in their midst. It was the only way he could find out where Herod and Valerian had gone. No one knew where Valerian disappeared to but the Scatha Cruors knew that Herod had gone to Central America. That was all they knew. Then a few days ago, D'Argyl returned to the British Isles and with him was Dac Valerian.

He looked out into the distance, his Cruor vision sharp as though it was day. The last time he saw Herod was in the Isle of Man. He had watched the skirmish near the sea unfold, not wanting to get involved, but Herod forced his hand when he attempted to kill Deanna Logan, Roarke Hamilton's mate.

There was another Cynn Cruor he did not recognize that came to Deanna's rescue. He found out later that the stranger was Luke Griffiths, another Cynn Cruor searching for his roots.

An avalanche of mixed emotions had swirled inside his chest and gut during the confrontation. Part of him wanted Herod dead.

The other part of him wanted to ask…why?

But the sun had blushed the line that divided the earth and the sky, eager to take over from the night. He and Herod came to a stalemate.

Shouts came from the bowels of the building. He saw someone zip out, frozen in place for one moment in front of a car. The Scatha Cruor appeared to hesitate before taking out the car keys and flinging it as far away as possible. That moment's pause was enough for other Scatha Cruors to emerge from the building's hollows. Their faces transformed, their hands morphing to talons before engaging the lone Scatha Cruor to a fight.

The Scatha came closer to where he was hiding. Instinctively, he reached out to his back, a motion he used when taking out his sword. But his back was empty. There was no scabbard, no sword. Only air. He had left his sword in Manchester. He did not believe he deserved to keep it.

Did not believe he had earned it after finding out the truth of who he was.

Frustration and anger tightened his jaw. Bloody hell, he would need to use his bare hands. His mouth lifted to a lopsided grin, looking forward to tactile satisfaction of the impact of his fist against a Scatha's jaw. Dux, Finn, Graeme, and Zac would have also had a field day. Roarke would probably chuckle. Finn and Graeme would…his grin subsided, a gust of loneliness searing into him. If only…

The pillar near him cracked and crumbled from the force of the body being thrown against it, bending the truss rods exposed by the crumbling concrete. The lone Scatha was on the ground while three more stood around him.

"You're dead, Greene." A piercing yowl came from the Scatha.

Good, I'll have some entertainment.

But something was not right. He cocked his head to one side, his nose flaring.

Cynn Cruor? Impossible!

Yet his olfactory sense zoned in on the Cynn Cruor blood inside the Scatha. Very faint, almost non-existent.

Still it was there.

Just like he had Scatha blood yet became a Cynn Cruor.

He did not think. He just did. His training kicking in when bloodlust bled into his eyes. He left his hiding place and growled, launching himself at the three Scatha Cruors. He broke the neck of one on impact. He rolled away and crouched, in his element. Closed-in fighting. He did not wait for the two to get their bearings before colliding into them. Dazed, the Scatha looked like rag dolls before he gripped tufts of their hair and smashed their heads as hard as he could. He had no blade to behead them. It did not matter. When they woke they would wish they had been decapitated.

Leaving the unconscious Scatha Cruors, he turned to the Scatha with Cynn Cruor blood. He winced at the deep slashes on the man's stomach. He took one step.

"Stay away from me, Cynn Cruor. Be thankful that I spare your life this night."

He looked at the push dagger in the Scatha's hand. He raised a brow. "You're a Scatha yet you have Cynn Cruor written all over you."

"I am not a Cynn Cruor!" the man hissed.

"Your dagger says you are. Leeds? Colin Butler? Ring any bells?"

"Shut the fuck up!"

Suddenly they heard shouts from the building. The Scatha rolled on one knee before hoisting himself up unsteadily, still holding his stomach, his dagger in front of him.

"Looks like they're looking for you." The Cynn Cruor faced him again. "Had a change of heart? Or are you planning on suicide by Cynn Cruor?"

"They're looking for someone and she's with the Cynn Cruors," the Scatha answered, his arms slowly lowering, his gaze still mistrusting.

"How do you know that?"

"Because I brought her to them. Now I need to warn them that Valerian is about to attack."

His eyes narrowed. "Why should I trust you? You're a Scatha."

"You don't." The Scatha shrugged. "But I'm doing this because of the woman I want to protect."

"So you can destroy her the way you Scatha have destroyed the lives of so many innocents? She's with Butler and he'll take care of her. Leave her be."

The Scatha's face tightened, a muscle ticking in his jaw. "Right, like the way he took care of me."

"What?"

"None of your fucking business."

They glared at each other before the Cynn Cruor relented. "I better get you to Leeds then." He dry scrubbed his face and scratched his beard. "I'm going to bloody regret this."

"Not as much as I. I'm betraying my kind. So we're even."

"But you are traitors." The Cynn Cruor scoffed. "That's in your gene pool."

"Are we going to trade barbs all night because you can be my guest and get mauled by the rest of my brethren and I'll make my way to the Faesten."

"I've got a beat-up car. At the rate you're bleeding it's going to take you a long time to get to Butler. How much time before they attack?"

"I didn't stay to find out but my guess is either tonight or tomorrow evening."

The shouts were coming closer. He and the Scatha Cruor hid behind the remaining pillars. His Cynn Cruor skill of throwing off their scent covered them. He would need to bed a willing partner to get his strength back soon or get his hands on some adriserum. But first things first.

He inhaled harshly when he saw his quarry. Herod D'Argyl stood by the entrance of the Scatha's lair, his neon green eyes like an incongruous beacon from a lighthouse guiding an errant druggie who cared to enter the sea of debris surrounding them.

"We better go." He nudged his head. "Just by the broken fence. Can you handle yourself with your guts spilling out?"

The Scatha's chuckle smacked of evil. "I still have my head, haven't I? Here," he flipped the dagger and handed it to him, handle first, "a gesture of goodwill."

He snorted, taking the dagger. "Will wonders never cease? Does that goodwill extend to telling me who you are?"

"Mack...Max. Max Greene. You?"

The Cynn Cruor hesitated slightly. "Blake...Strachan."

Chapter Twenty-Three

Amaryllis could not wipe the smile off her face as she entered her room. If what she had with Colin was anything to go by, one night, two nights stand, sex with Colin was mind-blowing. He knew where to touch her, knew how much pressure to put that stoked the fire inside to burn her alive with his passion. And his length and girth…holy crap! She did not think she would be able to take him in, but she did and the more he thrust inside her, the more she rose, heading towards heaven on earth.

It was going to be harder to leave.

"Oh, stop it, Hart," she snapped at herself. "This is just sex, nothing more. You can't stay. He needed you to strengthen him. Is all. Yes, just sex…just sex…"

"Whom are you talking to?"

Amaryllis squeaked then scowled. "Seriously, Seth. Isn't there a rule here about opening doors?"

Seth snorted. "The men won't dare."

"And you would." Amaryllis arched a brow, sarcasm trickling.

"Oh, come on!" Seth sighed. "Do you know what it's like to be surrounded by so much testosterone? You can develop muscles by just being with them."

Amaryllis giggled. She scrutinised Seth from head to toe. "You can hold your own. Be right back." She took a pair of new underwear from the bag. Maybe another shower would remove the shine on her skin. Her forehead puckered in concentration before she closed the bathroom door.

She came out moments later wearing the new pair of lace lingerie under Colin's shirt, her legs bare, her skin flushed from her shower. Still the shine had not disappeared. She had nearly finished the body wash and scrubbed her body until the loofah had probably cried out for mercy and still the shine could not be removed. Sighing, she had finished her bath, vowing to keep trying until it disappeared.

Amaryllis undid the clip in her hair, letting it cascade down her back. Seth was by the window, her reflection pensive.

"Seth, are you okay?"

"Hmm? Oh yes, I am." She walked to the bed and sat down. "Just wanted to hang out with a girl."

Amaryllis sat beside her. "Really? Is that why your eyes are puffy?" She smiled gently. "What's up?"

"Allergies," Seth quipped then grinned. "So you and Colin, huh?"

Amaryllis gave her a long hard look before letting Seth's deflection slide. Her cheeks heated. "Seeing that you're an adult, I can tell you it's a one night stand."

Seth rolled her eyes in scepticism.

"Okay, twice."

"Amaryllis." She sighed. "That's not what I meant." She took Amaryllis' arm, lifting it. "What do you see?"

"My arm."

"I know that. C'mon." She rolled her eyes but still insistent. "Tell me even if you think it's silly."

The thin milky film that shone with sands of light shimmered against Amaryllis' arm. "I've been trying to get this out. It's like I doused myself with shiny lotion. Ugh!" She wrinkled her nose. "Do you have anything I can remove it with? I don't like looking like I've been to a glitter party or something."

"You can't remove that. It might end up being part of your skin."

"What?" Amaryllis' eyes widened. "Why? How the

hell did I get this then?"

"Colin," Seth simply said.

"Excuse me?" Amaryllis blinked.

"You had sex that's more than a one night stand or a two night romp. That's what happens. Now go to the bathroom. Think of whatever you did with Colin and look at yourself in the mirror."

"Seth!"

"Humour me and tell me what you see." Seth gave her a gentle push towards the ensuite. Moments later Amaryllis returned. Her mouth agape.

"I have the same gold flecks I saw in Colin's eyes." Seth smiled.

"Why would sex with Colin make me look like a walking glitter ball with gold sparks?"

"Because you're his mate."

Amaryllis' eyes became as round as discs. "Excuse me?"

"You can 'excuse me' all you want, but that's proof that you belong together." Seth smiled. A genuine light of happiness brightened her eyes. "About time Dux had one."

"Whoa...whoa!" Amaryllis stood, her body starting to shake with disbelief. She strode to the window then pivoted to the woman sitting nonchalantly on the bed. "No one said anything about a mate. That's what guys call each other."

"Sure, they do. That's what you call the other half of the whole too. Man and woman. Cynn Cruor warrior and mate."

Amaryllis shook her head. "That can't happen."

Colin's mate? The thought warmed her, pleased her, made her giddy. But she did not want to get her hopes up. Did not want to wake up from this beautiful dream even if she was being chased by creeps and monsters half of the time."

Surprise flickered in Seth's eyes. "Why ever not?" Her mouth straightened into a disapproving line. "You don't like Colin?"

Her arms wrapped around her waist, her shoulders curving. "It's not that I don't like Colin." Amaryllis sighed before muttering, "I'm liking him too much."

"So, what's the problem?" Lines knitted Seth's brow.

"It's too soon."

"I see." Understanding replaced the confusion on Seth's face as she nodded.

"Do you, really?" Amaryllis inclined her head to one side.

Seth shrugged. "Time is immaterial when a Cynn Cruor warrior finds his mate. It can be a day or two. It can be weeks even months. Sometimes it takes just hours to know that they are meant for each other."

"No shit."

"Despite your sarcasm, that's how things are with the Cynn Cruors," Seth said, her mouth quirking. "And that bond lasts for eternity and beyond." She paused. "Have you spoken to Colin about this or has he?"

Amaryllis shook her head. "There doesn't seem to be time for us to talk at all. It's like duty, fight, fuck, duty, fight, fuck."

Seth laughed and Amaryllis' mouth tugged with mirth.

Seth mellowed. "That's the life of a Cynn Cruor warrior and his mate by extension." She inhaled and spoke in a breath. "It won't always be like that. It just so happens that Valerian has come out of the woodwork and the Cruor wars have ensued again."

"Who is this Valerian? Does he have anything to do with the monsters that came here?"

"Look at the tapestry outside. That's our story." Seth nudged her head towards the door.

"Seth, come on! It's not like I can decipher some of the figures there that look more like I'm reading hieroglyphics." Amaryllis rolled her eyes.

Seth giggled before sobering. Her eyes had a calculating gleam. "Me thinks there's more to you than you show people."

"Me thinks, you better start yapping," Amaryllis said drily.

Almost two hours later, Amaryllis stared at Seth, her mouth agape. Her mind swirled with the origins of the Cynn Cruors, the breakaway of Dac Valerian and the formation of the Scatha Cruors, the disappearance of the Scatha Cruor leader and his discovery by Eirene Spence of the Manchester Cynn Cruors. Seth told her about the siege of Dac's fortress that led to Colin and Craig joining the Manchester Cynn Cruors to the Honduras to look for the special silver that nearly killed another Cynn Cruor, Graeme Temple. Finally, Seth told her how the warriors found their mates and the importance of sex. Amaryllis looked down in bemusement at the pillow she hugged to her chest. She had not even realized she was hugging the fluffy contraption or that she was leaning against the headboard. If she could sink down into the mattress like a marshmallow floating in hot chocolate, she would. With all of the information now floating inside her head, she would not be surprised if she imploded.

"Wow..." she breathed. She straightened her legs. "Oh shit, shit, shit! Pins and needles!" Ants seemed to be crawling all over her calves, tickling her. "Seth!" she squealed, jerking her legs away. She tittered at the intensity of the sensations in her legs when Seth's hand made as though she was going to slap her legs. "Bloody fucking hell, don't!"

Seth pealed with laughter. Amaryllis did not know whether to give her friend a baleful glare or to chuckle. "Oh shit." Amaryllis sighed. "I feel like I've been branded."

"Oh God, don't even think that way!" Seth sounded affronted. "That means you're special."

"Yeah, a special fuck buddy." Amaryllis snorted.

Seth planted her hand on Amaryllis' thigh, causing her to grimace. "Amaryllis, you're not getting it. That is your connection to Colin. No woman he had in the past will have that sheen that coats your skin or the gold that enters your eyes."

"Why?"

"Because—"

"I'm his mate, I get it." Amaryllis leaned her head back against the headboard, gnawing on her lower lip. "What if he doesn't like me? What if I leave?"

"Answer to your first question, he's stupid if he lets you go. Answer to your second question, you're stupid if you let him go," Seth wisecracked, standing from the bed, causing the mattress to bounce a bit. "Besides, remember I said I might think of something to help you move away from your current occupation? I'm taking you under my wing to help me manage some of the Cynn Cruors clubs. The pay is phenomenal enough for you to put a down payment on your own place immediately."

"Really?" Hope surged through Amaryllis at Seth's pronouncement that she seemed out of breath. Her own place, something she could put her personal stamp on. Somewhere she could just stay put and not run away. Where she could have her own garden or a huge yard where she could put obstacles to continue her parkour training. And maybe a small patch in the corner for an herb garden.

"I can see that it appeals to you." Seth's mouth widened in amusement, her arms folded over her chest.

"Yes, it does," Amaryllis replied, a soft smile on her lips. She looked up. "Does it have to be here? The club, I mean? Do you know of any other place outside of Leeds?"

The smile was wiped out of Seth's annoyed face. She huffed. "Now why do you want to do that when you know that Colin is here in Leeds?"

Mate or no mate, how could Amaryllis tell her she did not know herself? When she was with Colin, the sex was so intense that she could be burned alive, willing to be reduced to ashes. Then what next? She squirmed, her belly clenching at the delicious memory. No, she needed space. Needed time away from all of this, a world she was thrown into which she never thought existed.

"Ugh! Both of you." Seth pointed to her and the space beside Amaryllis as though Colin was there. "You're both a pain in the arse. So bloody stubborn."

"I have my reasons." Amaryllis cringed.

"Yeah, whatever." Seth sighed. Her scowl disappeared. The wistfulness Amaryllis saw earlier returned, making Seth look worn out. "You have something special going on, Hart. Don't let go of it. It's very rare to have a connection like you and Colin have, like two moths dancing around a flame, never far apart, and willing to be burned knowing that the other will always be there. Because if you let go…" Seth's voice cracked. "Okaaay! I have to go."

Seth was out the door before Amaryllis could ask what she meant.

Amaryllis groaned into the pillow. To stay or not to stay. Colin scared her, excited her, made her feel things that were so alien and so addictive. Every breath she took against Colin's mouth even when they did not kiss was like an invisible drug she could feel immediately lighting her up inside. Bloody hell, Colin just had to look at her with those eyes that promised a carnal Eden she would not want to leave.

But was what she had with Colin enough for her to stay?

* * *

"What do we have, Liam?" Colin asked as the glass doors whooshed at his entrance. There was work to do and he needed to concentrate on keeping the Faesten as well as the rest of the Cynn Cruors safe.

"We have guests." Liam manipulated a few controls, enlarging the camera feed onto the LCD.

"Bloody hell…" Colin looked at the feed in stunned amazement at the man he saw. "Blake?"

"Butler, you there?" Blake Strachan growled.

"Deactivate the wall and open the gate," Colin ordered Liam before rushing out the Faesten, Craig and Cormac not far behind.

"Blake." Colin walked to him and encompassed him in a man-hug, ecstatic to see him. "Good to see you, mate. Where the bloody hell have you been? I've not seen you since you visited Graeme. Manchester'll be happy to see you, that is if they recognise you under all that facial hair and curly top."

Blake smiled before raking his fingers through his thick and curly hair almost self-consciously, chuckling. He gave Craig a man-hug, slapping him on the back. "Craig."

"Strachan." Craig cracked a pleased grin. "Been a long time. I'll make sure one of the guest rooms is prepared."

"I'm not staying," he said with rueful apology. "I

just had to bring someone here."

Colin frowned. He did not see anyone with Blake. "Who?"

"Hello, Butler."

Colin stiffened. His gaze turned to Blake. "Nice touch using our cloaking ability." *What now?* He scowled. His jaw tightened in anger. He did not know if he could forgive Mackenzie's attack on the Faesten the night before. "You two know each other?"

"I was watching the Scatha's lair when I saw him." Blake volunteered, hands on hips.

"What the hell were you doing near a lair when you didn't have backup?" Colin asked angrily. "You're my responsibility if you're in Leeds, Strachan. You're any Dux's responsibility if you're in their area. You know that's part of our code." He swore under his breath. "Roarke is going to have my hide for this."

Blake scowled. "I wouldn't have been if I didn't show up, Butler, now ease up a bit. What I do with my time away from Manchester is none of your business." He straightened to his full height, nearly as tall and as bulky as both Leeds Cynn Cruors.

"Blake—" Colin balled his hands into fists to control his temper. He swallowed. His only responsibility was to keep a Cynn Cruor safe. Blake was not part of the Leeds Faesten and therefore he could not order him to keep within the Faesten's walls. "Have a care and don't give me any white hair. Need backup? Call."

Blake grunted as though it did not matter before turning to the man slightly behind him. "I need some adriserum too if you have any to spare. Cloaking can be a pain. I know he's a Scatha Cruor, but you think Liam can check on his wounds? He nearly got pureed and decapitated if I didn't intervene."

Cormac moved like the wind and returned with a dose of adriserum. Blake gratefully reached for it and nodded his thanks. He rolled his sleeve back down, closing his eyes momentarily as the serum started doing its job.

"Why the hell would you do that?" Craig eyed Blake and Mackenzie warily. "Have a soft spot for them lately?"

Mackenzie stiffened, but he did not say a word.

"The original Scatha Cruors were once Cynn Cruors, Shaw." He inclined his head at Mackenzie. "And because he's got Cynn Cruor blood written all over him," Blake replied quietly, his eyes steely. "If they can be brought back, why can't we try?"

"You don't know what you're saying, bro'." Craig shook his head, looking away.

"Believe me, I do." Blake's hard look made Craig fidget where he stood.

"I have to agree with Shaw here," Mackenzie butted in, entering the sphere of light that spilled from the open door of the Faesten and from the carport making the earth glow in amber. "You see, we haven't been properly introduced." He took his hand away from his wounds that had already subsided to red welts across his abdomen, and offered his bloodied hand to Blake. His mouth widened, his grin evil. "Max Green."

"You already told me your name." Blake looked at his hand, askance, automatically stepping back.

Max hooted. "But you don't know my real name, do you, Blake? Shh…it's a deep dark secret, you see. No one must know." His eyes rounded, feigning innocence before they crinkled with evil. "It's Mackenzie Butler. Younger brother of Colin Butler, Leeds Cynn Cruors' Dux. And to top it all off, what an irony it is that I'm the head of the Scatha here in Leeds…well, until before tonight."

"Mackenzie...?" Shocked, Blake looked from Mackenzie to Colin, whose stance had dipped but still had his narrowed gaze at his brother. "I thought you were dead. Colin, I thought your brother was dead. You mourned him after you returned from the Crimea. We all did."

"Aye, that we did." Colin raked his hand wearily through his short cropped hair before dry rubbing his face, his hand moving back and forth the five o'clock shadow that covered his jaw.

"I am." Mack shrugged. "Dead to the Cynn Cruors and maybe in a few hours' time, dead to the Scatha Cruors too."

"What do you mean you're dead to the Scatha?" Colin demanded. "You should be lauded for finding out where we are. You told them where the Faesten was and we were attacked last night. Why would they want to kill you?"

"I didn't tell them where the Faesten was! I was in Hull." Mack's eyes began to morph. "That's all you believe. Both of you." He pointed accusingly at his brother and at Craig. "You always think I'm the one to blame. A human told my brethren about the Faesten. Jack Crawley, before he died." Suddenly, he cackled. "Looks like the Cynn Cruors are fallible after all. What happened? Couldn't wipe their memories like you used to? Whoever was responsible for that is a decrepit hack."

"Right." Colin turned away, but he was beginning to think how they could have faltered. Craig immediately stepped in front of Colin, his attention on Mackenzie.

"I didn't," Mack roared. His breathing came hard and fast, his face hardening as though he was finding it difficult to keep his inevitable transformation at bay. But it was a losing battle. His face contorted as his jowls distended.

Colin's chest squeezed so hard he thought he would lose whatever air was inside his lungs, but it did not matter. His chest cavity was huge enough for him not to breathe at all for several minutes. What mattered was that in the split second before Mack's eyes completely transformed, he saw his brother again. Saw the internal battle Mack waged. Saw the anguish that had carved itself a place inside his mind and would remain there.

For one moment, Colin Butler saw his youthful brother, who always looked up to him. Who wanted to measure up to him. Measure up to the Cynn Cruors. And that was why Mackenzie had followed Colin on to the battlefield in Balaclava, Sevastopol, Russia. Unbeknown to the human soldiers, after the Russians withdrew, the battle between the Cruors continued during the night after the dead had been collected and the humans had retreated. Colin, Craig, Liam, and Cormac, who were part of the Sutherland Highlanders 93rd Regiment, were about to be killed by the Scatha Cruors, a motley crew of both British and Russian soldiers. Mackenzie had hacked his way through using the Leeds Cynn Cruors' push daggers he held in both hands as he deftly decapitated several Scathas. That had been his forte, much like Cormac who was in his element when fighting in narrow spaces. Colin bellowed at Mackenzie, pushing his way through the ashes that scattered around him to get to him, but it was too late. Mackenzie had not seen the Scatha that came from behind. Mackenzie fell to the ground with a roar as Scatha claws from all sides embedded deep into his body. Colin could still hear the Mack's tortured cries in his mind. He had screamed his torment at seeing his brother fall and dragged away by two more. At that moment the Scatha deluged them and Colin believed that he was going to die had it not been for Liam and Cormac finally reaching them having disposed of the Scatha several meters away. They had found Mackenzie's body not too long after, his throat slashed, dead eyes unseeing through half closed lids. They brought him to their camp, preparing his body to be taken with them back to England but when morning came Mackenzie's body was gone. The Leeds Cynn Cruors scoured the area, eager for another skirmish with the Scatha but the next time they had found a group of their enemy, Mackenzie had become a part of them. The shock at seeing his brother was enough for Mackenzie to launch himself at Colin and stab him with his newly acquired claws. Colin roared but not from the physical wounds inflicted on him, but because of the gaping hole Mackenzie carved into his heart.

"This is your doing, brother," Mackenzie had hissed into Colin's ear. *"Because you didn't save me I have become one whom you must kill."*

Then Mackenzie disappeared only to resurface in the last few days.

"Believe what you want to believe," Mackenzie snapped, bringing Colin back to the present. "I came here to warn you that the Scatha are coming and Dac Valerian is with them." He pivoted, zooming into the darkness.

"Mackenzie!" Blake shouted and Mack stopped. He glared at Colin. "He's telling the truth, man. That's rare for a Scatha."

"Why is it so easy for you to believe him?" Craig's gaze darted at the figure that looked unsure whether he would wait for Blake or not.

"Because I was there. I saw Herod come out of the lair and that means Dac isn't far behind." Blake seethed.

"I don't know what went down between you and your brother, but now's not the time for fucking family reunions. I'm hoping that the one taking the war here is a moron and it will take longer for them to latch on to the Faesten's coordinates. So if you both just took out your heads out of your cracks, you'd start gearing up."

"You staying to fight with us?" Colin asked.

"Just because I help one Scatha who's more a Cynn Cruor doesn't mean I won't kill the rest." Blake's mouth twitched before sobering. "First, I need to tend to your brother if you can't tend to him." He jogged away. "Mack, wait."

Colin sucked in his breath, Blake's words as sharp as a Scatha's claws going for the beating muscle inside his chest.

"Should have straightened Strachan out," Craig hissed angrily. "That was unfair."

Colin shook his head. "He's right, Craig. If I made sure he stayed put, he wouldn't have been turned."

"We were in the middle of the fucking Crimean war!"

"It didn't matter," Colin said. "My brother was my responsibility." He switched to telepathic mode. *Liam, bring up the shields. Cormac, alert the mortals. The Scatha Cruors are coming.* He turned his attention to Craig. "I need to get to Amaryllis. Let's hope Blake is correct and time is on our side."

Chapter Twenty-Four

The door to Amaryllis' room banged open, causing her to jump up from the bed. Heart racing at the interruption of a daydream in the evening, the person that filled her every thought strode towards her.

"Heavens, Colin. There should really be a rule about people entering other people's rooms." Amaryllis did not know whom she should be angry with, Colin or her breathless voice.

Colin smirked. "If I was going to make another rule, no one but me can enter your room, Violet." He pulled her towards him and Amaryllis' breath hitched. Disappointment followed at the heels of her excitement when Colin bent down only to brush his nose against hers. Her mouth straightened in frustration. He chuckled. "If I kissed you now, babe, we'll never get to leave this room."

Her body awakened, her skin heating up beneath his hands that skimmed her waist before cupping her ass and squeezing it, bringing her closer to the proof of his lust. Colin bent his head down and Amaryllis closed her eyes as his mouth and slight stubble grazed the sensitive spot just below her ear, her throat, and she moaned softly when his tongue licked the pulse at the base of her throat before sucking it. She encircled his neck to bring him closer, needing him to kiss her. Suddenly, the air between them shifted, changed, and Colin embraced her so tightly Amaryllis could not breathe. She noticed the tinge of desperation in the way he held her, the way he smoothed her hair, kissed her temple, her cheeks, her eyelids. Except her mouth.

"Colin? What's wrong?"

But Colin kept caressing her, his hands roaming all over her body, his breath fanning her skin and she could not help but follow where his mouth moved. It was like a cat and mouse game. Mouths evading, yet chasing. Breathing each other's air as though it was the only source of oxygen.

"Colin...you're scaring the shit out of me." She held on to him. Oh God, was this goodbye? Was this how he was going to dump her? Was that the reason why he refused to kiss her? The thought of Colin leaving her stabbed through her, the pain starting as an ache incomparable with anything physical she had ever known, blooming outward from her heart. She swallowed against the ache. Suddenly, she could not breathe. The shock of this new reality numbed her. She pushed against his chest. He did not budge. She pushed harder.

"You know you belong to me, don't you?" he whispered against her temple.

"You have a bloody ugly way of showing it," she bit out. She pushed again.

"No, Amaryllis."

"Let me go, Butler."

"I'm not letting you go," he said firmly. His hands cupped her face. "Look at me."

She kept her eyes lowered. *Fuck it, don't fucking cry!* No way was he going to see how much he had hurt her.

"Please, Amaryllis." He rubbed his thumb against her lower lip and her mouth parted.

Amaryllis hated her traitorous body. She hated her betraying eyes when she closed them and tears slipped through the shut lids. She heard Colin sigh, an exhalation of breath that fanned the anguish growing inside her chest. She felt him move closer, felt his breath again only centimetres from her mouth. If this was the only thing he would give her, air to breathe which was not even enough for her to move on, she would take it. It did not matter if he said that he would not let her go. His actions were just the opposite of what he had said. So when he brushed his lips against hers, her eyes opened in surprise. A butterfly of a kiss, fleeting, tentative. He raised his head, his green eyes deepening, the sides crinkling slightly. Amaryllis' heart was in a turmoil, her pulse beating erratically in both pain and hope. With a groan, Colin took her mouth in a searing kiss, sweeping inside and claiming her completely. She opened up to him, holding him close while tears coursed down the sides of her face. She sucked on his lips, tasting him, a hint of scotch, of mint, all Colin Butler. Her arms snaked around his neck, drawing him as close as she could get him. Heart and blood thundering in her ears, she nipped at his lips, moaning when he sucked on hers. Their heads slanted against each other, trying to get as much as they could, making up for the lost moments when they could have kissed each other's doubts away. He groaned when she sucked his tongue into her mouth. He lifted her. She hooked her legs around his waist and rubbed her opening against his denim covered erection. Her nether lips throbbed, her vaginal walls clenched, seeking Colin, desperate for their joint release.

"Colin," she said between kisses, through heated breaths.

She did not need to beg any further. In one swift move, she was dumped back on the bed, her new but already soaked lace thong torn from her. Colin undid his jeans, dropped them and leaned forward. He hooked her legs over his arms and thrust deep into her liquid heat, groaning as she cried out, her back arching at the pleasure and pain of his claiming. Amaryllis' body was on fire, a flame so all-consuming and fanned by the urgent and hard thrusts of Colin's cock. He grabbed her wrists and roughly placed them above her head. The bed creaked mercilessly, their combined breaths and erotic sounds coming from their throats propelling them higher. Amaryllis clenched against Colin's lengthening and hardening cock, her orgasm building around the hardness pounding into her, her whimpers increasing every time she felt his tip deep inside her. She loved the feel of him entering her up to the root. His sac slapped against her upturned thighs, his hips thrusting hard and fast. He let go of her wrists and he spread her legs wide as he continued to fuck her.

"Damn, Amaryllis. I love the way your pussy swallows my cock. You fuck good." Colin's breath was ragged, and he threw his head back, his eyes rolling as his lids closed.

"Colin..." With his body above her, all Amaryllis could do was to fist the sheets. She whimpered. "More!"

Colin's breath came hard and fast. Amaryllis watched the sheer pleasure and lust in his face, the gold flecks that dominated his eyes, feeling her own impending release surging through her, taking her higher and higher, giving her wings to reach the sun.

"Colin, I'm going to..." She didn't finish the sentence as her climax ripped through her, robbing her of thought and time. Something inside her grew. A notion, a gut feeling to bite Colin because it was the right thing to do. Instinctively, she opened her mouth and her gums moved. She whimpered when her incisors inched their way out, elongating against her mouth. It was itchy. It was painful. The urge to sink her teeth overwhelming. Excitement instead of fear, bemusement instead of terror filled her. "Colin?"

His gold flecked eyes latched on to hers, looking at

her in wonder. He slowed down.

"Don't stop," Amaryllis whispered. Her eyesight blurred as though something entered her lids, causing her to blink several times to clear the offending particles. Was that the gold colour entering her sight? Her heart soared when she saw Colin smile. He tore at his shirt, the buttons flying and landing on the floor like hail before he held himself on his arms above her. His body rippled with muscle, his hard abs flexing with every push into her.

"Amaryllis…"

He thrust. She moaned, her eyes rolling before her lids closed.

"I don't want you to go," he said softly, his voice a deep velvet cloaking her entire body.

"Don't let me," she whispered. "Don't leave me, Colin. Please don't leave me."

"I won't." Colin leaned forward on his elbows as he slowed his thrusts, his cock teasing her inside with every undulation of his hips against her. "I can't, Violet. You've completely captivated me. You leave and I will just be a shell of the man I used to be before I met you."

He surged into her and stopped before flexing several times inside her. Amaryllis arched against him, ecstasy building inside her.

"Then take me completely, Colin. Take me. Make me yours," she said, her breath shortening, coming in gasps of pleasure.

Colin did not need further prodding. As though he had not slowed down, his hips moved fast, his cock slick with her sex juices banging in and out of her, feeding her lust, fuelling her desire, her climax coiling in the area of her pelvis, her quim begging for release.

With the next thrust, Amaryllis cried and rose up, snaking her arms around Colin's back before sinking her teeth by the side of Colin's heart. And her mind exploded both with the most intense orgasm she had ever had in her entire life joined with the taste of Colin's blood against her mouth. She trembled uncontrollably, but she still held on to the man above her. Her throat opened as she swallowed greedily, every swallow intensifying her climax. There was no gagging reflex at the thought of drinking human blood. A burst of sweetness filled her mouth not the coppery taste associated with it. Her pussy clenched around Colin and with a guttural shout he came, his seed flooding her channel once more, warming her, claiming her as his own to her immense contentment. Fresh tears formed in her eyes when Colin's life streamed through her consciousness. She saw the death of his father, the loss of his mother, the bewildered look of Mackenzie, and Colin's grief while Craig stood stoically to one side of their old home, allowing them to mourn. She saw the kaleidoscope of death that befell the Cynn Cruors in the hands of the Scatha, the constant training, the dangerous missions Colin and Craig went to. She saw and felt Colin's anguish when Mackenzie transformed, the heartbreak of a brother losing the only family he had to the very race he vowed to annihilate. Amaryllis felt her gums around her fangs open and an unbroken stream of her own blood gushed forth into the puncture wounds by Colin's heart. He groaned, his arms nearly buckling as he leaned forward to accept Amaryllis' blood. In Amaryllis' mind, she saw Colin's heart grow in size, her blood pumping into it, nourishing it, watching it distribute her own life force through Colin's veins, strengthening every muscle and sinew. And when she felt that what she gave was enough, her fangs detracted from Colin's chest, receding into her mouth and returning to normal incisors. Amaryllis licked at the puncture wounds and watched in fascination through half lidded eyes as the wounds closed, securing her blood inside Colin's body. She fell back on the bed, her legs spread beside Colin, who lay on top of her, their hearts still racing, their chests heaving as they took huge gulps of air. Colin raised himself on one elbow while his other hand ripped his shirt from her body. Amaryllis shuddered at the cool air that skittered over her heated skin and her pussy clenched once more around Colin when his mouth took one nipple, sucking and playing with it. She held his head to her breast, her hips moving against his when his tongue flicked fast against her tight bud, bringing lust rushing down into her core, inflaming her.

"This might hurt a little, my sweet." Colin's hand caressed the under swell of her breast before holding her back to lift her.

"What will? Oh…" When she opened her eyes, Colin's irises were nearly dominated by the gold flecks and in his mouth were razor sharp fangs. Amaryllis tentatively touched one fang and purred when Colin's cock flexed inside her. "Damn, I don't mind touching them if your cock keeps twitching inside me." Colin chuckled. "Mmmm…that too," she purred, smiling. She watched his desire swirl in his eyes and the strain of waiting corded his neck. She beamed when she cupped his face and he leaned into her palm to kiss it. "I believe it's your turn to bite me?"

With a chaste kiss against the inside of her wrist that made her pulse flip flop, Colin nodded, his golden gaze slightly curious. "Doesn't my transformation frighten you?"

"No," she replied softly. "It doesn't." She caressed his face, raising her lips to his in a sweet kiss. "Make me yours, Colin," she said against his mouth. "For always or for as long as we can possibly be. Or I'll keep haunting you wherever you go."

His laugh cracked through the room. He reached behind her back and lifted her against his mouth. "Granted."

Before she could catch her breath, Colin sank his fangs against the side of her left breast. She gripped his shoulders hard as a fiery pain pierced her skin, making her cry out and pant for breath. She trembled underneath him, her body straining, her senses centring on the agony of his fangs in her. And then the pain was gone. Amaryllis felt the bed once again behind her back, Colin's mouth latched on the side of her breast. He started to suck blood from her. Every pull was an erotic signal down to her pussy. The more he drew blood from her, the more her quim contracted around him, causing him to growl low against her. A sensation so in tandem with each other that Amaryllis had no other choice but give in to the exquisite way she was being pleasured. Colin's hand moved again, his rigid cock hardening more inside her, his hips moving faster. She was curled in a position that should have been uncomfortable, but she did not care. Delight danced at the languid beat trickling up and down her spine and she gasped when she felt Colin's fingers on her clit, rolling it and spreading her juices against the sensitive nub. Despite the quick fast thrusts of Colin's cock inside her, his fingers on her clit more than compensated in adding to her growing climax. Her pleasure built when his fingers and his cock rocked her sanity, the intense desire combined with Colin drinking her blood made her arch her back and scream. Her body shook with the force of her orgasm even as Colin groaned his release and fed his blood into her heart. She flopped back on the mattress like a satiated rag doll, floating in a sea of bliss while

Colin continued pushing his blood into her. Her limp hand caressed his hair, his sweat and heat rising from the beach blond tendrils, entering her system through her nose. Her lips parted in surrender as her body allowed his essence to cover her completely, feeling a renewed strength inside her that made her feel she could do anything. She groaned when Colin's fangs detracted, anticipating the harsh pain, but there was none. She hummed softly when he licked the punctures closed. When he eased out of her, a wave of loss filled her and there it was again. The sensation that Colin had taken a piece of her with him. She had felt it then as she felt it now. She had been intrinsically linked to Colin all that time. Once she accepted the fact that she belonged to him and no one else would have a hold on his immortal heart, she felt a peace that settled deep into her bones.

Amaryllis.

Her eyes snapped open. She looked at Colin, who was beside her, his head propped on his hand as he looked down on her. The gold flecks in his deep green coloured eyes reminiscent of the sun twinkling through the trees.

"What's with the smirk?" She arched her brow.

Can you hear me in your mind?

"Oh shit!" She vaulted to sit on the bed, gasping in amazement at how swiftly she was able to do so. "Colin?"

"Shhh...Violet." He sat up and opened his arms. Immediately she entered them. "I didn't mean to frighten you."

"I'm not frightened." She swallowed.

He chuckled. "Yes, you are. I should have told you but bloody hell, Amaryllis. When I am near you all I want to do is keep you inside my room, your room, and fuck you hard until you can't walk."

The throbbing between her thighs beat up a notch.

Not now, pussy. I need to know more about this world I've entered into.

A deep rumbling laugh left his chest. "Yes, you do."

She made a half-hearted attempt to thump his muscled chest. Like that was going to make a dent. "I forgot you could read my mind."

"And now you can read mine." He kissed her hair, caressing the dishevelled tresses coursing down her back.

She pulled away. "I can?"

Try. And you can speak to me through your mind too.

She gasped, her eyes searching his, her wonder growing in increments. *Colin?*

Colin gave her a lopsided grin. "So a thief, huh?"

Amaryllis' smile faltered. "Does it matter?" She searched his eyes, afraid of what she might see. "If I'm a thief?"

"It all makes sense."

Her brows knitted. "What does?"

"You being a thief. You knew how to steal my heart."

The smile he gave her burst through her, brightening the dark recesses of her soul. Those pockets of doubt that egged her to believe that she was not worth cherishing were replaced by slivers of light coming through a disintegrating wall. Her teeth clamped down hard on her lower lip to try to stop them from trembling.

You are worth cherishing, Amaryllis Hart. Anyone who says otherwise is the fool's fool. Anyone who tells you that after today, I'll sock in the face.

Full blown laughter spewed from her. She threw herself at him and true to his word, he caught her when she fell into his arms. Her heart wanted to burst with happiness, yet there was still the tiniest weed at the back of her mind that refused to budge no matter how much she pulled. She mentally flipped her finger at it because she knew one thing. Everything would be all right from hereon after. The thought of being by Colin's side brought a smile to her lips. Yes, she would be by his side. She was his as he was hers. He was her home, her haven, her midnight immortal warrior who would protect her always. Who would be with her wherever she went. Who would keep her safe for as long as they were alive.

There was no reason for Amaryllis Hart to run away anymore.

"Colin?"

"Hmmm...?"

She trailed her fingers up and down his chest and abdomen, a puff of soft laughter coming from her when Colin's skin shivered underneath her touch. The sheen she and Seth talked about was more solid, covering Colin and herself.

"Seth told me...ow!" Amaryllis slapped her hands over her ears, rolling away from Colin. "What the hell is that noise?"

He bounded up to put on his denims, his chest bare. The immortal who made love to her, replaced by the warrior who killed his enemy without remorse. "We need to suit up, Amaryllis."

"Suit up?" Her grimace did not leave her face as she stood. "What is that infernal noise? By the time I leave this room, I'll be deaf."

Colin rushed to her side and gave her a heart thumping and toe curling kiss. Amaryllis had to hold on to his shoulders for dear life.

"That's the bat signal," he said between nips, licks, and gentle sucks of her lips.

"Don't tell me you're Batman too." She sighed.

Colin chuckled. "Being part vampire and part werewolf is enough. No human would have heard that silent alarm, Violet. You heard that because you have my blood inside you." With one last hard kiss he strode to the door. "Seth will come to help you suit up."

"You keep saying to suit up. Why can't I use just jeans and a shirt?"

Colin's eyes tightened. "Mackenzie has come back and so have the Scatha Cruors."

Chapter Twenty-Five

When Seth returned to Amaryllis' room, she was wearing a dark grey body hugging suit not too different from that of a diver's suit. She gave Amaryllis one and asked her to wear it.

"It's an amorphic aramid material that will protect you from bullets and even a sword swipe. If you do get hit by a sword it's going to hurt like anything but with this suit, you'll only get a nasty bruise," Seth had said while Amaryllis dressed. "It's time you wore one. You're now Colin's mate."

As Amaryllis entered the command centre she could not stop gaping at the expanse of the place. If Armageddon happened that day, the centre would be the safest place to be in. A bar and a comfortable set of sofas were to her left. A long softly illuminated corridor was just off by the bar, leading to the restrooms. Another sign beyond said 'Quarters' leading Amaryllis to think that that was where the warriors and mortals stayed if they pulled in long shifts. What looked like a small armoury hidden behind a wall of glass was to her right and her eyes rounded at the impressive display of weapons that appeared to have been collected through the centuries. In front was a huge LED screen which had several camera feeds of the Faesten's surroundings and outside the walls. Above the screen was a heraldic crest that reminded Amaryllis of long forgotten knights fighting all over the British Isles. A griffin and wolf faced each other on either side of the crest on a background of dark blue. Between them was a spiked battle mace crossed over a double ball flail and underneath it were two crisscrossing oak leaves like hands cradling the animals and weapons above it.

All of the men wore the same dark grey suit Amaryllis wore, the material wrapped around their muscular bodies, the crest emblazoned on the upper left arm, but only one drew Amaryllis' eyes. Her breath came out in a sigh while she appreciated every muscular contour of the warrior she had fallen for. From his wide shoulders to his narrow waist down to his firm ass and muscled thighs. The sight alone was a gastro-erotic delight. She watched as he gave instructions quietly to Liam but with authority that brooked no argument.

Craig was inside the armoury, strapping several weapons on his body and so was Cormac. Amaryllis noted that Seth was looking at their direction.

"Will you be all right here?" Seth asked absently, her gaze pinned on the weapons area. "I need to get the mortals in place."

"She'll be fine." Colin had a predatory glint in his eye as he approached them. Amaryllis beamed at his cynosure, her heart jackhammering inside her. Taking her by surprise, Colin hooked his arm around her waist and drew her for his kiss. Amaryllis willingly opened, welcoming his plundering tongue, savouring his taste, and melting in his arms. Her arms went around his neck and she moaned as she drew him to her.

"Oh, yes, she will," Seth remarked dryly, shaking her head as she left them, the glass doors closing softly behind her.

"I'm making the most of this because I don't know when I'll get another chance to kiss you again," Colin said between kisses.

"Don't say that." Amaryllis objected in a whisper. Oh God, the feelings that ran riot inside her wanted to burst forth. She felt like she was facing the sun in Colin's embrace. Warm, fiery, all consuming. "As soon as this kick ass session is over, I want to go away with you. That is if duty allows."

Colin raised his head, the warmth of his gaze adding to the love already in Amaryllis' heart. He caressed her cheek with his knuckles.

"It will. I'll make it so," he said before a brief shadow passed through his face.

Colin, is something wrong? She gasped in surprise. *Wow, I didn't think it would be so easy.*

You're a natural. Colin grinned.

There's something wrong.

He opened his mouth.

Don't deny it.

"I wasn't going to," he murmured.

"Dux, we've got company." Liam's fingers flew over the keyboard.

"Friend or foe?" Colin's gaze never left hers.

"Friend." The voice shimmered. Colin's head snapped up, the interruption breaking their embrace, but he kept his fingers entwined with Amaryllis'. Everyone stared at the corner of the room by the armoury's door where Luke materialised. He wore the same body armour in black with a sword strapped to his back, but he did not have any crest. He sauntered to Colin and Amaryllis. "I thought you might need help."

Colin exhaled harshly. "Hamilton—"

"Don't blame Roarke, Colin," Luke said sternly. "This was my call."

"So you calling the shots now?" Craig mocked as he walked to Colin's side as he inserted a magazine clip into the Sig Sauer he held. "Mighty big of him."

"Roarke and Deanna are in Scotland visiting The Hamilton," Luke said evenly then he spoke to Liam. "Care to open the gates for Finn and Graeme? I felt I needed some backup."

"Why are you meddling in our affairs, Griffiths? You're not even one of us." Craig sneered.

Amaryllis saw hurt fleet through Luke's face before it disappeared and his face hardened. "You're right. I'm not." He looked at Colin. "But if what has happened here is anything to go by, the Scatha will return and you'll need as many warriors on your side."

"Why?" Colin's features were guarded.

"I know your brother is alive," Luke's gaze was steady, "and that he's a Scatha Cruor."

"The hell!" Cormac moved with such speed even Luke did not anticipate himself getting slammed against the wall, wincing as the sword on his back imprinted itself against his body. "What the fuck's wrong with you?"

"Me?" Luke pushed back, growling. "What about all of you? Hiding this from the Ancients!"

Cormac pulled away, his face a mask of anger. Liam's silver eyes bored disapprovingly at Luke. Neither of them spoke.

Amaryllis' chest tightened as she looked up at Colin. She nearly winced when she felt his fingers squeeze her own.

Colin, your grip is too tight.

Colin stared at her as though he did not recognise her before his grip relaxed and remorse pinched his features.

"It's okay. I'm here," Amaryllis said softly. "I'll never leave you."

"How did you find out?" Colin turned his attention back to Luke.

"The Archives," Luke replied. "When I was researching my origins." His mouth lifted in a semblance of a smile. "I went through all of the documents on the bloodlines, yours included. I thought maybe we could even be related." He expelled a long drawn out breath before he started to pace. "You don't know how frustrating it is not to find any trace of where you could have come from. I still can't find any trace of what made me a Cynn Cruor." He stopped. "A lot of us noticed something was wrong with you, Butler. Roarke, Finn, and Graeme said that you were not yourself in La Nahuaterique."

Luke sat down on the couch. The Leeds Cynn Cruors and Amaryllis remained standing.

"I decided to find out why. So sue me," he quipped. "Roarke was angry when I decided to interfere. He said that it encroached on your ability and leadership as Dux."

"He's right," Colin said, his voice devoid of emotion.

"Well, call it my training as a spook." Luke hitched his shoulders. "But when something doesn't feel right, it just doesn't feel right. While looking through your history, I saw a painting of both you and your brother, Mackenzie. It was reported that he died in the Crimea." His eyes bored into Colin's. "A few days ago, I saw the very same person with the Scatha Cruors."

"He could have been anyone," Craig spoke.

"Then tell me that it wasn't Mackenzie Butler I saw, Shaw." Luke challenged as he stood up. "Look me in the eye and tell me that Scatha wasn't Colin's brother and I'll back away."

A muscle ticked in Craig's jaw.

"I thought so," Luke said quietly. His voice held no reproach, only understanding. "Please, you have to believe me when I say that I will never interfere unless I feel it's necessary. You'll need me to shift from one place to the other without the Scatha knowing. You need me to help defend the Faesten."

The leather creaked as Colin sat down, his head in his hands. Amaryllis felt the sudden loss when he let go of her hand, the still air as cold as the arctic wind between them. A connection so harshly severed.

"Colin, don't, please," Amaryllis begged in hushed tones as she sat beside him. With a wan smile he kept her to his side.

"Why didn't you tell them?" Trouble creased Luke's features. "The Ancients? If you didn't want the Ancients, then Roarke? Finn?"

Colin barked with bitter laughter. "You fucking kidding me? Roarke is The Hamilton's son. The Hamilton is the most trusted adviser of the Ancients. They'd swoop down here and take Mack without another thought. And Finn." Colin rubbed his neck. "Man, if you saw him hack down the Scatha and the werewolves during the battle for the Silver cave…" He drew a breath. "I watched him nearly cut a werewolf in half before he seemed to stop himself and spared it."

"You forget Tommy, Kate's friend," Luke said kindly. "Manchester knew he was turned against his will."

"And Kate killed him, didn't she? She had no choice?" Colin asked on a breath, chuckling bitterly. "I made a promise I'd keep Mack safe. When he changed…"

Amaryllis felt the shudder that thrummed through the man she loved. "My brother is a fucking Scatha, Luke! Our mandate is to kill as many of them as we can. The last time I saw Mack was in Sevastopol. He resurfaced only recently. All this time, I thought he was dead."

"We've been looking for him for a long time," Craig added grimly before his mouth twitched. "Mack was always very good at hiding."

"I was going to keep him locked up—"

"How could you?" Amaryllis gasped.

"Only until I could find a cure." Colin squeezed her hand in reassurance.

"Once a Scatha, always a Scatha. I doubt if there's any cure," Luke noted, his tone quiet.

"No, Mack didn't become one willingly. That doesn't count," Colin shot back. "I can still see the Cynn Cruor in him battling against the evil that's slowly eating him inside. He brought Amaryllis here and asked that we protect her against his brethren. His own Scatha brothers, Luke! No Scatha has ever done that."

"Betrayal is part of their code," Liam mused. "To betray one of their own to the Cynn Cruor? That is indeed unusual."

Colin leaned back on the couch. Amaryllis had never seen a man brought so low by his loyalty to his kindred. Her heart ached for him and all she wanted to do was to take his pain and make it hers. Her gut instinct told her that shit was about to hit the fan. She stubbornly brushed the thought away, refusing to let it take hold of her.

"Where is he now?"

"In the dungeon and he went there willingly. The Scatha are now after him as well," Colin's said flatly. "Blake Strachan is with him."

"Strachan?" Luke asked, disbelieving. "Him too?"

"No, he's still a Cynn Cruor," Craig answered. "But he's the one who could see Mackenzie Butler not Max Greene, when all of us had almost given up."

Luke squeezed his lower lip between his thumb and forefinger in contemplation.

"What's going on in that mind of yours?" Liam rose to his full height, nearly dwarfing everyone.

"He's another conundrum," Luke murmured. "How

did he get involved in all this? The last time I saw him was in the Manchester Faesten before he disappeared again. Roarke and the rest have no clue what's eating him."

"That's what I'd like to know too," Colin agreed. "He was staking out the Scathas' lair when he came across Mack being mauled by the Scatha."

"And he helped?" A crease formed above Luke's brow.

Colin nodded. "He did."

"Why?"

"Because there is still a lot of good in him," Blake replied, the door to the centre opening with a whisper. "Griffiths, still getting involved in other people's business, I see."

"Good to see you too, Blake." Luke grinned, clasping Blake's arm in the Cynn Cruor greeting. "We seem to bump into each other on the cusp of a battle or a fight."

"Coincidence, nothing more." Blake shrugged. He turned to Amaryllis, his lips forming into a warm smile. "I have no doubt you'll be very good for the Dux of the Leeds Cynn Cruor. I'm Blake Strachan."

"Amaryllis Hart." She shook his hand. "Thank you. So," she exhaled, pinning everyone with her gaze, "when do we start kicking ass?"

Blake's eyes twinkled merrily. "Eirene is going to like you. She's the Manchester Cynn Cruor's kick ass expert."

"You better suit up, Strachan." Colin nudged his chin at him as he and Amaryllis rose from the couch. "This might just be a mighty bloody fight."

"I'll be fine." Blake looked down at his denims, T-shirt, and plaid shirt he wore over it. "What I can do with is borrowing some daggers. You know how I like to get up close and personal with the Scatha I ash."

"Blake," Colin warned.

"I have your protection, I know, but force me to wear one and I walk." His dark eyes were like flint. "What will it be?"

"Manchester has arrived." Liam sat in front of the consoles, the gate's camera feed showing the headlights of a dark Range Rover bounding towards the gates. The gates slid open, allowing the vehicle into the compound. Amaryllis noticed Blake suddenly becoming subdued. Her mind was swirling. So many things were happening. It was like a make or break situation and she could not stop the helplessness suddenly rising up and threatening to swallow her whole. No, she had to be strong for Colin. She had to find a way to make things right.

Some tall order that was for a human.

She watched as more warriors alighted from the Ranger Rover. Men as muscular as Colin, Craig and Cormac, but not as huge as Liam. There was also another man, impressively dressed in blue and green trews and a white shirt. Wrapped around him was a huge tartan with the same blue and green colours as ancient trousers that followed the contours of his muscular thighs and legs. "Oh shit," Craig hissed. In one stride he was in Luke's face. "I thought you said Roarke was in Scotland."

Luke held his hands up defensively. "He is...was when I left Manchester."

"Man, we are so screwed." Cormac cast a baleful glare at Luke and Blake.

Amaryllis looked at all of them in bafflement. She noticed the genuine surprise in Luke's face and the stillness in Blake's frozen features. Blake, she thought, looked like he wanted to bolt. Suddenly, his eyes turned to her. He was afraid. Then it was gone. In place was a placid smile that left Amaryllis wondering whether she had just imagined it. She looked at Colin and he also looked apprehensive, yet with one huge breath he steeled and changed as though some invisible mantle of authority was now clipped on his shoulders. The sudden changes in the men from exposing her to their vulnerability to being the warriors that they were fascinated her. Extremes merged into one formidable being that could kill without mercy.

"Colin? Can you tell me what's going on?"

Instead Colin took her in his arms and embraced her. Panic trickled down her spine. Something was seriously wrong.

Babe...

Colin raised his head, his eyes sad yet there was a flicker of amusement. *Babe?*

Yes, babe. Amaryllis telepathed with a slight scowl. *What's happening? Why is the temp in this room suddenly colder than the Arctic?* She looked at the LED. *Those men, they're from Manchester, right? I thought you were good friends with them. Aren't they here to help?*

Colin nodded. *When all is said and done, Amaryllis, I don't know if that will still be the case.*

You're bloody scaring me, Butler. Spit it out in plain English. Why can't it be the case?

Colin looked at the screen. "Because that man with Roarke, Finn, and Graeme? The one wearing the tartan?"

"Yes."

"That's The Hamilton."

Chapter Twenty-Six

Colin met the Manchester contingent and The Hamilton in the foyer. Except for The Hamilton, all of them wore body armour as well. His face remained stoic but inside he was about to lose it. He refused to look at Amaryllis, refused to see the love burning in her eyes. For him.

All for him.

What good would it do now to have her for his mate? The moment he saw The Hamilton, he knew that his life was now forfeit. What irony that he was one of the best reconnaissance Cynn Cruor warriors, his tracking abilities sought by so many of Faestens around the world. Yet he could never find his own brother. Kindred and people a warrior loved caused them to be weak, unable to see the flaws, willing to forgive any indiscretions until it was too late. He knew the moment he lost Mackenzie, he could not allow himself to feel love or be loved by someone else.

Yet Amaryllis came traipsing, nay, free running into his life and into his heart. And soon he would leave the mortal realm in payment for his transgressions and his sins of omission.

"My Lord, this is an unexpected yet pleasurable surprise." Colin extended his arm and The Hamilton took it. Of the same muscular build as his son, The Hamilton's chiselled features broke into a warm smile. He looked no different in age as his son save for the few greys that wove through his dark mane he wore long to his shoulders, tied in a queue at his nape. The blues and greens of The Hamilton's tartan were draped and wrapped comfortably around his body with the handle of his long sword peeking out like a sentinel at his back. Where his son had silver blue eyes, The Hamilton's eyes were dark, almost midnight blue.

"Colin." He pulled Colin into a bear hug, slapping him hard at the back. When Colin oomphed, he gave a hearty laugh. "Back still weak, I see."

"Nay, my Lord, only not used to your man hugs after so many centuries." Colin coughed discreetly. "Roarke, heard you and Deanna visited Alba."

Roarke embraced Colin and slapped him on the back but not as hard as his father did. "Aye. Still a land of beauty."

Colin pulled away and nodded. "It's high time I visited. Been very busy here." He turned to the rest. "Finn. Graeme. Welcome."

They gave Colin man hugs as well, which made Colin chuckle. "I've never had as many hugs from my brethren in less than a minute than I have had now."

They all laughed.

"And who is this rare violet eyed beauty?" The Hamilton approached Amaryllis, who stood beside Colin. The Hamilton inhaled then beamed. "A fine Cynn Cruor mate, Butler. My Lady, I am The Hamilton."

Colin watched the blush creep up Amaryllis' neck to her cheeks, her eyes bright. Pride of having her to call his own, despite what may come, swelled inside him.

"Amaryllis Hart," she replied, her voice strong. "Damn, you're huge."

The Hamilton threw his head back and laughed.

"Sorry, my filter's not working." Amaryllis lowered her eyes, though Colin could see her trying to stop the smile from breaking.

"Dinnae worry, lass. I like ta see that Cynn Cruor warriors' mates can speak their own minds, within reason." The Hamilton beamed, raising his finger to a point. He turned around and offered his arm. "Ye must be Luke Griffiths. The Ancients speak verra highly of ye."

Luke took his arm, nodding respectfully. "A pleasure to meet you…"

"Och, *duine*." The Hamilton waved his other hand, addressing Luke with the word for man in Gaelic. "Hamilton will suffice. You are welcome ta take your search ta Scotland, to Hamel Dun Uiamh. Maybe you will find your answers there. As long as I ken you will be there."

"Thank you."

"Amaryllis, my name is Roarke. And mister spiky hair here is Finn Qualtrough and the old man over there is Graeme Temple."

"Finn, Graeme." Amaryllis extended her hand. "Why do they call you old? You don't look like someone over thirty-five."

The men snorted.

"That's because he was born long before the First Crusade started," Finn replied dryly.

Amaryllis' eyes became huge. "Seriously?"

Graeme's mouth twitched. "I'm afraid so." Then his smile became happier when his gaze alighted on another warrior. "Blake?"

"Hello, Temple. Finn, Dux." Blake's face broke into a smile.

Graeme barrelled his way through. "Bloody hell, mate! Where in Ancients have you been?"

"Long story but can't tell you right now." Blake exhaled. "Suffice to say, I will be here for the duration of whatever's about to come down."

Colin saw The Hamilton's smile falter for a split second when he saw Blake, but he had no time to understand why when the huge Scot strode to Blake.

Graeme just stepped out of the way just in time before The Hamilton gripped Blake's shoulders and pulled him into his arms.

"It's verra good ta see ye, Strachan," he said quietly. "Verra good indeed."

Blake nearly stumbled when The Hamilton, his smile taut, pushed him away from his fold. "Are ye well, lad? The world treating ye as it should even without us?"

"Aye, my Lord. It is." Blake nodded and for once, Colin saw Blake as the young boy Finn had fetched from Edinburgh after his mother's burial. All of them had trained under The Hamilton, all of them in awe at the immortal Scot's presence. No one felt that keenly than Blake. Colin saw the light in Blake's eyes slowly dim as though he grappled with secrets of his own.

"Aye, right!" The Hamilton's voice boomed. If anyone noticed how his voice choked they kept silent. Only their furtive glances at each other like young boys keeping a secret showed their perplexity at The Hamilton's show of emotion. "Butler, I have never left Alba and I'm in dire need ta taste its waters." Then his eyes hardened. "If I am to help ye, level with me. That is if ye want to keep your heid. I willna allow your beautiful lass ta wither away."

Colin swallowed, nodding curtly. Amaryllis looked bewildered in a sea of men. "It will be all right." He brushed her hair way from her temple and gave her a sweet kiss on the mouth.

It was show time.

* * *

Amaryllis watched Colin lead the way to the lift that would take them to the nerve centre. She whirled around at Luke, who remained with the rest of the

Manchester contingent.

"What the hell did you tell him?" She blazed, her eyes shooting sparks.

"I didn't tell him anything." Luke raised his brow. "I've not met The Hamilton before today."

"Colin welcomed you to his home. Gave you his protection because you're a Cynn Cruor far removed from where you live." Amaryllis did not care what Luke said. "What is going to happen to him now?"

"He needs to answer for his crimes." Roarke's silver blue eyes regarded her. "As his mate, you'd understand that."

"No, I don't, because I've only just become his recently. As his mate, I'd fight with him and for him," she snapped.

"Spoken like a true partner." Finn observed.

"And what crimes?" Amaryllis scoffed in disbelief, her glare piercing all of them. "As his mate, I understand that you are about to punish him for something he did because it was the right thing to do! What kind of justice system do you have, penalising someone standing for what he believes in?"

Roarke merely lifted a brow. Amaryllis nearly stomped her foot in frustration. Where was Seth when she needed bloody backup?

"He lied to us, Amaryllis," Finn said quietly.

"He didn't lie to you," Blake spoke beside Amaryllis. "He just didn't say anything."

"And that is a lie by omission," Roarke said, his voice brooking no argument. "You of all people should know that, Blake."

"Aye, it's become crystal tonight." Blake conceded, his mouth bitter. "No amount of reparation will be enough to compensate for wrongs committed. There is no way a warrior who has veered away for so long only to find himself back on the right path will be forgiven by the Council of Ieldran, is there? He dies with an apology on his lips and remorse in his heart. And still it will not be enough."

"What are you on about, Blake?" Graeme clamped his hand on Blake's shoulder, stunned, hurt flashing in his gaze when Blake shrugged his hand away.

Blake merely shook his head, making Graeme look at a troubled Finn.

Roarke sighed, raking his hand through his hair. "We are not here to drive him away. I went to Scotland to seek The Hamilton's advice. He was the one who decided to leave my mother and come down here to speak with Colin. Da never travels away from Scotland unless he is summoned by the Ancients to go to Anglesey and even that has to be negotiated. In the end, it's the Ancients visiting my father in Alba. Scotland is his blood. Stepping outside the borders doesn't sit well with him and for him to do so on this account means that this is important."

"We are trying to help Colin find a way to fix this," Luke said.

"Some way you're showing it," she said angrily, wiping the tears that ran down her cheeks. She pivoted on her heel to follow Colin and The Hamilton then stopped. She looked back at them. "Looks like you have an idea of what Colin's secret is. If not, Luke the snitch, I'm sure will be more than happy to fill you in." Luke's gaze did not waver, but he appeared to turn ashen then flushed afterwards.

Serves him right.

Amaryllis sucked in her breath, swallowing against the lump of desperation in her throat. "And even if you say that Colin lied, I'm sure you know that his reason was sound. Have any of you been in a situation where you were willing to forsake everything just so that the person you loved could be saved from death?"

They kept silent.

Amaryllis smiled tremulously. The tears continued spilling down her cheeks. "I thought so. Think about it. Because if I were in his shoes, I would've done the same thing."

With that she left.

* * *

Colin gestured to The Hamilton to precede him out of the lift. Nodding curtly, the most trusted adviser of the Ancients stepped into the dank corridor and waited. He followed Colin through the cold stone path, their footfalls muffled by the hard yet smooth cobblestones beneath their feet. There was no electricity here, the pathway lit by torches attached to the prison walls. Their breath fogged in front of them, the only sign of the bone deep cold of the place. Every movement of their bodies and the weapons they carried alternately whispered and echoed eerily in the stillness of the long forgotten place.

Before taking The Hamilton to the dungeons a floor below the command centre, Colin brought him to meet the rest of the Leeds Cynn Cruors. Craig was enveloped in another bear hug while Liam and Cormac, who did not train under The Hamilton. They clasped his huge arm in greeting, both of them in awe of his commanding presence.

Colin brought out a bottle of his best scotch and a squat glass before setting it on the table before The Hamilton.

"Join me," The Hamilton commanded everyone. Cormac went to get more glasses from the bar and returned. The Hamilton poured the rich amber liquid to each of the glasses. He raised his glass in a semi-circle and toasted, "*Slàinte.*"

"*Do dheagh shlàinte,*" the men replied, toasting to The Hamilton's good health, before throwing back their drinks.

"Och, thank ye." The Hamilton sighed. "Ye do me honour with your warm welcome. Now." His face lost all joviality, pinning Colin with a look that would make a lesser immortal wish for death at that very minute. "My son is of the opinion that there is something ye want to tell me. What he told me in passing was enough for me to leave Alba, so this better be good."

Training under The Hamilton gave Colin the advantage. This was the man's concerned look. Still it did not stop Colin nearly quaking in his boots.

Colin looked at his men, their face grim yet accepting.

"Aye, my Lord, that I do. However, I have one request."

A thunderous brow rose. "Are you coming from a position of strength, Colin, when ye ask that of me? I still hae no heard what ye hae to say."

"Nay, my Lord," Colin said quietly. "Only from my belief that you will grant my request because of your reputation of fairness."

The Hamilton's huge chest heaved as he inhaled. He closed his eyes. "Verra well," he said, exhaling. "What is it?"

"Spare my men."

The Leeds Cynn Cruors started, their faces stunned.

"Colin, no!" Craig growled in anguish.

Colin's hand cut the air. He did not look at Craig, his gaze locked with The Hamilton's. "What I have to tell you involves them but only because of their loyalty. I did not force them to do what they have done. So I set them free now for they are without fault in this matter.

The blame lies entirely with me."

The Hamilton glared at Colin. Blood rushed up Colin's head, threatening to unman him, but he stood his ground. He returned The Hamilton's flint like gaze with his respectful but firm one. He balled his hands into fists at his sides, squeezing them so hard it would not surprise him if his knuckles broke through his skin. After what seemed like an eternity of waiting, of dead silence that had the Leeds warriors stop breathing, The Hamilton nodded.

"Aye, ye have my word."

Colin closed his eyes as his breath left him. He felt his burden lift from his shoulders, felt peace with his decision for his men. His mind was clear.

Even if his heart was heavy.

By saving the lives of his men, he had forfeited whatever happiness he had with Amaryllis. He would only know a glimmer of the love Amaryllis felt for him. And he did feel it in the way she gave herself to him, in the way she looked at him across a room. He felt it from the way she spoke to him, how her voice raised in irritation, or lowered seductively. He noticed the electricity in the air that made him come alive every time she was in a room, making him want to stay with her every minute and every second of the day and every moment of his life. He saw it in the understanding in her deep violet gaze that only had eyes for him and no one else. His only consolation now was that once he left the mortal plane, his mate, the woman who had finally given meaning to his life would soon follow him in death. What he would not do to have the same enduring love he and Mackenzie saw in their parents.

A screech and hiss brought Colin back to the present.

"We're here, my Lord," Colin said as they stopped

in front of one cell. The cell's door was made of iron encased silver bars riveted in place by steel pegs.

The Hamilton's leather soled booted feet creaked as he moved closer to the cell door. The torches light flitting in and out, casting his face in shadow or bringing it in harsh relief. However, the light did not reach the interiors of the cell, which remained pitch black. Without warning, a body slammed against the grill with such force for The Hamilton to growl but he did not step back.

A shrill cackle bubbled from the throat of the Scatha who had flung himself against the grills before landing on his arse on the freezing stone floor.

"Ahhh…that felt good." Neon green eyes stared up at the imposing figure of the Highland immortal. "Welcome to my humble prison, my Lord. You look well." He then turned to Colin, his grin widening to show the jagged teeth crowding his jaw. "Seriously, Colin? You think this will absolve you or me?"

Colin's face hardened in an effort to tamp his emotions. Desperation and frustration coiled around him tightly the same way The Hamilton's tartan wrapped itself around the man's body.

"Mackenzie."

The name was spoken softly, without a trace of anger. Only sadness.

Colin shut his eyes and inhaled sharply. He blinked several times to stop the mistiness away from his eyes.

Mackenzie's eyes snapped to The Hamilton's. "Mackenzie's dead."

"No, he isn't." The Hamilton bent down on his hunches so that he was level with Mack. "He's still there." He paused, pointing at Mackenzie's heart. "It's been a long time, laddie."

Mackenzie's eyes lost the glowing green colour,

gradually returning to amber. He turned his back and leaned against the grills. His skin hissed at the contact.

"Shouldn't ye move away from the grills? You're sizzling."

Mack gave a short laugh. "Like you care. Besides, my time with the Scatha has made me appreciate pain."

"Your time with the Cynn Cruors was much longer, Mackenzie. You have to remember that."

"What do you want, Hamilton?" Mack huffed. "I don't belong to the Cynn Cruors. Respect isn't part of my vocabulary anymore."

"Do ye hear me complain?" The Hamilton made himself more comfortable, arranging his tartan around him, sitting his arse on the cold floor. "Talk ta me, Butler."

"I'm no more a Butler." Mack shot back in anger. "What did my dear brother bribe you with for you to come all the way from Alba to sit inside a dungeon? Whatever it is, it will never be enough to get me to break my oath to the Scatha."

"The moment ye informed Leeds that Dac Valerian was coming to attack the Faesten, ye broke that oath, Mack," The Hamilton said smoothly. "I'd say your loyalties still lie firmly with the Cynn Cruors."

"Can't you smell the stench, old man?" Mack asked over his shoulder. He leaned forward. "God dammit, I'm so fucking tired!" In less than a minute he faced The Hamilton and Colin. His eyes accusingly pierced his brother. "You did this to me!"

"Aye, I did," Colin agreed. "I agreed that you could come with us to the Crimea. Against my better judgment, I allowed you to fight with us. I did not foresee how many Scatha Cruors would embroil themselves in the war." Colin let out a deep sigh. "I rushed to you. Ancients! I bellowed and hacked my way to get to you, but I was too late."

"You promised Mam you'd protect me." Mack's voice suddenly became timid, a young boy once again.

Colin crumpled on his knees, his shoulders hunched. The dam he built to tide the tears that collected inside him through the years, had cracked. "I tried, Mack. I tried to save you." His voice a broken whisper, blood tears splashing on his armour.

"And he's still trying to save you, laddie," The Hamilton said. "I hae agreed for Leeds ta keep ye prisoner until ye can be transported to Perth. Ye will stay in my dungeons until a cure can be found."

Mack's laugh cracked like lighting, echoing across the Scottish countryside. It went for a long time before he sobered. "I wonder how the Ancients will take it that you have a Scatha in your midst."

"There have always been Scatha prisoners in Faesten dungeons." The Hamilton rose to his full height. "They just doona survive, though I hae no doubt ye will. Besides, I ken ye, Mackenzie. Be glad I do." He turned to Colin. "Stand up, Dux. Ye have a battle to lead."

Colin and The Hamilton were mid-way through the passageway when Mack shouted. "What did my dear brother give you in exchange so that you kept me prisoner instead of killing me?"

Colin stopped, staring straight ahead. The Hamilton darted a look his way before he replied.

"Your brother gave me his life in exchange for yours."

313

Chapter Twenty-Seven

Amaryllis paced the nerve centre in agitation. Colin and The Hamilton had just left to see Mackenzie in the dungeons when she arrived. Unable to wait any longer, she rushed to the lifts only for Craig to block her path.

"Amaryllis, no," Craig said gently. Torment flitted across his face before it disappeared.

"What?"

No one wanted to look at her. A sense of foreboding slithered down her spine. Her heart plummeted and she could feel the blood drain out of her face. "Craig?"

"Colin will be back."

"I want to go to him," Amaryllis said stubbornly. "Move out of my way."

"I can't."

Amaryllis' eyes glittered, growing fury for not being allowed to be with Colin suffusing her with heat she had never known. Strength she never expected to feel. Authority she did not realise she had.

"Don't make me do this, Craig."

Craig's forehead puckered in a frown before truth dawned. His mouth straightened, his eyes accepting, grudging respect in his gaze.

"I am your Dux's mate." Amaryllis heard the rest of the warriors' sharp intakes. "Stand aside."

How Amaryllis knew that she could command the Cynn Cruors under Colin came from deep down inside her. As Colin's mate, they would protect her. At the same time, she held the same clout as the Dux unless he relinquished his position as leader of the Faesten and the Cynn Cruors under his command.

As Craig reluctantly stepped away, the lift opened

and Colin and The Hamilton emerged.

"Colin!" Amaryllis flung herself at her mate, embracing him tightly. Colin held on to her as though she was his lifeline.

"Hey," he whispered in her hair. Amaryllis felt his lips move to a smile against her cheek.

"I was going to follow you down to the dungeons." Her voice was muffled against his suit.

"I'm here now, babe," Colin replied. "But we have a battle to prepare for." He leaned away to look down at her, his thumb caressing her jaw. For once, Amaryllis saw the mocking glint return in his eyes. "You up for it?"

Amaryllis kissed Colin with all the love she had in her heart. "Let's kick ass so that we can finally have time alone."

"That's my girl." Colin grinned before it mellowed. "I love you, Amaryllis Hart. For as long as I live."

"As I you." She gazed up at him with a bemused smile. "You say it like this is the end."

"It's just the beginning." Colin leaned his forehead on hers. "I promise."

"Butler," The Hamilton said. "It's time."

"I beg for one more moment with my mate, my Lord." Colin's chin rose slightly. "Please."

"Aye." The Hamilton inclined his head at the warriors. "Take yer positions around the Faesten, Cynn Cruors."

Amaryllis watched nonplussed as the warriors filed out after The Hamilton, entering both lifts. The warriors' faces were stoic, their eyes lowered, their faces harsh and tortured.

"Dinnae take too long, Butler." The Hamilton reminded. "Ye are still the Dux."

Colin inclined his head in a grateful nod. "Aye, my

Lord. Thank you."

The Hamilton acknowledged his gesture just as the lifts closed.

Colin?

Amaryllis searched his face. His eyes shone with a different light, the warmest green she had seen. And his love…the tenderness and adoration in his eyes made her breath catch in her throat.

But there was another truth that was blatant for her to see. She gasped at the pain that ripped through her, stunning her to momentary speechlessness. Tears welled and spilled quickly down her cheeks.

"No!" she screamed. She pushed him away, but Colin refused to let her go. She fought and clawed at him. "Tell me it isn't true! Tell me that the thoughts in my head aren't bloody true!

"Amaryllis—"

"God damn you! Why? Why!" Amaryllis could not breathe. How could she when the sun in the centre of her universe was about to be extinguished. The moonlight that kissed her at night was going to disappear forever. The haven that she had found was being pulled from underneath her. She screamed and screamed, every cry a tear in her soul, every sound blinding out the only voice she longed to hear for the rest of her life. Colin kept his arms around her, not letting her go, talking to her softly until his deep voice penetrated the thick blanket of torment that covered her heart. Finally, Amaryllis flung her arms around him. Oh God! Her agonized screams bounced off the walls of the empty command centre. Her heart was being torn to shreds. If she could only be part of his skin. She squeezed him, held on to him, refused to look up at a face forever etched in her memory.

"Amaryllis…"

She continued to sob, her arms falling from his neck to grab hold of the suit, fisting them in her hands. She wanted to crumple on the floor and curl into a ball. The pain...there was no way to describe the agony of one's heart being broken into a million pieces knowing it could never be fixed again.

"Amaryllis, look at me."

She lifted her puffy eyes while tears continued to fall down her face. Colin cupped her face in his hands, his thumbs sweeping the trail of heartbreak from her cheeks.

"I had to, my love." The intensity of his feelings for her and the weight of the choice he had to make evident in his eyes. "There was no other way. I chose to keep Mackenzie alive. Someday there will be a cure for him and he can move on."

"But what about us?" Fresh tears fell, soaked up by the armour she wore. She choked, "You said this was going to be the beginning."

"And it is." Colin stressed, kissing Amaryllis on the mouth and the tear trails. "You're bound to me now, remember? If Mackenzie and I die, there will be no more Butlers to join the ranks of the Cynn Cruors. I cannae let that happen, Amaryllis. I owe it to Mam and Da." He smiled. "Call it a macabre love story but when I die, so will you. You will be with me forever in the pantheon."

Death. She was going into battle with only her faith and love for Colin to keep her strong only to probably find death on the other side. Souls forever entwined. She searched his face, locked every detail of who he was and his essence into the deep recesses of her psyche. Amaryllis did not know what was waiting for her on the other side. She never really thought about her mortality. Heck, she was only twenty-six to Colin's what? He was already fighting in the Crimea which was over three hundred years ago. She had never really asked, too engrossed in this thing between them and which they had made permanent. The irony of being mated to an immortal only to die in the end was not lost on her. And yet, Amaryllis doubted whether she could still live without him by her side. He was a part of her now, his blood and his memories flowed side by side with hers. If she had not agreed to belong to Colin and he died, she would be left behind. What kind of life would she have? Before Colin she had been alone. After Colin she would still be alone. No, this was the best outcome. To be by Colin's side.

Because not being beside him would make her dead inside.

Straightening, she edged away. Colin let his arms around her fall to his sides.

Amaryllis sniffed then exhaled. "You better damn well gear me up." She sniffed then started to breathe through her mouth when Colin chuckled. "Yeah, yeah, so my nose is clogged. That happens when you cry, you know?" She cupped his face and planted a loving kiss on his mouth, enjoying the feel of his firm lips on hers, still shuddering at the tingles of bittersweet pleasure his tongue gave her. She ended the kiss on a sigh. "The Hamilton said we shouldn't be long. Gear me up with all the weapons I need, Butler. I'm fighting by your side until the end."

Love and pride swelled in Colin's gaze, blood tears misted his eyes until he blinked them away.

"Until the end."

As soon as they emerged from the lift, they were greeted by all the Cynn Cruor warriors including The Hamilton, their faces a mixture of sadness and misery. Amaryllis' heart squeezed at the emotion they showed.

"Dux, your call," The Hamilton said. He had his broadsword in front of him with the point on the floor.

Amaryllis held on to Colin's hand, squeezing it as her emotions threatened to run away with her. She could hear their thoughts in her mind, all of them in solidarity with Colin despite knowing what was going to happen to him after the battle. Behind the Cynn Cruor warriors were the Cynn mortals and Amaryllis saw Seth leading the front, tears streaming down her face. She held a Glock in one hand and her short sword in another, her face a mask of determination and grief.

"Dux." Craig stepped forward. The smile he tried to give looked more like a grimace. "Lead us."

Colin looked at Amaryllis. She gripped his hand tightly, inclining her head and smiling.

Lead them one more time. I will be by your side. Always. I love you.

Colin nodded curtly. Taking a deep breath, he started firing instructions.

"Seth, are there enough mortals to man the clubs? This can just be a diversionary tactic by the Scatha to start abducting humans while they keep us busy here."

Seth nodded, wiping her face on her armour's sleeve while she moved forward. "They're all in place as is our communications protocol."

"Good," Colin said. "We may be thin on the ground and we don't know how many Scatha we'll encounter, but we've got Manchester with us." He pinned Roarke and the rest of the Manchester Cynn Cruors with a look. "Will you fight with me?"

Roarke stepped forward, extending his arm. "I will be the first to slap your arse if you don't allow us to do so."

There was a titter of laughter around them. Colin grinned, his eyes lighting up. "Thank you."

"We wouldn't miss it for the world, Butler," Finn added, respect and sadness in equal measure reflected in his eyes.

Colin nodded with gratitude. He looked at the Leeds Cynn mortals. "Gareth and Etienne, man the nerve centre. You will be our eyes where we can't see." He paused. "We have a Scatha prisoner. Keep one camera on him at all times. Don't let him out of your sight. Keep the shields down."

Gareth and Etienne nodded and ran to do Colin's bidding, making sure their ear pieces were in place.

"Seth and Donovan. Go with Finn and Liam." Colin turned to the Cynn Cruor warriors. "All four of you are crack shots. Take positions on the roof. Liam, you'll lead this team. I want to make sure that we can pick out as many Scatha Cruors before they land inside the wall."

"Let's go, little children. Choose your sniper weapons from the armoury," Liam drawled, his silver eyes starting to bleed to blood orange.

Finn snorted and chuckled at the same time. "You call yourself little?"

He and Liam continued ribbing each other while Seth and Donovan followed. Mid way, Seth stopped and twisted around to look at Colin and Amaryllis. Her mouth was in an uncompromising line, her warm brown eyes filled with purpose. She inclined her head to them as though acknowledging that Colin and now Amaryllis still had her loyalty before she jogged to where Liam, Finn, and Donovan were waiting.

"My Lord, perhaps you should change to the armour." Colin suggested. "The rains will soak you to the skin and you may be hard pressed to fight if your…" He flushed at the displeased frown on The Hamilton's face.

"The tartan stays in place, Dux," The Hamilton

replied sternly. "I hae been fighting wearing this," he gestured at himself, "even before ye trained with me." His face softened. "I appreciate the thought, Butler. The rains of the twenty-first century are no different from the rains of the past. It's still water."

"Aye, my Lord." Colin straightened before turning to Amaryllis.

"Oh no." Amaryllis scowled, shaking her head. "No way are you leaving me inside this bloody house when all of you are enjoying yourselves. I'm fighting beside you."

"Spoken like my true mate," Colin murmured. "Okay, Hart. Let's go and kick some Scatha butt."

Chapter Twenty-Eight

The rain fell without let-up. Herod ran his hand through his long hair, sweeping it away from his face and growled when strands stubbornly fell back down over his face. Commanding his hand to turn to a claw, he sliced the offending strands and grunted in approval as he flicked his cut hair away. The Scatha Cruors were watching the Faesten from the opposite side of the road.

"Are you sure this is the place?" Dac asked softly.

"Aye, sire." Lee nodded. "This is the place where Crawley followed a few Cynn mortals and wounded one of them."

Herod's eyes narrowed at the sight in front of him. Nothing was out of the ordinary yet at the same time something was.

"How did you extract the info from Crawley?" Water ran down his face, his leather great coat the only thing keeping his body dry.

Lee cackled with glee. "Let's just say I have certain abilities when it comes to mind games. I can dig out repressed memories in a human's mind to get a truth." His chest expanded. "That's how I manipulated Crawley's mind to think his sister was still alive."

Herod grunted, eyeing the Faesten once more, making sure his mind was shut down from Dac's prying. Lee Harris might just prove to be a liability for him but an asset for the Scatha Cruors. No sooner had he thought this when Dac spoke.

"I misjudged you, Harris," Dac said with reluctance.

Herod's mouth lifted imperceptibly. Mighty big of Valerian to admit he was at fault. La Nahuaterique and his short-lived partnership with Kamaria must have messed him up.

"Tell you what," Dac piped up again. "Get me Max Greene and I don't care where in the world he is. Find him and bring him to me. After I kill him, you'll take his place as head of the Scathas in Leeds. If you don't bring him to me, I'll cut your balls and feed them to you before I kill you."

Herod watched Lee's wide grin falter as he cupped his junk, smiling at the way the man's Adam's apple bobbed in the middle of his throat as he shifted his weight from one foot to another.

"To sweeten the deal, you'll get first taste of the women, men, and children any Scatha brings in plus a cut on every pussy or cock sold."

"You got it, boss." His initial discomfort at the thought of castration was replaced by the lascivious look of greed. Anticipation made him smack his lips together.

Herod shook his head subtly. Lee's head movement reminded Herod of those toys with bounding heads found in many human cars. Greed. Got them every time. Having a taste of nubile flesh…well, that was a different matter. No matter what Dac promised, he and Herod always got first digs. Except for Deanna Logan. Dac made sure of that. Herod had had a soft spot for Deanna and it had been out of character of him to give her some respite from Dac's degradations while she had been their prisoner. The only one he never touched. Sometimes he and Dac shared the merchandise, taking pleasure in the sobs and begging wails of those who screamed for their lives. In the end, they were just like lambs to the slaughter. Those who refused to bend were drugged, held in place by chains, suspended from the ceiling during the auction, and released when the hammer came down sealing their fate.

Until there was one whom Herod saved from a

similar misfortune. Someone he did not tell Dac about.

No, he refused to go down memory lane, turning his attention back to the Scatha Cruors who stealthily reached the walls, ready to clamber up.

Dac, this doesn't look good.

"Chicken, D'Argyl?" Dac did not bother sending it via the telepathic link. Herod could still hear him despite his voice nearly getting lost in the torrential downpour.

Herod's mouth pursed. "It's too quiet."

"Of course it is. They're not expecting us."

Herod swung his head sideways, glaring at Dac. "After that botched up attack two nights ago, they won't be on high alert?"

Dac sliced his hand through the air, the droplets slamming against his limb. "The Cynn Cruors will be spread thinly on the ground. The rest of the Scatha are already wreaking havoc in town." He arched his brow. "Unless you didn't tell them to cause mayhem to do their damnest tonight."

"Don't be ridiculous," Herod snapped. "You were there when I gave the order."

"How many Cynn Cruors does Colin Butler have?" Dac shrugged. "Four maybe five?" His eyes turned to slits. "I am Dac Valerian, Herod, and you're just a lackey. Don't ever forget that."

Herod bristled at the insult. "And you owe me your life, General. Don't forget that." He gave Lee a withering glare before he stalked towards the Scatha Cruors lining the walls.

He had enough. Dac was getting sloppier by the day, almost like he was throwing everything they strove to build down the drain. He was now sure that something happened to Valerian in the Honduras. Every move Herod made was now suspect. He had weathered Dac's bouts of jealousy in the past, laughing it off as the rants of an immortal losing his hold on sanity, not that they were sane most of the time. Back then, Dac should not have had any reason to be suspicious of him.

The present was a whole new ballgame.

Lee zoomed beside Herod, a blur under the dim streetlights.

"We'll split up." Herod did not bother to look at the Scatha beside him. "You want to prove yourself to Dac? You prove yourself to me that you don't deserve to eat your own gonads." He bellowed, "Take the Faesten!"

Some of the Scatha Cruors transformed completely. Others, who held weapons, kept to their human form but their eyes took the unholy green glow. Herod closed his eyes, sighing in pleasure at the sound of breaking and reforming bones, at the screeches coming from the chasm of the Scathas' throats. The Faesten's twenty foot wall was slick but the Scatha's claws had enough traction to scale it like gigantic monstrous spiders from Doctor Moreau's forgotten experiment. The rest whizzed toward the gates, their claws finding purchase on the elaborately curled grills. Those who remained partially human jumped over the walls and gates. Herod braced, waiting for the Cynn Cruors to flood the grounds with lights or pick them with silver bullets as they landed on the other side.

Nothing happened.

The Scatha began clicking their tongues against their razor teeth. Herod inhaled, some of the raindrops that pelted him entering his nose. He snorted them out. His mouth widened as his teeth elongated and his eyes took on the neon green hue of his kind. Instead of giving in to changing his hands to claws, he drew out a huge double razor edged sword from underneath his leather overcoat. Screeching once, he roared the next command and the Scathas immediately covered the walls completely. With one hand and foot he gripped and stepped on the gate and catapulted himself over the barrier, somersaulting mid-air to land crouching inside the Faesten's grounds. He straightened and as he did, the cruel smile that superseded the sweet taste of triumph froze on his maw.

The Hamilton!

* * *

The rain beat down on the impromptu battlefield.

Incessantly.

Colin looked beside him. Amaryllis had her hair in a high ponytail but the water trickling down her face did not detract from her beauty and determination he saw on her face as she glared at the intruders by the wall. He glanced about. The Hamilton's hair, as well as the rest of the warriors', was all plastered to their heads. He noticed Blake, still puzzled why he refused to wear the armour all of them wore, noticed the hesitation and the grim resignation that flickered across the young warrior's face when Colin had told him to suit up. He turned his attention back to the Scatha Cruors. Kill them first, then ask Blake questions later.

Colin opened his telepathic link to all Cynn Cruor immortals, including Amaryllis so they could hear each other. They still wore their ear pieces because as soon as the battle commenced, they would be too far apart and too engrossed in the enemy. The earpiece would be their only source of communication with the nerve centre and the rest.

"Dux, three lines of Scatha are starting to scale the wall." Gareth's voice came through their earpieces.

"Steady." Colin's deep voice came through calmly. "Liam?"

"On your signal, Dux."

The Hamilton suddenly inhaled sharply. "D'Argyl!"

Colin's attention snapped to the gate and saw Herod D'Argyl freeze. He cast a sideways glance at The Hamilton and the highland warrior was starting to shake. Whether from fury, mirth or a mixture of both, Colin was not sure.

"My Lord," Roarke spoke, addressing his father, formally.

"Keep yer eyes peeled, Cynn Cruors. Dac Valerian willna be far behind. Knowing the kind of coward he is, he willna come in unless he can claim the victory for himself."

"Hamilton!" Herod shouted across the distance, a smile in his voice. "I hae na seen ye in a long time."

For someone who forsook Alba millennia ago, he still speaks like a true born. The Hamilton telepathed before he bellowed back. "D'Argyl, no wonder the world is still a shite place. Yer still alive."

Herod hooted. The Scatha Cruors watched them warily. Others snapped their jowls, impatient for the skirmish to begin. Herod held up a hand abruptly. The Scatha Cruors stepped back against the walls, growling.

"Came over to take over Butler's command?"

"Nay," The Hamilton said. His hands were crossed over each other, relaxed over the cross guard of his sword. "I came here ta assist him kill ye. He's the Dux and whatever he commands, I follow."

Colin looked sideways at the highland immortal, stunned.

"Very generous," Herod drawled. "The esteemed adviser of the Ancient Cynn taking orders from an underling."

"No different from Valerian, hiding behind yer skirt." The Hamilton snorted with derision. "Coward much?"

Snickers erupted from the Cynn Cruors and Herod growled.

"Ye were once one of us, Herod," The Hamilton said, his voice carrying through the breeze that suddenly whipped the drops from the branches and sprinkling them with the rain that had stayed stubbornly on the waxy leaves. "You ken all Dux and Faestens are autonomous but their fealty belongs to the Ancients."

Liam. Colin telepathed.

"Targets chosen and acquired." Was Liam's response, dead calm through the ear piece.

Herod's eyes glowed and so did those of the Scatha Cruors. Their eyes looked like fireflies that were dipped in nuclear waste lighting them up eerily. Herod cackled.

"Butler has found a mate," he drawled, his grin widening at Colin's growl. "Violet eyes? Intriguing. I will have her just like we had Deanna Logan for centuries."

"Butler, you better damn well give the fucking signal." Roarke's bloodlust eyes darkened with fury, his lips drawn back against his teeth. Two Desert Eagles were gripped hard in his hands. "I will have his neck."

"Fall in line, Hamilton," Colin shot back, Beretta APX gripped in both hands. "My Faesten. My right."

"Eight of us and more than three dozen of them?" Graeme posited, his Mongolian Ilds crisscrossed in the scabbards on his back. He held Sigs in both hands.

"Gives a whole new meaning to the phrase 'thin red line'." Cormac was in a jocular mood. His silver laced misericordes were strapped to his waist. They winked from the light thrown by the Faesten behind them. Cradled in his arms was an M249 Squad Automatic Weapon. Blake had the same weapon. "It'll be fun."

"Cynn Cruors," Colin barked. "Brace!"

They positioned themselves in an inverted V line.

The Hamilton would be the hinge with his broadsword in the middle. Those inside the line would wait until the Scatha Cruors were close enough to shoot at, leaving the snipers to pick their targets and for Cormac and Blake to give suppressing fire from the edges of the line. This would force the Scatha to amass in the centre, crushing those already causing a stampede and confusion among the Scatha's ranks. Only when their silver bullets had been emptied would they start using their swords.

"Amaryllis?" Colin gritted.

"Give the order." Amaryllis' voice was arctic. "The Faesten's ground will be bathed in green ash tonight."

Colin's lips twitched to a wicked lopsided grin. "At the ready!"

Everyone braced their feet apart, their arms extended, weapons cocked and prepared to fire.

Herod roared. "Scatha, the ground is yours!" They sprinted towards the Cynn Cruors' line of defence.

Colin bellowed. "Now!"

The Scatha ran on all fours, their claws and feet kicking wet gravel and putting grooves on the soaked manicured lawns, their screeches carrying through the night air. In the melee, the rain eased as though surprised that something else could make a more fearsome sound than it could. The clouds parted to show the full moon casting its blessing on the carnage below. Screams rent the air with the roars of the Highland immortals. Spits from the assault weapons putting silver rounds into the oncoming horde were lost amid the sizzle and painful yowls of those hit. Cormac and Blake continued with their suppressing fire, their M249 Squad Automatic Weapons jolting against their bodies with its force. On the Faesten's rooftop, Liam and Donovan concentrated on Scathas pouring in from the left wall while Finn and Seth took down those running from the right. They all had AS50 sniper rifles that picked their targets easily in spite of the throng that flooded the grounds. As planned the Scatha Cruors converged in the centre, stampeding over their brethren already taken out by the silver bullets. Tried as they might, the Scatha shot at the snipers and always fell short, grazing the Faesten's roof and facade, the bullets stumped and lodged in the mortar.

The Cynn Cruors were not without pain. They got hit by the stray silver bullet, grunting in anger, but their armour protected them, the bullets bouncing off the amorphic material. Graeme rushed to Blake, who continued firing at the Scatha.

"What the hell are you doing, Temple?" Blake roared, scowling.

"You're a pain in the arse, Strachan," Graeme shot back. "You should have worn the armour to stop the silver from entering you."

"Maybe I just want to be shot at and decapitated."

"What the fuck is wrong with you? What's with the death wish?" Graeme faced Blake, shoving him back. Then he sucked in his breath, a look of surprise on his face before looking down at the tip of a sword protruding from his belly before it slid out. The skin around sizzled.

"No!" Blake roared furiously but was stunned when Graeme took his ilds as he twisted and decapitated the Scatha behind him.

As the dust immediately settled, Graeme turned around, his red orange eyes glaring. "I'm immune to silver now, Blake. I'm going to be your human shield while we both kill the Scatha, whether you fucking like it or not."

Several metres away, Colin, Roarke, Luke, and The Hamilton slashed their swords through the Scatha already shot by the snipers. The Hamilton hacked his way closer to Herod, who strolled toward him without a care in the world.

Amaryllis stayed by Colin's side. With his blood inside her, she tirelessly wielded the wakizashi, a shorter Japanese sword against the Scatha, wincing when a bullet slammed against her shoulder but it did not leave a gaping wound because of her suit. The blood lust sang in her veins. She surged forward, using the injured Scatha as leverage. With the Scatha crouched, she gained a foothold on its thigh before catapulting herself over it, taking its head with her blade. Taking the pommel in both hands, she surged and parried, her blade and the Scatha claws sparking like flint to a stone on contact.

"Amaryllis!" Colin's angry shout made her pause. She was far away from Colin and Scathas were coming from every side. Just as one launched himself toward her, he was pushed mid-air, disintegrating into ash even before he landed. Blake rose from his crouched position, his back facing Amaryllis.

Then Amaryllis screamed in pain, startling Blake. Her head pivoted over her shoulder, eyes blazing in fury. The Scatha was slack faced, disbelief in his eyes that his claws had not penetrated the suit. It was the precious seconds Amaryllis needed to lunge her sword with both hands into the fiend, flinching at the shushing sound of steel and silver running through flesh and blood, hitting bone before exiting at the back. With a flick of her wrists, she sliced across the torso. The Scatha knelt in front of her, clutching his innards together. Hatred spilled from his unholy eyes before he disintegrated to dust.

"Behind you!" Blake shouted, unable to sprint to her on time.

Amaryllis turned. Two more Scathas flew towards her. Colin launched himself against them but only nailed one. Amaryllis stepped back but lost her footing, falling hard on the ground, dislodging her sword from her hand. She lay on the ground, her chest and stomach an easy target for the claws that came barrelling to her.

"No!" Colin bellowed in anguish.

Something shimmered on top of Amaryllis. The next second, Luke swung his sword in an arc, slicing the Scatha in two. There was no way the Scatha Cruor would live, but Luke brought his blade down on the neck.

To be on the safe side.

Luke stepped beside Amaryllis' prone body. He extended his hand to help her up. Gripping it, she let go to brush the grime off her body.

"You okay, Hart?"

Amaryllis twisted her body and landed a punch on Luke's jaw.

"What the hell was that for?"

Her eyes flared with violet fire. "That's to say fuck you for causing a lot of shit to hit the fan and thank you for saving me." She spun on her heel, running for the next Scatha.

Luke massaged his jaw. "You're welcome." He shook his head, joining the fight again.

Chapter Twenty-Nine

The Hamilton and Herod circled each other. Bloodlust red and radiation green eyes tracked each other's move. All around them the Cynns and Scathas fought. Liam, Finn, Seth, and Donovan had left their sniper perches and fought on the ground. The Scatha kept pouring in. Etienne and Gareth left the command centre, unable to stop their desire to join their immortal brethren.

Dac Valerian was nowhere in sight.

The Hamilton and Herod, both titans, were oblivious to the sounds around them, uncaring about the number of souls called by death for their reckoning. Herod eschewed his claws for a deadly looking two sided razor edged broadsword. The Hamilton had his sword at the ready, his upper body turned at a ninety degree angle, his weapon by his shoulder.

Without warning, both roared and rushed forward. The clang of metal clashing against each other brought sparks that briefly lit their faces. Both immortals held fast. Unyielding. Unforgiving.

"Give it up, D'Argyl," The Hamilton grunted, his trews-encased muscular thighs straining, his feet planted on the wet ground. Herod hissed, the ligaments on his throat cording in similar effort.

"You're shite, Hamilton." Herod grinned, his sharp teeth gnashing as he spoke. "I hae the advantage."

Despite their dead lock, The Hamilton chuckled, his shoulders shaking with mirth.

"I wasna talking about this unusual embrace we hae going. Being with Valerian has made ye addle brained or logically impaired." His laughter gurgled from his throat.

Herod pushed back with an angry growl. The Hamilton did the same. Herod rushed forward again, his sword raised high above him before bringing it down. The Hamilton parried the blow, the clash of weapons reverberating, adding to the barrage around them.

They fought ruthlessly, each one trying to find a gap. They grunted, shouted, hurled expletives and insults. Still, no one wavered. Again they barrelled forward, their faces framed by their swords. Their breathing laboured.

Suddenly there was a long screech.

"I found him! I found Max Greene!"

Both immortals froze. The Hamilton noticed the change in Herod and pushed him away. Before Herod could react, the sharp tip of the Hamilton's broadsword nestled against the hollow of Herod's throat.

"Greene is here." Herod's chest heaved, pulling in huge gulps of air. His eyes narrowed, turning back to their normal colour. His jaw readjusting itself. "Why?"

"That is no concern of yours," The Hamilton replied, his nose flaring as he too inhaled deeply. "Shite, you Scathas really smell like rotten eggs." He watched emotions run through his enemy's face.

"He was changed against his will." Herod concluded softly. He chortled.

The Hamilton did not answer.

"Butler, I'm going down," a voice hollered.

Herod growled, moving his head, twisting to the direction of the voice, watching the Cynn Cruor pursue Lee Harris into the carport at the side of the mansion. The Hamilton's sword nicked Herod deeply, his blood welling in the hollow below his Adam's apple before trickling down his massive chest.

"What will it be?" The Hamilton asked.

"Save him," Herod hissed in agitation, facing the Cynn Cruor warrior. "Harris' orders are to kill Greene."

"Why do you care?" The Hamilton scoffed. "You hae killed so many of yer brethren with nary a blink. What's one more?"

Herod growled. "Do it!"

"Greene's life isna forfeit. Someone else will take his place. One who lied by omission."

The battle continued a distance away from them, as though they had been forgotten.

Herod sighed, looking around then laughed. His face gradually changed, losing its harsh planes and the evil that identified him as a Scatha Cruor. In its place was the face The Hamilton remembered from long ago.

"Then your life is forfeit as well, is it not? You omitted to tell the Ancients about my secret."

The Hamilton's jaw clenched in irritation. He sighed, bringing his sword down. "Yer a bloody shite, D'Argyl."

Herod shrugged. "Always have been. What difference does it make now?"

"Because a Scatha Cruor has made me bloody think!"

"Don't think now. Hit me." Herod scowled. "Fuck you, Hamilton, do it! Dinnae be a pussy!"

The Hamilton held his sword in both hands. With a shout, he impaled Herod. Herod gasped, his body concaving against the blade, his sword falling to the ground as his hand immediately morphed into claws against the wound. The Hamilton placed his booted foot against Herod's abdomen before violently sliding the blade out. Herod fell to his knees, bellowing as the silver smoked his skin from inside out. The Hamilton took out a syringe from inside his tartan and plunged it close to the wound.

"That should arrest some of the silver's effects," he muttered.

"Now save him." Herod wheezed. "Bloody hell, this pain is good!"

"And the Cynn Cruor?"

"When I said 'save him' the first time, he was the one I meant."

* * *

Max raised his head. His nose flared at the incoming smell.

Scatha Cruor.

He listened as the muffled sounds of the battle raging outside reached him. He yowled to be let out. Transformed and flung himself against his prison bars, his anger fuelled by the silver that singed his skin. In the end, he retreated to a dim corner, curling into himself, snivelling and whimpering like some caged animal in the brink of despair of ever being set free.

"Greene, I've come to get you out," someone hissed.

"Lee?"

"Fuck!" Lee's hand smoked as soon as he touched the bar.

"Silver."

"I guessed that, dumbass," Lee snapped. "Let's go."

"I'll stay here. Take my chances with the Cynn Cruors."

"Are you out of your fucking mind?" Lee asked incredulously. "They're going to kill you here! They think you stormed the Faesten two nights ago." He glanced furtively at the darkened hallway. "Come on!"

"How would they know that unless someone told them? You got a spy inside the Cynn Cruors?"

"You fucking with me, Greene? I have no spy."

"Then how do you know this place was attacked precisely two days ago?" Max ambled to the bars, his head inclined to one side. "I was in Hull until today."

Lee exhaled sharply.

Max snickered. "Who's the dumbass now?"

"You are so fucking dead!"

"Nope." Max shook his head and nudged towards the dungeon's exit. "You are." The feeling of being pulled apart started to grow in his gut. What Max would not do for Lee to die, then again he could not help the rage that coursed through him at the thought.

Lee should die by his hand.

Lee whirled at the Cynn Cruor that emerged from the shadows. His shirt was tattered, his hair partially covered in ash. His kilij, a Turkish scimitar ran with blood that dripped to the floor as he loped towards his prey. Lee backed away, looking from side to side. There was no escape.

"Strachan, no," Max said quietly.

"Yes, he must die," Blake retorted. "He's your enemy now too, remember?"

"He will die by my hand!" Max growled, slamming against his prison bars, hissing and snarling at Blake while his claws burned.

Lee looked askance between Blake and Max.

"Touch him and I don't fucking care if you saved me." Max lashed.

Blake hitched his shoulder. "Either way he dies."

"I will kill you!"

Unexpectedly, Blake was shoved to the side. The whisper of a blade slicing the air softly stirred the cold heavy air followed by flesh sliding against flesh. From shoulder to waist, Lee slithered from his lower body. He jerked around uncontrollably, spewing his life essence on the ground beneath him. He disintegrated to ash as soon as The Hamilton brought his sword down against Lee's neck.

"There," he grumbled. "That'll stop ye both."

"You're dead," Max screamed.

"Aye, good," The Hamilton snapped. "Let's see ye try."

Max continued yelling even after The Hamilton and Blake left the dark confines of the dungeon.

"Why did you do it?" Blake queried, his footsteps becoming brisk to catch up with the huge Highlander as they traversed the underground parking lot of the Faesten. His hand clamped down on The Hamilton's shoulder, swinging him around, past caring of the snarl that left The Hamilton's lips. "He was mine!"

"And cause enmity between you and Butler's brother?" The Hamilton sighed wearily at Blake's guilty look. "Colin told me and ye ken as well. No reason to make Cynn Cruors fight."

"He's a Scatha Cruor," Blake said in a flat voice, looking away from The Hamilton's sharp regard.

"And you dinnae kill him earlier. Ye saw that he was more the Cynn Cruor than a Scatha."

Blake remained silent. Outside, the battle appeared to have died down. The rains started again as though making their own contribution to washing away any traces of the battle fought within the Faesten's walls.

"What's going to happen to Colin now?" Blake looked down at the ground.

"His life and that of Amaryllis are forfeit in exchange for Mackenzie living." The Hamilton's eyes sparkled with the weariness of a decision he did not want to make. "Colin believes that there will be a cure for Mackenzie and when he is cured, he can live a life of the Cynn Cruor and find his mate. Colin has found Amaryllis and that is more than enough for them both.

They die when the sun rises later."

Blake closed his eyes at the abject sadness and regret he felt. "All too soon," he whispered. "Immortal and mate have only found each other only to be separated all too soon."

"It's a heavy burden I bear as the Ancient Eald's adviser and enforcer." The Hamilton's face looked beaten. The lines on his face became more pronounced, showing his real age of over seven hundred years than a youthful thirty-five.

"Surely you can make an exception." Blake insisted. "The choices we thought were best at one time in the past will always bite our arse in the future."

A ghost of a smile flitted across The Hamilton's handsome features. He clamped his hand around Blake's nape and pulled him close so that they were nose to nose.

"Someone reminded me of that." He pulled away and started for the carport's exit. "I hae some thinking to do."

"Who reminded you?" Blake called, his voice echoing in the cavernous parking lot.

"Someone who has yer best interests at heart," The Hamilton shouted back before disappearing into the pre-dawn darkness.

* * *

The rains had stopped, satisfied with flooding the land for the moment. Colin walked across the ground covered with grey packed mud instead of the gardens' green grass. Sculptures that dotted the landscape were riddled with slash marks and bullet holes, fissures and cracks marking where they were hit. While most of the Scatha Cruors had either been killed or escaped, a few Cynn Cruor mortals would also not see the sun rise again. Casualties of a war fought within the borders of a country relatively living in harmony with the world. The Cynn Cruor mortals working with the West Yorkshire Police immediately sanitized the area. Connections with the media made sure that the deaths were sound bites easily forgotten. Colin would need to speak with the parents of those who died.

He stopped mid-stride.

It was not his responsibility anymore. That duty now fell to Craig.

Colin strode over to the woman he loved, who was kneeling over the Cynn mortal now eternally at rest. She placed her hand over the warrior's sightless eyes before bending down to kiss his forehead.

"*Reposer en paix, Etienne,*" she whispered softly. "Rest in peace."

Colin's heart squeezed and he swallowed hard at Amaryllis' kind gesture. He touched her shoulder. She looked up, her violet eyes welling with unshed tears, her face smudged with ash and mud. She had her share of using her knuckles to misalign several jaws but with Colin's blood in her, she had quickly healed.

Unfortunately, the Kinaré would not be able to heal the wounds permanently written in their hearts and souls.

Amaryllis stood, immediately entering Colin's waiting arms. He kissed her forehead, caressing her damp hair and taking in her sighs as his elixir of life. He looked over Amaryllis' head. Seth sobbed against Craig's chest, holding him tight around the waist. Craig's own eyes were filled with his own heartache. Brothers in arms looked at each other for a long time.

One had the face of a hardened immortal bracing for another bout of pain.

The other wore the smile of someone at peace.

The breeze rustled the leaves in the trees. Some of them fell immediately to the ground. Others shook off the remnants of last night's deluge. Dawn peeked over the houses' rooftops. It would soon bask the Faesten with gold. Humans would be waking. Parents would be preparing children for school before going off to work.

An ordinary day for those the Cynn Cruors protected.

The Manchester and Leeds immortals and mortals surrounded Colin and Amaryllis.

The Hamilton presided over the group. "It's time."

* * *

The postie whistled as he got out of his van, carrying a parcel for delivery. He pressed on the doorbell several times and banged on the door. Suddenly bellows and screams pierced the morning air, causing him to drop the parcel on the floor.

"Shit!"

The cries came again, coming closer. The postie looked around, his eyes wild. The curtains of all of the houses moved but no one opened their doors. He turned his back and banged on the door again. What sounded like tortured screams rent the air again. Dread trailed up and down his spine and his heart wanted to pop out of his chest. Swearing, he took out a red card to write the details of the delivery office where the parcel could be collected. His hand shook while he wrote but before he could finish, the shouts rose again.

"Ah fuck it!" He strode quickly to his van.

"Arrrgh!" The door handle slipped from his hand several times before it opened. He switched on the ignition and floored the accelerator. The tires screamed, leaving black marks on the wet street, splashing water into the sidewalk from the pools that collected on the uneven ground.

Unless someone ran down the streets and started shouting, "Fire!" no one would bother finding out what the dreadful noise was all about.

Chapter Thirty

Taigh a' Chnuic (the Hill House)
Altnaharra, Lairg, Scotland

Snow fell in violent swirls, capping the crags with white, basking the darkness with light. The bungalow in the middle of the vale sprawled across a good patch of land. The wooden porch wrapped around the main house and beams made of Scottish oak held the shingled roof above. The walls were interspersed with floor to ceiling windows that allowed people to look out but the sun not to shine in. Inside the bungalow was a flurry of activity. A woman wailed and screamed, cursing her mate to the high heavens. Outside in the wooden patio several Cynn Cruor warriors waited with the expectant father. Every time a scream cleaved the air, they flinched.

Colin Butler pulled at his hair before running his hands down his face and a few weeks growth of beard.

"Here." Graeme handed him an unopened bottle of Dalmore, which Colin mutely took. But when Amaryllis screamed, Colin's fingers let go. Liam, who was nearby, and Graeme nearly collided with each other as they reached for the bottle at the same time.

Craig and Finn looked at each other, snickering and shaking their heads. They were both leaning on the pillars by the porch stairs.

"Graeme told Butler some time ago he'd have the last laugh if Cupid caught him," Finn said wryly.

Graeme chuckled. "What he's going through pretty much sums it up. No need to rub it in."

"Why she refused to go to the hospital, I'll never know," Colin mumbled before leaning back on his chair, his face ashen with worry.

Cormac looked up from his wood carving. "You want other doctors poking—"

"No," Colin replied gruffly. "I don't like that Zac's doing it as it is."

"Faith's with him," Liam piped in.

"Your woman is very wise." Cormac nodded sagely, his eyes twinkling. "And your child is very impatient wanting out after only eight months."

Liam looked away towards the loch, his silver eyes narrowing. There was no let-up in the snow swirling around. "They've arrived."

Their sharp hearing detected the crunching of snow under booted feet. Soon, The Hamilton and Roarke appeared over the hill, making their way towards the bungalow.

"I never thought I'd be so scared shitless in my life," Craig spoke on an exhale. His gaze tracked the highlanders walking to them.

Finn turned his head and gave his brother in arms a long look before facing the blazing white garden. "Agreed. Even after eight months, my heart remains heavy. I thought Colin and Amaryllis would die."

"Thank you, Finn," Colin spoke softly behind them. "I thought the same thing after telling The Hamilton and all of you about Mackenzie. Banishment is just as painful."

"I'd rather you were banished than sent to the pantheon, Dux." Craig twisted on his waist, looking back at the warrior who was as much of a brother to him as Mackenzie was. "I don't relish the thought of dying just to kick your arse."

They all chuckled.

Craig and Finn left the porch and strode to meet The Hamilton and Roarke.

"You've become a great Dux, in your own right."

"That honour will always remain with Colin, Qualtrough," Craig said, shaking his head the farther they walked. "I'm too much of a hot head."

"Seth will likely calm you down." Finn hazarded a guess. "You've not put your scent on her yet everyone sees the fireworks between you. If you have a care, better claim her before she agrees to be claimed by someone else."

Graeme spoke just as the four immortals returned to the house as though the earlier conversation had not ended.

"You can't die either because you'll soon be the father of a Cynn Cruor warrior or a Cynn Cruor mortal." Graeme winked.

"Conceived during the month of Beltane and born on the month of *Am Faoilteach*, the Wolf Moon?" Liam arched his brow. "A formidable Cynn Cruor indeed."

As though on cue, everyone heard the strong and lustful cry from strong lungs. Colin stood and stalked to the sliding door then stopped. He started to pace.

"What the hell are you waiting for?" Cormac's eyes widened in disbelief.

Just then Zac came out wiping his washed forearms and hands on a towel. His face broke into a pleased smile.

"Congratulations, Butler." He reached out his arm and Colin took it in a daze. "You have a son. The Cynn Cruors have gained another immortal."

There were whoops, man hugs, and back slapping. Laughter amid swigs from the Dalmore joined the pelting snow.

"My Lord." Colin's eyes glistened, unsure whether to go or stay.

"See to yer bairn, Colin." The Hamilton laughed,

crossing his huge arms over his muscled chest. "Yer father first and foremost now."

Colin rushed into the room faster than the North wind.

Soft laughter flitted around the porch.

After The Hamilton commuted Colin's sentence, the Cynn Cruors went to work to count the casualties. Seth refused to let go of Colin and Amaryllis until Amaryllis told her she was choking. They all retreated to the command centre, the only place unscathed by the carnage. Liam carried Etienne to the hospital wing. Gareth and Donovan followed behind him, tears falling down their cheeks. Seth was a wreck and it took Craig to hold her still and threaten her with injecting her with a sleeping draught for her to calm down.

It was the first time any of the Cynn Cruors saw Seth completely crack.

Cormac and Graeme manned the computer consoles, getting reports from the clubs and restaurants of the casualties and informing the Cynn mortals working with the police to check other places where skirmishes with the Scatha transpired. Then they took a break so that Roarke, Finn, and Graeme could speak with their women and request for more assistance from the Manchester Cynn mortals. Eirene said she would inform Jay Nevins so that he could arrange for the mortals to leave for Leeds. They would meet up in the Faesten where Deanna had her fleet of cars at their disposal. Kate called her contacts in the media in Leeds, calling markers to make sure that the news did not make the front page. They were all sad to hear what happened to Colin but relieved that an execution was not in his cards.

Dac had disappeared again. The Hamilton was right. Not once did the Scatha Cruor leader enter the fray. Herod left as well. No one knew what had happened to him, each immortal too engrossed with the Scathas they fought. What they did know was that The Hamilton had fought him. They had no intention of asking the formidable immortal what had happened. Not even Roarke. With Colin's life in the balance, it was best not to court his ire.

"How's Mackenzie?" Craig asked, stomping his feet to rid his boots of the cold.

"He still has a long way to go," Roarke replied. He pinned his gaze on Zac. "McBain?"

"Still testing." Zac threw the towel over his right shoulder, his voice slightly raspy. "Faith wants to keep using her firebinding gifts to extract the Scatha's poison." His face became troubled. "She gets very exhausted afterwards. She has been looking through her grandmother's things to see if there are more like them. If there are, she might be able to ask them to come out of hiding."

"On Colin and Mackenzie's behalf and that of the Leeds Cynn Cruors, thank you. Mackenzie Butler was one of us. Losing him that way is something we will never forget," Craig said with sincerity. "We will take what is offered." He turned to the Hamilton.

"I have broached the subject with the Ancient Eald and he has seen reason. As long as Mackenzie is under my protection, he will not be harmed," The Hamilton replied to the query that flickered in Craig's eyes. "In the meantime, let Zac and Faith take their time."

* * *

Colin neared their bedroom. It was the first room he built with his own hands and when he found out that his mate was pregnant he built the nursery with a connecting hallway to the master's bedroom. But in the meantime, his bairn would sleep with them, in the crib he had built and honed lovingly while Amaryllis already heavy with child watched him with adoration and love in her gaze. Colin closely worked with the Cynn mortals from the various Faestens in the Highlands. Deidre and The Hamilton visited often, speaking to them of their responsibilities as Cynn Cruor parents, one of the growing number of warriors and mates who decided to risk having a family in the midst of a millennia long war. Huge oak beams held the ceiling high above the bedroom. An iron cast chandelier in black hung over the centre of the chamber. The huge sleigh bed which Colin built from cherry wood stood against the recessed oak and slate wall and underneath it was a huge luxurious rug in reds, blues, and yellows. He had also built the side tables completing the ensemble. To the right of the bed was the huge ensuite and walk in closet. In one corner of the room was a huge fireplace made of slate and above it was the tartan that warmed Duncan Butler under the Scottish skies all those centuries ago. The only thing Colin took with him from the Leeds Faesten. The fire in the hearth crackled merrily, bringing warmth in the love filled room. In deference to Amaryllis' discomfort of closed spaces, Colin built a huge bay window that looked out to the sprawling gardens and Amaryllis' obstacle course so that she could continue with her parkour. On the opposite corner were French doors that opened to the private patio. The specially made glass automatically dimmed when the sun hit it, allowing any Cynn Cruor immortal inside the room to stay and not get burned.

Colin stood at the threshold. The remnants of childbirth still clung to the air. The women, all the mates of the Manchester Cynn Cruors were busy helping Amaryllis ease back to the bed after taking out the soiled cotton and plastic sheets and replacing them with fresh ones. Even Seth was there, all soft and gentle, a far cry from her kick ass attitude as the head of the Cynn mortals. He laughed softly when Amaryllis protested at the way she was being pampered, a frown forming on her face, a brittle smile which looked more like gritting teeth plastered on her mouth.

"Ladies, please." She exhaled. "Please!"

They merrily tittered and cooed at the babe in her arms. She rolled her eyes in defeat until they fell on Colin. Her face changed, lighting up. Her eyes glimmered with love pouring in buckets that washed Colin's lingering anxiety away. Ancients! She looked exhausted but the happiness that brightened her features was like the sun breaking through the clouds.

Deanna, Eirene, Kate, Faith, and Seth turned and parted to let Colin into the all-female circle. Elation filled their faces and for once Eirene was tongue tied.

"Meet your son," Amaryllis spoke softly.

"We'll be outside," Deanna said, beaming. "He's a strong bairn, Colin. Congratulations."

Colin acknowledged the women's congratulations, accepting their warm embraces with unease at the sight of the growing scowl appearing on Amaryllis' face. It matched the scowl on his son's face.

The women laughed at Amaryllis' soft growl, only knowing too well how it felt when other women embraced or flirted with their mates. Seth stood one side, a smile quirking her mouth that did not exactly reach her eyes. Soon they all left.

"Come on, Dux, hold him," Amaryllis said as soon as the women left. She winced, sucking her breath sharply when she adjusted herself on the bed.

"Amaryllis!" Colin rushed to the bedside. "Should I call Zac back? Faith?" Colin resembled a wayward top pivoting towards the door then back to the bedside several times. Bloody hell, he could face and laugh at the Scatha anytime.

Seeing Amaryllis in pain was going to lead to his untimely demise.

"Sit your arse down, Butler." Amaryllis sighed with indulgent amusement. "It's just an afterbirth contraction. Here." She reached out her arms. "Your son is waiting."

Colin slowly sat down on the bed, the mattress dipping under his weight. He carefully held out his arms. He frowned, hesitated, unsure of how to carry this new life.

"Watch the neck," Amaryllis murmured as she slid her arm away from under their son's body.

Their son must have sensed the change in who was carrying him because his face crunched in displeasure, fidgeting in Colin's arms. Soft tufts of black hair cover his small head. Soft dark brows tilted at the end were lowered in a frown. Dark thick lashes lowered over chubby cheeks. His nose wrinkled before his mouth opened, preparing to let out a wail. His fist escaped the blanket wrapped around him and shot up, hitting Colin on the chin. Their son jerked in surprise as he hit Colin's beard and immediately opened his eyes and Colin was floored at seeing his own dark green depths mirrored in his child. Father and son regarded each other. One set of eyes looked up in curiosity, the old soul still lurking in their green depths before memories of a past life disappeared, relegated into the subconscious as new life surfaced to take on the world it was born to. The other set of eyes lost its battle to weariness, the responsibilities brought to bear on shoulders for centuries. It its place was an enthusiastic curiosity, a more significant understanding of purpose, and a fierce conviction to protect the woman and son who were his haven, who chased midnight's shadows away that had been with him for so long.

"Colin?"

"Hmm...?" He and his son continued to gaze at each other. The bairn brushed his tiny hand against Colin's beard. His heart wanted to sing to the rafters. He wanted to run to the crags, raise his son up to the Scottish sky and roar out his joy. He would teach his son all, if not more, than what his father taught him and Mack. His son would learn about the Cynn Cruors, his legacy, his immortality. It would break his heart the moment his son left them to train. The Hamilton had offered to be his mentor. How could Colin refuse?

"I never understood why the Hamilton spared us." Amaryllis pulled at the loose threads of the thick handmade blanket that covered her from the waist down. "I was so sure we were going to die." She leaned back on the headboard and her fingers absently went to play with the violet streak of hair. "Everyone already said their goodbyes and returned to the Faesten before the sun really rose."

Colin looked up. Amaryllis' violet eyes stared at the ceiling. "I still remember the feeling of the sun and watched as you flinched and started hyperventilating, waiting for the wave of fire to touch you."

Colin remembered it as well. Even before the sun had even shone on them, the daylight had made his blood simmer inside him.

"I have no idea." He looked down again at his son, whose eyes continued to look at his face, as though memorizing it. "I'm as bewildered as you are. When the warriors and the mortals came out shouting, I thought they were going to kill us. I've never seen an execution done that way. Immortals were always left to the mercy of the sun. But they were like a mob about to lynch us."

He drew a ragged breath. He had held Amaryllis in his arms, his hold on her tight against her shaking body. "Now I know how it feels to be at the receiving end of a Cynn Cruor battle cry."

"When in reality they were there to take us back to the Faesten as soon as they could so that we could all rejoice," she said, lost in thought. Her mouth pursed. "How's Mack?"

At the mention of his brother's name, Colin exhaled, raking a hand through his longer hair. "I've no' spoken to The Hamilton because I wanted to see you and this bundle of love you've given me." He smiled at the blush on Amaryllis' cheeks. "I will find out later. I know that he's being treated well for a Scatha Cruor."

"No one knows he's your brother?" Amaryllis' face filled with concern.

Colin shook his head. "I dinnae know how The Hamilton does it. Apart from all of us here, The Hamilton and Deidre, no one knows, though I willna be surprised if the Ancients eventually find out."

"Your burr's returned." Amaryllis teased.

"Aye." Colin gave her a wicked grin then waggled his brows. "And ye like it."

Amaryllis giggled then sobered.

"So the Ancients..."

"The Hamilton told them he caught a Scatha and he has asked Zac to see if there was a way of reversing the Scatha blood's effects especially if they were not turned willingly. They probably talked about it while I came here. I also have Faith to thank for that. I will forever by indebted to them. All of them," Colin said.

"We," Amaryllis stressed, chiding him gently, "are indebted to all of them. You have a family now, Colin, remember?"

"Aye." He grinned, standing to move closer to her

and lean on the headboard, carefully cradling his son. "This near death experience has brought things to perspective. I am glad that you agreed with me to start a family." He leaned down and gave Amaryllis a warm languid kiss that had Amaryllis moaning and his son protesting that suddenly he was in between two unrelenting bodies. Colin and Amaryllis chuckled, reluctantly breaking away as their son squirmed, biting his tiny fist.

"He's hungry," Amaryllis said softly.

Colin watched as Amaryllis took their son from him. She opened her bodice and lust flared in him. A fleeting moment when he saw her breast but disappeared when his son latched greedily, causing Amaryllis to wince.

"I've got competition," he groaned.

Amaryllis gave a beatific smile. "No, you don't. These belonged to you even before they belonged to him."

"See? Competition from my son."

"Duncan Mackenzie." Amaryllis eased her bodice away from her son's mouth. She caressed the still soft head with her finger.

"What did you say?" Colin's eyebrows rose in stunned surprise.

She looked at him and his chest tightened at the beauty he saw. "Duncan Mackenzie Butler. Our son's name." She paused, becoming serious. "Unless you want another name, we can—"

Colin kissed her hard, this time making sure his son still comfortably fed. When he finished they were both breathless. His other head down south had thoughts of his own. Damn, Colin did not know how long he would have to make do with his hand.

"It's perfect." He rasped. "You're perfect." He

leaned his forehead on hers, caressing her face with his thumb. "I love you, Amaryllis Hart-Butler. I'll love you even after death. You've given this weary heart a place to rest. A haven when I thought my life would only be filled with despair and heartache." He looked away. "I have nothing to give you except this land that has been in my family for centuries. No longer a Dux—"

"Only for a little while." She pressed a finger over his mouth. "Call it a slap on the wrist." She made herself more comfortable, gingerly shifting her weight. Baby Duncan still latched on to her nipple. "And I don't care if you're Dux or not. I have you. You are mine. All of you are mine." She smiled. "The Hamilton was right. Our son needs us both. Craig will always keep you posted about what's happening in Leeds. And with the nerve centre you built underneath this house that'll probably rival MI6's…"

Colin's left brow rose a fraction.

"Well, okay, I exaggerate." Amaryllis laughed. "But seriously? Satellite tracking?"

"Hey, it's a Cynn Cruors satellite." Colin defended. "We had that in Leeds too and Manchester's hooked up to it. Dan made it so."

"Warriors and their toys." She huffed, shaking her head. "By the time you're all done, you won't know who won the pissing contest."

Colin guffawed, startling Duncan, who let go of his mother's breast and wailed.

"Och, laddie." Colin took his son from Amaryllis and stood. "There'll be more booming laughter before I'm through with ye." He chuckled, teasing Duncan's chin with his finger. Swiftly, Duncan caught the offending digit.

"Ancients, he's got a strong grip!" Colin exclaimed.

"Nope. He's just saying, quit, Da," Amaryllis

declared wryly.

They both laughed, enjoying the miracle nestled between their two hearts.

Amaryllis was blissfully happy watching her alpha warrior reduced to a gentle lion in the presence of its cub.

"I love you, Colin," she said, love burning in her eyes. Colin returned to the bed and leaned against the headboard so Amaryllis could nestle inside his arms as well. She leaned up, taking his mouth in hers, kissing him like there was no tomorrow. He returned her kiss in kind, her toes curling in delight.

If Colin had found his haven in her, she had found her own haven with him. She did not know what the future held for them. For the entire Cynn Cruors race. A bigger war was imminent, that was certain. The undeniable fact evident in all the Faestens that were on more than a red alert, if there was such a thing. She was going to make the most of Colin's banishment from Leeds. It was not what she was hoping for when she told Colin she wanted to go away for a while, but this was much better. Craig was more than capable of filling in for Colin. With Seth by his side…that was another thing Amaryllis was going to talk to Seth about when she found the Cynn mortal alone. Roarke and the rest of the Manchester Cynn Cruors were there to help Leeds. Theirs was a bond that ran deep, that not even time could sever. Amaryllis knew she still had a lot to learn about the world she now called her own.

In the meantime, she was going to make sure that Altnaharra would be her perfect haven with her Midnight warrior.

Epilogue

Blake and Luke watched the *Taigh a' Chnuic* from afar. Two figures approached them. They knew that the Manchester and Leeds Cynn Cruors had tracked them what with Liam having the sharpest eyes. They could hear the celebrations and got a glimpse of the newest Butler when Colin and Amaryllis came out of the room to present their bairn to the rest of the Cynn Cruors.

"Duncan Mackenzie," Luke commented. "Nice name."

"Duncan was their father killed by the Scatha by the loch there." Blake pointed behind them to the Naver.

They both waited for the two Cynn Cruors trudging to where they were. The Hamilton and Roarke crested the hill opposite the house and closer to the loch.

"You are both welcome in Colin's home," Roarke said quietly, his arms crossed over his massive chest, his hair covered with snow.

"I still have to go," Luke said.

"Colin doesn't take that against you."

Luke snorted. "You're shit at lying, Roarke. You didn't want me to interfere but if I didn't then we would never know that Mackenzie was still alive. In some bloody perverted way, he was saved, but I lost the friendships I developed with Leeds."

"Give it time, Griffiths." The Hamilton's voice boomed over the falling snow. "Ye had good intentions. And I ken that no one takes it against ye. Colin and Amaryllis most of all."

"Spare me, my Lord," Luke muttered. "I don't like myself one bit at the moment."

"I better go." Blake walked away from the group.

"Blake, why can't you tell me what is wrong?" Roarke asked in exasperation. "We are your brethren."

"Leave it," The Hamilton said quietly. "Blake has to do this for himself."

Roarke's eyes narrowed. "There's something you're not telling me."

"As is my prerogative, Roarke." The Hamilton's voice steeled.

Roarke's face hardened, but he nodded.

Blake returned and extended his arm to Roarke. "Soon, Roarke." He smiled, his eyes sad. "Soon you will know why."

Roarke gripped his arm and pulled him to an embrace. "Take care of yourself. Do you know where you're going?"

Blake nodded, his dark beard and hair already white. Snow drifted on the shoulders of his denim jacket. "I won't be far."

"Manchester's resources are still at your disposal, Strachan. Use them."

Blake shook his head. "I must decline, Dux." After Roarke stormed a few feet away in frustration and then came back, he added, "It's for the best."

He turned to Luke again, giving his arm in the Cynn Cruor greeting. As Luke gripped his arm, he said, "I hope you find the peace that seems to elude you."

"As do you," Luke returned.

Blake nodded before pivoting and going down the hill.

The three Cynn Cruors watched until Blake was merely a speck.

"Where are you going now?" Roarke turned to Luke, a troubled sigh coming out of him. "Eirene is going to chew my hide."

Luke's mouth lifted in a small grin. "Finn will make

her understand." He looked away towards the loch. "I'm going to follow a trail I picked up. It's very slim that I will find what I'm looking for but at least it's something."

Roarke nodded. "Where does it lead this time?"

"America."

"Really?" The Hamilton's dark brows lifted. "Where did you find that piece of information? In the Anglesey archives?"

Luke shook his head. "In Hamel Dun Uiamh."

The Hamilton scowled. "Without my permission. I told ye to tell me if you were going inside. Was that so difficult to do?" He blew out an annoyed breath. "I hate spies."

Luke shrugged. "So do I, even if I'm one. Maybe if I disappear for a while, things here will die down and you'll all be in a better frame of mind to accept me back."

"We never told you to leave." Roarke riposted.

"True," Luke agreed. "But I've put a damper on so many things. Making myself scarce at the moment is a good idea."

"And what about Adara Kerslake?"

Luke gazed at a point between the two warriors. "If she doesn't want to be found, I can't find her."

"Says the spy," Roarke said with a tinge of sarcasm.

Luke huffed a chuckle. "Yeah, says the spy."

"Be off with ye, *duine*," The Hamilton said gruffly. "Ken that no matter what ye did, ye will be missed. Even Cynn Cruors make mistakes."

"That's pretty loaded," Luke commented.

"Take it for what it is and be off with ye," The Hamilton growled.

Luke laughed before he shimmered in front of them, disappearing.

"What did you mean by that?" Roarke asked his father. They started making their way down back to the house.

"What?"

"Did you make a mistake allowing Colin and Amaryllis to live?" Roarke asked quietly.

"No, it has nothing to do with them at all." The Hamilton continued walking.

"With Blake?" Roarke stopped walking.

The Hamilton continued walking before he realized his son was not beside him. "I need Alba's water to sharpen my mind, son. Let's go."

"Da."

"Let's go, Roarke."

"Blake is my responsibility," Roarke said, bothered. He and his father hardly fought but when they did, they were like two wild deer with antlers locked in battle. And Deidre was not there to pull them apart.

"No, he is no'," The Hamilton looked at him, his tone brooking no argument. "For the moment, he's mine."

THE END

Thank you for reading Colin and Amaryllis' story. I hope you liked it! If you could kindly leave a review on Amazon or Goodreads. Reviews help authors gauge the quality of the stories as well as help us make our stories better. Thank you.

About the Author

Isobelle Cate is a woman who wears different masks. Mother-writer, wife-professional, scholar-novelist. Currently living in Manchester, she has been drawn to the little known, the secret stories, about the people and the nations: the English, the Irish, the Scots, the Welsh, and those who are now part of these nations whatever their origins. Her vision and passion are fuelled by her interest and background in history and paradoxically, shaped by growing up in a clan steeped in lore, loyalty, and legend. Isobelle is intrigued by forces that simmer beneath the surface of these cultures, the hidden passions, unsaid desires, and yearnings unfulfilled.

Connect with Isobelle Cate Online:
Isobelle Cate's Facebook Profile and Page:
https://www.facebook.com/AuthorIsobelleCate

Follow Isobelle Cate on Twitter:
https://twitter.com/Isobelle_Cate

Isobelle Cate's Amazon page:
http://www.amazon.com/Isobelle-Cate

Find Isobelle Cate's Books on Goodreads:
https://www/goodreads.com/author/show/7191925.Isobelle_Cate

Email:isobellecate@gmail.com

Buy links to other books by
Isobelle Cate:

The Cynn Cruors Bloodline Series:
Rapture at Midnight: (Book 1)
Amazon US http://amzn.to/1neSbAD
Amazon UK http://amzn.to/1mRDFx3
Amazon CA http://amzn.to/1C1DKe7
Amazon AU http://bit.ly/1C1Dbkm

Forever at Midnight (Book 2)
Amazon US http://amzn.to/RE1jES
Amazon UK http://amzn.to/1e4kwIY
Amazon AU http://bit.ly/1BAcVZ1
Amazon CA http://amzn.to/1FeFQIF

Midnight's Atonement (Book 3)
Amazon US http://amzn.to/1nxcqwT
Amazon UK http://amzn.to/1iR0tAh
Amazon CA http://amzn.to/1L60dIv
Amazon AU http://bit.ly/17iO8Aw

Midnight's Fate (Book 4)
Amazon US http://amzn.to/1tpt4zg
Amazon UK http://bit.ly/Midnight_sFate_UK
Amazon CA http://bit.ly/Midnight_sFate_CA
Amazon AU http://bit.ly/Midnight_sFate_AU

Contemporary Romance
Love in Her Dreams
Amazon US http://amzn.to/1qOEufk
Amazon UK http://amzn.to/1cpBLTd

Second Chances Series
Be Mine (Book 1)

Amazon US http://amzn.to/1LiDvLy
Amazon UK http://amzn.to/1BxfqPu
Amazon CA http://amzn.to/1xTa2Bo
Amazon AU http://bit.ly/1utgiyh

You and I
Amazon US http://amzn.to/1yWptcH
Amazon UK http://amzn.to/1A1GacD

Dying to Live
Amazon US http://amzn.to/1K0GcG6
Amazon UK http://amzn.to/1xbihgF

Historical
Lakam (The Mana Series: Book 1)
Amazon US http://amzn.to/S6cy90
Amazon UK http://amzn.to/1vrZRnr

Made in the USA
Charleston, SC
02 July 2015